SANCTUARY

Grace J. Agnew

Woodhall Press
Norwalk, CT

woodhall press

Woodhall Press, 81 Old Saugatuck Road, Norwalk, CT 06855
WoodhallPress.com

Cover design: Asha Hossain
Layout artist: LJ Mucci

Library of Congress Cataloging-in-Publication Data available

ISBN 978-1-949116-50-2 (paper: alk paper)
ISBN 978-1-949116-61-8 (electronic)

First Edition

Distributed by Independent Publishers Group
(800) 888-4741
Printed in the United States of America

For Teal, Luke, Harrison and Channing.
Your generation will fix the mistakes
that my generation made.

PROLOGUE

Was this the right place? She hadn't visited this street in three years. Everything looked different, sadder, more decrepit. Like Miranda herself. She was probably imagining things. She shook herself, and as she did, she woke the tiny package, wrapped in a used scaleskin and tucked against her chest. It had been shivering nonstop, like something electric, but now it stirred and extended its claws out of the cloth. Miranda tried to tuck the arms back in. The waving arms froze and then attacked. Miranda saw dots of blood well on her arm. It had been a while since she saw blood, but this blood was nothing compared to—

She stopped herself from thinking about the past. It was enough that she dreamed about it every night. Time to finish her errand and go home, or what was left of home, without—

She was doing it again. She pressed a communications button, intentionally choosing an unknown flat. She didn't want to face anyone who knew her, who would ask inconvenient questions. She turned her head to one side when an unknown woman answered, sounding put-upon.

"Yes, what is it?"

Miranda mentioned a name in response.

"You have the wrong flat. Turn your head, please, I can't hear you."

Miranda shook her head, but she repeated the name and what she needed more clearly. It didn't do to face people. She had seen the end of the world, and the horror was reflected in her eyes.

SANCTUARY

When she knew her message had been reluctantly received, she put her bundle down and watched it scurry away. It wouldn't go far. It was fitting that the story ended as it had begun. With a cat.

CHAPTER ONE

Designing the dog was easy. The cat took a lot of work. But here it stood, pretzeled into Zen calligraphy, purring with pleasure as Miranda stroked its thick fur. She worked her fingers down to the spine, feeling each knob as the cat arched its back and leaned against her arm. Density, that's what she was feeling, richness. Which was perfect, because of course the fur was holo. Real fur would catch every passing microbe, clog the venting systems, and produce allergies in people who hadn't seen a pet in thirty years. Microscopic jets of forced air created the tension of fur that was brushed against the grain. And totally self-sustaining. Each time the cat moved, it created and stored its own energy.

As a final test, she grabbed a clump of fur and pulled. Resistance. Perfect. The cat narrowed its eyes and hissed. A paw came up, claws curved to attack. Miranda pulled back, even though the claws, gleaming like enamel, were also holo and couldn't actually draw blood. But the immediate reaction—the hissing, the indignant look in eyes that had been half lidded with drowsy contentment—this was practically perfection after months of disappointment. New behavior, new appearance, new color. A tiny triumph, maybe, but the design had been a struggle. Not like the dog, tucked away in a cupboard. She looked around, unbalanced, as if she could hear the dog scratching to get out. It wasn't trapped, for God's sake; it was turned off.

The flat alarm, a pleasant tinkling during the day. Alex was home. She felt his eyes on her from the doorway. "Look," she said, "the latest model."

He stood there, leaning against the narrow frame; tall, skinny—too skinny for a sixteen-year-old, according to the health charts. She made a mental note to check his diet stats from his DP. She narrowed her eyes and peered around him. Where *was* his DP? Turned off again. She pursed her lips. This was the sort of thing that got you noticed.

Alex watched her in turn. She was sitting on the flat sofa, so basic and colorless it was hard to distinguish from the floor. Everyone they knew had lots of holo decor because it was so easy to design and project from the story cube. You could change it on a whim or when company came over. He admired his mother for keeping it simple and basic, although he knew a lot of that was probably in response to his complaining about the phoniness of projected junk. He watched her lips moving. In, out, in, out. Miranda's features were finely drawn, her mouth thin like a pencil line across her face. She had told him how kids teased her when she was little. The lip pursing was a nervous habit to plump them out. Something she did when she was angry or uncomfortable. Angry . . . with him?

She looked up from the cat, directly at him. Those eyes. Even though she was his mother and he saw her almost every day—unless he could avoid it, and frequently he could—those eyes never ceased to amaze. Large and blue, like the best sky she had ever designed. You forgot everything else about her when she turned those eyes, gleaming like grow lights, on you.

"What do you think?" she asked. She stroked the cat again.

"Is that the final version? Nice." He tried to put some enthusiasm in his voice. He hated how he had to fake everything with his mother. Otherwise, he was just a total disappointment. He avoided her now because everything about him that was real she disliked.

8

He turned to head into the kitchen for a packfruit.

"Is that it?" Her voice stopped him. Five minutes in the house, and he had already done it. Made his mother mad. He had to make a friend or two, just to have another place to stay sometimes.

"You know how long I've worked on this. How important it is to me. Is that all I get? 'Nice'?"

He sighed. "I said it was nice, and I meant it. It's what you do. Build things. You always have something new. Do I have to get excited every time?"

Her lips tightened. "I build things—"

"For the good of the city," he finished her thought. "I know, Mom. I just don't get all the effort you've spent on building animals. You hate animals."

Miranda was pushed back, as from a physical blow, by his judgment of her. When did all this start? Twelve? Thirteen? She knew it had been growing, but she hadn't realized how much it had solidified. The distance between them wasn't air any longer, it was concrete. She took a deep breath. They were not going to fight every time she saw him.

"First of all, I don't design for myself. I design for Sanctuary. People love animals. Loved animals," she corrected herself. "And I don't hate animals. When I was a little girl, I had a pet. A dog, Fred"

"Your DP," he said, without much interest.

"No, a real dog," she said. "A flesh-and-blood, scratchy nailed, drooling dog."

Alex looked at her, meeting her eyes for the first time since he'd walked in. "I can't picture you with a dog," he said. "You're afraid of animals. You see an animal and your first thought is 'Call animal management.'"

"Maybe because I remember animals the way they used to be," she said. "Not the way they are now. Fred was my best friend. He did everything with me, slept with me at night."

"I thought Tara was your best friend . . ." His sarcastic voice trailed off as he left the room. She heard him rummaging around in the kitchen.

"I got a loaf today," she called to him. "And some melt." Loaves of bread were created from the hydroponic rice in the Sanctuary gardens. Packfruits—luscious, concentrated sweetness, loaded with every nutrient you needed—were the daily meals, supplemented by treats like loaves and long stalks of celery, to maintain dentition and digestion. She actually got two loaves because they were small, but when she set the bakery bag down, a ferrat was on it in an instant, stealing a loaf and disappearing in a quick streak of brown around the corner. She disinfected the remaining loaf. They would eat it tonight; you didn't waste bread.

Alex brought in the loaf, coated in melt, and two plates. He broke the loaf in two and pushed a plate toward her, carefully avoiding the cat, which leaned over to sniff the bread.

"I thought you would be interested in pets. You had a blue rabbit for your DP for the longest time."

"When I was four," he said. "And you're talking about digits. We exterminate anything that's real, like ferrats, and make more things that are unreal, to keep all the human animals happy in their zoo. Listen, we have animals now. Real animals. Ferrats are actually pretty cool; they stay together as families even when they're grown." Ferrats, colonies of smart, agile rats that had somehow invaded from the outside, were one of the banes of Sanctuary life. Alex, of course, liked them.

"Adapted to hunt, to take precious food and water resources," Miranda said.

"If you hate animals so much, I don't see how you are going to design something cuddly that everyone wants," he said. "Ferrats aren't the only animals. There are coyotes and wild dogs that roam parts of the city, if you know where to look, and more that get in every day. You could tame them. There's life in this place; you don't have to make it."

"More that get in," she repeated. "What do you mean?"

"Oh, come on, Mom! You know there are holes in the city wall. You can shut your eyes to the big, bad world out there, but you can't shut Sanctuary. Not completely."

"Have you seen those holes, Alex? Have you been . . . through any of them?"

He looked at her. "You can't live out there," he answered. "You know that. That's why animals are sneaking in. To enjoy the survival we've created for ourselves. Nothing lives outside."

"You're being sarcastic, but it's true. I know. I lived outside, when I was—"

"Younger than me. I know, Mom. Nobody can live outside anymore, except . . ." He stopped.

She busied herself with melt. She knew what was coming.

"Except maybe my dad."

"How do you know this?"

He paused. "I didn't learn it from you. You never tell me anything about my dad. You always make it sound like he didn't exist at all. Like maybe I was something you created in your lab. Maybe I was your first android."

She whirled to face him. "Alex, you can't believe that! I never talk about him because he left. He abandoned you when you were just a toddler. In all these years, he has never once tried to see you. If he even survived, because he—"

"Because he went outside. Where no one can survive," he finished.

"That's right. And not for any noble reason, if that's what you're thinking. Not from any desire to save mankind. Sanctuary is what saves mankind. No, he went outside because he never cared about his role; just drifted about, claimed the city made him claustrophobic, viewed one too many stories about cowboys riding across the prairies into the sunset. But there are no prairies, no sunsets; just howling winds and dust poisoning the air so you can hardly breathe. The outside sounds so romantic when you are sixteen, Alex, but it has nothing."

"Except my dad."

"Not likely," she said, before she could stop herself.

"What do you mean?"

She paused, measuring her words. "Alex, it wasn't good when I lived outside. It hasn't gotten any better, only worse. Nothing could survive out there for long."

"There's City of the South," Alex argued. "And Asia City. And probably others."

He named the cities within a week's travel from Sanctuary. Both cities had begun well. Asia City controlled its environment and the people who could live and mate there. People with genetic issues were ruthlessly forced outside the city walls. And yet, before Alex was born, the city had fallen to rampant drug abuse and disease and now was a largely abandoned shell.

City of the South, depending on what story you believed, was either a tragedy or a joke. It was ruled by lazy and venal rulers. The people who lived there were either serfs or outlaws. There was no in-between. The city was falling apart, besides, barely providing shelter from the rains, the dust, and the wind. People who survived didn't live very long. Some people romanticized it. Easy enough to do if you never had to live there. Miranda had seen refugees from City of the South, quarantined in a special section of the city for the outside diseases they carried. They all looked old, even the children. She had no idea what became of them, but they didn't mingle with the citizens of Sanctuary. And after a while, refugees stopped banging on the wall.

She didn't bother to reply.

Alex changed course. "People like you don't care about anything but Sanctuary. You suck what is left from the outside to keep your precious city alive. Sanctuary sits like a tumor on the world, depending on the world to survive. You can call everything else 'outside' like it is something else, like it doesn't matter. But the outside is everything real. And sooner or later, it's coming in."

He sounded like a pamphlet from the 2084 protest group. Miranda took a breath, trying to salvage the evening.

"That's not true," she said. "In fact, there's a special role, perhaps the most important, that is focused on developing a mutual relationship with outside, harvesting and reusing what is good. Healing what is not."

Alex snorted. "If believing that makes you happy."

"You could be part of that, Alex. You could have the role of outside integrator." It was a demanding role, hard to get into, but Miranda could pull some strings, and Tara could pull even more.

He shrugged. "I've already decided, with the role counselor. I'm going to be a story maker." His voice was flat, uninterested.

"A story maker?" Miranda was amazed at her own disappointment. She knew that stories made life more interesting and worthwhile for many people. Some people lived the best part of their lives in story. Still . . .

"C'mon, Mom, do you think what you do is so different? What is Sanctuary but a giant story? A great big ball of make-believe."

"You don't mean that, Alex." She forced her voice to be steady and even. "You're sixteen. It's natural to push against boundaries. But people ultimately want to thrive, and Sanctuary is the only place left where we can do that. What else is there? You may not see it this way, but Sanctuary is our best hope for tomorrow. Not just your tomorrow, but the tomorrow of the children you will have."

He stared at the bread, getting soggy under the rapidly cooling melt. "How old was my dad when he left?" he asked.

"Twenty-eight." She'd known one day they would be having this conversation, after she'd discovered his secret DP when he was ten:

a six-foot-tall version of Alex. He couldn't possibly remember his dad, but the result was so close it took her breath away. Alex had quickly turned it back into the fuzzy ball he normally used, and they both pretended she hadn't seen the other DP.

She had always deflected questions about his father, dismissing him as someone she barely recalled. As Alex got older, he quit asking. She hoped he had only a few memories. But she couldn't forget the night terrors, when he woke crying hysterically, for years after Peter left.

"And how old was I?"

"Four."

He rolled the spongy bread into inedible marbles. Almost a week of her salary.

"Why did he leave, anyway? Didn't he want anything more to do with us?" *With me*, he meant.

Miranda sighed and decided on the truth. "I don't know. He was too big for the city, taller and broader than any other man I knew. I used to see him on his rounds and wonder how he fit into a magcart."

"What was his role?"

Miranda hesitated before answering. "Disposal," she said reluctantly. She was sorry to destroy whatever romantic vision Alex had of his dad.

Alex just laughed, surprising her. "Good for him!" he said. "Maybe I could do that."

"Don't be ridiculous," she said.

"I'm not," he answered. "It's an important role. Gotta throw things away that people no longer need, or else the city gets cluttered. Anyway, I'd like to know where the stuff goes that we throw away. Is it just heaped in piles outside Sanctuary's walls?"

Miranda had seen the immense towers of garbage a short magtrain ride from Sanctuary. When the city managers wanted everyone focused on building things that could be recycled, they were taken to see the slag heaps as incentive. Now, 90 percent of the city's matter was recycled, from packfruit skins to magcarts. Even human waste was filtered and reused. She tried not to think about the 10 percent.

"Disposal man," Alex said. "Clever, Dad."

She couldn't tell if he was admiring or sarcastic. Maybe both.

"So how do you know he isn't alive?" he asked. "If he was in disposal, he went outside; he probably figured out a thing or two. Unless he was really stupid." He gave a short laugh, but Miranda could tell by his eyes, the eyes of four-year-old abandoned Alex, how carefully she had to tread with her answer.

"No, he wasn't stupid," she said slowly. "Actually, he was the smartest man I ever met. He just refused to do anything with those brains. To adapt. This is life now. Outside is over."

She sighed, trying to put her memories of Peter into perspective. "He used to bring me things from outside, a rock or some weed still growing, like other women got holoflowers. He could talk for hours about where he found these things."

He collected things she had no hand in building, things she didn't know the backstory to, such as who invented it, how it got approved, how well it tested in the city. Things she didn't have to analyze for flaws, as if they were a personal success or failure. Was that the attraction he'd held for her?

"He was an adventurer," she finally said. "Someone who didn't want to know the ending to things. He had the explorer gene, loved to visit other cities. When they started closing those off . . ."

He had saved his salary for magtrain trips, content to let her pay all their expenses. She remembered his last trip to City of the South. He was two days over schedule. She was trying to save his job, papering over his absence with stories of illness, juggling full-time childcare and a major assignment at work.

15

When he finally showed up, he had a nasty gash on his cheek and an oozing, bandaged arm.

"Where's your DP?" she asked.

"They turned it off," he answered.

"Who is 'they'?"

"The people who did this," he answered. "Before I returned. They don't want any records. They knew just what they were doing when they jumped me. First thing they did was jam the DP."

For some reason, the DP loss horrified Miranda more than the oozing sore on his arm. Her own DP was moving forward with an antiseptic spray. Peter impatiently waved it aside. Her DP paused, waiting for Miranda's instructions.

"Don't be an idiot, Peter; you can't afford an infection."

"Fine," he said shortly, letting the DP unwind the makeshift bandage. Miranda gasped at the red, swollen, oozing sore. The worst she had ever seen were ferrat or dog bites, from the feral offspring of pets smuggled into the city. Fortunately, most of those had been rounded up and dealt with humanely.

"People did that to you?"

He laughed shortly.

"What were you doing to place yourself in a situation like this?" she asked. "Where were their DPs?"

"In City of the South, the only DPs are spies and jailers. The first thing anyone learns to do is jam them up. Even the ruling families have turned theirs off." He waved away the ministrations of her DP. "Enough. Get that thing away from me."

She looked at her DP. "No record," she said. The DP flattened into a line and disappeared.

"I don't know how to react to this," she said. "Two days without word. We've been going crazy here. You could have been killed, Peter. You have a son."

"I know," he said. "But it looks worse than it is. Listen, I have a plan."

16

She looked at him and saw the familiar wild, excited look, the gap-toothed grin. The man had a plan. Again.

Miranda sighed and backed away. "I'm going to bed," she said. "Alex is fortunately asleep. He had nightmares every night you were gone. You have to be up early for work. I managed to lie convincingly to your boss—"

He grabbed both her arms. "Fuck the job," he said. "Let's move."

"Move? You don't like the flat?"

He shook his head at her obtuseness. One of the things she hated about him was how impatient he got when his brain was racing with ideas and her slower, more practical mind couldn't keep up.

"To City of the South," he said. "Let's move there."

"Are you joking?" she asked. "We have a four-year-old son. Are you planning to train him to win knife fights?"

"Eventually," he said, "but not right away. Don't believe all the stories you hear about City of the South. Sure, the rulers are absolute shits. But the kids have a great life there. Playing in gangs, studying in street schools, learning to evade the ruler spies. Living by their own wits, not their DPs."

"Sounds lovely," she said, her anger beginning to catch fire. "A great life for your son. What about the life expectancy numbers from City of the South? Are those just 'stories we hear'?"

He was silent for a moment, marshalling his arguments. "Most kids don't have two parents. With two adults, and his own brains, Alex will be at a tremendous advantage. And City of the South is much more porous. People go in and out of the city. They aren't trapped in a city aquarium, dependent on digital babysitters. If you have skills, like we have, you are valuable there."

"We're valuable here. At least *I* am."

He shook her slightly. "What's your endgame, here?" he asked. "What do you mean?"

"This." He waved his hand at their climate-controlled flat, with the lighting automatically calibrated for conversation rather than reading. "This can't last forever, Randi. You know it can't. The kids of City of the South, they know the score, they're prepared."

"Prepared to be slaves to the rulers, to work at jobs that crush their health, to have babies and die young," she said bitterly. "Illiterate."

He studied her. "They are literate in what matters," he said. "Survival."

"You and I have different ideas of survival," she replied. "Do you think I don't know Sanctuary? Of course I do. I make it. Yes, it may not last forever, but it will outlast you and me. It will outlast our son and his future children. None of us can ask for more than that."

"When you lived outside," he asked, "did you have a pet?"

She shook her head. It was late. She was tired and disappointed. She needed to get up in a few hours. The last thing she needed was to think about Fred.

"I'm going back to bed," she said. "You better do the same if you want to make your shift."

"I had an aquarium," he said to her retreating back. "My parents wanted to have pets that didn't have to suffer because of what was happening to the world. That didn't have any idea. Last thing we did before moving to the city was throw the fish down a drain. They lived and they died never knowing what a fucked-up world they lived in."

Miranda didn't even turn around. "We'll talk in the morning."

"Night, Randi," he said to her back. "Sweet dreams."

She'd laughed shortly at that.

The next morning, he was gone. Whether outside to wander or back to City of the South, she didn't know.

"Gone to find something better for my son" was all the note said. Nothing about her and their life together, not even a signature with an endearment.

"Love, Peter" she said aloud, finishing the letter for him. "Sorry I am such a complete and utter asshole. Sincerely yours, Peter."

Another letter, sealed, was addressed "To Alex, when your mother feels you are old enough to read this." She still had the letter, unopened. But Alex never seemed old enough. She rarely thought about it, but when she did, she would freeze in her tracks with guilt. Many times, she thought about throwing it away. But looking at his tense, bitter face, seeing how much he had suffered with just the two of them . . .

Alex downed a packfruit, squeezing the contents into his mouth in a single gulp. "Well, I'm off to bed."

Miranda checked the time on her newsline. Seven thirty. She doubted he was off to bed. No doubt some role-playing story that made the outside seem better than it was. He was so like his father, who he barely remembered. How did that happen?

She decided on an early night herself. She turned on her DP, a misty blue square, just before bed, as she frequently did, to make sure she didn't forget anything. DPs, or digital personas, were three-dimensional sentient support systems that managed most of the circumstances that got you through your day. If they also documented your daily history for the Sanctuary archivists to store and mine, you tried your best not to think about that.

"I want to get together with Tara tomorrow night after work." A slight sharpening of its misty edges, visible only if you looked for it, showed that the invitation was issued, her calendar updated. Thank God, Tara was free. She rarely was these days. But Miranda needed advice about Alex. Before he committed to that ridiculous role. Story maker!

In his room, Alex turned on his story cube with a glance, just as his mother suspected. He jumped from story to story, barely staying long enough to leave a trail, moving past the newsline—the daily information feed calibrated to your age, needs, and personal interests—past the interactive stories he stored, drilling deeper into the unvisited places, the root of the newsline, with great blanks instead of data, until faint lines drifted out of the cube, shaping themselves into letters, images, musical notes. Alex hastily turned the volume down as his fingers played through the tangle of lines. There it was: a coyote moving furtively along a line. Small and gray, barely visible against the empty walls of his room. He arrested it with his finger, and it spoke.

"How are you doing?"

"Okay. I settled on a role today. With my role counselor. Story maker."

"Story maker," the coyote repeated. Alex frowned. Was he disappointed too?

The coyote chuckled. "Good choice, Alex. People need stories. They help them make sense of things. Adjust. Very good." The two chatted in whispers awhile longer. Alex fell asleep with his father's approbation in his ears.

CHAPTER TWO

Alex was lost. This wasn't a reason for panic. Sanctuary was huge, and you needed your DP to tell you to turn left at the green glass building and then right at the large story parlor with the Grecian columns. The alternative was the magcart, where you said the address and it scooted along on a magnetic track below the level of the streetway, so all you saw were people's legs striding past. Alex didn't like the closed-in feeling that gave him. Sanctuary could be difficult for a person who got claustrophobic in tight places. He knew Sanctuary so well, had memorized the available maps, that he could turn off his newsline and his DP and still get from place to place, even places he had never been.

If you walked by yourself, without your DP, it was easy to get lost, so almost no one did. Everyone on the streetway was paired with a DP of their own design. You would see a man striding along, ignoring the beautiful woman loping easily by his side, or clutching the hand of a cherubic child who managed to look helpless and trusting but still keep an eye on traffic and other people. It could be difficult to tell the DP from the human, except with children. You would see a small child all alone accompanied by a watchful rainbow-haired nanny or a loping purple-spotted giraffe. The only person who provoked a stare was the one without a DP.

"The cheese stands alone," he said aloud, causing a gleaming lion walking beside a small girl to twitch its tail and growl a warning. Alex dropped back. The lion didn't scratch or bite, but it could summon a guardian, which was worse. Alex couldn't afford a warning for scaring a child. Not when he had just signed up for a role.

Today he wasn't trying to get lost, as he sometimes did when he was at loose ends or trying to think through a problem with school. He glanced periodically at directions on the newsline, on the cuff of his scaleskin. Most people had eye implants to project the newsline on the cornea, but Alex was squeamish about his eyes, squinting, splintered green behind thick lashes. His mother had dropped the crumb that his eyes were just like his father's. All he saw of his dad was the coyote avatar he used to prowl the root, so he sometimes stared at his eyes in the mirror as if he could see his dad staring back. He hated looking into people's eyes and seeing small letters and numbers flashing in the corners. He once walked out on a date, one of the few girls in school he hooked up with, when he realized she wasn't staring meltingly into his eyes but was absorbed in a sordid story of sex slaves in City of the South.

He turned down a narrow street, which caused the lion to purr with satisfaction and rub its head against the little girl. "I'm a guy without a DP," he muttered; "so what? That makes me scary?" He knew the answer. The city had very little crime. DPs were programmed to prevent illegal acts. Marginal people, those without roles who needed coins to survive, outsider groups intent on protest or other mischief, had to turn off their DPs to do anything dodgy. But even those couldn't be sure that their DP wouldn't show up to save them from themselves. Of course, people in the know—world builders, city managers—seldom if ever used DPs, and when they did, they were generally small and unassuming, geometric shapes rather than anything mammal.

He ran his fingers through his bristly brown hair and straightened his shoulders, trying to look like someone who didn't have a DP because he didn't need one, not because he was up to no good. He wasn't in the mood to be stared or growled at. Without realizing, he had taken several turns that presented themselves, and now he was lost in what looked to be the crumpled edge of the city.

Almost as abruptly as a holo scene, the city changed from gleaming buildings with doors and window frames in a rainbow of colors to small gray buildings, shabby and hunched in the waning light. He realized he was the only person on the street except for a man in a nondescript scaleskin the color of the roadway who emerged from a door overhang and approached him, yellow teeth bared in what Alex hoped was a smile.

"Goo eve, suh. Spa coi or pafru?"

"What?" The man talked like a bowl of mush. Alex leaned forward to hear him better. A voice that managed to be both emotionless and sharp spoke behind him.

"Guest 3789. You have been disciplined and warned about begging on the street. I will summon a guardian in five seconds."

Whatever language the man spoke, he understood Alex's DP well enough. The DP he was convinced he had turned off except for the health and bodily danger override. Was this sad, hunched little man, now scurrying around the street corner, a bodily danger, or had his mother tinkered with his override? He suspected the latter.

"What language was that man speaking?" But the DP, true to its instructions, had already disappeared now that harm was averted.

Alex shrugged and focused on his plan for tonight. He was attending his first meeting of the Earth Firsters in a long time. He had quit going, in disgust, because all they did was talk; but tonight's discussion, "Story Making as Rebellious Art," might be something useful.

It felt good to be going someplace without his mother. When Alex went anywhere with her, Miranda was frequently recognized. People would nudge each other. Some would come up and shyly compliment her on a new foliage design or a curving streetway. Not all of those were Miranda's invention, but enough were. She was everywhere at Festival time, introducing new fabrications to remind people of the outside before it soured. Which had happened so quickly. She told him once about attending a pumpkin fair when she was five, everyone joking that the pumpkins were bigger than she was. By the time she was eight, cultivated fields were gone, destroyed by blight and by windstorms that tore vegetation from the ground and blotted out blue sky, by torrential rains that flooded homes. He remembered her face as she described the flood alarm the grandparents he had never met had installed at the front door and how they would scurry upstairs to avoid the water first seeping, then rushing in, until the alarm itself rotted away from all the wet. He accused her of exaggerating. The stories of yesteryear had pumpkins, gleaming orange in the sunlight, but not muddy water flooding in.

"Yes, well, those are stories," Miranda had replied, "of yesteryear. As in, no longer exists. If it ever did. Sometimes, I'm not sure myself. I was so young when it all fell apart, maybe I just imagined it." She said this as she worked on the dog's fur, black with white markings, thick in places and patchy in others. Like a real animal. You had to give her credit. Her creations weren't romantic like the sappy stories he secretly watched over and over. Her designs may have been as fake as the fruits they drank every night, but she did her best to make them seem real.

Alex stumbled against a magcart track. In the better part of the city, the tracks were a dark gray that contrasted sharply with the silver streetway. In the outer district, near the city wall, the streetway looked bruised and tarnished, blending in with the magtrack, hiding the three-foot difference in elevation. Alex was lucky the lip prevented him from stumbling in and breaking something, luckier still that no magcart was whizzing past. He looked at his newsline, 7:05. He was already late. He looked around. There were no parks in this shadowy part of Sanctuary to orient himself with. He focused on the newsline directions.

The door looked like every other door in this part of the city. No complementary colors to amuse the eye as you drifted from building to building. He hesitated a minute. He knew Earth Firsters were considered harmless. His dad had steered him away from 2084, where real protests supposedly happened. But if there was any chance auditors were still watching Earth First . . .

The door opened before he could knock. Faces stared at him—young, old, male, female, yet all looking alike. "It's Alex," a voice said, and Alex picked out Noel, a student a few years behind him at school that he sometimes hung out with. The other voices murmured a welcome that sounded relieved.

He sat cross-legged on the floor. A man at the story cube was projecting stories they were seeding into the newsline, about survival on the outside.

"We need people to get used to the idea that it is possible to survive outside. That a city like Sanctuary can remain enclosed but still provide managed access to the outside."

Alex raised his hand. The man nodded in his direction.

"What are the stories based on?"

"What do you mean?"

"Are they based on anything real? Have any of you been outside? I mean recently," he added hastily as several older members who had come to Sanctuary from outside started to answer.

"I have requested a reconnaissance visit. With guardians, of course, all the necessary precautions," the speaker answered bitterly. "Thus far, they haven't even given me the courtesy of a response. That is why we need to flood the newsline with stories."

"Stories they already know aren't true," Alex said. Out of the corner of his eye he saw Noel whispering to his neighbor. The man straightened up and look suspiciously at Alex. He knew he had been outed, yet again, as the son of Sanctuary's top world builder. The speaker bent down to hear a muttered comment then straightened up, his eyes narrow.

"Who did you say you were again? And what is your interest in Earth Firsters?"

Alex shook his head. "Earth Firsters? My mistake. Wrong meeting." He was too late. People had already begun to gather their things.

Rabbits, he thought. How would they face down the Sanctuary Council if they were scared by a teenage boy wandering in from the street? He remembered a story he did with his mother when he was little, "Thousands of Rabbits." That's what they reminded him of. As he backed out the door, another image came to him, the coyote loping along the root. His dad.

CHAPTER THREE

Miranda had been sitting at the bar for fifteen minutes before Tara arrived. She forced down any irritation, because she knew her face would give it away. Tara was a busy woman. Miranda was lucky she was available on such short notice. The Lavender Bar was a popular place, but the stools on either side of her were empty. This was the price she paid for being the top world builder in Sanctuary. She knew that people appreciated what she designed, but they wanted to take it for granted. Interacting with Miranda reminded them of the artifice.

Tara on the other hand, was almost invisible to the people in the bar, even though she was a tall, graceful blonde with a rhythmic, gliding walk. And, of course, a city manager, who could have anyone in the bar removed from their role, even arrested, with a flick of her eyelashes to summon a guardian. *How does she manage it?* Miranda wondered, as she did every time she saw Tara. *Carry so much power so invisibly?*

"Wonderful evening," Tara said. "Beautiful twilight. Just the right breeze. Yours?"

"My team," Miranda answered.

When Tara was a world builder, she designed most of the things that made Sanctuary the city it was, things everyone still used, like the packfruits they drank every day. Even now, Miranda suspected that Tara could design rings around her, but the admiration in her

SANCTUARY

voice was genuine. Miranda felt her tensions melting as her friend, boss, and occasional lover hopped up on a stool.

"So, what are we drinking?"

Without waiting to be asked, the bartender placed two small glasses of the drink for which the bar was named in front of them—a splash of alcohol-infused liquid followed by bursts of lavender-and-citrus-scented vapor. Orange and purple swirled as they clinked glasses.

"To Alex," Tara said, "and his amazing new role."

Miranda frowned and set down her glass, untouched. "Why would he pick story? There are so many other options, engineering, cityscaping. You offered to help him." She couldn't keep the reproach from her voice, even though they had been drifting apart for some time and tonight was a chance to restore the old friendship.

"I did." Tara set her glass down and brushed bubbles from her upper lip. I spent a whole day with him, introduced him to masters in many of the roles you proposed, things I thought would engage him."

She didn't add that Alex had been openly indifferent, checking the time on his newsline whenever he thought Tara wouldn't notice. They had been close when Alex was a small child, but when Tara became a city manager and Miranda a master world builder, things had to change, particularly her relationship with a subordinate and that subordinate's child. Tara had never explained to Alex why the trips to the park and the nights spent at Tara's flat, had become less frequent and finally nonexistent. She only hoped that Miranda had.

She didn't feel she had to explain to Miranda. Miranda was ambitious, and busy in her new role. And Tara had never believed Miranda cared as much as she did. She drifted into an affair with Tara because she was bruised by her failed relationship with Peter and at her age, past peak childbearing, unlikely to attract a new husband. But Alex? She relived the same stab of guilt she had felt at Alex's too polite greeting and behavior during that awkward day. Tara had talked too much and too quickly, engaging in conversations with various role masters, to cover the silence.

"I'm afraid Alex didn't take an interest in anything," she said to stop her own thoughts.

"Story making wasn't even on the list," Miranda objected.

"Your list," Tara said gently; "not Alex's list."

"That's not fair," Miranda said. "I asked Alex for ideas, and he refused to give me any, but I tried to include roles I knew he would like and do well in. Outside integrator, for example. I thought that would be perfect for him."

Tara paused and sipped her drink before replying. "I didn't think that would be a good idea. For one thing, it's a popular choice and highly competitive." She raised a hand to stop Miranda's defensive response. "And yes, he would probably be good at it. But given his history, I don't think anything to do with the outside would be suitable. Alex is obsessed with the idea of outside."

"All teenagers are obsessed with outside," Miranda replied. "Until they actually see it and realize that outside is simply an irredeemable mess. There are other cities, of course. We used to be able to visit them. I went to Asia City with my dad, before I started my apprenticeship."

"And now Asia City is a ruin." Tara responded. "Do you ever wonder what happened? Do you wonder why other cities fail while Sanctuary thrives?"

"We thrive because of people like you," Miranda responded impatiently. "And me. Some cities don't know how to plan for the future, much less manage for today. But what's the alternative? Outside? You and I know better. We grew up in it. Remember when the winds started blowing hard, churning up the dust into funnels? Our hair stood up from our heads with grit. I can still taste it in my mouth sometimes. You couldn't play with any toys outside; they would blow away, or the moving parts would clog with debris. And we weren't allowed outside for days after a rain, until it all evaporated."

"I'm older than you," Tara responded, "so my childhood was different. But I remember the sun hoods to block the sun's radiation—a sun we couldn't even see for all the clouds. It felt normal at the time, but when we went into the city and I took my hood off, I understood freedom for the first time, because I realized that until then, I didn't have it."

Miranda was silent.

"Alex has real potential with story. I stumbled on one of his stories in the root directories. There was no name to it, there never is at the root, but I knew it was his." She didn't elaborate, but the mother in the story was clearly Miranda, even down to the huge blue eyes.

"Karnofsky, one of the most interesting of the master story makers, is a friend of mine. He's reinventing story for a new generation of Sanctuary dwellers. He really liked Alex's story. He's going to take Alex on as an apprentice."

Miranda shook her head to clear it. This was too much to take in. And the vapors from the unaccustomed drink were making her head swim, even though she hadn't touched the small amount of viscous liquid at the bottom.

"Alex is hiding stories in the root?" she asked. "How long have you known this? That's totally illegal." The root was the unbuilt part of the Sanctuary newsline, with blank spaces that people could find and fill with whatever they wanted, where groups like 2084 and the Earth Firsters posted cryptic messages for their followers and people shared things—stories, art—that might get them in trouble at work or school. Root was one of Tara's greatest inventions, a place for people to let off steam, to share ideas that sounded rebellious if not outright seditious. It was also the easiest way to identify troublemakers. Three full-time archivists mined it daily for information. Miranda had worked on the project. She was still squeamish about the manipulation involved. She had warned Alex repeatedly to stay away from the root directories. He had been scathing about how stupid it was, how everybody knew it was a tool for the city managers, and yet here he was . . . And no one had told her . . . not even . . .

"I guess he hasn't shown it to you?"

Miranda shook her head. "I know he likes to watch stories, particularly the role-playing ones. I had no idea he was designing them." She sipped her drink to swallow the disappointment flooding her throat. Story maker! And it was so hard, almost impossible, to change a role once you picked it. She had such hopes. The strong liquor made her cough, which was good, because it gave cover for the tears sparkling her eyes.

"Story isn't just silly role-playing anymore. It's a way to explore what it means to be living in an enclosed city, to be human and alive when we have lost so much."

"What's the point of that?" Miranda protested bitterly. "Mistakes were made. Obviously. Our parents, their parents, didn't take care of what we had."

"Destroyed what we had," Tara interjected quietly.

"But we rebuilt. That's what humans do. We survive. We move forward. We can't do that if we are always looking back."

"We live in a city with a false sky and high walls you can't get close enough to touch. Sanctuary rescued us, and I for one remain forever grateful, but you can't ask a generation who never knew life on the outside to be equally appreciative. This is all they have ever known, so it is natural to focus on its limitations."

"But all those stupid stories of yesteryear," Miranda objected. "How do they all end? People going into the sunset. And why?

31

Because they were never satisfied; they always wanted more. Because of them, children miss the whole point of Sanctuary: being grateful for what you have, surviving on less."

"But I see all the requests, some of which get transmitted to you. They ask us to create things to make us feel like we have no limits," Tara said. "Like the outside never happened."

Miranda was silenced. She thought about some of her current projects and couldn't argue.

Tara put a hand on her arm. Miranda flinched at the unexpected contact. It had been quite a while.

"We've had an unspoken ban on the outside. Teaching it, except in carefully approved school lessons; exploring it in art. We can't see it or experience it in here, and visiting other cities is no longer allowed, so it is easy to pretend it doesn't exist. There's no actual law against discussing it, but it's frowned upon, and that's almost worse."

Miranda thought about the sessions with the school psychologist, very concerned and helpful, with suggestions for weaning Alex from his "unhealthy obsession." Miranda barely heard him. She was focused on the intent look of his DP, which meant it was taking detailed notes. Notes that would exist forever in Alex's file.

"I've been arguing against it. The prohibition has created a generation of children fixated on outside and mostly getting it wrong. I want the next generation, Alex's generation, to confront what we did to the world. Our parents got us into this mess. Alex's generation, and their children, will find a way out. Story making sounds like a silly, escapist thing, but stories like the one Alex created, these are our future. Ask him to show it to you."

Miranda shook her head. He had hidden it from her for a reason. She could imagine his reaction, the fight they would have, if she asked. She looked oddly at Tara. One of the things she admired most about Tara was her confidence in Sanctuary and the things they built for it. Life outside Sanctuary had never occurred to Miranda as an option. She would give everything she had to keep Alex safe from what the outside had become. And here was Tara, a member of the Sanctuary Council, saying the city wasn't enough.

Tara played with her nearly empty glass. "I think you should let Alex bring what he is thinking out into the open. He has the potential to transform Sanctuary even more than you. But he needs to be able to dream fearlessly. He won't do that if he's always dreading your reaction. He might not set limits on himself, but he will let himself be limited by you."

Miranda had nothing to say.

"Alex loves you, Miranda. He's going through the whole independence thing that teenagers do. You don't recognize it because you lost your mother before you were Alex's age, but my mother suffered through my teenage years. I remember. It's called 'adolescent rebellion.' Get your DP to brief you."

Miranda smiled slightly.

"I remember you as a young world builder. You were so full of ideas. There was no point in telling you no. It just made you more determined." Tara smiled sadly at the memory.

"You tell me no often enough now," Miranda said in a teasing voice to lighten the mood.

"You tell yourself no more than I do," Tara replied.

Miranda was silent. Was this true?

Tara picked up her glass again. "Your biggest worry was that Alex wouldn't pick a role. Well, he has a role. And we should be celebrating. I predict that he will do great things."

Miranda raised her glass and clinked with Tara. All that was left were gassy bubbles that made her cough.

Tara could tell by Miranda's mood that she was unlikely to go home with her tonight. It had been a long time. She wasn't even sure if she wanted that, but she missed Miranda, the warm feel of her in her bed. She softened and melted like the candles they had been forced to rely on at night, on the outside. Tara had always loved rolling and shaping the wax that dripped as the fire burned. Stroking Miranda after sex gave her the same feeling, sleepy and safe.

She had assumed, from the invitation, that Miranda was feeling the same. But of course it was about Alex. It was always about Alex. Tara wondered if Miranda even realized that Alex was another reason they had drifted apart. As he got older, and figured out the relationship between them, his easy relationship with Tara had soured, flaming into open hostility toward a replacement for his absent father. She knew that Alex's messy adolescence had hit Miranda hard. Tara had no wish to contribute to the situation.

She signaled the bartender, a tidy DP with a handlebar moustache and a lavender-striped shirt, for another special. A thin black stripe stretched across the stool next to Tara, widening into a black square that dissolved into a small man, no more than four feet tall, in a coat and tails.

"You have the anacoccus infection," he announced. "We are treating it with an effective and additional nutrients in your diet. No more alcohol for a fortnight and adequate bed rest. At least nine hours a night." He looked pointedly at the newsline above the bar, proclaiming 7:00 p.m. Miranda looked around. People were starting to leave the bar for home and dinner.

"I generally turn Jeeves off," Tara said. "I apologize." Tara, the inventor of DPs, was famous for her bossy little butler DP, an anachronistic early model that was difficult to control. She resurrected him occasionally for social events, but never in public. She was one of the very few authorized to actually turn off her DP at will. Tara muted Jeeves with a nod. "No recording of this," she said crisply to the bartender, who nodded blandly as he took away their glasses.

"I had him set to low-level monitoring, which of course means health sensors, but he should have waited until I was alone. I have to recalibrate him."

Miranda was startled and uneasy by the unexpected appearance of Jeeves—and his scolding, almost hectoring tone! Nobody talked to Tara that way. Why hadn't she replaced her DP? She studied her friend as she stood up from the barstool. Tara had always been thin, but was she thinner than usual? When had she last really looked at Tara? They were both so busy, they didn't meet up often.

A squirt of terror propelled her off the barstool. Tara needed to go home and rest. She couldn't imagine Sanctuary without Tara. Only Alex mattered more. She took Tara's thin elbow in her hand as if she needed guidance out of the bar. Tara gently brushed her arm away. They walked out into a skillful twilight, the sky darkening subtly from blue to violet, with rose clouds at the horizon. Two more days and there would be more clouds, starting as wispy gray cirrus clouds touched with flame at twilight, finally massing into heavy cumulus smudged with charcoal. She had approved the pattern in art several months ago. People seemed satisfied. No need to rethink it. She shook her head irritably. Lately it seemed impossible to turn off work thoughts.

She and Tara parted ways at the door. Tara didn't clasp her hand. With a viral infection, of course she wouldn't. She did look tired. There were shadows under her eyes, mimicking the cloud cover massing in the sky. Cloud cover was a bad idea. Everything staying the same was better, Tara staying the same. She watched her friend walk away until she was out of sight.

SANCTUARY

CHAPTER FOUR

Miranda woke the way she always did, instantly, as if she'd been poked by the morning. A headache was pounding behind one eye. She never had headaches. It must be the unaccustomed liquor. Miranda had always done everything full strength, including the end-of-week partying with Tara or her work team; but when she turned forty, her tolerance for liquor vanished overnight.

She struggled up and into the bathroom. Her short brownish-blonde hair looked snarled and dingy. She needed a glow rinse, but not this morning. She stared at her left eye. Pink rimmed. And was it larger than the other? Fear needled her skin, and she shivered involuntarily. What was that health alert?

She nodded, and a blue misty cube appeared and announced blandly, "the anacoccus virus. If left untreated, it can cause blindness, cancer, and result in death. Your infection is in the very earliest stages. You started the effective course last night. If successful, you should be healed by 12:00 p.m., May 16, 2070."

"Prognosis?"

"Risk of contagion for others is minimal at 3 percent. Your immune system is at 85 percent performance, so likelihood of cure is 90 percent."

Miranda frowned. Only 85 percent?

"Immune system at last check?"

"Ninety-three percent."

Miranda stared at herself in the mirror.

"Checked nine months ago," the DP reminded her. "You are three months overdue for another scan. You are in the top 5 percentile for women aged forty-two in the city."

"Thanks," Miranda said, and then stopped and looked at her DP. It folded into a black line and disappeared. Speaking without being spoken to, reassuring her when it sensed she was scared. Miranda had stripped her DP of all its empathic programming, but apparently some of it was built into the core. *Not good*, she thought. *I won't be turning you on anytime soon.*

Still, it was comforting to know this was a short-lived infection, and her odds of beating it were strong. Could she have gotten the virus from Tara? No, it was too soon; anyway, the risk of contagion was minimal. She should ask her DP about the risk factors, particularly for Alex, but she didn't feel up to it. She set the shower to heavy pulse. She needed to feel energized today, to change the conversation after yesterday's disappointments. Pulses of light, as hot as she could stand, beat against her skin. She shut her eyes as the light tattooed her face, stinging her enlarged left eye and making it water.

Miranda considered calling in sick, but she didn't want the gossip of a sick day. No one called in sick unless it was so serious, they often ended up never coming back, the subject of whispered conversation and then a slow and steady drift into oblivion. Miranda shivered again. Even though she was at the top of her game, she was in a young person's role. Work proceeded at a relentless, never-ending pace. At forty-two, Miranda was the grand old lady of world building, but no one questioned her right to remain as the head of design, at least not openly. Tara looked great, thin and strong with gleaming blonde hair, despite the virus. In all these years, Miranda had never asked her age, but she had to be at least fifty, if you did the math on her career. And in world building, everyone did the math. Tara had moved on to city manager a few years ago. Miranda assumed that would be her own path, but she was in no hurry. She liked doing the work, not just overseeing it.

She glanced sideways at the newsline, which she kept on low and projected from a magnifying eyelash to her scaleskin sleeve. She never wanted to be one of those distracted people, muttering to themselves about viruses, sun showers, drug lords and famine on the outskirts of Asia City, and the price of rice bread. Her newsline showed 9:05 a.m. She was late for work. Alex had already left, based on the empty packfruit skin on the table. She picked it up to recycle it, remembering the awful ant infestation that had taken months to resolve last year. It was too late to walk to work. She sighed and unfolded her magcart.

In front of the building, she met her next-door neighbor, struggling with her magcart. Her DP, a woman even older than she, was murmuring anxiously. "Careful there, love. Set it down gently now." Of course, given the heft and size of the magcart, the DP couldn't do anything to actually help, but she looked indignantly at Miranda, who hastily put down her own magcart and grabbed Mrs. Hooper's. It was one of the smaller models but still quite heavy. She set it down on the magtrack in front of the building, where it unfolded so that Mrs. Hooper could climb in. Miranda offered her an arm, but she waved it away.

"I'm fine," she said. "How are you, dear? We haven't seen you around lately."

We? For as long as Miranda had known her, Mrs. Hooper had been a widow. She looked at the DP, fussing and clucking as the magtrack connected to the cart and began to glow slightly. She must mean her DP. Some of the older people considered them actual friends.

"How is Alex?" Mrs. Hooper asked, leaning forward to keep the magcart from moving. "I haven't seen him in a few weeks. Does he have a role picked out yet?"

Miranda didn't answer. She still had to talk with Alex about his role.

As if reading her mind, the DP gave her a reproachful look and sniffed. Mrs. Hooper looked embarrassed at her DP's manner, although it was probably just reflecting what Mrs. Hooper herself was thinking.

"Well, I'd best be off," Mrs. Hooper said. "Bridge club." Her magcart settled into the slightly depressed track that ran along the streets. Only her hunched shoulders and curly gray hair showed above the track line. Miranda's lips tightened. The pewter-gray track, a few shades darker than the wide streetway, blended in too well at night. People were stumbling into them and bruising, even breaking things. *Maybe a dark blue. . . .* Mrs. Hooper's DP gave her one last indignant glance, folded itself into tiny imp size, and hopped, squeaking, into the cart.

"We'll have coffee soon," Miranda said to the retreating cart, her voice pitched so that the empty promise, meant for her own conscience, wouldn't be heard by Mrs. Hooper's aging ears—or her officious DP. Fortunately, Mrs. Hooper's head never turned back. *I'll talk to Alex,* Miranda thought. *Mrs. Hooper is a favorite of his. He should check in with her more.*

When Alex was a small child, Mrs. Hooper had been a lifesaver. Her friends at work thought she was silly, when a DP could alert you and summon emergency aid, instantly. But she had worked as an apprentice on the development of DPs. She knew all about design flaws, malfunctions. Many a night she came home to find Mrs. Hooper snoring in front of a story with Alex in the next room, forgotten. Still, she felt reassured that Alex was with Mrs. Hooper.

When she reached her floor, she found her work team: eight men and women in their twenties and thirties, with their short hair fashionably styled into bristles and their scaleskins mostly in edgy, stylish blacks and grays—an intentional contrast to the bright colors of Sanctuary buildings and furnishings. They were gathered around Shelley, a glum, whiny woman with a patrician beak of a nose. She spent all her time focused on her peers rather than designing anything worth adding to the world herself. Miranda found her hard to bear on good days. Today, she looked different, with a glow about her, as if she were finally getting the attention she thought she was due. No one noticed Miranda walk in until she caught Shelley's eye. Shelley took a moment to give the others a warning glance before she smiled, a little too broadly for someone who disliked Miranda as much as Miranda disliked her.

"You're late," she observed. "Everything okay at home?" Her eyes drifted up and down Miranda, assessing the design, her hair, stopping for just an instant at Miranda's left eye, which began to throb slightly from the attention.

Miranda forced a smile in return. "Everything's fine," she said. "Just one of those days."

Shelley looked at her skeptically. She was always on time coming in and on time leaving.

To change the subject, Miranda asked, "Is that a new design?"

Shelley twirled around. Miranda knew she had ambitions to be the team leader when Miranda eventually moved up to city management. She had grandiose ideas about what that meant in terms of "professional" behavior. It wasn't like her to prance about.

"Do you like it?" Shelley asked.

"Very nice," Miranda said. In truth, it was a pedestrian design, geometric patterns in gray and pink; some of the patterns were muted or missing, creating a slightly patchy effect that surely couldn't be intentional. Time for a new scaleskin, obviously.

"It's just something new I thought I'd try," Shelley responded. Behind her, Len snorted as he smothered a laugh, and Mikel turned away to hide his grin.

"Did you design it yourself?" Miranda asked politely, hoping that Shelley hadn't, because she had run out of lame, forced compliments. What was wrong with everybody this morning?

"Actually, Len did."

"Really?" Miranda was surprised. He wore his own scaleskin in solid black. She never thought of him as having an artistic side and, given the awful pattern, he didn't.

"Not the design. That's mine," Shelley said. "No, Len designed the fabric, or actually the lack of fabric."

"I don't understand," Miranda said. "That's not scaleskin?"

"Virtual," Len said. "Shelley is wearing tiny projectors that scan her contours and then project the design onto her body. With weather and surfaces totally controlled, who needs a fabric anymore?"

Shelley tilted her head, and Miranda could see that the cluster of tiny silver balls at each ear were projectors, not jewelry. Miranda started to say something, but Len interrupted. "I know we haven't completely got it down with the projection; there are glitches here, and here." He pointed out the bald spots on the design. "But we're close."

"Who green-lighted this?" Miranda asked.

"Well, I've been doing it at home, on my own time," Len said. "Shelley has been helping me." He looked at Miranda anxiously. "What do you think? Am I on to something?"

Miranda was concentrating on keeping her temper. Someone in her work team was developing something not at work, giving up his limited free time, because he didn't want her advice or criticism, didn't want her sharing any of the credit. Because he was replacing scaleskin, her first big achievement. *Breathe*, she told herself. She forced a smile. It was her own fault. She had been working on a project for months, at Tara's direction, that took her away from the group, a project of importance that didn't involve them. Of course their feelings were hurt.

"It's definitely something," she conceded.

Her eye was throbbing in time with her pounding head. Her work team. In what other ways were they shutting her out? She prided herself on being a fair manager, one who praised others' achievements. She had worked for months with Bethany on weather pattern variations. When Bethany finally achieved a rainstorm that gave the effect of being caught in a shower without using water, she had arranged the demonstration for the entire role community and given Bethany all the credit. And here was Bethany turning away guiltily, not meeting her gaze.

Len was looking at her expectantly. He was a first-class pain in the ass, moody and contemptuous of anything anyone else created, particularly her. Yet here he was, clearly expecting her praise while he demoed the application that would replace her scaleskin. Not her latest achievement, but an important one. And what had she done lately? A dog? A cat?

She forced a bigger smile. She was the team leader, after all, and Len was a top-notch, extremely hardworking, world builder. "It's really good, Len," she said. "And you're right, with the climate totally controlled, who needs a fabric any longer?"

Scaleskin, thousands of tiny, reflective feathery scales that could be infused in a moment with any design and shaped into a shirt, pants, or a dress, was thermostatically controlled to be airy yet warm. But scaleskins were expensive and specially fitted. If you gained or lost weight, you had to buy another. Who needed it, anyway?

"Well, I'll leave you to it," she said, and walked stiffly toward her office. "How is the cat coming?" Shelley called after her. Miranda pretended not to hear. Her glass office walls were checkered with floating holo awards, giving her at least the illusion of privacy, but Miranda knew better than to sit at her desk with her aching head cradled in her arms. She stole a look back at her team. They were crowded around Shelley in that ridiculous getup. They weren't intentionally ignoring her. They had forgotten about her entirely.

She studied the awards on the wall. The security award in particular pleased her. When the 2084 movement caught fire, the city managers were almost frantic with concern. Miranda had never been called into their meetings so often. A strong minority wanted to crack down, but Tara's cooler head had prevailed. She hadn't been a member very long, but Miranda could tell she was already a leader. The 2084 movement was studying the city wall, looking for weaknesses. Tara turned to Miranda. Together they opened the root area of the newsline to give people a place to be subversive, and stage-managed its accidental discovery. The archivists mined it for information that the city managers could use to track, and then marginalize, the leaders of 2084. The movement held open meetings the first Tuesday of every month now because, why not? Almost nobody attended.

Under her direction, Len designed a deterrent to keep people at least two feet from the wall. Children could still dance in front of its beautiful mirrors, but anyone who crossed the red warning strip would think twice about trying that again. It was a multipronged approach, and it seemed to do the trick. But lately—

A knock on the cubicle glass startled her. Tara was at the door, her face concerned, as if she could read her thoughts.

"Everything okay?" she asked. Tara was a conscientious city manager and visited all the Sanctuary work divisions at least once a month. But she had said nothing about stopping by last night. Tara was more than a boss, but Miranda wasn't sure how many people knew that. She had taken Miranda under her wing when her father died, leaving her orphaned just as she was starting her apprenticeship. She hadn't approved of Peter. Well, none of Miranda's friends did. But when Peter left, Tara had taken an interest in Alex, to the point of showing up for school events and awards. And as their relationship became closer, it morphed into something more. Not surprising, when carefully regulated birthrates turned sex into something you calculated with mathematical precision. Many people turned to immersive stories to recapture what sex could, and should, mean. Miranda was surprised and delighted to manage a physical relationship with no worries about unintended consequences. Her only problem had been keeping it from Alex.

She sensed he would see it as a betrayal of his father, maybe the reason his father had gone away. The secrecy had added to the surprising, addictive physical thrill of sex with Tara. She was a different person at night. But it all ended when Tara became a city manager. She carried the whole weight of Sanctuary's survival on her thin but capable shoulders. Miranda had been disappointed, but also, as the sex had become routine, sometimes even tiresome, she had been a bit relieved.

She forced a smile. "I got a late start," she said. "I guess I'm too old for the bar scene." Tara didn't reply.

"I was admiring my team's new development," Miranda added, determined to be the one to announce it to Tara.

"Ah, yes, the new scaleskin," Tara said.

Miranda's eyes widened. "It was intended to be a surprise. Do you truly know everything that goes on in this place?"

"I know a lot," Tara said. "But don't worry. I also know how to act astonished." She studied Miranda's face for a minute.

"Scaleskin was a wonderful invention," she said. "Design projection builds on what is best about scaleskin, the creativity of design, but with even less waste. Your team has learned well from you. They are building forward on the principles of design you model for them every day. You should feel quite proud."

Miranda's eyes sparked with tears, making her left eye burn. Tara really did know everything that went on in this place, even inside people's heads.

"How is the cat coming?"

Miranda shrugged uncomfortably. Her eyes roamed the awards on her walls again. Scaleskin, security, trees, weather. She remembered the shabby stuffed animals from her childhood. They grew soggy and moldy in the damp rainy season and were the first of many things to be discarded. How had she been reduced to designing toys?

Tara was studying her as she waited for a reply.

"Fine," Miranda replied. "I'm ready to start testing, I think."

Tara hesitated and looked at the motto that scrolled across Miranda's office wall in unending projection, interleaving between the awards and the portraits of Alex at various stages of childhood. "Technology is neither good nor bad. Nor is it neutral," she read aloud. "Kranzberg's third law. Have you ever wondered why we don't deploy robots for everyday use, instead of DPs?"

DPs, digital personas, were Tara's enormous contribution to city life: three-dimensional projections that used small, focused air concentration to appear, to move, and to handle small objects. They were plugged into the newsline and focused on you and your needs so that they filtered everything of importance to help you through your day. Nobody, even Miranda, who found her DP a daily annoyance, could imagine life without them.

"You know what they say about DPs," Tara said. "They *know* everything, but they can't *do* anything. If we morphed them into androids, we'd have a physical presence that knew everything and could do everything. Why don't we do that? We can create anything from growfiber. Light, strong, grown from genetically engineered cells to be almost indestructible and impossible to distinguish from human tissue, except it doesn't decay. We construct parts of people from growfiber all the time. Why not a whole person?"

Miranda thought about her neighbor, Mrs. Hooper, and her DP clucking at Miranda to lift the magcart. What did they do when people like Miranda weren't around? Unless you registered as disabled, you didn't get robot assistance. And a robot, unlike an android, didn't look like a person and lacked the sentience and omniscience of a DP.

"I've always assumed it was a materials issue," she said cautiously. "Even though we create our own growfiber, built things use energy, take up space. You don't even get a robot unless you really need one."

"You're partly right," Tara conceded. "But even when we give someone a complete robot to replace their mobility, they aren't androids. You still need a DP, even if you use a robot for physical activity. We're capable of building androids, so why don't we?"

Miranda's pulse quickened. For the first time that dismal morning, she forgot about her eye and the infection coursing through her body. Was she being asked to design the first production human android? Were the pets just a stepping-stone to this?

Tara brought her back to reality with a thump. "Don't worry," she said. "You aren't being asked to design a human android. I've done designs, as have others. We even have wonderful working prototypes with growfiber skin so soft and lustrous the only way you can tell they aren't real is that humans generally don't look this good. This isn't a new idea. It's one we've discussed a lot and discarded."

Miranda started to ask a question but stopped.

"Think about the possibilities," Tara said. "If you had a bad birth number and couldn't have a child. You see people with child DPs, but imagine a warm-skinned android child, with your family features, holding your hand crossing the street, looking lovingly into your eyes. Maybe it always stayed that way, or maybe you replaced it every few years with an "older" android child. And this android could do everything your DP does—feed you the newsline, get you from place to place, monitor your health, keep your calendar. But it also keeps your home clean, your food stocked;

it protects you on city streets. It could even go to work with you and do your designs, turn in your assignments. If you have real children, you no longer need to worry about them, because the android is always there, keeping them safe."

Miranda imagined Alex with an android companion. Not having to worry if he came back late at night. She smiled at the thought.

"And what would we be doing?" Tara asked.

"Pardon?"

"While our androids are out and about doing amazing things, conquering Sanctuary on our behalf, what would we be doing?"

Miranda thought about it. She pictured an android that looked just like her, but without the throbbing eye, the short temper—picking up food for Alex, reading him stories when he was small. She could have used an android when she was a single parent working long hours. When Alex was little, the slightest alarm from her DP, synced up to Alex's blue rabbit DP, could send her scurrying home, wondering if she would make it in time.. An android that looked like her, who could handle any problem—from soothing a nightmare to insisting on study time—would have been a lifesaver. And yet . . .

Tara was watching her face. "Exactly," she said. "We don't do androids because we can."

Both women were silent for a moment. "Now that I am a city manager, you haven't seen much of me. I'm sure you have wondered what goes on over there, to take up so much of my time?"

"I'm sure its important stuff," Miranda said cautiously.

"When I meet with the other city managers, we talk mostly about the work of people like you, the leaders of divisions—cityscapers, role counselors, food provisioners, disposers, guardians, outside integrators, archivists, story makers, healers. We talk about how things coordinate for the good of Sanctuary. Everything we design, everything we build, has consequences. We work closely with a special branch of healers in Psych Services who keep their fingers on the pulse of the Sanctuary psyche.

"I know it's popular, particularly among the young, to talk about 'big brother.' We know all about the latest movement, the Earth Firsters, who are convinced we should return to the outside and heal it. And do you know what our biggest concern is?"

"What?" Miranda asked cautiously. "Alex experimented a bit with Earth Firsters, but it didn't mean anything. Just rebellious teenage stuff." She suspected he might even be a member of 2084, although that group was fading. She shuddered and steeled herself to hear that Alex was being monitored.

"Our biggest problem," Tara continued, "is that there aren't more of them. More collaborating in groups around a shared belief system. The city psyche is becoming insular and self-satisfied. People are choosing DPs—who can be anything or anyone you like, who can be turned off when they argue too much or disagree—over messy, unsatisfactory people. Our numbers in certain areas—independent reasoning, empathy, personal attachment, and outward focus—are sinking dangerously."

Her voice trailed off as she frowned at something Miranda couldn't see. "No, we'd never do androids. That would tip us right over the edge. We need to develop things that counterbalance this tumble into narcissism." She looked at Miranda.

"You may be feeling funny that the successor to scaleskin has been developed," she said, "but don't. The greatest successes, like DPs, have terrible consequences that rob their creators of sleep every single night. I notice you mostly keep yours turned off."

Miranda nodded guiltily. She started to explain, but Tara waved the explanation away.

"You're smart," she said. "You understand the DP is just a tool. Unfortunately, most of the city takes these beautiful, all-knowing creatures very much to heart. So, we must work with that, to meet them where they are. We want to use android technology to create empathy and awareness of others. That's why I asked you to create a very special class of android, the household pet. And because we want people to care about their pets, to see them as real, I asked you to design it quietly and to not involve your team. I know there have been consequences to you and to the team's dynamics, but we felt the cost was worth it."

"You did really well with the dog," she continued. "I think it can be released at Festival, where it will be a big hit. Where are you keeping it? Are you and Alex playing with it at home?"

Miranda thought guiltily about the dog, stuffed away in a cupboard, where she thought about it as little as possible. It was Fred to the life; and yet, it wasn't. Better not to answer at all than to lie.

"I think it's ready," she responded. "I'm focused on the cat now. It's almost there."

"Do you have it with you? Let's see it."

Miranda pulled it out of her pack and placed it on the desk. The cat looked up at the women with wide eyes and meowed.

Tara's delicate hand moved across the fur and then reached in and gave a strong tug. "Amazing!" she said. "It feels like I am pulling on something real."

The cat ducked its head and arched its back in pleasure at Tara's touch.

"How did you pull this off?"

"Right above the follicle air jets are tiny cross-hatch jets. Fewer, but emitting a stronger pulse of static current. The crosscurrents come into movement when you tug and create powerful resistance."

"Brilliant!" Tara said, smiling her wide, curved smile. "So, what else can the cat do?"

"It pays close attention to its owner and can gauge the owner's mood against the standard fifty-point psych reference scale. It will

50

gaze at you and offer you comfort when the gauge registers sadness, rub against you and demand attention when you are distracted or focused on something else, look chastened when you are angry, and act playful, which I interpreted as mildly predatory, when you wave a ball or feather on a stick in front of its face. There are twenty different actions and ten body changes based on the fifty-point scale."

Tara buried her narrow face in its fur. "I can't get over the warmth of this fur," she said. "If I didn't know it was currents, I could believe it was real. And the jets?"

"Self-ejecting and self-cleaning," Miranda answered. "Exceeding city health standards."

Tara smiled. "I knew I could trust you for that," she said. "Hygiene Mary."

Miranda was annoyed. "Is that my nickname? Because I honestly don't—"

"You were the single mother of a son," Tara responded. "You lost your mother to an outside illness. Of course you wanted to keep him safe. And you did. Alex had almost no illness growing up. The other parents were envious, I think."

Tara continued stroking the cat, which arched it back against her hand and purred. "I am envisioning a line of amazing fur coats in time for Festival. I can see all the ladies strolling around City Center Park, their white furs reflecting the Festival lights. I'll send a designer to you this afternoon."

Miranda smiled. "Great idea." Covering up virtuskin, which she pictured in that patchy pink-and-gray design. She didn't like herself for taking satisfaction in trumping Len and Shelley's invention. She smoothed her face so that she didn't look like her own cat after it pounced on the feather attached to the stick.

SANCTUARY

CHAPTER FIVE

Alex had spent the last four years schooling himself not to expect anything much. Ever since he turned twelve, and his mom loosened the reins a little, he had explored the city from end to end, hoping for something different, something out-of-the-way and worth investigating. Even the outskirts of the city, where the streetways were surprisingly narrow and the people didn't meet your gaze, were more sad than mysterious. He had combed every inch of the wall, from the polished, mirrored perfection fronting local parks to the places where the mirroring was chipped and doused with grease and debris from the garbage magtrains leaving the city every day. There was nothing left to see.

Still, his pulse quickened as he approached the arts complex, where story making was one of the many roles taught. His first year would be all classes, learning the ins and outs, and then the all-important second and third years would be spent following someone in the field. If you got a good mentor. . . . He shook himself mentally. There he was again, hoping for something that wasn't there. He had played in enough stories, and seen many more, to know that storytelling was just another way to keep everyone in line, marching in rhythm from birth to role to marriage and, if you were lucky, children. And then, where? To death, quietly, probably painlessly. Nobody talked much about it. Visitors to that floor of the healing centers were strictly regulated. Close family members only, for a very short visit at the end. The health of the city was the excuse, but Alex knew better. They didn't want anyone questioning the point of it all.

He interrupted the thought and looked around, as if someone were watching him and reading the inside of his head. Alex had spent most of his teenage years protecting his privacy. He had watched his mother closely with her DP and learned how to make his DP—a gray, fuzzy ball that blended in with the streetway—as stupid and utilitarian as possible. But even when he turned it off, it was in standby mode, in case he got hurt or did something stupid. He suspected it reported things to his mother, so he didn't turn off recording. Instead he scrubbed the memory selectively, using the records he kept to craft a story of each day. It was kind of fun, actually, and gave him the idea that story making might be something he would like to do. As he entered the building and stepped onto the stairs that moved when his feet were firmly planted, he wondered what he would need to scrub about the day. Maybe nothing at all.

He entered the training room casually, mad at himself that his heart was beating faster. *Expect nothing*, he reminded himself. Role students were pulled from all over Sanctuary—different neighborhoods, different schools. And Sanctuary was a big place, even if it didn't always seem like it. He looked around the room and was relieved to see that he only knew a few people of the twenty or so students gathered in the room waiting for Karnofsky, the instructor. Guys and girls looked him over appraisingly and then looked away.

Alex knew he was nothing special to look at—tall but too skinny, with his mom's thin features. But not her eyes. His were deep green slits, fringed by long lashes. Like his dad's, his mother admitted. One of the few things she told him about his father. He rarely bothered with his unruly hair other than to keep it short. Smith, a guy from his school, nudged the girl standing next to him and whispered in her ear. Her eyes widened as she stared openly at him.

When she saw him noticing, she reddened and turned away. A jerk, just like the others. Too bad, because she was kind of cute.

Smith strolled over. "What are you doing here, Davis? Your mother couldn't get you into world building?"

Alex shrugged. "No interest," he said.

"So, you're interested in story making?" Smith asked skeptically. Story making was viewed as a fallback for people who couldn't cut it in more-demanding roles.

Alex shrugged. He had already said as much as he wanted to Smith. He was hoping he would see nobody he knew, that he could leave his mother and her reputation behind for at least a little while.

"I guess your mom can't fix everything," Smith said with a laugh. He tapped Alex on the shoulder and moved back to the cute girl. She wrinkled her nose sympathetically at Alex before turning to talk to Smith. He should have asked Smith what he was doing here. Couldn't get into cityscaping? He slumped his shoulders. Who cared, anyway? Story making was going to be just like school. Sitting around waiting . . . for nothing at all.

Karnofsky charged into the room. He was a little man with a large stomach that folded in waves under his scaleskin, and with flyaway hair that couldn't conceal his balding, bony head. He rubbed his hands together.

"All right, let's get started. We'll dispense with introductions and why you chose story making, particularly since most of you probably didn't. I'll either get to know your names as we progress, or . . . I won't." His eyes, under curly gray eyebrows, were unexpectedly sharp.

He gave them a brisk history of story, from the cave dwellers making sense of being human; to classical and Renaissance eras; through the golden age of art and industry, when man believed he could do anything to the world he had conquered; to the twenty-first century, when man began to realize exactly what he had done and stories took a dark and twisted turn; to . . .

"To the age of Sanctuary. Where we have fixed things so life is once again good, as long as we stay inside the magic circle. So, what do we make of storytelling in this wonderful predicament in which we find ourselves, Mr.?" He studied a list streaming across his wrist. "Mr. Davis?"

Alex jumped. He was slouching in the back, playing a game, hoping to make it through the day unnoticed. But he had been listening. All eyes turned to look at him. He took a breath.

"It's a distraction," he said, "and a control mechanism. To keep us from realizing." He stopped. This was a bad idea.

Karnofsky was listening carefully. "Realizing what, Mr. Davis?"

Alex waved a hand. "This. All of it. Nothing here is real. There's no point to any of it. To roles, to stories. We destroyed what was real, which is out there, and kept just enough to build a fantasy world for ourselves. But it can't last. How can it? We are the heroes in our stories. We do great things in the stories of yesteryear, and it makes us feel better because, really, we can't do much at all anymore except survive." Alex amazed himself as everything he thought came pouring out.

"And if survive is what we do, even all that we do, isn't that something?"

"Not when we ruined everything else. We should be figuring out what made us do that, not just living our lives like nothing happened."

"And you don't think story can have a role to play in figuring that out?"

Alex shrugged. He had already said too much. His mother would be hearing from Karnofsky, and then he'd be hearing from her.

Karnofsky turned from him to the rest of the class. "What do the rest of you think of Mr. Davis's theory?"

An angry babble resulted. The voice of the cute girl seated next to Smith rose higher than the rest. "If story is a distraction, what's wrong with that? My mom works long hours in disposal. I take care of my brother while she's gone. If we relax together as a family over a story, what the hell is wrong with that?" She turned around in her seat to glare at Alex. Her face was red, her eyes liquid with angry tears.

"Nothing," he murmured, his eyes fixed on his shoes.

"I disagree with Davis," Smith spoke up. "We do stories of yesteryear to understand what we had. Sure, they're fun, but they also tell us a lot about the world that was. If we are ever going to rebuild it, we have to understand it."

"A very good point," Karnofsky said. Other voices chimed in, agreeing with Smith. Alex shrugged. If participating in stories about people on horses that no longer existed riding into sunsets that no longer occurred made you feel like you were going somewhere with your life, who was he to argue otherwise?

At lunch, Alex sat by himself and sucked a packfruit. The other students broke into groups naturally. The few students he knew from his school clustered around Smith. Nobody looked around for him. He tilted his head back and shut his eyes, letting the warmth of the fabricated sunlight play on his face. His mother told him the light was calibrated to stimulate essential nutrients in the body. He didn't care. It felt nice and warm. A shadow loomed over him, blocking the light. Alex sat up hastily.

"My apologies for startling you," Karnofsky said.

Alex stood up, almost knocking into the smaller man. It was the expected deference of the student to the master, but now he towered over Karnofsky, who had to tilt his head to speak. He had been surprised to get an invitation to study under Karnofsky, who had made the best of the role plays he sometimes indulged in. They were alternately funny and scary, but with twists that hinted at a deeper purpose. He had been disappointed that the man's appearance didn't match his stories. But he was open to the experience of learning something new in a way he hadn't been since he was twelve, and school began projecting you into a slot you would occupy the rest of your life. The morning's lesson had been disappointing, but he didn't say that out loud.

If it bothered Karnofsky to look up at Alex, he didn't show it. "I was impressed with the story you submitted," he said. "You have a very interesting perspective on the outside. You take it very seriously without romanticizing it. Have you ever been outside?"

Alex shook his head.

"Interesting. I have. And your understanding is that of someone who has spent some time out there. No doubt your mother—"

"We don't talk about outside," Alex said quickly. "She hasn't seen the story."

Karnofsky lifted an eyebrow but didn't reply. "Well, lunch is ending soon. I should have a little nibble myself." With a quick nod, he turned to walk away. Without turning back he said, "Keep asking your questions, Mr. Davis, and sharing your thoughts. Try to learn something from the lessons here. Don't dismiss the stories we watch out of hand. If no one can answer your questions, maybe it is because there are no answers yet. But if *you* are asking, so are others. Try to answer your own questions, in the stories you design."

Alex watched him walk away. Story making might be bearable, after all. At least it would be better than school.

CHAPTER SIX

Alex's mother was waiting for him when he got home. She followed him into the kitchen as he grabbed a grape packfruit. He assumed she wanted to hear about his first day in story making, so he gave her a short report. He intended to be neutral about what was, on balance, a pretty good day, but he found himself getting a little excited as he explained Karnofsky's approach to story.

"He told me to go beyond entertainment, to answer for myself the questions I ask that nobody else seems able to answer." He paused, realizing that Miranda might take this as a criticism of her parenting, but instead she seemed distracted.

"That's great, Alex," she replied.

"What's up?" he asked. Usually she was too focused on him and his activities. For the past year he'd had to brace himself daily for interrogations about role tests and interviews. He knew she had wanted a more prestigious role for him. She'd never got over that award he'd won for an outersuit, intended for people to wear in a mass exodus from Sanctuary. She had wanted him to go after a role in engineering, but when he realized the city had no intention of planning for its ultimate demise, he lost interest. Before he knew it, he was sixteen—and practically the only student with no role lined up when he left school.

He knew his mother believed his reluctance to choose a role was intended to deliberately hurt her, but if he was honest with himself, he was just scared. In Sanctuary, everyone doing their roles, day in and day out, was an intricate dance that couldn't be allowed to break down. Once you were trained up in a role, there weren't very many mechanisms to change. If you were discontented, or a poor performer, you were given lots of counseling, because if you were let go, you ended up as one of the marginal ones—cadging a life on the outskirts of the city or being supported by family and friends. It was every kid's nightmare. But choosing a role was so . . . final. It was accepting that Sanctuary was the answer to the conundrum of life on a ruined planet. It was an answer Alex just couldn't accept. Maybe because his father hadn't.

His mother continued to stare into space, her huge eyes narrowed and her mouth pursing, in, out, in, out.

"Cats," Miranda said. "Or rather, one cat. The cat I've been designing for a couple of months. I think it is almost there; maybe it's actually there. I don't know. I need a test case. What do you think? Do you want a pet?"

He recoiled at the idea of some robot cat following him around, rubbing up against his leg, but he stopped the instant denial before it was spoken. His mother looked so vulnerable in that ratty bathrobe, not a scaleskin but something the grandmother he'd never met had brought with her from the outside. "Let me think about it," he said. Then he had a brainwave.

"I know this older couple," he said, "bridge buddies of Mrs. Hooper. They are always talking about the cats they had outside. I'll get in touch with them tonight. They would probably be delighted to give it a whirl."

Miranda looked at her son curiously. He had never had a gang of friends, but there were always a few boys and girls he played with when he was little. As he got older, and rebellious adolescence kicked in with a vengeance, they melted away. Miranda had been almost too busy to notice. A year or so ago, he had shot up six inches in height. He was a good-looking boy, almost a man, but she didn't know if he had ever had a girlfriend. And yet he was friends with people old enough to be his grandparents. Old enough . . . to tell him all about the outside. She shivered and pulled her bathrobe more tightly around her. It would be a good idea to spend more time with Alex and to meet his friends, whatever their ages.

"That sounds perfect," she replied. Please set up a meeting as quickly as you can."

Alex was as nervous as a cat himself as he waited for his mother to arrive at the Fiskes. He insisted on meeting her there rather than arriving with her. As he waited, he looked around their shabby flat critically, as his mother would do. Miranda wouldn't say anything, but those enormous blue eyes would take in everything, including the shabby couch covered in real afghans—not holo designs, afghans Mrs. Fiske had made on the outside, colorful designs that showed skill despite the inevitable fraying with age.

The Fiskes were fussing about, moving things from one table to another, bouncing on their plump feet with excitement. They were a round couple. Round, jolly faces; round little ringlets of cropped curls on their heads; round bodies with protruding bellies. They could have been twins rather than husband and wife, except that the husband was tall and broad shouldered while the wife was tiny.

Miranda was right on time, arriving shortly after work ended. The Fiskes greeted her with the eagerness of people who didn't get many visitors. You were provided for when your roles were finished, but since most people socialized within their role groups, your social life could end abruptly. Something a pet might help with, Miranda realized, and thought of Mrs. Hooper.

Of course there were the DPs. The Fiske's DP, a tidy little man in a green velvet suit, was busy presenting small cups of coffee essence to everyone.

"Thank you, Harmonium," Mrs. Fiske said. The man bowed and replied with a light, somewhat tinny musical stanza. The Fiskes looked at Miranda's face and burst into laughter.

"We like the music!" Mr. Fiske said.

Miranda looked at Alex. He hadn't blinked an eye. He looked entirely at home, sprawled on the Fiskes' patchwork sofa. Miranda realized he was probably a frequent visitor and thought guiltily again of how little she knew about her son's life when he wasn't at school or in their flat.

"So, you wanted to know about our kitties," Mrs. Fiske said. "Starlight was our favorite. You're leaning against her."

Miranda jumped and realized she was indeed leaning on a cushion, remarkably lifelike, of a black cat with white spots.

"Her spots looked like stars in the night sky," Mrs. Fiske said. "She was very regal. Knew her worth, you see. Didn't approach just anyone. He was her favorite." She nodded at her husband.

"Albert Fiske," he reminded Miranda, because their first names had been lost in a flurry of welcomes. "I was in streetways. We worked a lot with world builders, so of course I've seen you about, although you wouldn't have noticed me."

Miranda murmured something noncommittal and smiled the way she did when people came up to her on the street. She might have seen him, since they did a lot with streetways design when Alex was little, but when focused on a job, she didn't tend to notice the people milling around.

"Albert retired three years ago," Mrs. Fiske (*What was her name? Adele, that was it.*) said. "You can't think how he misses it. He's got nothing to keep him busy now. We loved our cats. The cushions are such a poor substitute."

Miranda turned over the cushion of Starlight and gasped. The front was entirely furred with something deep and nappy. As her hand brushed through the curls, puffs of dust arose. She hastily put the cushion back and tried to wipe her hand unobtrusively on the sofa.

"Tell me about Starlight," she prompted.

"It wasn't only Starlight we had," Adele said. "There was also Peter."

"Old Peter," Albert said. "Like the story."

"Story?"

"The Irish folktale: 'Old Peter's Dead, Now I'm the King of the Cats.' We had a Tom, also, but he died of the cat fever that went around the outside. No vets anymore. It was all you could do to find a doctor for your own ailments." Adele teared up and wiped her eyes on a cushion that Miranda could see was a calico cat, fortunately unfurred.

"Peter also left us," Albert Fiske said. "He didn't do well without his sparring partner. And then, finally, Starlight."

"She knew," Adele murmured. Albert patted her hand.

"So then we came inside," Albert said. "We wouldn't have left our babies, but once they left us. . . . You wouldn't know it to look at me now, but I was a strong one. Lots of muscles. I was put to work right away building streetways. I remember when the world builders started changing them from simple roads that people walked to broad silver ways with magcart tracks built in. I remember seeing you as a young world builder. "

"It was quite a treat when Alex said you wanted to visit," Adele said. "Old home week for Albert." She nudged her husband, and he blushed.

"I notice that Starlight has actual fur," Miranda said. "How did you manage that?"

Both Fiskes burst into peals of laughter. "Every time we had a haircut," Albert said, and shook his curly head in her direction. Miranda fought hard to keep the distaste off her face and again rubbed her hand unobtrusively on the sofa. Alex noticed and smiled sardonically to himself.

"Would you want another Starlight if I could create one?" she asked the Fiskes.

They exchanged solemn glances.

"N-o-o-o," Albert said finally. "I don't think there could be another Starlight. She was a little miss, she was. One of a kind."

"What would you say to a gray cat?" Miranda asked. She pulled the prototype out of the bag and turned it on with a glance. It jumped off her lap and onto the floor, where it arched its back and looked around curiously.

Mrs. Fiske gave a gasp. "Oh, my word," she said. She reached a tentative hand to the cat. It backed away but not so far that her hand couldn't reach. She stroked the fur, and her eyes instantly teared up. "I never thought I would feel that again." She turned away, her shoulders shaking.

"You will have to forgive my wife," Albert said gruffly. "She's a bit overcome. When we lost Starlight, we never expected to have a pet again."

"Are you willing to give this one a try?" Miranda asked.

Albert's gnarled hands played on the fur. The cat arched into his touch and purred. He turned away to his wife so that his face was hidden from Miranda and Alex.

He blew his nose noisily into a handkerchief before turning back. "I suppose we might as well," he said. "Not much to do these days, except attend memorials as the old streetways crew dies out."

"These people are fantastic," Miranda said to Alex after they said their goodbyes.

"I like older people," Alex said. "They have much better memories of outside than you do. Before things went so bad."

They walked along the streetway silently. Miranda glanced surreptitiously at her son. Surely, he was taller than last month? "But you do have friends your own age," she said, making it a statement rather than question. "That boy, Parker." When was the last time he had stopped by the flat? It must have been at least a year.

Alex hesitated before replying. "He got a role early," he said. "He's apprenticed in engineering now. We kind of lost touch."

"There must be someone you hang out with," she said. "Is there a girl you like?"

"Not really," Alex responded. He looked down at her worried face and took pity on her. "There's some cute girls in my training, though." He couldn't tell his mother that his most important relationship was with a coyote. A coyote who would soon take him away from this claustrophobic place. His mother looked smaller in the twilight, or maybe it was the two inches he had put on this year. The magnitude of what he was about to walk away from suddenly hit him. He took his mother's hand, which felt small and fragile in his. She didn't pull away, although they weren't a physical family. They walked hand in hand back to the flat as the darkness deepened and grow lights haloed all the trees.

SANCTUARY

CHAPTER SEVEN

Alex seemed to perk up now that he had embarked on his role. Neither he nor his mother were morning people. They barely managed a greeting if they bumped into each other—both running late—in the mornings. But Alex began to wait for her to eat dinner, and he talked eagerly about what he was learning from Karnofsky. Miranda listened and was reminded of sharing her stories of Tara with her dad. Alex looked so much like her dad, with his lanky frame and wild, wiry hair. She was quite excited when Alex told her the Fiskes had asked them to coffee. It was like the old days, when the two of them went on excursions around the city together.

———————

"I don't understand," Miranda said. She fought to keep her voice neutral. She petted the rich gray fur of the cat absently, and it purred in response.

The Fiskes' eyes grew rounder with dismay. "We're really grateful you chose us," Albert hastened to say; his wife clucked and murmured in response. Harmonium showed up with a plate of cookies and coffee essence. He nudged her politely with the tray.

"No, thank you," she said stiffly, although the Fiskes had clearly gone all out to mitigate the disappointment.

Alex took a cookie, solidified and shaped packfruit paste, and nibbled. "Delicious," he murmured. Harmonium wheezed politely in response.

"I don't understand," Miranda repeated. "The fur, the eyes. It looks exactly—"

"All the pieces are perfect," Adele Fiske said gently. "It's just the whole package."

"What about the whole package?"

"It follows us everywhere. Tries to guess what we're thinking," Albert Fiske said.

"And cats don't do this?" Miranda asked.

Both Fiskes burst into laughter. "A cat walks by itself," Albert said.

"You have to win over a cat, not the other way about," Adele said. "They make their own choices. And they play favorites. Albert was Starlight's favorite, although she would make do with me if he was working late."

"Whereas, Old Peter," Albert chimed in. They looked at each other and fell silent.

"She looks right and feels right, dear," Adele said. "But she's not her own person."

"She's not an old soul," Albert said. "A cat always reminds you that before people came along and built their cities, there were whole civilizations of cats."

"I think you maybe put a DP in a cat's body," Adele finished. "She's eager to please, that's for sure, but a cat is a creature *you* want to please. To reach a mutual understanding."

"A cat is a friend, you see," Albert finished.

"Yes, well, I'll take these concerns back to the drawing board," Miranda said. "I think I can see the problem, and with some reworking of the psych scale response . . ." *Randomize*, she thought; *add some capriciousness.*

The Fiskes smiled politely.

"Well, let me take another few weeks, see what I can adjust," she said.

The Fiskes looked at each other again. Mrs. Fiske nodded at her husband.

"If it is all the same to you," he said awkwardly, "Adele and I won't participate anymore. We've changed our minds, you see."

"We think we are better off with our memories," Adele said. "We wouldn't want to spoil them with a robot cat."

"If you give me a chance, I really think I can design something," Miranda said.

"I don't think we want anything designed," Adele said. "We thought we did, but the problem is . . ." She looked to her husband for help.

"You can't design a soul, you see," Albert said.

Miranda picked up the cat and stood. She pressed her thin lips together. "Well, thank you for your time and effort," she said stiffly. Alex grabbed her arm and guided her out of the Fiskes' flat. The Fiskes followed Alex and Miranda to the door, murmuring their thanks, such an honor to be included in this wonderful project, wishing Miranda all the luck and success in the world.

Before Miranda knew it, she was sitting on the couch in her own flat with a glass of something Alex had brought her with a strong vapor that made her cough. How long had that stuff been around, and why did Alex know where it was stored?

"So, that's that," she said.

"Well, I guess we both should have seen they would be a tough sell," Alex said. "My fault. I should never have suggested the Fiskes."

"I don't know what you mean," Miranda said. "They were perfect, right up to the end, when they pulled the plug on three months of very hard work with sad little smiles and a plate of cookies."

Alex studied her. "But they had lives on the outside, before all the troubles," he said. "They knew and loved real cats. You probably could never have competed with memories."

"That's ridiculous," Miranda said. "You really think the Fiskes prefer their dusty stuffed pillows and memories to what I can develop?"

Alex was silent for a moment. "Where's the dog you built?" he asked. "Robot Fred. Is he still locked in the cupboard?"

Miranda stiffened. "Okay," she said. "I can see the mistake I made. And you're right. I've been afraid of this assignment. Afraid to tackle the ghost in the machine. The soul of the cat, I think Albert called it. They were right to say it's a DP in a robot body, except the blue rabbit you had when you were a toddler had more spirit and personality than this so-called cat." She aimed a little kick at the gray cat winding around her ankles. It looked at her in wounded surprise and scuttled under the sofa. "So, back to the drawing board." She narrowed her eyes and pushed her lips in and out.

Alex watched his mother with both admiration and a touch of alarm. *This is why she's a world beater of a world builder*, he thought. "I think the Fiskes might have been serious about not participating anymore."

Miranda opened her eyes. "That's fine. Don't worry," she said. "They've been very helpful. More than helpful."

"You're very scary, do you know that?"

Miranda smiled. "You have no idea." She packed the cat back into its case and headed to her bedroom. Alex's voice stopped her.

"There's something else I wanted to tell you. Something different about my role work."

Miranda turned to face him.

"They're starting something new with the first years. Psychological profiling, to make sure we are a good fit for our roles." Alex looked down and didn't meet her gaze. "Next week we'll start spending two afternoons a week with Psych Services. We're one of the test groups. You probably already know about this."

"No," Miranda answered slowly. "This is news to me. Were they planning to alert the parents?"

"We were told it's not a big deal," Alex said. "According to Karnofsky, the most recent crop of apprentices is having trouble settling

70

down in their roles, and the city managers want to know why. To help us, apparently." His voice was dry.

Miranda knew he was telling her this because he was scared. *He's hiding things, and not just from me.* She thought about Alex's rebellious attitudes, the unexplained gaps in his DP's memory files, his open contempt for Sanctuary. The psych evaluation might be fine for some, but not Alex. Definitely not Alex.

SANCTUARY

CHAPTER EIGHT

Alex slipped in the door at 2:00 a.m. His head was whirling from the story bar. He had finally made a few friends, guys and girls as disenchanted with Sanctuary as he was. They shared the stories they were really working on, the stories they hid even from Karnofsky. He was grateful for the craft he was learning, but the stories they studied were old, tired—

He jumped. "Jeez, Mom, you totally startled me. Are you sick? Do you need something?" Old and tired. His mom, wrapped in an insulator, with eyes narrowed over a cup of coffee essence. Had he done something? Defensive anger and irritation replaced the momentary fear. *I'm a first-year story maker now. I don't have to account for my comings and goings.*

"I have a meeting in the morning. I wanted to talk to you, so I thought I'd wait up." Her voice was mild, reflective. "Coffee?" she asked.

Some of the tension eased, to be quickly replaced by the familiar guilt. They had been sharing a lot of stories, having fun almost like his younger days, when they explored the city each weekend, sometimes with Tara as a quiet but commanding presence in the background. After the old people decided they didn't like her cat, she'd binged on every story he could find that even mentioned a cat. Then she didn't want to watch anymore, didn't want to discuss it. Was it his fault she couldn't design a cat? And now he was making stories he definitely didn't want to show her. So where did they go from here?

Miranda told him. "I figured out what my cat needs," she said. "A story."

Alex made himself a cup of coffee essence. "Pardon?"

"These stories we've watched, they have protagonists, a plot, a narrative story arc. The people and cats behave the way they do because of the story."

"Okay."

"And people watch and get involved, as much as anything, to figure out the plot, to understand why everyone acts as they do."

Alex limited himself to nodding cautiously over his cup.

Miranda reached over and clutched his arm. "Alex, what about embedding a story in the cat? I have to trigger behaviors somehow, so I was having the cat respond to the actions of humans. If you're sad, the cat comes up and rubs against you."

"Like a DP," Alex said.

"Well, not intentionally, but apparently that's what I was doing. The Fiskes twigged to that right away. They said the cat lacked a soul."

"You can't design a soul," Alex said. "I mean, you're good and all . . ."

She punched his arm lightly. "I know," she said. "But think, Alex, what do the healers in Psych Services do? They ask you questions about growing up, interactions with people. They want your story. Because your story explains you, and why you act as you do."

Alex nodded. He was fascinated by the gleam in her large blue eyes. Normally her eyes were narrowed in confrontation or suspicion, at least where he was concerned, or abstracted, lost in the story they were watching together. Now he had a glimpse of the mother he used to see when he went with her to work, the mother he'd bragged about at school when he was much younger.

"Like grow lights," he said.

She looked at him.

"Your eyes, large and shiny, like grow lights on trees." For a minute, he felt sorry for Tara. On some level, even as a child, he had understood that the relationship was more than friends. Poor Tara never had a chance. Neither did his dad.

Miranda blushed and talked faster to cover her embarrassment. "I've been watching these stories from the wrong angle, from the human angle, what the human does to cause reaction in the cat. Instead, I need to see things through the eyes of the cat. Why do we watch stories, Alex? I'm sure Karnofsky has told you that?"

Alex thought. "Well, obviously, like you said, to lose ourselves for an hour or two in the lives of others, to figure out their story."

Miranda started to say something, but Alex wasn't finished. "But mostly to learn about ourselves. The story maker uses symbols that human beings recognize on several levels, conscious but also below the level of consciousness. Humans push away a lot of self-knowledge at the conscious level. A good story breaks down barriers so we can learn things about ourselves that we may not want to know or may even run away from."

Miranda shook her head, puzzled. "I'm not quite getting that," she said. "That may be too deep for a cat, but what the heck, pack in a few symbols if you want."

"If I want? What do you mean?"

"I talked to Tara about an idea I had. They are making changes to the role training program, making sure that apprentices don't get isolated in their roles, that they learn to contribute across roles. They're starting up cross-mentoring in other roles. You're only a first year, but she said they already see tremendous potential in you, Alex. So Tara is willing to take a chance, pull some strings."

Alex readied himself for what was coming next.

"Also, I haven't done my bit as a mentor. I'm frankly not that good with people I don't know."

Alex waited.

"But I know you, Alex. At least I used to. So, like I said, Tara pulled some strings."

Uh-oh. Whatever was coming wasn't—

"It's only part-time so that it doesn't disrupt your first-year studies, but two days a week you're going to work with me. Helping me put the story into the cat."

Good. He finished his thought and flashed on his friends at the story bar. *Not good at all.*

"Are you sure a story maker is what you need?" he asked, stalling for time. "Seems to me a psych apprentice, or a role counselor, someone who really understands people . . ."

Miranda didn't look at him. Those large, shiny blue eyes were focused not on him but on her own thoughts. "No, that's not what I need," she said decisively. "I'm not interested in what people think. I need to know what they feel."

Alex looked at her. This was his mother—but a part of her he really didn't know. When he used to go to work with her, he mostly saw her interacting with her team. She was always uncomfortable, a bit shy, unless they did something really well, and then she bent over the idea eagerly, looking just as she did now, turning those grow-light eyes on the dazed subordinates. He remembered how the juniors competed to get her attention. It was astonishing to watch, even a little scary. His own pulse quickened a bit.

"Maybe it won't be so bad," he responded cautiously. "We can give it a try. For a week or two," he added hastily, giving himself an out. "A month, at most. You shouldn't need longer than that."

"For heaven's sake, Alex, I'm not a disease you need to recover from," she said. But her voice was teasing. When she was wrapped up in her work, she was a different person. *Like I am at the story bar,* he realized. He had always rejected any likeness to his mother. And yet . . .

"When does this start?" he asked, resigned.

"Next week," she replied. "I talked with Tara and with Karnofsky. While your cohort is meeting with Psych Services. I didn't want to interfere with your actual apprenticeship, so they agreed to delay the psych work while you work with me. No more than a month. You'll soon catch up. After all, since you have known Tara, a city manager, all your life, your history is more of an open book than most."

She said the last hurriedly. Alex looked at her. *She's protecting me,* he thought, and blinked his eyes against the unexpected moisture. He was amazed at the relief he felt to delay Psych Services. The way Karnofsky had looked, his apologetic voice. Something didn't ring quite true. He and his cohort were already building personal story walls for Psych Services, internalizing simple stories that created an impenetrable structure, they hoped, that the psych healers couldn't breach, working from hints Karnofsky was giving them every day. As the son of the top world builder and a renegade outsider father, he would come in for more scrutiny than most. Having an extra month to build his internal wall was a good thing.

He laughed and put down his cup. "I'm looking forward to it," he announced. He tugged his mother's hair, tangled from an argument with her pillow.

Before she could respond, he was in his bedroom, closing the door softly behind him.

Alex needed several steps to jump from newsline to root and then deeper still, to the tenuous connection to COSLine, in City of the South, but the delay was worth it when the coyote slunk across the line, out of the monitor, to appear for him alone. Once—just once—he saw his actual father, a man who looked nothing like him, except for the splintery green eyes and the unruly, cowlicky hair. He had only appeared to prove to a wary and hurt Alex that it was really he, that he had been watching him all these years, that he really did care. But that was all past, and now they just talked hurriedly and made plans. Tonight he had a lot of news for his father. He explained about the cat, and Miranda's plans for the two of them.

The coyote cocked his head to one side and listened without interruption, something his mother never did. When he was a kid, his mother had carelessly revealed that Tara had known his father. He had pestered Tara for information, something she shared reluctantly, and only when his mother was far away and both their DPs were turned off. Tara described a Peter who was reckless, full of enthusiasms but no follow-through. The outside had clearly changed him. They wouldn't recognize this man, this coyote.

"Your mother is a clever woman," his father said. "I was worried about Psych Services. They were likely to discover me."

Alex bristled at that. *Give him a little credit.* He explained about the story wall he was building, about the constant scrubbing of his DP and his root tracks.

"You are a smart one, Alex, a planner. You get that from your mother. But you take risks. You get that from me. You have left tracks in Sanctuary, just as I did. Psych Services would discover those tracks and follow them."

Alex started to interrupt. The coyote shook its head vigorously to stop him. "They can't afford to have the top world builder's son questioning Sanctuary. They need your mother too much. Unfortunately, they don't need you. How long is your project?"

"I think Mom said a month."

"I need you to get a better date. It's time for us to make our move."

Alex's pulse quickened. This is what he wanted, what he was working toward. And yet . . . he couldn't imagine walking into a flat and not seeing his mother, at her design table, at a story cube, huddled over a packfruit. He couldn't imagine calling any other place home if his mother wasn't there waiting.

"Does it really have to be just me?"

The coyote was silent. "She won't leave with you, Alex. In fact, she would stop you. And trust me, you don't want to be one of the rebellious ones that Sanctuary catches."

"Why is she like this?" Alex burst out in frustration. "Why does she believe this place is the best we can do?"

"Because she builds it to be the best we can do," his father said. "She refuses to believe there is any other way. My way isn't perfect, Alex. I told you, the rulers in City of the South are shit. I work for them so I can work around them. And a lot of what I do isn't pretty. But it makes a difference. Not just for City of the South but for all the outside. What your mother is building can't last. What I am building just might."

Alex was silent.

"The choice is yours," Peter said. "Whatever you decide, I'll accept."

"I've made my choice," Alex finally replied.

"Good. The next time we talk, I'll have instructions."

SANCTUARY

CHAPTER NINE

It felt strange to be in his mom's office. It wasn't like he remembered. These walls were bare, the tables uncluttered. Gone were the awards, the ribbon cuttings, the amazing sunsets and storms that played along one wall. This office was pristine in its neutral gray. His mother pulled up sketcher on the cube.

"So, motivation for a cat," she said. "We know they are capable of loyalty; they need love as every creature does, but you have to win them over. Why? What makes them feel threatened? How do you earn their trust? How much is the instinct of their species? I've arranged for us to talk to a big cat expert at the zoo about that last, on Thursday. But in that story we shared the other day, *The Three Lives of Thomasina*, the love of the little girl—"

Alex stopped her. "Seriously? Mom, you are not going to get anywhere by just watching hokey before stories."

"What do you mean?"

"Do you ever think about stories? I mean, not the stories people say they watch, but the ones they really watch. The romance porn, the happy tales of yesteryear?"

"What about them?" Miranda asked cautiously, wondering if she had scrubbed the story cube cache recently.

"In case you haven't noticed, we don't live there. Where are the stories about us, about the lives we live? People make them, but no one watches them. You're a world builder, Mom. If the city you built is so great, why does nobody ever want to think about it?"

Miranda was silent. She rebelled instantly from what he said. They had a great life. She should know. She had vivid memories of outside. And yet . . .

"Because it's what they know," she said slowly. "People like to experience what they don't know."

Alex looked at her with new respect. "You're right," he said. "I was going to say something about the phoniness of the city. But you're right. It's the sameness that gets everybody down. We all know our roles, we all know what we are going to do every single day, we all have DPs who can predict our every move and stay one step ahead of us at all times."

He stood up and leaned over her. "What about this for a story? A cat that comes from the outside and experiences the city for the first time. How would it react to people? There aren't very many people outside, and those it encounters would probably try to eat it. What would it think of DPs? Would it even see a DP? Could it evade ferrats? Coyotes? How would it acclimate to life in the city after a life outside? Would it let a human adopt it? Would its owner be its ally or its enemy?"

Miranda felt her face heating up with excitement as her son loomed over her. *When did he get so tall?* "You're onto something," she said. "A cat as outside refugee. Pitting its natural instincts against the city. We need to read everything we can about the cat's response to its environment." She summoned her DP with a nod of her head.

"Mind if I go home for a bit?" he asked. "I study best alone."

"Of course not," she replied, pushing back against disappointment. "I'll see you at home later, and we can share results."

Alex patted his mom's shoulder awkwardly. "We're onto something here," he said. "I can see why you like world building. It's a chance every day to change things up."

She smiled gratefully at him. "We make a great team," she said to his retreating back. She closed her eyes against the relief that suddenly flooded her. She and Alex were getting on better than they had in years. She should have known that work was the way to bring them together. He was her son, after all.

The next week flew by. They talked about his studies and everything they'd learned about cats. Miranda had arranged a private tour of the zoo. The animal manager at the zoo was waiting for them, although they were a little early.

"Roger McNaught," he boomed at them with a wide smile, revealing gleaming, square teeth. He was a large man, perhaps a little older than Miranda, with a hearty handshake and brown eyes that darted between the two of them.

"Nice to see a young apprentice taking an interest in the zoo," he said. "Do you know my apprentice, Alicia? Perhaps you went to school together?"

A pretty young woman with short blonde hair and large, round hazel eyes smiled at them uncertainly.

"Did you go to Center City school?" Miranda asked Alicia.

Alicia turned to her instantly and caught her eye in a bland, attentive manner that made Miranda start slightly before she recovered herself and listened to the girl's answer.

"No, ma'am." She named a different school on the far eastern side of the city.

"So, what can I do for you?" McNaught asked. "I understand why you are here," he said to Alex. "You're a story making apprentice, right? You people often turn to the zoo for ideas. But I am seldom graced by the presence of a world builder. Of course we have lots of ideas for the next-generation zoo. We have sent them to world builders time and again, but you've never shown much interest before. More important things to do, no doubt."

Amazing. In one short speech, he had managed to antagonize both of them. Miranda shot a glance at Alicia and saw that she was blushing.

"Well, as I said when I set up this meeting, I am interested in cats. Pet cats. I need to know what makes them tick. Their instincts. How they interact with other species, with humans. I was told you are an animal behavior expert, so I came to you."

"Cats?" McNaught barked incredulously, as if he had never heard of the animal. "I'm afraid you've come to the wrong place. I don't know anything about cats, if by cats you mean *Felis domesticus*, the common house cat. I work with big cats. Lions, tigers"

"But aren't they the same family, just writ large?"

He laughed shortly again. "Okay," he said. "Believe that if you want. Maybe the closest big cat to a house cat is the tiger. Both are largely solitary and the dominant species of their environment. The tiger was a marvel of construction. It was the apex predator of the jungle. It could jump fifteen feet from a standing position. Fifteen feet!"

"You!" he pointed at Alex. "Walk backwards." Alex looked quizzically at Miranda, who nodded at him. He started walking backwards and continued as McNaught's testy hand waved him back further. He passed Alicia and exchanged a commiserating glance with her.

"Stop!" McNaught said. "That's fifteen feet. Amazing!"

Alex nodded politely.

"Believe it or not, the house cat is in a similar position in the home. There is nothing it can't climb or get into. It appreciates and resents its captivity at the same time, so anything that interests its owners will interest the cat—at least until the cat has mastered it and made it its own. Humans appreciate the cat because they recognize superior strength, agility, and mastery of the environment, and because they can still feel superior because the cat is smaller and weaker than a person. In the jungle, all animals freeze into silence when the tiger walks by. In the home, there is a constant struggle for mastery, with the cat throwing the owner the occasional bone of affection to retain the balance of power in the cat's favor."

This battleground view of cat ownership didn't quite square with the round and jolly Fiskes, but Miranda let that pass. When McNaught talked about animals, he lost his pomposity and resentment. She was learning something.

"So, do you have some tiger holos we can watch?" she asked. "This is really interesting."

McNaught laughed bitterly again. "You haven't been listening," he said. "The tiger is pure predator, pure instinct. The house cat was one of the earliest animals to be tamed, and so its instincts were corrupted by centuries of domestication. It's also a natural mimic, so it is hard to know what is cat instinct and what is human. Natural selection favored adaptable cats, the ones that could understand and take on the habits of their captors. The tiger never adapted to human habitation and was one of the first casualties of the twenty-first century. Of course, ultimately, domestic cats didn't fare any better. They developed a level of trust in humans that was seriously misplaced."

Alex and Miranda were silent.

"But if you want to see tigers, I can show you holos—watered down, as our city masters dictate, for the sensibilities of the school children who visit."

"Please," Miranda said politely.

McNaught shrugged and led them down a path to a large empty room. At a nod, the room dissolved into a green and leafy lair, with a quiet stream running through and patches of color where birds darted among the trees. The calls of monkeys and birds made a haunting, staccato song, accompanied by the murmur of the stream. Suddenly, immediately, everything went still. Miranda heard a low, throbbing growl at her side and turned to look into the leaf-lidded golden-brown eyes of a tiger. The head was immense, the long white teeth barred in a snarl. It leaped and Miranda screamed. The tiger dissolved.

"You show this to children?" she asked in a shaky voice.

"Well, older children," McNaught said. His eyes gleamed with pleasure as Miranda struggled to regain her composure. "Believe me, they love it. They ask for it."

"Not your standard house cat," he said.

Miranda tried to imagine an android tiger that could jump fifteen feet. She shuddered slightly.

"How many visitors do you get at the zoo?" Alex asked politely.

"Quite a few," he replied. "It's like what you do. A nice story. People like to see the animals of yesteryear."

"School groups?" Alex asked, his voice a purr, very like a house cat. Miranda shot him a look.

"School groups," McNaught said defensively. "But people do come on their own. People who find the city too tame. Who miss the wild places. But I admit that visitors beyond school children are falling off. We need some attention from world builders. We need to reinvent the zoo. People don't like to think about animals anymore. They need to remember, to respect them."

"But if they can't ever have them again?" Alex pursued. "If they feel guilty about the destruction of these former fellow travelers on our planet?"

"Yes, they like them in stories, like what you will churn out. Animals made in their own image. But you're right. The victor doesn't always relish the spoils. Is that what you want me to say?"

Alex didn't respond.

"Do you have any, well, actual, animals?" Miranda asked cautiously.

McNaught was silent a moment. "A few," he said. "Some reptiles and of course insects. Our only mammals are a few rodent species."

"Can we see them?" she asked.

McNaught smiled again. "I'm sorry," he said, not sorry at all. "Real animals are strictly off-limits. We can't risk contamination for the few species we have left. I believe I explained this to you when you set up the appointment. And now, I'm behind on my regular work. Alicia will show you out." He turned on his heel and left.

"What's it like to be a zoo apprentice?" Alex asked Alicia, timing his steps to hers.

"All right, I guess," she said. "The animals in their settings are beautiful."

"But do you wish you worked with real animals?" he asked. "Did you have that choice?"

She turned at the zoo entrance and looked at him. "What's real?" she asked and turned away.

Alex stared after her and shrugged. "Imagine having to follow that ass around all day. Remind me never to complain about Karnofsky."

Miranda turned away to hide a smile.

"What?" he asked suspiciously.

"He doesn't have an apprentice. Alicia is his DP."

"What?" Alex repeated. "Why didn't you say something?" He glared at his mother and then walked ahead of her in a huff. Miranda let him go. She was still thinking about the holo tiger, its bared teeth inches from her face, as they unfurled their magcarts for the ride back to Sanctuary center.

SANCTUARY

CHAPTER TEN

The next morning, Miranda rose early, but Alex was already gone. He had recycled his packfruit skin and left a note on her newsline that he had to run an errand before work but would see her at her office around nine o'clock.

Miranda walked to work, lost in thought. She was remembering her dog, Fred, and how he got her through the long and lonely days. She dreamt last night about the tiger. The holo was so real, she could imagine the animal prowling a jungle teeming with available prey. She had adjusted to a life without animals. It was surprisingly easy. The nonhumans that invaded Sanctuary—ferrats, the occasional coyote or wild dog, the ever-present ants that infested apartment buildings—were rightly viewed as threats. No one argued with their swift, if not very effective, extermination. But was she doing a good thing? Was Tara, by reintroducing animals you had loved, that had gotten you through the worst of the outside? It might rouse people from their sleepy self-absorption, but to what end? Would the work she did, that everybody did, to re-create the idealized outside that no longer existed be the saving of Sanctuary or its end? She shook herself mentally and decided to walk to work to clear her head of the animal-fueled dreams of the night before.

Alex was already settled at the story cube in her office. "So, to really imagine the cat, we have to imagine the outside," he said. "What did it live on? What grows there? What's still alive?"

Miranda thought back to her last days on the outside, and to her only visit to the outside after she moved to the city. She didn't romanticize the outside, or even give it much thought. It was the stuff of nightmares—of Fred wandering emaciated, cowering, dodging wild animals and even hungry people. The pet center had been the right choice. Of course, it was. Anyway, if they hadn't moved to Sanctuary, she wouldn't have Alex.

"City to Mom," Alex said gently. "Outside. What do you remember?"

"I took a magtrain once to the slag heaps," she said. "The city managers were concerned about the amount of trash the city was throwing away. We could stay on the train, which was climate controlled, or step out with our guide and explore the heaps for a little bit."

"Did you get out?"

"I did," she said. His eyes widened. He hadn't expected that answer. But the guide had been tall, with a rangy, athletic body; bristly brown hair; and long-lashed, narrow green eyes.

"He told us about the heaps, and then we were able to walk around, just a little. We had to wear masks because of the trash, but also because the air was full of dust."

"And was it moldy, decaying?"

Miranda closed her eyes to think. "No," she said. "It was all fused together; well-preserved. Sculpted into towers and canyons by the dust-filled air. We didn't throw food way. It could be repurposed. This was stuff that didn't decompose. It was huge, a lot of interconnected hills and valleys. There were crevasses, holes you had to be careful of, stuff that would crumble under your feet. It was large and gray against the white sky."

"So, the sky was white?"

"Well, colorless. Everything seemed bleached out after the colors of Sanctuary. This sculpture of refuse was gray and dead, like the bones of a thousand animals."

"Poetic," Alex said quietly. "I'd like to see it."

"But the thing is, Alex, stuff was moving."

"You mean it was shifting?"

"No, small things, like blowing balls of dust, would scurry around corners as we approached. The guide said that anything alive in the outside was a scavenger, drawn to the slag heaps."

"So, our cat would have come from the slag heaps," Alex said. "And maybe it jumped on a visiting magtrain and was carried into the city. How would it react to the city after the slag heaps?"

Alex's face was absorbed in the sketcher as he drew a three-dimensional slag heap that looked remarkably like the real thing. The way he drew her memories out of her, he could have been in Psych Services. Miranda shuddered slightly. For the first time, she was truly grateful for story making as a role. It was a safe role. If it didn't do much good, at least it didn't do any harm. And it had brought the two of them together. She realized with a start that she was spending all her free time with Alex these days. She hadn't seen Tara in more than a week. They'd never gone this long without at least talking.

Unwillingly, she found herself remembering that fateful evening in the bar when she had bumped into the guide from the slag heaps field trip again. He had a gap-toothed grin, and his face was already weathered, with cobwebs of lines around his eyes from the time spent outside. Miranda peered at his face and was sure she could see the microscopic dust that silted the outside air gathered into the lines around his nose and mouth. She shuddered slightly and turned away. She was there with Tara, but they were just friends back then; anyway, the guide ignored Tara completely, which made it easy for her to do the same. Miranda noticed other women in the bar looking their way—calculating their own attraction and whether it was worth brushing past the table. He solidified the air around them, flattening the rest of the bar into swirling wallpaper.

Miranda's eyes quit circling the room; she couldn't meet his gaze, so she focused on his hands. They were big hands, with long, tapering fingers. She pictured those hands moving up and down her body and shuddered. She looked up. His eyes were deep slits in his face. It was like looking down into a slag heap crevasse. She fell into those eyes and couldn't climb out. Tara looked at the two of them, excused herself, and went to the bar for another drink.

"So, is this bar in your neighborhood?" he asked casually. Miranda could feel every inch of her body responding, stiffening but turning toward him. *Fight or flight*, she thought. Probably both.

"Not far." Her voice was a croak. She looked over at Tara, sitting alone at the bar. Tara smiled tightly and lifted her drink in a sketchy toast before turning away.

Miranda hadn't felt anything but sad since her dad died. But now the grief was pulled roughly away, leaving her exposed but sparking like the last days of electricity on the outside, when touching an appliance made you tremble and shudder. You touched them because you weren't supposed to, because you liked the oddly alive feeling when the fading, uneven power coursed through your fingers. Why wasn't everyone looking at her? The change must be obvious. She looked back to the bar for rescue, but Tara was gone. "I've been struck by lightning," she told the slag heap man.

He smiled. "Not yet," he replied.

Miranda shuddered in remembrance. Three days when she never left her flat. Called in sick at work. Unheard of. He explored her like a slag heap, finding and filling crevasses in her body and spirit she didn't know she had. Alex was conceived sometime during those three days. She shook her head ruefully. Eventually they had to get out of bed, make a hasty registry, and then the nonstop fun really started. She looked at Alex, intent on his sketcher. He had the same eyes as his dad, deep green slits in his face, with tiny, almost transparent lines already wrinkling the corners. She wondered who the girl would be that got lost in those eyes.

Alex needed to see the outside so he could lose whatever romantic notions he had of the world. People went outside—disposers, integrators, ambassadors to other cities. She was such a loner in her work that she had few connections, but Tara had many. She'd ask Tara to arrange it.

SANCTUARY

CHAPTER ELEVEN

Miranda called Tara on her newsline on the way to work. She expected to reach her DP, and to wait several days for an appointment, but Tara responded right away.

If Tara was surprised by a call from Miranda she didn't show it. "Miranda! Good to hear from you. Do you have a finished cat to show me?"

Miranda hesitated. "Not yet, unfortunately. We've hit a bit of a wall with the design. I was hoping maybe I could get an appointment, talk the design through with you."

Tara paused. "Well, my day is pretty busy. In fact, the whole week . . ." She tilted her head to one side, as she often did, consulting her internal calendar. Miranda was continually amazed that the woman who invented DPs really didn't need one herself.

"My first meeting of the day is in about an hour," she said. "I don't suppose you could come over right now?"

"Of course. I'll just shoot a message to Alex and be right there."

"Alex," Tara responded. "How is he doing? Never mind, tell me about him when you get here." She blinked off. Some people favored a slow fade. Not Tara.

Tara's office was large and spacious, but her walls weren't opaque. Two walls looked out on the city, but two walls were open to the people and DPs walking past. No one drifted in city management. Everyone was moving fast and with purpose, alone or talking seriously in groups. Awed apprentices, interns from different departments, hurried to keep up.

Tara looked up from her cube with a smile. "Come in," she said, as Miranda hesitated at the door. "So, give me an update. How is the cat doing?"

"Well, I ran into a bit of a snag in testing."

"Ah, yes, the Fiskes. How did they react?"

"The Fiskes?" Miranda asked. "I didn't know I'd mentioned them by name. I know they weren't on your recommended list of testers."

"It's okay," Tara said. "I know Albert Fiske. He was an amazing streetways builder. He still comes to all events with his old team, mostly funerals these days, sadly. But he was telling everyone that he and Adele had been specially chosen to test the new cat, which is eagerly anticipated. You couldn't have chosen a better representative of the retirement community to get the word out."

Miranda studied Tara's face, open and smiling and apparently genuinely pleased. "They were an accidental find, but they really understand cats. They are sentimental about them, but at the same time, they can't be fooled by something makeshift."

Tara patted her arm. "You did perfectly," she said. "They are one of the key demographics for pets. Sanctuary places such emphasis on having a role and being useful to the city that it is difficult when you have to give that up. A pet will give retired workers a new interest. I think it's brilliant. The other demographic of course is the young, just choosing a role or starting out in one. They need an undemanding presence to share their anxieties, help them blow off steam in a game of ball in the park, something to take care of at night after a long day at work." She looked expectantly at Miranda. "So, what's the problem with the cat?"

Miranda hesitated. "The Fiskes didn't feel the cat responded to them like a creature with its own reality. It did everything they wanted it to do, but not what it wanted to do."

Tara tilted her head again in thought. She frowned. "I see the problem. I mean, I guess I do. But I don't see an easy way to solve it.

GRACE J. AGNEW

Maybe people who knew cats aren't the best test case. The people we want to reach first are the young. We have some apprentices here that might be good—"

"But if the goal is to take people out of themselves," Miranda objected, "then a cat that is just a reflection of them . . . "

"Good point," Tara said. "It's like a more solid DP."

Miranda shuddered involuntarily. Tara's prescience was actually scary.

"So, is the dog completely finished? What have you done with it?"

Miranda hesitated. "The dog is . . . fine. I think it is ready to go. Right now, I'm concentrating on the cat, to have both ready. Give people a choice."

"I thought the dog was really impressive. Maybe concentrate right now on releasing the dog model at Festival. In lots of shapes and sizes. A dog is a lot more eager to please its master. The unfortunate resemblance to a DP won't be as noticeable. How did you test the dog? Who were your test subjects?"

"I tested it on myself," Miranda admitted. "I had a dog. Outside."

"That's right. Fred, wasn't it? How did he get his name?"

She really did know everything. Or at least she remembered everything you said. "He was a black-and-white collie. A sheepherder dog," Miranda replied. "Daddy named him. He had a white mark on his neck like a bowtie that reminded Daddy of that yesteryear actor Fred Astaire. 'I'm putting on my top hat, tying up my white tie.'"

"'Polishing my nails,'" Tara finished.

"Well, that part didn't fit," Miranda said. "Fred had long, raggedy nails. When he got scared, he'd climb in my lap and scratch my arms and legs to pieces wiggling around with those nails." She smiled at the memory.

"How old were you when you moved into the city?"

"Eleven. Most of our neighbors had gone. Our neighborhood

97

was flooded. We were lucky. Our house was on high ground. But every time it rained . . ." She remembered the water seeping under doors and bubbling up through the floorboards, chasing them as they retreated upstairs.

"Anyway, my Mom started coughing. Her doctor had already moved inside."

"And Fred," Tara prompted gently.

"They told us," Miranda swallowed and started again. "They told us that the city wasn't balanced for pets. Everything was calibrated to supply the inhabitants, just enough but no more. And pets are unpredictable, and they get sick . . ." Her voice trailed off.

"Did you take him to the pet center?" Tara asked.

Miranda nodded. "It was partly for Fred that we chose to move to the city. He couldn't go outside anymore. I couldn't go outside, even when the floods receded. So many people had abandoned their pets when they moved inside. The small pets, cats, little dogs, were eaten. The big dogs roamed in packs. They could come up on you, just like that."

"So, the day came when it was time to move" Tara prompted.

Miranda nodded. Her eyes were stinging. "Daddy took Fred alone. I stayed upstairs. I didn't even pet him goodbye. I couldn't. He would have wondered where he was going, without me."

Once it got too dangerous to play outside, Miranda lost touch with her school friends. She and Fred played endlessly. He didn't mind dressing up; he played a mean game of hide-and-seek. The thing was, when they weren't playing, he'd lie by the door and whine to go outside.

"They told us it was quick and painless. Just going to sleep. Daddy said he was with him the whole time. He wagged his tail as he drifted off." Even at the time, Miranda had wondered if that part was made up for her benefit.

When they got to the city, the shiny apartments, playmates, the parks with trees and swings; in the excitement of exploring it all, Fred was forgotten . . . except at night. She would dream of dog packs, not scary packs but happy, running, barking dogs, with Fred in the lead. She would run after them, calling for Fred. He would look back briefly but then turn away. He always turned away.

Tara was watching her closely. "I think perhaps testing pets with people who had pets outside is a mistake. Too loaded with memories of before, of . . . the surrender. Maybe put the cat aside if you are stuck and focus on different dog models in time for Festival. Small dogs."

Miranda didn't say anything. She hated to give up on a project, and she was very reluctant to pull the black-and-white collie out of her closet.

"Your target demographic should really be young people, the current crop of apprentices. How did Alex react to the dog?"

"He wasn't very interested," Miranda responded. "He's a lot more interested in the cat. Perhaps because he's helping to design it. He's putting a story into the cat. I think he is really on to something. I was thinking about taking him on a field trip outside. Maybe with an integrator. Or possibly with disposers. Is that a possibility?"

Tara looked away from her. "Many of the next generation, apprentices, even younger, have a curiosity about the outside. Curiosity is a good thing, an emotion to be cultivated. The goal of apprenticeships is to channel that curiosity into work that benefits Sanctuary. In most cases, it works. But for some people, outside becomes an unhealthy obsession."

Miranda stiffened. She reminded herself that this was Tara. Her mentor and former lover but, more than that, also her friend. Tara had helped her through the dark days after her father died. She didn't care for Peter—well, none of Miranda's friends did—but when Peter disappeared, Tara was a big help, particularly with Alex. She invited both of them to all the unveilings that would delight a child, and she came to programs at Alex's school. She was there when he won his outersuit award.

"I feel like he has really been missing his dad, turning him into some sort of outsider hero, and no doubt blaming me for his absence."

Tara didn't say anything but tilted her head to show she was listening.

"I've told him that if his dad went outside, or even back to City of the South, that there is no way he would have survived this long . . ." her voice trailed off.

Tara didn't respond.

"I mean, there is no way, right? He was an adventurer, a risk taker, but not a survivor, and anyway, the life expectancy stats—" Stopping suddenly, she asked, "Have you ever heard anything about Peter?"

"There have been rumors," Tara said. "Nothing I could ever confirm, and therefore nothing I would share unless you asked, and you never did. And you didn't seem to be looking. In fact, it seemed you wanted to put Peter behind you and start a new life with Alex, so I respected your wishes."

"I did," Miranda said. "I do. Peter gave me the best thing in my life, but otherwise he was bad news. Disconnected, unhappy, but not someone who steps up and fixes the things he doesn't like. Instead, he ran away from problems. I never wanted Alex to become someone like that."

"Alex was raised by you," Tara said. "He'll never be a clone of Peter. He's troubled about his future in Sanctuary, and he's lashing out in all directions, but he's not running away."

"But he might," Miranda said. "It's my biggest fear. Especially if . . ."

"If what?"

"If Peter reaches out to him."

"What?" Tara's voice sharpened. "Has Alex heard from Peter?"

"No," Miranda answered. "Not that I know of. I thought all you heard were rumors, nothing substantiated. Is Peter alive? Is he likely to come back?"

Tara thought before answering. "Nothing is certain," she said, "but there are some survivors—living a wretched existence, believe me—on the outside, and one of them is the appropriate age and appearance to be Peter. Most of them want to come back. It's quite pitiable, really. But we don't think it's a good idea. They made their choice as adults, and we think everyone needs to honor that choice."

"Is Peter one of the ones wanting to come back?"

"We don't know that it is Peter," Tara answered sharply. "But no, there are some deluded ones who don't want to come back, despite the wretched conditions outside. If anything, they want recruits to replace the ones trying to sneak back in. Many have made their way to City of the South, where there are no standards for citizens other than survival of the fittest."

"How do you know all this?" Miranda asked.

"Well, of course we keep tabs on outside," Tara said. "It's important to do so. But we've also let a few of the returnees who crept back into the city remain, and they've told us quite a bit. It's not the wonderful life the outsider groups would have you believe."

"I'm sure," Miranda replied.

"But Alex isn't. He's still a child, with a romantic view of outside. Outsider groups are fine when they safely balance people's conflicted values of safety and a future versus the illusion of unlimited freedom. It's when people become totally invested in that illusion that those groups are dangerous. Because it is an illusion. When your sole focus is on drawing breath and finding a bit of clean water to drink, believe me, Miranda, you aren't free. People who choose that life quickly learn the error of their beliefs. Alex will outgrow his discontents. But if he goes outside, he will never recover. Your decision to completely forget Peter when he left is the right one. Alex is lucky Peter is out of his life."

Tara turned back to her desk. "I think Alex should get back to full-time story making. I'm told he's good at it. He should explore the outside through story. It's better for him, and it's good for the city. His fellow apprentices are questioning where he goes two days a week. I'm told he's made a few friends, but he is in danger of losing them because he appears to be getting special treatment. You make your deepest connections in first year, the ones that last. He needs time to explore those relationships right now. Let's put the cat on hold for a while and just build a few more models of the dog. Small dogs." She smiled and looked down at her work.

Miranda took the hint. She closed the door softly behind her.

CHAPTER TWELVE

Miranda walked the streetway to her office lost in thought. She had really blown it with Tara. There must be some way to keep Alex on the cat project—if she still had a cat project. She didn't like the idea of Psych Services probing the tender mind of her child. She wasn't sure what they would find: the natural rebelliousness of a teenager, or something else? She stopped, causing a man behind her to walk into her. He glared at her and then almost simultaneously at his DP, an anxious young man taking notes on a pad. "Why do I bother to turn you on?" he muttered.

"Sorry." Miranda and the DP answered simultaneously. The man snorted and hurried away, his DP changing pace immediately to keep at his side. Miranda stopped in her tracks and watched them. Were other people as bored and impatient with their DPs as she was, as this man seemed to be? She looked around at the few people on the streetway in the middle of a workday. They were walking aimlessly or hurrying like this man. She counted. One, two, three, four. Only one of them had a DP turned on. Three out of four, no DP. When did this start?

A DP looked the way you wanted it to look, responded to you, but it also monitored you, kept you on track. She realized that having a DP could be like being pursued by your 3:00 a.m. thoughts all day long. Or what was it Alex called his DP? His nanny. Maybe Tara was right. A pet that you looked after rather than the other way about could be just what people needed. She realized with a start that Alex was right too. She was so used to taking care of the citizens of Sanctuary, herding them this way and that like sheep—for their own good, of course—that what she had designed was a DP in fur clothing. Only Alex got to the heart of the problem: The cat needed to be separate from the people who adopted it, to have dreams of its own. He was better at this than she was.

Her heart squeezed with pride, but also with panic. It wasn't just Psych Services that had her feeling bereft. It was losing this precious time with Alex. Her son had disappeared completely the past few years, replaced by a moody, contemptuous stranger who hated his life and everything about it, including her. Especially her. And now, maybe, she had him back.

Miranda always believed, or claimed to believe, that once you had your purpose, once you knew your fit, you embraced Sanctuary and discovered everything you needed for a whole and wonderful life. It had been true for her. Becoming a world builder had changed everything for an anxious, motherless girl. It had even enabled her to deal with the loss of her father shortly after she started her final apprenticeship. And with Tara Jordan! She hadn't realized at the time how lucky she was, but the jealous stares of the other apprentices soon set her straight.

She thought back to the outside that Alex romanticized so fiercely—the thick cloud cover, the stinging insects that seemed to be the only life that flourished in the twilight days, the heat, the torrential, poisonous rain, the gray dust, and the biting winds. She embraced the new world, without sun hoods and a restricted indoor existence, but also where every action had a consequence. But in her dreams she had to acknowledge that she missed the hours of aimless fun with Fred more than she wanted to admit. Even so, when her family first came in, her thoughts were already centered on determining what talents and skills she could bring to the city. Alex had been like her at twelve, even at thirteen, but by fourteen it had all changed. What had happened, exactly?

GRACE J. AGNEW

At fourteen, Miranda had been totally focused on fitting in. Maybe too focused? She leapt eagerly at every role that was presented. She frequently scored the highest in her class on aptitude tests. She remembered her dad sitting her down solemnly and telling her, "You are one of the lucky ones, Miranda. You can be whatever you want. We sacrificed a lot to come here, so choose well." But for Miranda, it wasn't a question of choosing. She was still waiting to be offered a role, while other students found theirs and began to naturally clump together with their peers.

"I don't get it," she wailed to her father. "My scores were high everywhere, especially in creativity. You said!" She glared accusingly at her father. He laughed and ruffled her short, mousy brown hair.

"Just wait," he said. "All things come to those who wait."

So she waited. She ignored the remarks of other students. "Never mind, they haven't filled disposal yet," accompanied by a piece of trash dropped on the schoolyard. "To give you practice."

And then Tara showed up at school—

She shook her head impatiently to disperse the past. She might never know what happened to Alex, except her detective mind had pieced together that he began to change when she and Tara—very surreptitiously!—introduced the root. Maybe it had been a mistake to give kids an outlet to express their dissatisfaction. But now, finally, he was growing up, and things seemed to be shifting.

She knew Alex was making friends in story making. And some of those friends were girls. This was as it should be. Alex would find someone. They would marry and hopefully have a family, if the birth numbers aligned. This was also as it should be. But she had a brief time, disappearing with each passing day, for reconnecting with Alex, to make sure she was part of his life in the years ahead. She stood as if planted in the streetway as people and DPs eddied around her. It was lunchtime, and people were exiting buildings to enjoy the manufactured sunshine. If she hurried, she could catch Alex and maybe take him somewhere special for lunch, for something besides a packfruit. She had at least a week more before orders came down. Tara would give her that time to break the news to Alex. Instead, she saw it as a week to make real progress on the cat—and to change Tara's mind.

Alex's face as he bent over the sketcher was gray. Miranda's heart squeezed tight. Was he ill? So far, the virus seemed to be afflicting mainly adults, particularly the elderly, but if it took root in the city . . .

Alex looked up and smiled. She realized with relief that the pallor was just reflection from the sketcher. She leaned over to see what he was designing: a gray cat twining through trees in a park, darting past tiger and clown DPs, and watching children playing on swings and slides. It was the city, but sad in the twilight, as the cat threaded among indifferent children. Miranda wondered why they didn't react. "They think it's a DP," she said. Alex nodded. The cat flashed back to another cat, larger but emaciated, resigned, lying on its side as it sheltered behind dusty gray slag as this cat and another kitten, a rusty tabby, suckled voraciously.

"Milk," Miranda said. "The cat needs milk."

The cat wove its way through the playing children and their watchful DPs and jumped lightly onto the magtrack, where it was almost run over by a magcart carrying an older woman who had slowed to watch the children.

"What's her story?" Miranda asked.

Alex answered without hesitation. "She's unmarried, was a leader on the outside; organized things, kept spirits up, stockpiled food and water for community use. The city courted her because it wanted her organizational skills. Joining the city was a difficult decision because so many people afraid to move inside really depended on her. But ultimately it was just too hard to remain outside. She had to give up a beloved cat, her constant companion. A lot of what is beautiful and colorful about the city can be traced to her management skills, but she questions her choice every day, particularly now that she is retired and the city moves on without her. Every day she sees the things she built replaced. Every day she rides by the playground to watch the children. She tells herself that these children are the reason she helped to build the city, but she doesn't know if she is thinking more about their future or her past."

Miranda stared at Alex. He recited the facts of the slender, white-haired woman in the magcart without pause. As if he had been thinking about her a long time, as if he knew her. But as he was talking, he was changing things about her, straightening her, slimming her, making her taller, adding some color to the hair and then cropping the gray-white hair into a sleek bob so that she looked less like Mrs. Hooper and more like a woman of uncertain age that neither of them knew.

"Did you just make that up?" she asked. In his short recitation, she saw traces of herself, even of Tara, but this woman was her own person.

"We have to give the cat someone to play off if we are going to design its instincts, its behavior," he responded. "This woman is nobody's fool. She knows instantly that this is no DP, that her life is about to change."

Almost without thought, the woman scoops the cat into the magcart. The cat arches its back and hisses. It scratches the woman, who clutches it to her, burying its face and paws so it can't claw or bite. She huddles over the cat, closing off all escape routes. "Home," she says to the magcart in a muffled voice.

Miranda couldn't wait to see the woman's flat and how she occupied her day. She would get a preview of what her own life would be like when Alex registered with a young woman and started his adult life. In little more than a decade, Miranda would step down from her world builder role and either move up into management or be forced to build something else—a life without a role in the city. The thought was a cold wind. She thought about the Fiskes, Mrs. Hooper. So much of your time was spent engaged in your role. When you weren't living it, you were generally thinking about it. What did people do when they retired from roles? For once, she thought not about the cat but about the people she was designing the cat for.

"You're good, Alex," she said. "Very, very good."

Alex looked up, surprised and pleased.

"You build a character with just a brief narrative and a sketch that leaves me wanting to know more."

"I wish I knew more about her life on the outside," he said. "Why would the cat matter so much to her that she would risk having a contraband pet in Sanctuary? All I know are the stories of yesteryear, before the troubles. It seemed like a great place."

"I don't remember much," Miranda said. "It changed when I was very little."

Alex studied her. "I'm sorry," he said.

Miranda made a cup of coffee essence and cradled the cup in both hands. "It was all we knew, so it didn't seem that bad," she said. "We had to wear protective clothing, but until the last year, we could go outside to play. Until the very end, there were still birds." Large, squawking black and brown birds. Muddy birds, the kids called them, but still . . .

"When a storm rose, whether dust or rain, the mothers called us in. Sometimes, if you were too far from home, you went to a friend's house, which was always different. Different food, different books." And worried parents, because the storm canceled all communication. But when you reached your door and your mother shut it strongly behind you, blocking out wind and dirt and rain, was there any better feeling?

"You should watch some of these old stories," Alex said. "You missed a lot."

"I've seen them," Miranda replied. "World builder 101. I spend my days re-creating a world I barely experienced. Although I did see a real sunset once." She shut her eyes, savoring the memory. "But what I most remember about growing up outside is how we all clung to one another. We were all we had."

"What made you come inside?" Alex asked. "I mean, if outside was so great."

"I didn't say it was great," she replied. "It was all we knew. And Sanctuary was so restrictive about who they would accept, at first. Until the city was largely built, if you didn't have the right skill to contribute, you didn't come in. And then, when the admission process got easier . . ."

"Yeah?"

"The problem was that the rules got harder. Sanctuary is a delicate balance. People coming and going were damaging the equilibrium. You had to agree to leave almost everything behind." She swallowed, thinking of Fred. "And you could never go back out."

Alex waited.

"To have no choice," she replied. "That was new, and hard to deal with."

"But people did," he said. "You. Tara."

"Well, loneliness," she said, "as the outside got worse and more people went in. And sickness. Sickness was the final straw." She stopped, remembering her mother, with the constant cough she tried to suppress.

"And I have no complaints. The job of my dreams. My wonderful son. My dad would be so proud."

Alex turned away. One of the problems with the taboo subject of fathers was that Miranda could never talk about her own beloved dad, and how much of him she saw in Alex.

Alex sensed that he had changed the atmosphere and it was up to him to fix it. He nodded at the story cube and the woman barreling home with her cat.

"Embedding a story in a three-dimensional object," he said. "It's a new place to take story. It opens up all kinds of possibilities. Of course, DPs are really designed as aspects of our own stories, so the concept isn't entirely novel. But giving an object a story, separate from you, is different. I really appreciate your giving me this opportunity."

Miranda stared at him, amazed. He sounded like an adult.

Before she could respond, the moment was dispelled when Alex got a message on his newsline. His face changed; it seemed to lengthen and harden as he scanned his wrist.

"I'm going to have to go," he said abruptly, standing up from the cube. "It's Albert. Mr. Fiske. He caught the virus. I've been helping Adele with him. She needs me now."

Miranda felt the cold tickle up her spine. She read about deaths from the anawhatsit on the newsline every day. "Alex, you can't," she said. "You're not a healer; anyway, if it's even slightly infectious—" She stopped as the glass door whispered shut behind him.

———

She was waiting up when he returned to the flat much later that night.

"How is Mr. Fiske?" she asked.

"About the same. At least he's not worse."

I did some reading on the anacoccus," she said. "It's getting better. Dying out. If he caught it at this late stage—"

"He's not getting better," Alex said. "And something strange.

110

His effectives."

"Yes?"

"Adele and I have been studying the list. It's a very short list, with nothing on it effective against the virus."

"I'm sorry," Miranda said sincerely. "Immune system boosters—"

Alex waved that away impatiently. "They've tried them all. The thing is . . ." He paused.

Miranda waited.

"I've combed through his medical history. He's been healthy. He hasn't burned through his effectives as a lot of people his age have. The effective that fights this virus was never on his list."

Miranda was silent. After losing her mother at an early age, she paid close attention to health. "That's not possible," she said. "We all start with the same list."

"I'm hoping it's just a bureaucratic mistake, but Adele couldn't get a real answer from the healer when she stopped by."

Alex turned away so that Miranda couldn't see his face. "It's tough," he said. "He sees his cats crawling all over the bed. He talks to them and pets them. I don't know. Maybe he'll get better." He opened a packfruit but just stared at it, too tired or lost in thought to eat. His eyes, when he looked at her, were as wide as the four-year-old with his night terrors.

"What do you think happens when we die?" he asked. "In nature, the plants that emerge each growing season are so close to the plants of the season before. Not like the children of those plants, but the plants themselves, just changed somehow."

Miranda paused. Her mother, her father were here one day, gone the next, and now were nothing but memories. The main reason she believed Peter was still alive was because, even unseen and unheard, he was messing with her life. If he were dead, she'd have no further problems in that direction. She looked at Alex's haunted eyes, bright with tears behind those thick lashes, and answered carefully.

"I believe we have our memories to comfort us, and that people live on through the impact they have on our lives. But I do believe we only get this one shot, and we have to do the best with it we can."

Alex didn't respond, but his lips tightened. "Albert Fiske is a good guy. He is all his wife has. He's barely sixty, not much older than Tara. We've got to beat this. You have to help."

"What can I do?" Miranda asked. "I don't really know anyone in Health."

"You know Tara," Alex said. "Rumor is that she's not just a city manager, she's *the* city manager. The only one that counts. I know that a mistake has been made somewhere. She'll be able to get it fixed."

"I'll ask," Miranda promised.

"Tomorrow?"

"If she's around," Miranda replied. "She often isn't."

"Can you send her a note? Tell her it's really important you meet with her."

Miranda blinked on her newsline. Two times in one week. She was stretching their friendship to the breaking point. Tara might very well say no. "What should I say? Do I explain about Albert?"

Alex thought, then shook his head. "Better not. Just ask for the meeting. Tell her it's really important, that you'll explain when you see her."

Miranda sent the note, inwardly wincing as she pictured Tara's surprised reaction, and was surprised and relieved to get an immediate response that Tara would see her at eight o'clock tomorrow morning. She knew Tara was wondering what was up, but she didn't ask.

Alex tilted his head awkwardly. "Thanks. I knew you'd be able to help."

"I can't promise to help," Miranda said. "But I can tell Tara the situation and see what she can do. I'm sure she knows very high up healers. But I think you exaggerate her influence."

Alex looked at her oddly. "Maybe," he responded quietly, "but we appreciate anything Tara can do. Make sure she understands time is running out."

Alex needed sleep if he was going to be any help to Albert and Adele, but he turned on his newsline and slipped quickly into the root, too tired to bother with the circuitous path he usually followed. For once, the coyote was waiting when Alex reached the COSLine. It wasn't slinking or hiding in the shadows but waiting silently for Alex to arrive.

"I spent the day with friends of mine," he told the coyote. "The man, Albert; I think he may be dying." When his voice broke on the last sentence, the coyote stiffened and cocked his head.

"People die, Alex," he responded quietly. "It will happen to all of us."

Alex shook his head. "But not like this. Not before their time. Something's wrong. I asked my mom for help. Because that's what my mom does. She helps people. Don't you think?" His voice trailed off.

The coyote paused before answering. "I am sure she will do her best."

"Is there really no way to tell her . . . ?" He didn't need to finish his thought.

"She won't come," his father responded. "Her life, her future, is bound up in Sanctuary. But not ours." He tilted his head, awaiting Alex's assurance.

"No, of course. I mean, I'm ready."

"Good. Because you should leave tomorrow."

"Tomorrow?" Alex's voice rose, like a child's. He thought he would have more time.

"I explained to you. It's dangerous to travel between cities. I had to time it with a shipment so we would have armed guards for the journey back." His voice softened. "It won't get any easier to wait," he said. "I know. I left once myself. And I didn't just leave your mother, I left my son."

Alex shook his head stubbornly. "I can't leave my friends. Albert, Adele . . . I'm all they have."

"Listen, whenever you make a decision to live your life the way you want to live it, you have to break old ties. You can't have a future if you don't."

Alex didn't respond. The coyote studied the defiant posture, the narrowed eyes. Alex was very like him, maybe too much. He sighed.

"I can wait a day or two for things to settle for your friends. But not for too long. It is dangerous at the Sanctuary perimeter, and my work needs me."

Alex nodded. "As soon as I can. What do I need to do?"

CHAPTER THIRTEEN

Miranda was surprisingly nervous about meeting with Tara. Not because she saw so little of her, but because lately she had seen her too much. These constant meetings were getting ridiculous. A role master who was this needy would never be promoted. She would be lucky if her role wasn't cut short. She hesitated at the door and almost turned away, but then she remembered the relief on Alex's face.

"Come in," Tara said, before Miranda could announce herself or knock. The door whispered open and Miranda walked in. Tara smiled, but her eyes were wary.

What's up?" she asked. "Trouble at work?" She didn't mention Alex.

Miranda paused, waiting for the right words to introduce the Fiskes and Alex's request.

"No," she said. "I made a lot of progress yesterday on the fur designs for Festival. I think you'll be pleased."

"Excellent! I can't wait to purchase one," Tara said. Her eyes strayed to her desk.

"The thing is," Miranda started cautiously, "I need to ask a favor."

"Of course," Tara said. "Something else to do with Alex?"

"Not exactly," Miranda answered. "You remember those cat test cases—the Fiskes? It's about the husband, Albert."

Tara's face went still. "I know he's not been well. I was really sorry to hear that."

Relief washed over Miranda. Tara already knew about it. Perhaps steps were already being taken.

"He has that virus that's going around, anawhatzit."

"Anacoccus."

"Yes. Lots of people had it, including me and even . . ." Her voice faltered before she said, "you. It responds very well to certain effectives. As we both know, it doesn't have to be fatal."

Tara waited.

"The thing is, none of the effectives that work with the virus are on his list. Not because he's built an immunity to them. They simply disappeared. We're sure there's just some bureaucratic mistake . . ."

Her voice trailed off as she watched Tara's emotionless face.

"We were hoping you could check."

Tara paused, clearly selecting and testing each word before she spoke.

"The effectives are a dwindling list," she said finally. "I'm sure you know that. It's a mystery to Health, to all of us, how these new infections develop. We have an enclosed environment, strict hygiene laws, carefully selected diets. Of course nothing is completely enclosed. We visit the outside—to dispose of garbage, harvest what is still usable, maintain relations of a sort with other cities so they don't invade us for what we have as their societies fall to pieces. Many think the species that exploit the holes are bringing these viruses in with them. Ferrats, coyotes . . ." her voice trailed off.

"Albert Fiske," Miranda prompted gently.

"Yes, well, health is one of the most difficult areas in which to maintain equilibrium in the city. We've made so many advances in technology since we built Sanctuary, but we haven't made the advances we'd hoped with health. Somehow the infections stay one step ahead of us. Do you understand what I am saying?"

Miranda shook her head.

"We have to manage the effectives statistically, for the good of the general population. We must fight against the frightening ability of viruses and bacterial infections to develop immunity to effectives. As people get older, some effectives are removed from their list."

Miranda stiffened with shock. "I've never heard of this," she said. "I guard my effectives list carefully, as you're supposed to, using them only when absolutely necessary, using just the right amount, and now you say that ultimately they'll just fall off my plate, and I have no say in the matter?"

"It's not quite that simple, and you do have a lot of say. Statistical analyses are balanced with individual characteristics—your age, your sex, your individual immunity, even your lifestyle. Effectives are administered for the ultimate good of the city. Albert Fiske was a very nice man. I will miss him at city events. But he and his wife ignored hygiene rules, never really adapted to Sanctuary, were too nostalgic for what they left behind. The next generation, your generation, who came at an earlier age to the city, is already better adjusted psychologically. This plays into the immune system more than you might imagine."

"So people with compromised immune systems will have more effectives removed than others?" Miranda thought of Alex, his thinness, his shadowed eyes, his refusal to eat properly, to get enough sleep.

"Many factors play in," Tara said gently. "Effectives are not removed lightly."

"Wait a minute," Miranda said. "You said 'was.' Albert Fiske *was* a nice man."

Tara paused before answering. "Adele took him to a healing center late last night, where he passed away peacefully early this morning, as was his wish. I'm very sorry, for you, for Alex, and for Adele, but also for myself. Albert was a wonderful streetways builder. He did beautiful work and was always friendly to people passing by. I'll miss him."

Miranda stared blankly at her for a moment. *I must get to Alex,* she thought, and turned to leave.

Tara's voice stopped her at the door. "I'm fifty-one," she told Miranda's retreating back. "I've already lost one effective myself."

Miranda stepped over the sill without looking back. The door closed silently behind her.

She was supposed to meet with the fur designers that afternoon, but she ignored her calendar and blew past Lesley, who wanted to show her the latest iteration of virtuskin. Her last look as she jumped on the stairs was of Lesley's surprised look, just starting to rearrange into offended. *Can't be helped*, she thought. She borrowed a loaner magcart from Security downstairs so she could reach the Fiskes' building as quickly as possible. She wasn't surprised that Alex answered their monitor. His tear-streaked cheeks caused her heart to clench.

"Alex, I'm so sorry. I just heard," she said.

"I'll come down," Alex replied. "Adele isn't really up for visitors."

"I wanted to tell her how sorry I am," Miranda said.

"I'll tell her you called. She'll appreciate it. I'm coming down."

The Alex who showed up at the street door and led Miranda to a small park square across the street was folded into himself and expressionless, more like a DP than a person. He moved deftly aside when she reached out to hug him.

"How is she doing?" she asked awkwardly.

"Just as you'd expect," Alex replied. "Adele never took to the city. She mostly kept to the house, grieving for her cats. Albert took her out of herself, got her to attend a few city events. I don't know what she's going to do without him."

"She's lucky to have you as a friend, Alex."

Alex's mouth moved, but he didn't say anything. He blinked his eyes rapidly and turned away. "I need to get back to Adele," he said. "I guess you saw Tara this morning. That's how you knew?"

"Yes, she said Adele took Albert to the healing center late last night."

GRACE J. AGNEW

"He was ready to go. Adele said he administered the FD himself."

"FD?"

"Final dose," Alex said. "C'mon, Mom. You must know all about final dose."

Miranda shook her head.

"When you know you are at the end, and the healers confirm it, you are offered a final dose that puts you into a deep sleep so that none of your body's defenses operate; you pass away peacefully. You have to administer it yourself, or a next of kin. Even I know about final dose. I assumed you probably invented it." His voice was bitter.

Miranda thought of her father's last day at the healing center. He was almost cheerful, despite his pain. He cupped her face in his hands and told her how proud he was of her and how well she was doing in world building. She left for work feeling relieved. Perhaps he was turning a corner and getting a little better. That afternoon she had anecdotes about her new team and a compliment from Tara stored up to share with him. The healers greeted her with grave faces. Her dad had passed quietly, peacefully, that afternoon. Had he . . . ? Without telling her and letting her be there? She felt sick at the thought.

Alex was studying her face. "I learned about it when I was looking at healing as a possible role. One of the healers showed me the area in the healing center where they administer it. They used it with pets when people were coming into Sanctuary. She said it took them a while to agree that humans deserved the same opportunity."

Fred. Miranda hugged herself. Her father leaving just like Fred, alone at the end, without her. Did he wag his tail also?

Alex changed the subject. "So, what did Tara have to say, anyway?"

Miranda paused. "She knew that Albert had passed," she replied evasively. "I left as soon as I found out. I knew I needed to get to you."

119

"I should have contacted you sooner," Alex said, "when Tara could have helped. But he went downhill so fast."

It was Miranda's turn to look away, but not quickly enough.

"Or would she have helped?" Alex asked. "Was his effectives list so short on purpose?"

Miranda didn't answer. "Alex, you need to be careful with exposing yourself to illnesses," she said, changing the subject, but not really. "You can't take good health for granted, even at your age and in a safe place like Sanctuary."

Alex snorted bitterly. "Safe place!" he replied. "Yeah, it was really safe for Albert. You know, he and his wife debated not coming in, just staying outside and looking for any stray cats that were still out there. He came in for Adele. And look what happened. Albert built half the streetways in this place, and this is how the city repays him in the end. Uses him up and throws him away."

"It's not like that—" Miranda protested, but Alex stood up and walked away in midsentence, back across the street to the Fiskes' flat.

"I'll see you this evening," she called to Alex's retreating back. Alex didn't even raise a hand in response.

Miranda stood there, uncertain. Should she go to the Fiskes' flat, offer her condolences, try to get through to Alex? And say what? That it was best for Sanctuary to let old people go? She didn't believe that herself. She went back to work, to lose herself in fur coat designs. There was still time to make that appointment. On the way she sent a message to Alex via the newsline, letting him know she would need to skip dinner, but she would check in with him when she got home.

Miranda grabbed a packfruit at her desk for dinner. She had a lot to do to get fur coats ready for Festival. It was after eight o'clock when Lesley and Len caught her as she was leaving. They were still hopeful that virtuskin would also be ready for Festival. She was distracted, but she looked it over and gave them a few pointers.

She pulled away as soon as she decently could and hurried home to her flat. Alex's door was shut, but she peeked in anyway. He was curled up in a ball in his bed, so much like the little boy Alex that she almost went in, but she didn't want to wake him.

She didn't see him the next morning, but it was a school day and their schedules weren't the same. Later he sent her a message that he was going to hang out after training with kids from his course. She was both disappointed and relieved. Albert's death was tragic, but Alex was already starting to move on.

SANCTUARY

CHAPTER FOURTEEN

She signed off on final designs for the fur coat and left early. She wanted to be home when Alex returned. The flat was quiet. Of course, these days it was always quiet, but tonight the silence was a hole. Even though his door was shut, she knew instinctively that Alex wasn't there. Her heart squeezed like a sponge. *It doesn't mean anything,* she told herself. *He's stopped by to see Adele.* But she had sent him a message asking him to be home by five, that they needed to talk. It wasn't like Alex to stand her up, no matter how angry he was with her. But he was getting older, and things were changing. She turned on her DP with a small nod.

"Where is my son, Alex?" she asked.

The blue cube shimmered slightly as it worked. "Unable to locate his DP," it finally said.

"Aren't you synced to his DP for health alerts?" she demanded. "Even if it's turned off, you should be able to locate it. Is it here?" She looked wildly about the room.

"It's not in the building," her DP responded. "And it isn't turned off. Not in the normal way. It's been disrupted."

"Disrupted?"

"All systems halted, including the emergency locator."

"Was this an accident or intentionally done?"

"Without a significant signal burst, a disruption is never accidental. In a large signal burst, I would also be disrupted."

"What have you recorded? When was Alex last at the flat?"

"Yesterday, at 6:45 p.m."

Yesterday afternoon. So, what she had assumed was Alex curled up asleep? Blankets? Pillows? "Yesterday afternoon. And you didn't tell me?"

"My instructions on behaviors to report are clear," the DP responded with an unmistakable stiffness, despite everything Miranda had done to remove personality. "Illness, illegal activity, twenty-four-hour absence from the home. It is 6:38 p.m. Alex has been away from the flat for twenty-three hours and fifty-three minutes. In exactly seven minutes—"

Miranda held up a hand. "Stop," she said. "What was he doing? Where did he go? Show me the recording."

Her DP turned to the story cube and waited for more precise instructions. Where did she even start with the recording? She didn't want to be alone with whatever the DP showed her. She shook her head to countermand her order. "Call Tara," she commanded instead.

Tara was clearly distracted, but she interrupted Miranda's broken explanation to say she would be right there. Once she arrived, she took control. "When was he last in the flat?"

"Yesterday, 6:45 p.m.," the DP repeated.

According to her DP, Alex was last tracked via his magcart to the Northwest Disposal Facility, on the outskirts of the city yesterday, at 7:27 p.m. Her DP scanned the flat and reported that his backup scaleskin and two insulating blankets were missing, as well as packfruits and waterskins from her emergency supply. Also, some of her stockpiled antiseptic puffs.

Tara turned to Miranda. "When did you see him last?"

"Yesterday morning at the Fiskes. But he left me a message. I had no reason—"

"I'm not judging," Tara interrupted quietly. "Alex is sixteen. You can't follow him around all day. I'm just trying to decide when to start the recording. "Yesterday, 4:00 p.m.," she told the DP, which was waiting silently for instructions.

At first there was nothing. The flat was still, then and now, broken only by the sounds of their breathing as Tara and Miranda stared at the screen. Miranda noticed how bleak and gray her flat looked. Gone were Alex's childhood drawings that used to adorn the flat. They had been replaced with artistic studies of her many inventions, which once she thought looked colorful and interesting but that now looked vague and predicable, like the decor you find in a healing center reception room. Why had she done that? Was that the message she was sending to Alex, that he mattered less than her job? Never, in a million, billion years. He was irreplaceable, the center of her being. So why did she never tell him that? Miranda wanted to jump up, grab her magcart, and go immediately to the edge of the city, where Alex's magcart last registered. Tara placed a restraining hand on her arm. They watched as Alex's bedroom door opened.

Miranda felt her heart tear at the sight of holo Alex. He looked solemn but focused as he moved quietly and efficiently through the flat, pulling down blankets from shelves and gathering pack-fruits. He knew where the sensors were—how could he not?—so he kept his head down, completing his packing. When he grabbed a handful of waterskins, he looked directly at a sensor and said quietly, "Sorry, Mom, it can't be helped."

Miranda jumped at the sound of his voice. "Where are you going that you need so much water?" she asked. But she knew the answer. Outside.

She and Tara watched in silence as Alex neatly packed his backpack. He looked directly at the sensor again. "I'm really sorry," he said, sounding as if he meant it. "I know how upset you are right now, but I've been preparing for this for a while; I know you sensed it. I'll be okay. I'll try to get word to you whenever I can. I'll miss you, and I know you'll miss me, but I had to grow up and leave home sometime. Try not to worry too much. Just live your own life. We'll see each other again." He started to leave, then paused and looked back. "Please check in on Adele. She's all alone now, and . . ." his voice choked as he turned away. The flat door closed quietly behind him.

Miranda sat still, taking it in, emotions and thoughts chasing each other. Her son, her reason for life itself, was gone, and he said to just live her own life? They would 'see each other again'? That was supposed to be enough? Everything she lived for had just walked through that door. Everything she feared, and tried to prevent, had happened. She was so heavy with grief and fear, she couldn't move. He was right, she realized; she had been expecting this. All the nagging, the fights, were because she was trying to prevent this day.

"What does he mean, Adele's all alone?" she found herself saying to Tara. "I'm all alone. His mother." She hated how whiny she sounded, but the fact that the only emotion he showed was for an older woman who was no relation tore at her soul.

"What's happening?" Tara asked. "Does he have a contact on the outside?" She didn't mention Alex's father—she didn't have to.

The thought of Peter galvanized Miranda. She had been sitting like a sack full of sand, unable to move, but suddenly she felt something, adrenaline maybe, coursing through her and jumped up. She ran into her bedroom and grabbed her own backpack. Why did she even have a backpack? That's right, camping with Alex's adventure group when he was little. They had a life together, memories like that one, how did he simply leave all that behind?

"What are your plans?" Tara asked at her elbow. "Where are you going?"

Miranda answered tersely. "Outside." She threw her spare scale-skin into the backpack. Would one be enough? She looked at Tara.

"Don't be my boss right now," she said. "Be my friend."

"Outside? How?"

"His dad," Miranda answered. Could she get hold of the coveralls the disposers wore to take out the Sanctuary trash? Maybe at the wall.

"Peter? Is he still . . . I mean are they in touch?"

"Yes, he is still . . . and clearly they are in touch. Alex wouldn't leave for any other reason."

He wouldn't leave me, she meant.

"But how?"

Miranda waved a hand impatiently. "Honestly, Tara, I don't have time. He's been gone since last night. If you want to be helpful, please get some packfruits from the kitchen."

Tara was her sometimes friend and former lover, but mostly she was her boss. Miranda had never given her an order before. She couldn't look at her as Tara turned on her heel without a word and returned a few minutes later with an armful of packfruits and waterskins.

Miranda braced herself, but Tara didn't try to talk her out of it. Instead she laid a hand on her arm. "Wait a day or two," she said. "Let me arrange something. I have contacts on the outside. I can probably locate him. And if not, I can arrange things to keep you safe."

Miranda took the packfruits one by one and counted them as she carefully packed. Two days to find him, another two days back. Unless they were already at City of the South. Needles of fear shivered through her. Could she survive outside long enough to reach City of the South?

"Did you hear what I said?"

Miranda looked at Tara. She had lost so much weight from her recent illness. She didn't look like her boss; she looked Alex's age, like someone needing protection and care. Not someone who could handle the worst thing to ever happen.

"No," she said decisively. "My only hope is to move fast if I want to find him."

"If he is with his father, he's safe enough," Tara replied. "Peter must have learned a thing or two about the outside over all these years. But you came inside when you were eleven. And you don't know anything about what the world has become. Let me contact Peter. We need to negotiate."

Miranda's heart sank. She could imagine Tara's idea of intervention—a Sanctuary-approved diplomat bartering with Peter and his friends for her son. And even if it worked, Alex would return as an outcast, his role stripped away, aimlessly wandering the city walls like the other hopeless cases. The only chance for Alex's future was to get him back before anyone noticed. She picked her words carefully. "I appreciate it," she said, "but I'm the only one who can persuade Alex to return. And it has to be face to face."

"Well, then, an escort. Someone to protect you."

"My only hope to survive is to move quickly and quietly. I can't outfight or even outrun whatever is out there, and neither can an escort."

She didn't look at Tara as she finished tucking away the pack-fruits and started with the water. You had only enough skins for an emergency, a breakdown in Sanctuary that thus far had never happened. You weren't allowed to hoard. One, two, three, four—

"There are eight waterskins," she said.

"Okay."

"I had twelve."

"So Alex took four," Tara said.

"Less than half," Miranda said. "Much less. And probably not as much as he needs."

"So?"

"You don't understand," Miranda said. She wrapped the waterskins carefully in the spare scaleskin and walked quickly into the bathroom.

"Half the antiseptic puffs are gone," she said,

"So, he wasn't greedy," Tara replied.

Miranda grabbed her shoulders. "Don't you get it? We don't need these things in Sanctuary. We never have emergencies. Alex used to tease me about this. "If Sanctuary is so great, what are you saving these for?"

Tara waited.

"This is the emergency," Miranda said. "The only emergency that ever mattered to me. Losing my son."

Her eyes filled with tears. "He knew I would follow. He left me supplies so I could."

"I think you might be reading too much—"

"I know my son," Miranda said. "These supplies are hard to come by. He would have taken them all if he wanted to stop me, or at least slow me down."

Tara didn't answer but went to the hall closet. She pulled out a reflector blanket and rolled it tightly. "You're going to need this," she said. She reached into her own elegant day pack and pulled out a bag that jingled. Miranda looked inside. Coins. DPs handled all legitimate transactions in Sanctuary, but on the shabby outskirts, where the marginals lived, they preferred to be paid in coins, tarnished, metallic remnants of life outside.

"Where did you . . . ? I don't want . . ." Miranda couldn't think straight; all she could see was Alex, alone outside in the dark—or maybe not alone.

"Take them," Tara said, pushing the bag into her hands. "You may need to buy food, or shelter." Miranda took the bag and hastily hugged Tara. Her shoulders were trembling. She was scared for Miranda.

Miranda couldn't think about what was waiting outside, if she even made it outside. She checked her backpack. Who knew if she had everything she needed? Tara turned away so that Miranda couldn't see her face. She knew Tara was fighting back tears. If she had any advice about how to escape Sanctuary, she would offer it now. Miranda waited, but Tara said nothing. She clumsily shrugged into the laden backpack and left the flat.

Tara was still for a minute, then shook herself as if waking from a bad dream. She hurried out of the flat and looked up and down the streetway. Miranda was gone.

CHAPTER FIFTEEN

Miranda stepped into the loaner magcart she had borrowed from work. She could have taken her own, but magcarts were tracked. She was really doing this. Going outside. A thousand memories flooded her. Playing outside or in abandoned houses, always accompanied by Fred. Reading books with Fred's head in her lap. His deep sighs when he wanted to play; she shushed him so she could read another chapter. Pressing a pillow against her ears when the cracked doorbell rang until it could ring no more, replaced by frantic knocks on the door that were even harder to ignore.

"Northwest waste disposal facility," she said. She had to say it twice before the magcart understood her quivering voice. It gave a little leap and headed down the streetway. *I'm off,* she thought. The magcart glided past buildings and trees but no people. Although there was no curfew in Sanctuary, it was understood that after dinner everyone not in their flats would gravitate to the entertainment districts, with drinks bars and story parlors for adults and concerts for teenagers. If you wanted to wander the streets at night, your DP would give you a dozen reasons why not, including the fact that the sanitizers were set to low at night, which meant the carefully calibrated evening breeze could be carrying microbes looking for a place to root. Miranda shivered, although the early-evening air was balmy. *What would the air outside be like? What was Alex breathing right now?*

The magcart slowed. Miranda stopped a quarter mile from the refuse facility, too far to recognize anyone or be recognized in return, except for the ubiquitous sensors. Miranda scurried under a tree. Most trees held sensors, but they were outward focused, so directly underneath was the safest place to evade scans. She looked down at her feet. Even footsteps were tracked, as she had good reason to know, having designed the streetway sensors herself. She knew Alex wore black-market shoe inserts to prevent footstep tracking. Miranda never said anything, but those inserts, worse than useless since they actually magnified footstep traces, were her design also.

The refuse facility was crowded. Miranda seldom thought about the workers—healers, guardians, even disposers—that worked at night while everyone else was tucked snugly in their flats. She would give anything right now for a boring night at home, watching something silly while Alex holed up in his room.

Miranda moved to a nearby refuse bin where she could stash her magcart and backpack while she reconnoitered. There weren't many refuse collection bins in Sanctuary, since most trash was disposed of from facilities inside flats and work buildings, but there were artfully designed bins around the city where people could dispose of bulkier things. There was a refuse bin painted like a dragon not far from their flat that Alex had loved as a child. "Daddy!" he would exclaim and run over. Maybe Peter had shown it to him, or perhaps they had walked by once when he was working. It was possibly the only authentic memory he had of his dad, so Miranda let him run to the bin without comment. This one was painted like a starry sky, in keeping with the stillness and gloom of this part of the city.

The disposal center was easy to find, the only building with lights and movement in the area. Of course this would be disposal's busy time, packing the waste to be taken outside to the slag heaps in

132

the early morning. All her senses were heightened, even her hair was alert to every stray breeze. In another time, for another reason, it would be exciting to be out and about. She thought about that safe outside adventure she had hoped to have with Alex: a visit to the slag heaps. What sort of adventure was he having now? She skirted the building with its chain of magcarts carrying trash in and leaving empty and headed to the wall itself. It wasn't a good idea to visit the wall, except for the specially designed parks at its safer edges.

As the lights from the building diminished, the streetway grew very dark, only a faint metallic sheen differentiating it from the dark shadows crowding in. No grow lights, Miranda realized, and no trees, living or virtual. Ahead, Miranda could see the curb as the streetway ended against a looming blackness. The wall. Miranda seldom visited the wall, although some of her designs were used there. As a boy, Alex had clamored to see the wall. Miranda took him a couple of times because she didn't want him going on the sly with his friends. She wanted to show him how innocuous it was—a large-mirrored surface that showed a mother with a strained smile and worry lines already etched in her face and a boy pulling on her hand and pressing his face against the wall, trying vainly to see outside. Other children made faces at the wall or pirouetted like ballerinas to watch their reflection in the mirror that stretched up into the sky. Miranda couldn't see the appeal. There were mirrors at home.

The wall always reminded her of the day it went up, when you could no longer watch your salvation being built, building by building, street by street. In the end, there was only endless guessing and gossip. There were a few people engaged in building the city who still came home at night. Those knocks you answered, and you shared what little you had, to learn about the homes being built, the shops. Miranda's mother had wanted to know all about schools. She was a teacher, so after the local school closed, Miranda had daily lessons inside. Arithmetic and sentence declension punctuated by slight, ladylike coughs. She could hardly bring herself to attend Alex's school events. All those children crowded into a single large room. She watched for the sniffle and listened for the telltale cough. She shook herself impatiently. Woolgathering, while Alex was out there, somewhere.

Another memory came to her, unbidden. Visiting the wall with Peter, when she was pregnant with Alex. "Study your reflection," he had advised. "We're looking for any distortion or warping in the mirrored surface."

"Why?"

"Those are the seams of the wall, where the pieces join together."

The wall had looked like an unbroken, shimmering surface. A frozen lake surrounding the city.

"And the seams are important why?"

"Some of them can be pried open," he replied tersely. "With help, and for a price."

She realized now, looking back, that he was already feeling trapped by her expanding belly. But now, when he finally had use for the contents of that belly, he had taken her son away. For good.

"Not if I can help it," she muttered grimly and studied the wall. Most of the light had faded from the sky. Miranda could hardly see the woman in the mirror, her hair silvered to gray by the dark, the worry lines visible only if she stepped up close. It all looked wavy and distorted. Looking at the smooth, vast expanse of wall, she felt despair that she would ever find a way out. And even if she did . . . She shook her head. Time enough for thinking when she had Alex back. While there was still some daylight, she had to find a seam. It was all that she knew to do.

A red stripe, roughly patterned with bumps that felt different on the feet from the smooth walkway, kept the path separate from the wall. She tiptoed to the edge, as far as she dared. A few years back, when the kids Alex's age began their ridiculous fascination with the wall, measures had to be adopted to keep them from touching its surface. It was sturdily built, but enough adolescent hands pressing for seams was not a good idea. Len, one of her best world builders, had developed a device, the peripheral defense strip, or PDS. She had green-lighted his ingenious tool for protecting the wall, but she hadn't taken much interest other than to make sure no actual physical harm was done to wall violators, who were mostly children after all.

She was pacing the wall as she was thinking. She would lose the light soon. She stopped to study her face. Sure enough, when measured against the nose, one eye was the tiniest fraction higher than the other. Before she could stop herself, she placed her hand on the wall. The reaction was instantaneous. The wall itself seemed to move in and press against her, and a similar wall seemed to spring up behind, pressing in until she was flattened between two invisible surfaces, her nose and mouth pushed to one side so she could barely breathe. As she fought rising panic, she remembered that there were strong forced-air jets lying beneath the red strip. She could feel her heart pounding as she forced shallow breaths in and out, but they were coming too fast. Her last thought before blacking out was, *We do this to children?*

She came to in a sitting position on the streetway, beside the red warning strip. A guardian was standing over her.

"Out a bit late, aren't you?" he asked. "What's your business at the wall?"

"Nothing," she replied. "Just talking a walk."

"You're far from home," the guardian replied, naming her address. Of course he knew who she was and where she lived.

"A world builder should know better than to touch the wall," the guardian said.

Miranda attempted a chuckle. "We've had some complaints about the perimeter defense system," she said. "I was at the wall, and I couldn't resist testing it myself. I approved the PDS, but I don't know that much about it."

"So, what do you think?"

Miranda thought for a moment. "It was terrible," she said. "I think they have a point."

"Funny that you violated the wall right at a seam," the guardian said.

Miranda didn't respond. Her acting skills weren't that good.

"Probably a good idea if you head home now." It wasn't a suggestion.

Miranda realized by the way he was studying her that he was filing a silent report. Twenty-six years as a world builder with an unblemished record, except maybe her hasty, unsanctioned registration with Peter. Her lips tightened. It figured. If she was going to get in trouble, it all came down to him. As she studied the guardian's expressionless eyes, her resolve wavered. Her bed sounded really good right now. Give Alex twenty-four hours to realize what a terrible place the outside was; take Tara up on her offer to negotiate for his return. Sanctuary had uneasy truces, even bartering alliances, with other cities, including City of the South. Tara would get him back. Miranda almost turned around.

Almost. The thought of Alex out there, in the dust and the wind, with night falling . . . Even if he was with Peter. She couldn't trust Peter to put his son ahead of his own survival, not the way she would. He was like his namesake from that children's story of yesteryear— the boy who never grew up, the eternal adventurer, but ultimately amoral, caring for nobody but himself. Her lip curled when she thought about the letter he left for his son, which she'd hastily read while packing. He hadn't forgotten how she'd teased him. Except he took it as a compliment. "When you are ready to join me, go to the wall by the Northwest Disposal Facility and say the word 'crocodile' until somebody hears you and responds, 'tick tock.'" *Was it really as simpleminded and foolish as that?*

Without thinking, she muttered "crocodile."

"What?"

She looked up, startled. She had almost forgotten the guardian. "Did you say something to me?"

"No. I was just . . ."she started to explain, to make something up, but she realized his eyes had changed, no longer expressionless but wary. And he was looking around suspiciously.

"Crocodile," she said loudly and firmly.

He covered her mouth with his hand. "Sh-h-h," he advised. "Tick tock."

Miranda stared in turn. Peter had been gone for twelve years. How did he have contacts in the guardians?

The guardian grabbed her arm and pulled her into the shadow of a nearby tree. "How do you know Peter?" she asked.

"Be quiet," he responded. "Don't mention names out loud. I used to be on the day shift, guarding garbage disposal."

He turned her to face him, his eyes gleaming with suspicion. "There's no activity planned for tonight. If I had been expecting you, I wouldn't have recorded this meeting."

Miranda took a deep breath. Honesty was probably the best strategy. "I'm following Peter," she said. "He has my son. Our son."

The man's voice rose a notch. "You're Peter's wife?" He looked her up and down. Miranda knew he was looking for the horns, the cloven hooves.

"You helped them escape last night," she said. "And now you're going to help me."

The guardian's eyes narrowed. She stiffened when he touched his weapon. It was designed to stun, not kill. A crime that required killing as a defense was unheard of in Sanctuary, but once she was unconscious . . . She stepped back.

"If you've looked me up, you know I am a leader in world building," she said. "I wouldn't be leaving without powerful help. People expect me to get in touch from outside. If I don't, there will be questions." It didn't make sense, even to her. Why weren't these powerful people helping her get outside? But she made the guardian hesitate. He wasn't sure what to do. His hand moved slightly away from his weapon belt. She pressed her advantage. "As you pointed out, you've already sent a report. I can help you fix that."

"What do you have in mind?"

"We'll record another report, where I apologize for alarming you and walk away. I can program my DP to show me quietly at home all evening. In reality . . ."

"In reality?"

"You show me how to get out of here."

She saw him thinking it through.

"You know I am one of the inventors of DPs." She pulled up her DP and wrinkled her brow in concentration.

"Play back, please" she told the cube.

"Playing back," the cube responded blandly. The cube showed the guardian stepping forward, his hands closing around Miranda's neck. Her face turned red, then blue. Her eyes bulged; her tongue, fat and purple, thrust out of her mouth—

"Hey!" the guardian protested. "That never happened! Turn that off!"

"Show me the way out, and my DP shows me going home and then reading quietly in bed."

The guardian pulled out his baton and Miranda jumped, but he walked past her to the seam of the wall. The guardian's cloak was protection against the PDS. He inserted the tip into the wall seam and began working it back and forth.

"Peter was right about you," he muttered.

"Excuse me?"

"Put my cloak around your shoulders. Get ready to jump over the red strip when I say."

"I left my supplies. I have to go get them."

"Better run. You have five minutes. I'm late for my round as it is."

Miranda ran.

The guardian eyed her sourly when she returned, red faced and out of breath. "No telling who is hanging around the city walls outside. Put on coveralls if you've got them."

Miranda shook her head.

The guardian looked at her in disbelief. "Do you have nose coat?"

"Nose coat?"

"And you a world builder." He pulled a half-rolled-up tube out of his pocket. "Coat your nostrils with this."

"What's this for?" Miranda asked.

"What do you think the air is like out there?"

The stuff was thick and shiny and started drying the minute it was exposed to air.

"Better hurry. That's all I have. I don't think it will get you to City of the South."

She spread the mixture experimentally on one nostril. The air turned viscous, and she had to suck it in.

The guardian was shifting his weight from one foot to the next. "Hurry up before a sensor catches the open crack. You'll get used to breathing soon enough."

She coated the other nostril. Her lungs tightened immediately in protest. Who developed this stuff?

"When you get outside, put a scarf around your mouth to protect your throat," he advised.

Miranda didn't have a scarf, but she didn't say anything. She could fashion something from her second scaleskin. She needed to get moving. The guardian helped her into the crack.

"Move fast. Don't stop for anyone. If someone comes toward you, run away. If someone is lying on the ground pleading for your help, step around them. It's most likely a trap."

Miranda nodded. She took her pack off her back, turned sideways, and edged into the gap. The wall edges plucked at her scale-skin. Even turned sideways, her body felt squeezed like a tube. It was like being captured by the PDS again, except she could wiggle and move slightly. But she couldn't breathe. She kept wiggling until she could move her shoulder an inch and use it as a lever. The wall shifted slightly. She pushed harder and continued to wiggle back and forth. She cautiously stretched out a leg and felt it push past the wall into nothingness, or at least nothing that caught at or squeezed her. Her leg was outside! She threw her shoulder where her leg had gone, and tumbled forward until she hit the ground, painfully. Her other leg was still caught in the door. She rolled on her back and began pulling at the leg. Something pushed the leg from the wall. The guardian. Her leg fell to the ground, and she heard the wall pop back into place behind her. She was alone in the dark.

The seam popped back open with a loud crack. "Hey" a voice whispered from far away. Something fell through the crack with a *thunk*, and then the wall snapped back a second time. She could hear the guardian's footsteps recede from the wall. She felt around in the dusk. His baton! She couldn't believe how much he had given her, first his cloak and now his baton. He'd never be able to explain these losses.

CHAPTER SIXTEEN

"Seven a.m. No appointments. No health alerts to concern you. Do you want to know what is happening in the city?"

The clipped British accent was momentarily disorienting after a night of terrible dreams. At one point, Tara was handing Albert Fiske the final dose, but the hand that reached out for the cup was Miranda's. She sat up in bed.

"A cloudless day," Jeeves continued blandly. Tara groaned. Her head, on the other hand, was full of clouds. She wondered where Miranda was now. Had she really left Sanctuary? Tara had smoothed the way, ensuring that a guardian who was a covert 2084 member was patrolling the gate where Peter's letter to his son had indicated there was a usable crack in the wall. She didn't watch the wall last night, in part so that no one else would, but also because she didn't want to know. Jeeves waited, the stillness of his posture conveying his puzzlement and concern that Tara wasn't up. She had to get moving. "Coffee essence, please, while I hop in the shower."

Jeeves bowed and walked away with a swish of his impeccable tails.

Tara watched him leave. She knew how to wipe the emotion from the DP, none better; but truthfully, Jeeves's fussy mannerisms were her guilty pleasure. DPs studied the missteps of their owners and calibrated their actions and responses to align them more closely to the city's expectations. Tara wasn't the model citizen in private that she appeared to be in public. In private she drank

SANCTUARY

too much, and she hated, absolutely loathed, packfruits, with the result that she was below the optimum weight for a Sanctuary citizen. She was such a frequent offender of Sanctuary health standards that Jeeves had become a clucking old nanny in tails. She should be bothered by Jeeves's disapproval, but mostly she found it amusing. In the privacy of her flat, she exaggerated her otherwise hidden eccentricities to bring out more personality in Jeeves, a trick she suspected many lonely people in Sanctuary employed. With Miranda gone, if she really was gone, Jeeves was all she had left.

That realization propelled her from her bed. It wasn't true, of course. She was a member of the city council and got on well with most of the members. She went to Sanctuary events with them and sometimes out to dinner before or after. She spent every day with her coworkers and latest apprentice, but Tara was too focused on the work involved in keeping Sanctuary stable and thriving to pay much attention to the people in the background. The beauty and mystery of what made Sanctuary successful when all the other cities failed never ceased to absorb her. People, on the other hand, were bland and interchangeable as they came and went, with the exception of Miranda, the apprentice who questioned everything with brow furrowed, whose designs were the puzzle pieces that linked together all the aspects of the furtive soul of the city, whose son went from trusting and charming to moody and hostile, almost overnight. She had invested too much in Miranda, more than Miranda was ever able to return. They were colleagues, then friends, and then briefly lovers, although Tara always knew that Miranda was just fiercely seeking the physical connection that had disappeared with Peter. Tara was the one who saw that it was going nowhere, who ended the affair and pulled away, but at some level, both women knew the truth. Miranda was the one who rejected what they had, and she was grateful that Tara shouldered the burden of blame.

Tara listened to Jeeves fussing in the kitchen. Fifty-one years on this planet, thirty-three of them in Sanctuary, and all she really had was a holo slightly more solid than something you experienced in a game . . . Her thoughts trailed off. This wasn't getting her anywhere. *A shower*, she reminded herself.

Jeeves was waiting with her robe and a cup of coffee essence as she emerged.

"Thank you, Jeeves," she said. The DP bowed again, this time more deeply, responding to the warmth in Tara's voice. As she dressed, the flat bell rang. She jumped at the sound. She never had unexpected visitors. Jeeves turned to her for instructions.

"Who is it?" she asked.

Jeeves switched on the newsline monitor in the bedroom with a glance. "Jonathan Royce," he announced, "city counselor."

"I know who he is," Tara answered. Jonathan obligingly turned full face to the door sensor. He didn't ring the bell again.

"What's he doing here?" Tara wondered. Jeeves didn't respond. Tara had trained her DP to recognize rhetorical questions. Tara nodded at a sensor to open the flat door. Miranda's absence must already be noticed. They were sending in the big guns.

"How are you, Tara?" Jonathan asked, too heartily. He made no attempt to explain his visit. Of all the council members to choose, Jonathan was the one she liked and respected the least. She stiffened as it hit her. That's why.

She knew from the question that this was a veiled reference to her recent bout with the anacoccus virus. City councilors were expected to take every precaution during any illness outbreaks. Sickness was a moral as much as a physical failing. "What can I do for you?"

Jonathan took a deep breath, and she realized he was nervous. "I won't take up much of your time, particularly if we can agree on the things I know and get that out of the way. I know that you met world builder Miranda Davis at her home after she discovered her sixteen-year-old son, Alex, was missing, and you helped her leave Sanctuary." He paused. "To go outside."

Tara said nothing.

"Thank you for not denying this," Jonathan said. "It saves time." He dropped the businesslike demeanor. He could never quite carry it off. "What were you thinking? A top world builder! She's taken half the secrets of Sanctuary with her."

"There's a thriving black market for Sanctuary inventions outside," Tara responded dryly. "The disposers and outside integrators make a tidy second income, I'm told. Miranda's inventions are huge sellers." She didn't say more, but she didn't have to. Jonathan was suspected by most of the council of having a hand in the black-market barter.

His fleshy face turned the color of a plum packfruit. "You think you know everything," he responded. "But I can tell you some things you don't know. Miranda Davis went outside last night at 8:03 p.m., shortly after leaving you. Guardians found and repaired the seam she used, so she won't be returning that way. Apparently, there was some altercation with one or more outsiders not far from the city wall. It was just beyond sensor range, so we don't know exactly what happened or how it concluded. There were no bodies. There was, however, blood. Miranda's blood."

Tara schooled herself not to respond or freeze with panic. "I think you are giving me credit for knowing a lot more than I do," she responded smoothly. "Her son had disappeared, and of course she was worried. I tried to convince her that he was probably still in Sanctuary, maybe hanging out with a protester group. He's just started a role he likes. Why would he leave now? But obviously she didn't believe me if she has left to pursue her son."

Jonathan consulted his newsline, as she hoped he would. She had no doubt hers was already censored.

"The boy Alex left at 9:45 p.m. the previous night through the same gap. He was met by three hooded men at the city wall. They were not picked up by sensors, so presumably had disruptors."

"Stupid boy!" Tara said with feeling. Inside, the phrase "Miranda's blood" was drumming in time to her own rapid heartbeat.

Jonathan's face softened. "I know these are friends of yours," he said. "There's going to need to be a conversation with the full council about this, but I was to let you know it can wait a day if you want some time alone."

Tara looked at him coolly. "I don't need time alone. And I will give any help I can to retrieve both of them. I'm sure it's the result of some misunderstanding. A mother-son quarrel. They can't have gotten far."

Jonathan tilted his head to one side and studied her speculatively. "Yes, well, this is the kind of mistake you don't really recover from in Sanctuary," he said unnecessarily.

"I realize that," she responded sharply. "But if we bring them back, at least they are safe." Miranda was the best of the current world builders. Better than Tara had ever been. She trusted her stubbornness and her talent to claw out a place for herself and her son when they returned. If they returned.

"If there's nothing else?"

Jonathan made an attempt at an "all friends here" smile. "I guess I will see you shortly."

Tara gazed at the door in answer. He took the hint and left.

She shut Jeeves down with a glance, feeling momentarily bereft as his expression changed from attentive to vacant before he folded into a vertical line and disappeared.

SANCTUARY

CHAPTER SEVENTEEN

One hundred ninety-seven . . . one hundred ninety-eight . . . Alex found that counting the steps between landmarks helped pass the time, even though, the farther they got from Sanctuary, the fewer the things he could count as landmarks. They were on the second day's walk, although the misty gray of the permanent cloud cover kept the world from getting too dark or too light, making it hard to tell night from day. At some point that first night, when Alex was so tired his smelly companion was practically carrying him, his dad had called a halt for some sleep. They shared a hunk of something smooth and creamy in texture and water bubbles similar to those Alex had in his pack. His father tossed him a blanket before spreading out one of his own beside his son. Alex brushed the rocks away before positioning his blanket, as he saw the other men do. He fell asleep almost as soon as he stretched cautiously on the makeshift bed.

In the morning, Alex offered everyone a packfruit for breakfast. The slithery hunk of whatever he had eaten the night before sat uneasily on his stomach, and the bathroom facilities—a stunted tree next to the campground—offered no protection from smells or sounds. They rolled up their packs and started walking as soon as everyone had visited the tree. Alex looked around curiously. His first real day on the outside. Dwarfish trees, mostly dead but a few with spindly branches and leaves, gave way to rocks, some of them large enough to sit on during their infrequent breaks. Ruined buildings choked with green and brown vines, the only things that seemed to thrive outside, looked more like hills than anything man-made. Alex couldn't imagine living in one of these and thought, not for the first time, of his comfortable flat.

Once a gigantic black bird flew closely overhead, making Alex duck in response. The man he was walking beside laughed. "We nah buzza fee ye," he said. The voice was scratchy and muffled by the cloth wound around his mouth and nose. The words were hard to understand, the final consonants worn away by the constant dust that the wind, and their feet, kicked up. The first time one of the men talked, Alex had started to ask him to repeat himself, but a shake from his father's head had stopped him.

His father! The rangy coyote was a good avatar for the tall man with the ropy arms and creased face, particularly around the eyes, which were deep green slits like his, fixed in a permanent squint on the road ahead. That and the unruly, cowlicky hair, were the only similarities he could find to himself. His father had full lips, the upper lip split slightly by a scar, unlike the lips Alex inherited from his mother. There was also a half-moon scar curving under his left eye and a deep scar gouge across his stomach that Alex saw when his father's shirt rode up during his restless sleep the night before. Peter didn't offer his son any explanation for his battered appearance, and Alex knew better than to ask.

His hasty exit from Sanctuary seemed like a dream, and not a good one—more like the dreams he had as a small boy when he would wake up thrashing and sweaty in the middle of the night to find his mother sitting beside him. He had followed instructions to the Sanctuary wall, only to discover it was patrolled by an overly conscientious guardian. He'd hid behind a dumpster, painted like a starry sky, and waited until the refuse facility shut down for the night.

His first thought, when the guardian just wouldn't go away, was that his mother had found traces of him in the newsline root, maybe even followed him onto COSLine, although his father claimed the biometric security was unbreakable. He had obviously forgotten the resourcefulness of his ex. But gradually he realized the guardian wasn't looking for him; he was waiting for something, or someone. Anyway, it wasn't illegal to be at the wall, even this late at night. The worst that would happen was that the guardian would call his mother and he'd have to try again in a few months. If his father was willing to wait. The idea that this might be his only chance to get away from Sanctuary made his courage flare like a match. He approached the man, who studied him without saying anything.

"Crocodile," he said.

Things moved fast after that. "About damn time," the guardian responded. "I expected you hours ago. You think it doesn't look suspicious, me hanging around like this?"

Before Alex could answer and explain, the man wrapped a guardian cloak around him and hustled him over the red strip. He felt a whooshing blast of air, which eddied around him before he landed roughly on his feet and stumbled against the wall.

"Get off of that!" the guardian said testily; "you'll set off an alarm." He pulled a thin, flexible rod from inside his guardian coverall and began expertly maneuvering an almost invisible seam in the wall while Alex watched dumbly. He should offer to help or something, but his arms and legs felt curiously weak. He was really doing this, going outside. Not on a safe field trip with his overprotective mother, but all by himself. And likely to never return. He tried to summon up his anger about Albert Fiske, but his quick, painless death in the healing center seemed less horrifying than whatever was waiting for him outside.

Before he could question his own decision, the wall popped open with a loud crack that Alex was sure would echo all the way back to his mother's flat. The guardian grabbed him roughly by the shoulders and thrust him into the crack, which was just wide enough for Alex to wiggle through.

"Wait!" he said.

"No time," the guardian replied. "I needed to be on my rounds a half hour ago. Either they're waiting for you or they're not. If you don't want to get squashed, start moving."

Alex was forced to move sideways, his nose mashed against the interior wall. He inched along cautiously, aware with each footstep he might step into—

An arm grabbed his leg and pulled hard. He cried out and struggled, but it was no use. *A trap!* his mind told him, and the world went dark with the terror of it. He revived when he hit the ground with a thump.

"Tho you wa n'er com." A brown face thrust into his was split by a grin showing a sprinkling of brown teeth. Alex wrinkled his nose at the man's musty breath. The man nodded. "Yo fa theah."

A man stepped out of the shadow. "Hello, Alex," he said.

The meeting should have been more dramatic. In stories of yesteryear, when family members reunited, music played. His father looked him over matter-of-factly. "Scaleskin and a guardian cloak. There's no time to change. It'll have to do." He unrolled two strips of cloth and wrapped them round Alex's nose and mouth, mummy fashion. Alex's protest was muffled by the thick, none-too-clean cloth.

"It's the dusty season," his father said. "Which is pretty much every season except the rainy season, and that's coming soon." He looked at the sky. "We expected you a couple hours ago. We were just about to move on when you popped out."

Alex started to explain about the guardian. His father stopped him again. Was he never going to get a chance to speak?

"We have a long tramp. Night is a dangerous time to move, with marauders. Although I doubt they will want to tackle us."

The man with the niblet teeth pulled a knife from his ragged pants and grabbed Alex by the arm, while his father led the way, and another man closed in behind them.

SANCTUARY

CHAPTER EIGHTEEN

Miranda shrugged the guardian cloak over her pack and looked around. It was almost dark, but she could make out misty shapes in the distance. That was probably the slag heaps. She could make her way there, maybe find some shelter to curl up in for the night. She had a headlight in her pack, but it seemed like an open invitation to whatever was out there, waiting. Marauders, gangs of outside survivors, occasionally attacked disposal workers. The guardians accompanying them made short work of the marauders, according to the news stories. Miranda shivered, imagining people so desperate that they would attack men with weapons. She clutched the guardian's baton and fingered the buttons cautiously. One of these would at least stun a marauder. She should be okay unless she was surrounded.

She moved away instinctively. Hanging around the huge wall was not a good idea. Not just the marauders, but the city would have defenses against outside vandals. She felt her neck involuntarily, thinking about the red protection strip for the inside wall. She had never been part of designs for Sanctuary's outside protections, but she could imagine. The thought propelled her down a dusty path in front of her, toward the slag heaps or whatever those tall outcrops were.

The land was flat, and silent. No birdsong, no insect noises, none of the sounds, calibrated for time of day, that formed the aural backdrop for Sanctuary life. When the wind, or her feet, stirred the

153

dust, it prickled unpleasantly against exposed skin. As she walked, she realized the world wasn't silent. The wind was a mechanical, whining noise that drowned out every footstep. The sound changed in timbre and volume as the wind rose and fell according to its own needs that had no interest in her. It sounded almost human, like it was plucking at her, complaining, demanding an explanation of what had happened to the world, and why.

Miranda found herself responding. "Don't ask me," she said crossly. "I wasn't responsible for whatever happened. I was just a child."

The outcroppings seemed to recede as Miranda walked, rather than get closer. How long was that magtrain ride? She wished she had paid more attention to the journey back then and less to the guide. Thinking about Peter made her pick up speed, although the walk through an inch or two of dust shifting under her feet was slow going. She slid several times and barely stopped herself from falling. She had to concentrate on her feet to make sure she felt a way forward without obstacles. This was ridiculous. She was going to end up falling down a deep hole because it was too dark to see changes in the path. And the wind would not shut up.

"Plea," it said. And clutched at her. Clutched? Miranda jumped and pulled herself away from the skinny fingers of a young girl. She pressed the button for light on the guardian baton. It was weak and wavering but revealed a young girl, not much more than a child.

"Pre lay. Wha you go they?" Miranda couldn't understand her. The girl reached for the pack on Miranda's back. Miranda understood that well enough and slapped the hand away. The girl dropped her wheedling smile and hissed at Miranda. The girl's teeth, scattered and brown from abuse, were filed to points.

"Who are you?" Miranda asked sharply. "Where did you come from? Where are your parents?"

The girl smiled, showing all her imp teeth. "I hun," she said. "Go ay foo?"

Miranda studied the girl while her heartbeat slowed down from a panicked cacophony to a loud *thump, thump* in her ears that drowned out the wind. Her features were hard to make out in the dusk, but her long blonde hair was tangled, and she was so thin that Miranda could see her ribs through her skimpy clothing. She had never seen a child so thin. Say what you will about the sameness of packfruit . . .

While her thoughts were racing, the girl was inching closer—her left hand out in a wheedling gesture, the other by her side. Miranda looked at the girl's right hand and saw she was clutching something that flashed as she sprang forward. Instinctively, Miranda pulled her pack around to her chest just as the girl's knife slashed. The movement was so quiet, they could both hear the ripping sound as the knife struck the pack, but the pack was multilayered and solid. It held together. The knife was stuck fast. Miranda stepped back as the girl twisted and jiggled the knife free.

"Hol sti, nassy bi," the girl said. Now that she was close enough to see features, she saw the girl was much older than she appeared, at least in her twenties. Her skin was wrinkled and spotted by constant exposure to sun and wind.

"So you can kill me?" Miranda panted.

"You hassa die. Thi my las cha." She sprang forward again, an emaciated frog, and this time the knife struck Miranda's arm, where the guardian cloak fell away. Her arm burned as if on fire. She touched the split skin, and her fingers came away slick with blood it was too dark to see. She almost dropped the baton. She felt along the buttons on the handle. Which one was "stun"? She pressed the largest button. Nothing.

"You alre dea," the girl snarled and lunged for Miranda.

"I have no intention of dying." Miranda swung the baton at the girl. The knife fell with a clatter as growfiber reinforced with metal alloy struck bone. Miranda saw a jagged white stick broken through the skin of the girl's arm as she fell to the ground with a shriek. Gagging as bile rose involuntarily, Miranda turned away to be sick.

The girl stopped shrieking and cocked her head. "Lis!" she hissed. "They com." She stared wildly in every direction, raising the hairs on Miranda's neck. The girl's fear was stronger than the pain of her broken arm.

Miranda knew that whoever was coming, she didn't want to meet them. Dashing the nausea tears from her eyes, she could see the gleam of the knife at the girl's feet. She snatched it up as the girl grabbed her ankle with her good arm.

"Don lea!" the girl pleaded.

Miranda hesitated, just a minute, but a spasm from her wounded arm pushed away any charitable impulses. She pulled her ankle away, kicking until the girl released her grip. She reached into her pack on impulse and connected with the small bag of coins Tara had given to her. She scattered a couple at the girl's feet.

"Good luck to you," she said grimly, and ran.

Miranda ran until she stumbled in a hole and fell, twisting her ankle. She lay there stunned, listening to the shrieking wind. Shrieking? She could just make out the word "Nooooo," howled over the mechanical whine of the wind, until it ended abruptly. She couldn't see her throbbing ankle in the dark, but she felt the points of the girl's fingers burning on her skin.

"Don't be ridiculous!" she said aloud to herself. If she had stayed to help, whoever was coming would have killed her too. It was the girl's job to set her up to rob and kill. The only way she lived was if Miranda didn't. Still, the sound of that shrieking "no," cut off abruptly, drowned out the wind and her thoughts. She forced herself onto her elbows and dragged herself to a clump of rocks. She curled behind them and hoped she was invisible as she clutched her pack and the slick knife to her chest. She tumbled into sleep.

Miranda woke the next morning to the skritching of rocks against dirt. Instinctively, she pulled her feet closer into her chest. Her ankle was sore and looked a little swollen, but she could turn it left and right without a problem. She heard a snuffling sound very near the rocks and poked her head out to see curious yellow eyes and a gray snout inches from her face. She could just see the long, lean body with its tail bristled in the gray gloom that signaled morning on the outside. Coyote! She had never seen one physically, but she had seen many holos. She pulled her head back behind the rock just as she heard voices on the path.

"Yah," a male voice yelled. "Oer tha!"

Miranda heard running feet and a desperate scrabbling, followed by frantic yelping and a squeal that reminded her of the girl from last night. She heard a soft moaning accompanied by chewing and gulping as well as sniggers and words garbled by full mouths. They were eating the coyote while it was still alive. Burning acid rose in her throat. She didn't dare swallow or spit—they were so close, they might hear. Finally, she heard the men rise and groan from full bellies. She heard bodies tumble together and heard one snarl as he pushed another into the rocks close to where she was hidden. The man scrambled up, cursing, but they both moved away without further fighting. Miranda waited until she was sure there was nothing but wind to rise up on her knees and heave until there was no more acid in her stomach to expel. She peered cautiously around the rock. The coyote looked like a bloody, chewed piece of cloth. The head had been cracked open and the eyes chewed out of their sockets. Only the wiry legs looked untouched. Miranda shuddered, imagining the girl from last night meeting a similar fate.

She stood up cautiously and placed her swollen left foot on the ground. The pain gushed upward like a Sanctuary fountain and flooded her leg. Except this was real, not holo. She took an experimental step. Now the pain was a zigzag, like the zap of a guardian baton. Another step. Doable. If she moved slowly. The thought that Peter and Alex were not moving slowly propelled her around the rock, where she almost slipped on the slick blood of the coyote.

She tested the guardian baton as a cane. Too short. She saw a stunted, dead tree a few feet away, covered in ropy vines. The girl's knife came in handy to hack the vines away and fashion a walking stick from the spindly trunk. She squeezed a packfruit quickly down her throat and felt better. She tested the stick on the ground. Despite the sickly look of the tree, the wood was strong.

Miranda started walking, following cautiously in the direction the men had walked. Droplets of coyote blood, dark against the dust, led the way. The wind picked up as she walked. She looked up at the sky. The gray clouds that pressed down last night like a blanket were breaking into shards and darkening. She knew from her childhood, but also from her recent work with sky designs, that this probably meant rain coming. She would deal with that when she had to. One step at a time. It felt good to be moving.

CHAPTER NINETEEN

After a while, the scenery changed. The path grew rocky and hard to navigate, particularly for someone used to the smooth sameness of a streetway. It started as pebbles, but the rocks got bigger until they were picking their way through boulders. And then through walls of rocks, twice as tall as Alex, creating caves that looked like paths until they dead-ended, costing precious time as the last light waned.

Alex had navigated rocky paths in holo, but that involved dexterous hand movements and, as he grew expert, a slight movement of his head or a sideways flicker of his eyes. This involved—ow! He bumped hard against a rock outcropping in the dark and felt a knot rise on his leg in response.

"Careful," his dad said, the first word he had spoken in hours. He studied his son and announced, "We need to stop soon. Let's find a likely cave."

The two men with them said nothing, but Alex could tell from the way they looked first at his dad and then at him, that this was way too soon to stop and entirely for his benefit.

"I'm okay," he said. "I can go a lot farther."

"Don't be stupid," his dad replied. "You were too well looked after in Sanctuary. You have the will and you have your wits, but the rest of your body is unprepared. You have to take the time to acclimate."

Alex stiffened at the words, sensing an insult to his mother as well as to himself. This wasn't the same man who had coaxed him out of Sanctuary on the forbidden COSLine. This was a man who kept his own counsel, hour after hour, seldom looking back at him, although he seemed to sense when Alex had had enough. And how did a rugged disposal man learn the word "acclimate"? All he did know was that he was miles away from the only home he had ever known, miles away from his mother.

His heart squeezed smaller than the pebbles he was scuffling through as he thought about his mother. She had seen the holo of his leaving by now, and she had certainly traced him to the wall, despite his precautions. The only question was whether she would persuade Tara to send a raft of guardians after him or follow him herself. As the hours passed and there was no sign of anyone behind them, he lost heart. He had told his mother not to follow, to live her own life, but he didn't believe she would. And as the second day wound its dreary way, he realized he didn't want her to.

Any curiosity about where they were headed and what it—and his future—would be like had been blasted away by the never-ending wind, which seemed to be picking up. Despite the cloth over his nose and mouth, the dust settled in his throat, and no amount of coughing could clear it. His chest was tight with the effort to breathe. Nothing in the stories of yesteryear, or even in the sordid news of gangs, rapes, and murders in City of the South, had prepared him for the endless gray, the dust, the rocks, the choking half-dead vines of outside. His mother was right. Of course she was. When was she ever wrong? The only satisfaction was that he would probably never have to face her "I told you so." He pulled the cloth off his face. It wasn't helping, and it was hard to breathe through it.

The broken-toothed man, who had matched his stride to Alex's while Peter strode on ahead, pointed up, nodding his head vigorously. He pulled a dirty hat from a pocket and offered it to Alex as he pointed skyward. Alex followed his bony finger with his eyes and stiffened. The sky was no longer a thick, gray blanket that blotted out everything except the wind. Instead, it was full of boulders, dark and tumbled together, some rounded, some jagged. And they were moving, rumbling as they butted each other. They were . . . clouds. But not the fluffy white clouds of story. Suddenly they broke apart and water, as hard and swift as a waterfall, came gushing down, knocking the hat out of his companion's dirty hand.

The rain stabbed their skin like needles. Alex couldn't stop himself from crying out with the pain. The other men, even his father, were pulling their cloaks tighter against their bodies. His father seemed to notice him only when he bumped into things, such as last night when he had banged his head on a rock outcropping where they had sheltered for the night. He had cursed freely while the men laughed. His father had said, "One more day should do it." It was the first encouragement since the hellish walk started. It wasn't much, but Alex clutched it to him like the blue bear he had when he was small.

Now Peter leaned closer to Alex to be heard over the drumming rain. "This is no good," he said. "We have to find somewhere to wait until the clouds release the excess they are holding." He nodded at the men, and they made a run for a bank of boulders. Alex followed as best he could with his head down so the rain, harsh and metallic, didn't blind him. His companion—nursemaid?— grabbed his arm and pulled him almost off the ground so that he was carried as much as walking. He shoved him forward into an opening between two large rocks that was surprisingly roomy.

"A bear den," his father announced, speaking loudly to be heard over the rain. "A family probably hibernated here once."

"Bears?" Alex asked, looking around. "Are there animals outside, then?" He looked around cautiously, thinking of the visit to the zoo, which seemed a million years ago, and the tiger baring those three-inch incisors. The cave smelled—a meaty, rank smell that reminded him of a nest of dead ferrats, curled up around each other, that he had once found.

"More than you might imagine," his Dad replied. "Turns out some animals are more resilient than we are."

"Ferrats," Alex said, "coyotes. We have them in Sanctuary too."

"Those, sure, but also bears. They are omnivores and can eat anything—plants, animals, insects. Some birds have done well, particularly the carrion birds. Vultures. Do you know what those are?"

"That huge bird that flew over us yesterday?" Alex ventured.

"Yes, that was a vulture. Coyotes of the sky. They feed off dead things. The outside doesn't have much, but one thing it does have is death."

"Then why did you bring me here?" Alex burst out. A clap of thunder drowned out his words, which sounded like whining, even to him. He was sixteen years old, practically an adult. He had chosen to come. He had made his bed—a shabby, smelly blanket that offered no protection from the rocks underneath. He would just have to lie in it.

"What?" his dad asked.

"Why did you choose this? Over Sanctuary, I mean?"

His dad thought a moment before answering. "You're seeing the worst of the world right now," he said. "A dead place, except for scavenging animals and people so desperate and diseased, they might as well be animals. Sanctuary, on the other hand, is a beautiful place. You must be missing it, and your soft bed, by now." It wasn't a question. He smiled as Alex squirmed on his lumpy blanket.

"I'll tell you something," his father said. "I miss Sanctuary. Every day. Of course I missed you and your mother most of all. In City of the South, we invented COSLine to talk to Sanctuary, to barter for things, but I worked hard on it so I could use it to watch you grow. But right now, with you beside me, I still miss Sanctuary. I miss believing the world can be like that. What it once was. But it can't. We have done too much damage.

"Sanctuary is make-believe. A protective bubble. And the thing about bubbles is that they burst. They keep the terrible world—the predators, the dust, the weather—out for a little while. But they can't last forever. Even with the philosophy of zero waste, Sanctuary is starting to fail. And people like you no longer believe in it. I know you think you came outside for me, but you really came outside for you. You didn't believe in Sanctuary the way your mother does. I didn't lure you outside, I helped you escape.

"City of the South has its troubles. It isn't pretty, and you may not like the decisions I have to make, but it has a future. When Sanctuary is gone, even when you are gone, City of the South will still be there. Why? Because we are in the world, working with it as it is, not shutting it out. We all walk on the same ground, breathe the same air. You either adapt, or . . ."

His voice drifted off. Alex shivered, thinking of his mother. He was all she had. He should have found a way to bring her with him.

They remained in the cave for another day while the rain stabbed mercilessly at the roof, sometimes hitting so hard that rocks and dust fell off the ceiling into the mouths they forgot to close as they lay on their blankets. The men, including his dad, seemed resigned to the inactivity, lying still on their blankets except to roll further away from the opening when a slash of rain, driven by wind, doused them with water.

Alex couldn't sit still like this. He sat up, shoulders hunched in the cramped space. He opened his pack and went through his supplies, noticing the things he forgot. No hat, of course. No one wore them in Sanctuary. His father held a hat out of the opening to capture some water for drinking or maybe to gauge the fierceness of the storm. It was torn to ribbons in seconds, and his fingers were bleeding from dozens of small cuts.

After a day, the rain slowed enough that they could walk again. His dad improvised a hat for Alex from a scarf in his pack, which protected his head and created a ledge over his eyes to keep the rain from dashing in. The eyes weren't the problem. The problem was his feet. His shoes were well made, given that each pair was designed to last for years, but they were designed for the smooth sameness of Sanctuary roadways. The soles were already thin from walking on stones, with holes pricked where the rain and wind had chiseled the rocks to points. The path was as smooth as ice in spots; in others, the rain sent the rocks scurrying underfoot like insects. He jumped and yelped as one rock extended claws to propel itself across his foot. His hairy, toothy guardian angel grabbed him yet again as he almost went down the side of the steep path. Alex reddened. What possible role could he play outside, except to entertain people who had never seen such a clumsy, weak—

His dad grabbed his arm. "Look!" he said. In the distance Alex could see lights, as wispy in the rain as cotton balls. City of the South.

"There are two parts to the city. The administrative compound, where I live and work, and the city itself. The compound is a city within a city, walled off from the town. There isn't much governance in the city itself. City dwellers go about their own business, but for their own safety, they mostly show allegiance to the family. They pay tributes of various kinds, and most people work for the family in one way or another. But they are left alone from day to day. City of the South has ways of keeping an eye on its subjects, to be sure they don't stray too far or rise up against the rulers."

"COSLine, Alex guessed.

"That's one way," his dad replied. "Another, crude but effective, is to take family members into service. Their treatment depends on the others, left behind. But the main way, the best way, is by teaching them trades and helping them survive to see another day."

"What does that involve?" Alex asked to break the silence. In response, his father placed an arm across his shoulder, almost the first physical contact since their journey together had begun days ago. Alex looked up into his face. His scarred mouth stretched into a broad smile. Another first. He was happy to be almost home.

"You're about to find out," he said.

SANCTUARY

CHAPTER TWENTY

On her second day of walking, Miranda saw clouds hardening into mountains that leaned ominously as if they would topple down and bury her forever. When she looked up, the sight of them rooted her in place with terror, so she stopped looking up. If she thought at all, she thought of Alex. He had a day's head start and was with his father. Would his father keep him safe? Or if Alex, a soft Sanctuary boy, was a disappointment or too much trouble, would he abandon him a second time? The thought kept her going, despite having spent a second restless night sheltering among rocks and despite her now-burning arm. She didn't have time to look at it or to fish an antiseptic puff out of her pack.

She walked for what seemed like days but was probably hours. The sky grew darker, and the wind flung debris into her mouth and hair and stung her face. She took off the guardian cloak and fashioned it into a headscarf that covered her mouth. She could only use one arm because the stabbed arm was too painful to move. After another hour, she was nothing but a gigantic throbbing arm attached to a hollow thing that was the rest of her. She was all out of thoughts, including caring whether she was going in the right direction.

Any semblance of a path was gone, obliterated by the dust whipping up to her knees in the wind. She was just putting her foot wherever it could fit on the rocky path. The dusty wind had turned her eyes to stinging, blurry slits. She could see just enough

SANCTUARY

to find her next step. Fortunately, the damaged ankle was blessedly numb. Otherwise, she would simply have lain down where she was and let the wind build a mound of dirt over her. She had no idea where she was headed and barely an idea why this had seemed like a plan a couple of days ago. She was going to die, she knew that, but she wasn't afraid. Sanctuary seemed like a mirage. Why had it seemed so solid, when just a few feet outside, you saw and felt what the world had really become? Her son was out here, somewhere, navigating the same wind and dirt that she was, or he was already gone, because nothing could survive for long.

Her foot stumbled on a raised patch. She could just make out something dark and cracked. She knew what this was, from streetway design, but her tired brain at first refused to make the connection. Tarmac! Although covered with dust and the roots of vegetation that had thrust itself through the concrete crust, it was a sign of civilization. All roads led somewhere. Miranda stepped gingerly onto the road. The sign that someone human had gone before gave her a new strength, and she pushed herself almost into a trot. When the first drop of rain fell, she looked up. Ahead she saw a blurry structure. A building!

A loud crack split the sky, startling her so that she fell and grazed her knee through the scaleskin. Rain began to slash down—not the pleasant tickle of moisture-laden air she had designed for Sanctuary but an army flinging weapons at her defenseless body. She rose on all fours and crawled to the building, a one-story house with its door blessedly agape.

She pulled herself in as far as she could to evade the stinging streams. The building was dark and stank of rot. She could hear things—ferrats?—scrabbling and squeaking in the walls. She shuddered and pulled her legs up against her chest. And then she smelled—smoke? She looked around wildly. How could anything be burning in so much rain?

168

She saw a thin trickle of smoke illuminated by the red tip of something that moved deliberately, forward and back. Something attached to a dark shape. The red tip went out, and she heard a snap and then saw a flare of light that illuminated a—face?

Miranda scrambled to her knees and turned to flee, leaving her pack somewhere in the smelly dark.

"Relax," the man advised with a wheezy chuckle. "No matter how dangerous I am, the rain is worse."

"I don't have anything . . ." she started to say, even as she fished around with her foot for the knife attached to her pack. She struggled to rise, but the effort was too much. She spiraled down into a chilly darkness, her fall broken by the rough stone against her cheek. She leaned into it gratefully.

Miranda swam up out of the darkness the way she had once swum cautiously with Alex in Sanctuary's carefully managed lake. Thankfully, Alex hadn't cared for the experience, so they never went back. She lay there, letting her mind process all the physical sensations. The bumpy and smelly ground beneath her reminded her she wasn't in her own soft bed. The noise, rhythmically crashing against the ceiling, what was that? Was she in a fabrication machine room? How had she gotten to work without remembering? Where was Alex? Everything came flooding back, and she struggled to sit up; she took a large gulp of air, thick with dust, and began to cough wildly.

"You get used to it after a while," a man's voice drawled. "You want to take short, shallow breaths."

She turned her head painfully toward the sound of the voice. A thin man with scraggly blond hair was leaning against the wall, watching her. Not her imagination. She scrabbled for her pack.

"It's behind your head," he advised. "Safest that way, and I know you Sanctuary folk like your pillows."

"Who are you?" Miranda asked.

He took a puff on something that smoked and created a haze of blue between them. She recognized it from stories of yesteryear. A cigarette, it was called.

"I'm the man who doctored your arm," he replied. "Smart to bring antibiotic puffs and bandages"

Miranda felt her bandaged arm cautiously. It still hurt but was back to normal size.

"I had to drain it," the man said. "You're gonna have a wicked scar to show your Sanctuary friends."

He reached around her and grabbed her pack before she could react. He rummaged through it and pulled out a water bubble. He bit though the skin and drank a mouthful and then handed it to Miranda, who sucked at it greedily before looking around for anything, a rock or a stick, to use as a weapon.

The man chuckled. "Relax," he said. "I could have killed you half a dozen times if I wanted."

"Why didn't you?"

"No introductions. You get right to the heart of things," the man said approvingly. "Why didn't I just kill you? Good question."

"So, what's the good answer?" Miranda asked. She was lightheaded and hungry but better. She felt her ankle cautiously. The swelling was down.

"Well, my dear, there's a reward for bringing you back that is more than double everything you got in your pack. You and I have a mutual friend, Tara Jordan. I have two weeks to return you safe and sound, and you wasted two days of it being passed out cold."

Two days! A squirt of adrenaline gave her the strength to scramble to her feet. He was between her and the door, and he had the knife she had taken from the marauder girl. She crouched into a spring, like the holo tiger in the Sanctuary zoo a lifetime ago.

"I'm not going back to Sanctuary!" she said through gritted teeth. "Not without—" She stopped.

"Your son. Alex. You been raving about him in your sleep." The man carefully pinched the glowing end of his cigarette and packed the remnants carefully in a dirty cloth. He stood up and grinned down at her. Miranda realized he was very tall.

"What the hell," he said. "Tara gave me two weeks to get the job done. We've lost a couple of days with your arm, but we have the time. What do you say? Let's see some outside."

Miranda looked around. The rain outside was lightening, and she could see details. The man was a raggedy scarecrow, but he reminded her of someone. With a start, she realized he reminded her of Peter. Is that what the outside did to you? Remove everything that made you an individual? What did she look like? She scrabbled self-consciously at her snarled hair. The man reached down a hand. She took it gingerly and then screamed before she could stop herself as pain burst like fireworks through her damaged arm.

The man reached an arm around her shoulders and pulled her up. "We'll take it easy," he said. "There's not that far to go."

"Where are we going?"

"City of the South," he replied. "That's where he's headed, if he isn't there already."

"Unless he's been killed and eaten," Miranda replied bitterly.

"I'm sure he's fine," the man said. "City of the South is ol' Pete's base. He can walk there in his sleep."

"Pete?" Miranda asked stupidly.

He looked at her without response.

The coldness in her arms and legs invaded her stomach. This man knew her ex-husband well enough to give him a nickname. Did he really know Tara or just of her, from Peter? Was all this a trick? She tried to casually reach for her pack.

The tall man scooped it up. "I'll carry your things for you," he said. "We'll move faster that way."

"So, you know Peter?" she asked, trying to sound casual.

The man grinned. "Everybody knows everybody out here," he said. "It's safest. Anybody out here, you are either dealing with them or killing them before they kill you."

He slung his pack and Miranda's over his shoulders and slouched out of the house. He held up a warning hand to hold her back while he looked in all directions and sniffed the air.

"Rain has chased away anything we need to worry about," he said. "But now that it's dying down, they'll be back. Let's get moving. We should make City of the South by tomorrow morning."

"What's your name?" she asked the man.

"You Sanctuary folk, you like the names," he said. "You think you are going to be around somebody long enough to know them."

"Two weeks, you said," Miranda replied.

The man gave a hoarse chuckle that turned into a cough. "Fair enough. Tara calls me Murray."

What do you call yourself?"

"Murray will do."

CHAPTER TWENTY-ONE

As they moved closer to City of the South, the path turned from mud and loose stones to something darker and harder but equally treacherous, with cracks and holes, some filled with weeds, others with muddy water that squelched unpleasantly through Alex's city shoes or caused him to stumble into one of his father's companions, who would either ignore him or shove him roughly away with a curse. Ahead the road seemed to be heaving and rolling with waves like Alex had seen in stories of yesteryear about the ocean, but with a peculiar humming sound, almost machine-like, only without the monotonous rhythm of a machine.

They climbed a small hill. "Look!" his father said. The heaving roadway mass resolved itself into something large and jointed, like a mechanical snake, except the scales broke apart as they moved.

"Carts?" Alex asked, just recognizing the resemblance to the sleek magcarts of Sanctuary. But instead of smooth, magnetic movement, they were pulled in a jerky fashion by hunched and hooded creatures in layers of rags.

"People? Where are they going?"

In answer, his father handed him a spyglass and turned his head to direct his gaze. Alex saw that the dense and crooked line that blended in so well it seemed part of the roadway was headed toward what looked like a hill of rocks, but with the glass he could see the rocks were pieced together to form a wall. In places where the rock had crumbled, or been pulled away, the holes were stuffed with sticks, cloth, and broken things—half a wheel, a rotting cart, a window frame—creating the appearance of a giant garbage dump. Alex thought of the smooth, mirrored wall of Sanctuary, with the pieces that snapped together perfectly at the seams. This wall was crooked, bulging in places like thousands of people on the other side were straining to break out. The heaving mass of people moved in a jerky, disjointed way, with lots of collisions and curses, toward a giant, rusty metal door, open just wide enough to let each cart in single file.

"Is this City of the South? Do they live there?"

"Some of them, returning from marauding. But in its own way, City of the South is just as discriminating about who gets to live there as Sanctuary. Most of these people are rejects, or refugees from other cities. They are coming to barter whatever they have scavenged from outside." There was a lilt to his dad's voice that Alex had never heard before, not even when they had first made contact. He was happy to be here. He was home.

"Refugees. From Sanctuary," Alex couldn't keep the skepticism from his voice.

His father tapped him lightly on the shoulder. "You are a refugee yourself. And you are no more guaranteed safe passage into COS than they are."

Alex looked up, alarmed.

"Come on," his father said. "We're going to skirt the main entrance and go in the back. And I'll tell you what you need to know to earn yourself a welcome."

Alex had silently questioned many things on the long, dreary trip. Why had he left Sanctuary in the first place? How had his mother reacted to his leaving, and what was she doing in response? And most of all, what would City of the South be like, and how could it possibly entice a smart man like his dad to leave his family and comforts to make a life there? But while he wondered if he had made the right choice, he had never wondered if the choice was not his to make. Alarm flooded his body like adrenaline. What were his options if City of the South turned him away? Would he be forced to make his own way back to Sanctuary without his father and his bodyguards? He was under no illusion that the two rough men were along for the trip to sightsee. Every scratch of gravel on the road, every snap of a twig, caused the men to stiffen and finger their knives. When they slept, one man stayed awake. Alex knew instinctively that the only reason they didn't encounter trouble on the trip was because his father and the men were bigger trouble. If they abandoned him, what hope of survival would he have?

They headed down the hill. At the bottom, as if they had read his mind, the two men turned away with just a nod to Peter and nothing at all for Alex and strode toward the caravan of people headed into the large doorway in the wall.

"Where are they going?" Alex asked, his voice coming out like a croak.

"They served their purpose," his father answered. "We're close enough now we don't need them. No one is going to try anything this close to City of the South. This isn't Sanctuary." He spit out some dust contemptuously. "We're going in the back way. My own entrance."

He turned and began walking, leaving Alex to follow. When they reached the roadway, people moved away from his father with averted eyes. Alex dodged carts covered with rags, with children clinging to the sides like ferrat babies on their mother's furry back. Alex stumbled into carts and tripped over feet so muddy and black they blended into the roadway. People cursed and shoved him. As he sprawled in front of a large cart pulled by a shrieking woman, an arm grabbed him and set him upright.

"You're going to have to move more nimbly than that," his father said. "No DPs to guide you in City of the South."

175

Alex's stumble had caused the woman's cart to overturn. She was screaming at him even as she beat away hands reaching for the clothing that tumbled from the back. She spit at Alex as he pushed past her to catch up to his dad. He felt the warm liquid, viscous with dust, trickle down his neck, but he had no time to wipe it off as he followed his father's straight back, towering over the hunched people crowding the roadway.

It was only when he broke free of the roadway and was once again matching his dad stride for stride across muddy ground that he had time to think about what he would do if he was turned away at the alternative entrance. Would his dad have a plan for him, or would he just move on without a backward glance? He was under no illusions that he could survive for long in the outside. His best bet was to try to barter his pack in City of the South for an armed guide to Sanctuary.

It was getting dark when his dad turned to a dip in the wall that proved to be yet another battered metal doorway, this one just large enough for one person to walk through. His dad rummaged in his bag and pulled out a key.

"Shine a light," his dad said, the first words he had spoken since they they crossed the road teaming with people and carts. Alex remembered that they had parted without words, from the men who would probably have fought to the death to keep him, a boy they had never met, safe from harm. What kind of man was his father?

"Today, Alex," his dad said, with the steely impatience of some- one who never had to ask for something twice.

Alex tried his newsline. It still worked for some things. He filtered the powerful beam into a concentrated ray, no wider than an arrow shaft, where his father directed. A large lock. His dad fitted the key and turned. The lock opened with a squeal that was answered by rustling and the soft stamping of feet on the other side of the wall, as if his father had a small army of people waiting for his arrival.

His dad pushed the door open, but the way was barred by a beam of light stronger than Alex's. Peter tilted his head up in response to a round sensor above the doorway. An eyebeam, Alex guessed. There were places in Sanctuary that required the same recognition. He just had time to wonder how much City of the South had "borrowed" from Sanctuary when his dad pulled him into a tight embrace and hissed "move with me. You're not registered here." They moved as one, but Alex felt the beam resist the pressure of two bodies. His dad's pull was stronger. They were through.

The wall wasn't as thick as the mirrored wall of Sanctuary, but the dark when you stepped through was just as deep. Alex couldn't see, but he could feel, and it felt no different than outside—the same dank breeze laden with more rain to come, the ever-present dust in the air.

As if reading his mind, his dad said, "You're still outside, but although you can't see it, there is a slatted roof to deflect the heaviest rain."

Alex sniffed. The air was different, filled with hundreds of mingling smells: the smell of wet hair, the rank and meaty smell of unwashed bodies, but intertwined with sweet and sharp smells, smells that filled your body like food. Alex had smelled something like this before. He struggled to remember, and it came to him. The hydroponic farms on school field trips, but that smell was faint compared to the earthy green sweetness filling the air.

Alex stopped, transfixed by the smells. He knew his mother and her team had spent lots of time on the scents of Sanctuary, but this was different. These smells came in waves that had nothing to do with calibrated diffusers. Things smelled in City of the South because they were attached to living things that gave off these smells, not because scents were created and carefully released. Tears came into Alex's eyes as he turned in a circle, sampling the smells. He had never realized how starved his senses were in Sanctuary. He began to understand his father's excitement at returning home.

A wavering light sprang up, not more than four feet off the ground, illuminating a small face with pointed chin and sharp cheekbones, thrown into relief by the flickering light. The small head was hooded as protection against rain and dust. The child turned to the side and tilted his light, which created another light, and another small person standing beside him or her, then another and another. Children! They were surrounded by children, no older than four or five, Alex guessed. At their age, he would have been tucked safely into bed, a blue bear sitting watchfully beside him that sprang into life whenever he woke up.

A chorus of tinny child voices rose up in greeting. "Weco mas," they seemed to be saying, with the same abbreviated diction of Alex's companions on the road.

"Enough of that," a woman's voice said sharply. "You four with the candles, come with me and light the way. The rest of you go back to bed. Chores start early in the morning."

Four children surrounded a short, stocky woman. She pulled her hood back, revealing a knobby face and a thin bob of gray hair showing pink scalp through the strands. She looked Alex up and down without smiling. "This is him, then?"

"Birna, this is my son, Alex." Peter said. His voice was as flat as if he were saying this is my pack or my waterskin. But if he didn't sound as proud as he did when announcing City of the South to Alex, at least he acknowledged the relationship.

Birna's expression didn't change as she reached for his pack. Alex clung to it instinctively, but she pulled it from his grasp.

"I'm not stealing it," she said. "You have no need for what's in it here. We aren't Sanctuary, but we can see to your needs."

Alex was embarrassed. "Sorry," he muttered.

"Are you hungry? Or do you want your bed?"

"Just bed, I think," his dad replied. "He needs to be rested for tomorrow."

The woman turned to lead the way and saw that the small hooded forms had ignored her command out of curiosity about the newcomer. Without speaking, she lashed out with a metallic object that glinted in the wavering lights. The children fell back, whimpering. One child fell down and lay there unmoving until he was pulled away by his companions.

Alex gave a cry and stepped forward. His dad pulled him back and hissed something in his ear.

The woman led the way down a path, preceded by two children carrying lights. Alex could hear the other children, still crying, as they fled into the shadows. She stopped at a doorway.

"I've put your son in here." The grim set of her mouth and her refusal to look directly at him told Alex she was angry with his attempt to intervene.

"I'll get him settled," his dad replied. The woman snatched a light from the nearest child and handed it to him.

As soon as their footsteps retreated, Alex turned on his dad. "Those were little children!" he said, his voice shrill with outrage. "Four or five years old, at most. What are they doing here? Where are their parents? Are they orphans?"

His dad didn't answer the question directly. "For your own safety, it is best if you just keep quiet and observe," he said. "City of the South is different from Sanctuary."

"Right and wrong aren't different," Alex said, thinking of the child who had been knocked unconscious, or worse.

"Everything is different," his dad replied. "Life is about survival, here, not make-believe. Childhood is different. These children are the lucky ones. They have enough food, a place to sleep. Useful work to keep them occupied. Most of them will make it to adulthood. Their lives won't be long by Sanctuary standards, but everything they do will mean we survive as a species. They don't tell stories or build pretty parks, but they are one of the reasons you have a bed to sleep in tonight."

The roughness and passion in his dad's voice silenced Alex. He lay down on the mat he assumed was his bed. His dad leaned over him, but Alex shut his eyes tightly against the light, which dripped something hot and soft that burned his forehead. After a moment his dad said, "It will seem strange for a while, but you'll adapt. You're my son."

As Alex drifted off to sleep, his father's final sentence, "You're my son," competed with the contemptuous "They don't tell stories" in his tired thoughts.

He woke to the patter of gentle rain on his cheeks. Not the slashing outside rain, but the rain his mother had invented. Although he would never admit it, Alex loved the rainy days in Sanctuary. The air, the sky, everything felt different, and different opened the way for new possibilities to disrupt the sameness. This felt just like Sanctuary rain, ticklish and cool but not really wet. Why wasn't it wet? The question made Alex sit up and look around, knocking into a small body as he did. The child pulled its dirty fingers away in response. Not rain, but a child, exploring his face.

The child backed away into another child, who carried a cup of something and a plate.

"Foo, mas?" the second child said, thrusting the things forward.

The cup held something hot and bitter but pleasantly warm as it moved down his throat to his stomach. The plate held bread and that moist white stuff that was thicker and harder than packfruit paste, but which Alex knew from experience would sit heavily in his stomach.

To make conversation, he pointed at the white stuff, which was hard and crusty on the edges but soft in the middle.

"What is this?" he asked the children. Both had long, tangled hair, grimy faces, and just a scattering of teeth. He couldn't tell the sex of either.

They looked at each other before one answered shyly, "Chee."

"Chee," Alex repeated. "I don't really want it. Would either of you like it? Maybe to split?"

The children looked at each other, puzzled.

Did they only understand the abbreviated English they spoke?

He broke the chee in two and held the pieces toward each child. They backed away in alarm, like it was poison. Alex pushed a piece into the nearest child's hand.

"Eat it," he said. "I don't want it. Don't let it go to waste."

The child took an experimental bite.

Behind them, the door pushed open, and Birna was in the room. The child dropped the chee on the floor.

Birna cuffed the child on the head. "Corn Seven! You know better than that. Your job is to serve the young master his breakfast, not eat it. You can work without rations this morning."

The child began to cry, and the other snuffled in sympathy. "Apple Twenty, the same can happen to you. Get out of here, both of you, and get to your chores."

She raised a hand, which caused the children to flinch and scramble out the door, but she made no move to hit them, perhaps remembering Alex's reaction yesterday.

"I made them take it," Alex said quietly. "I didn't want it, and I didn't want it to go to waste."

Birna looked at him, and the creases around her mouth deepened. "Oh, it won't go to waste," she said. "But we can't have the workers scavenging for food because it's been thrown away. That's good barter, there."

She stared at him challengingly until he got the message.

"That's right. You have to eat every bite." He smelled her sour breath as she leaned over him for emphasis.

Alex forced himself to eat the piece of chee in his hand. When he had gotten it down, she scooped up the piece the child had dropped. He could see the bite marks on the edge. He shook his head.

"Wasting food is a crime here," Birna said.

"I'll take my chances."

Birna's voice turned soft with menace. "It's not you that would pay the price, is it? It's Corn Seven."

Alex's stomach turned over, and not from the chee. He shut his eyes to blot out the tooth marks and the dirt and swallowed it in two large bites. His stomach heaved in protest, and he felt bile rising in his throat, but he shut his eyes more tightly and willed it down.

"Finish your tea, and then your father is ready for you." Birna took the plate and left the room.

Alex sipped his tea slowly. What was this made of? The dead trees they passed on the road? He knew better than to pour it out. Anyway, he was in no hurry to start his new life. For a long time, Alex had thought the day his father disappeared was the worst day of his life. He was beginning to realize that the worst day might prove to be when the coyote first appeared, loping furtively across his story cube.

CHAPTER TWENTY-TWO

Miranda was forced to cling to Murray as they stepped over the splintered threshold of the house. If anything, it was colder and windier now that the rain had stopped.

Murray sniffed the air. "Rain's not through with us yet, but I think we have a day before the next storm. If we make tracks, we can reach the suburbs of City of the South by nightfall and find another place to hole up for the night."

Miranda's heart sank. The outside was as vast and gray as an ocean and just as filled with strange creatures with nothing but their next meal on their minds. Every muscle and bone ached, but she tensed herself to follow where he led.

Murray made no effort to move. He reached into her pack, which he seemed to know as well or better than she did, and pulled out a packfruit. Apple. He squeezed half into his mouth and then gave her the rest. Tart and flavorful. She had never been so conscious of packfruit before. It seemed like weeks since her last meal. Or sleeping in a real bed. He rummaged further and found the half tube of protectant gel the guardian had given her, coated his nose, and then handed it over. She used it without speaking. He carefully folded the used packfruit skin and put it in his pack. Miranda saw that he looked around carefully for any debris that indicated their existence.

He placed his arm around her shoulder and walked with her until he could see that she walked without stumbling, even though she still had a limp. He handed her the walking stick she had lost on the path. How long had he been following her, and why hadn't he intervened before? She didn't bother to ask questions. She knew instinctively he wouldn't answer. She would use him to get where she needed to go, which was City of the South, but she wouldn't trust him.

They walked for what seemed like hours. It wouldn't be so hard if Miranda could catch her breath. Her lungs felt heavy, like half-full bottles of water she was carrying. Try as she might, she couldn't fill them with air.

Murray observed her. "Short, shallow breaths," he advised. "This isn't city air. Take what you need, but don't fill your lungs with it."

"How do people survive out here?" she gasped.

"There are places with better air, like City of the South. And even this air will keep you going for a while, until your lungs fill up with dirt."

"And then what?"

He gave her a quizzical look in response.

Miranda studied him. She knew there was a lot he wasn't sharing with her, but far from resenting it, she was deeply grateful. Without another word, they began the slow march to City of the South, punctuated by stops when he sniffed the air or pulled out a spyglass that looked like something from a story of yesteryear and looked around, motioning with his hand for her to be quiet.

She followed him over the rocks, up, down, left foot, right foot. She would keep going until he said to stop. She soon tired of counting, and simply stumbled along behind him. Her only thought was how bruised her feet felt in her Sanctuary shoes. She would give everything in her pack for a pair of shabby boots like Murray's. She mentally coaxed her screaming feet forward. They were barely inches off the ground. She had stumbled several times

GRACE J. AGNEW

when one foot rebelled, too tired and sore to lift from the dusty earth. Once she had fallen flat, and Murray had to pick her up. Her cheeks burned at the thought.

So far, she was nothing but a liability. She continued hobbling forward with her eyes focused on Murray's back until she stumbled into something built of cloth and sharp edges, which made her cry out. Murray was ahead of her, but he was at her side in a moment. He pulled her roughly away.

It was a small cloth-covered lean to, torn apart and flapping in the rain. Murray fingered the outside cautiously and pulled back quickly. He pried the flapping cover off very carefully, exposing a sharp knife on a spring.

"A marauder trap," he said. "This is a stroke of luck."

"What's that?" Miranda asked, shouting against the wind. She rubbed her barked shin, glad she hadn't actually stepped in the thing.

"They set these up on the path to City of the South, for newbies. Most times, they are just waiting in the shadows for someone to crawl in. Sometimes, they set up booby traps. If you had crawled in headfirst, this would have slashed your neck."

Miranda was silent. She looked around.

"This is good," Murray said, almost cheerfully. "We can use the lean-to and the knife." He folded them both up and placed them in her pack.

"We're closer than I thought. We'll reach COS tomorrow."

They continued to move, hours of walking in a world that seemed like rock upon rock to Miranda but was endlessly fascinating to Murray, who sniffed the air and craned his neck to look around like a ferrat every mile or so. He stopped and held up a hand.

"We're close to the suburbs. Know what that is?"

Miranda nodded, a cold pit forming in her stomach. "I grew up in a suburb," she said in a shaky whisper.

Murray nodded. "This is the outer suburb of City of the South. With luck, we can find a place to rest for the night where we won't be discovered. We need to move slowly but also look like we belong. There are small bands of people that go scavenging and hunting. We will walk as if we are the scouts for a hunting team, while keeping an eye open for an abandoned place. Follow my lead." He pulled a short bow from his pack and placed it across his shoulder. Then he strode ahead, his eyes darting forward and sideways.

As the day lengthened into afternoon, Miranda sensed evening coming by the increase in the cloud cover and the sharpness of the breeze. A smaller roadway crossed the one they were following. Murray turned off the path, followed by Miranda. The way forward resolved itself into an old road lined with one-story buildings, angled away for privacy. The buildings had gaping holes in roofs. Windows were filled with dirt, rocks, and sticks. "To keep the wind and rain and some marauders out," Murray said. A battered box on a pole tilted at the entrance to one building.

"A mailbox," Miranda said slowly. "We had one like it." She stared through the gloom at the building. The shingles had been mostly pulled away, revealing moldy beams and crumbling wallboard. Boulders and dead tree branches were holding up falling walls. A metal bar with faint streaks and markings, all that remained of the paint, resolved into the shaft of a bicycle. Miranda remembered riding a bicycle like that down a street very much like this one. She stopped on the road and turned around, staring at battered, crumbling houses. No curtains anymore in windows. No interior lights to show the way home. Was this her neighborhood? Was this all that was left of the life her parents and grandparents has built? The enormity of what they had done as a society hit her. She sank to her knees in the road. Murray ambled over and squatted beside her.

"I'm okay," she said, swallowing a mouthful of dust and gulping. Life had been hard outside, but there was order, some stability, everyone putting their own family first, of course, but also looking out for the neighborhood. When they moved to the city, she still pictured life outside as she last remembered it, which was bad enough. But this!

Her eyes teared up. Murray put his arm around her shoulders, and she leaned into him.

"This," she said. She was incapable of saying anything else, of putting her horror into coherent sentences. It was like losing her childhood all over again. All her memories.

Murray broke the silence. "It's a shock when you first see it," he said. "But this is what happens to any society when it is abandoned. The Incas of Peru, the ancient Egyptians."

Miranda shook her head. There was grandeur in the pyramids, the Parthenon, a belief in something mightier than the individual, something that mattered. This ruin around them was a tribute to small-mindedness, to short-term thinking, to a shabby, every-man-for-himself abandonment when things got so bad that you could no longer fool yourself into believing they would ever get better. She didn't know whose idea it was to build Sanctuary, but she remembered being grateful, even as a small child, that somebody had a plan.

She looked around again, and the hallucination of being in her own neighborhood disappeared. These houses had mostly been clapboard, where hers was all brick. And this was too far away from Sanctuary, where she and her friends rode on bikes to watch its building. Her suburb was already being scavenged for Sanctuary building supplies when her family left.

"I'm okay," she said, and stood up.

Murray stood up as well. "We'll stay in a place I know, away from the others. Safer."

Miranda nodded without speaking. As she followed, it occurred to her to wonder, *Incas? Egyptians? Who was this man?*

Murray led the way down a side street that culminated in a circle. "They called this a cul-de-sac," he announced. "Do you know what that is?"

Miranda shook her head.

"Some streets don't have a way to exit the neighborhood," he said. "To keep out trucks and people just passing through. Great for kids riding bikes. My—" He stopped himself from sharing something that might have been personal. "This will do for the night," he said. "Marauders don't like closed-off places. No escape routes." He went through what had already become a routine of sniffing the air, walking completely around the place and then going in alone to make sure it was safe, all the while holding up a hand to keep Miranda quiet. It wasn't necessary. You had to almost shout to be heard over the wind, and she had no interest in attracting the attention of anyone out here. She was extremely grateful they hadn't met anyone.

At last, Murray beckoned with his hand, and she stepped cautiously over the threshold and the remains of a rotted door.

"Nobody has used this place for a while," Murray announced, "but we'll go inside a ways so that if anybody shows, the place will seem abandoned."

The smell of the place made Miranda cough. It wasn't the meaty, sharp-but-alive smell of animal, but a scent both nasty and sweet. She wasn't sure she could bear it for a whole night.

Murray shook his head. "Mold," he replied, "from all the wet. It's a good stink. People don't like it. They'll keep away."

Miranda could feel the toxic smell clinging to her clothes and hair, seeping into her lungs, despite the nose coat.

"Is it dangerous?"

Murray took his time answering. "Well. I wouldn't stay here more than one night." Then he spread out his bedroll with finality, making it clear the sleeping quarters weren't open for discussion.

188

Miranda rolled out her blanket reluctantly. It was already dusty, torn, and an amalgam of all the horrible smells she had encountered in the last few days. She thought about the delicate symphony of odors in Sanctuary—morning smells, midday smells, evening smells—designed to keep you moving through your day, gently herding you from leaving the house to heading home. She had a sensitive nose and had never been a fan of scents, so they kept them subtle, but they were effective. She had seen how turning up the evening scent a small degree could send the dawdlers hurrying home to family and shelter. As bad as the wind and the rain felt as they beat against her disintegrating guardian cloak, Miranda thought the smells of outside would be what finally drove her over the edge. Alex had inherited her sensitive nose. She wondered how he was faring in City of the South.

Murray stretched out on his blanket without another word. He pulled out a battered, handmade clay pipe instead of a cigarette. The smoke it produced was pungent and bitter, but it fought the sickly, pervasive mold and won.

"What is that odor?" she asked.

"It's a kind of plant that smells a little like sulfur and a little like charcoal. Do you know what that is?"

She shook her head.

"It's a lot like gunpowder," he said. "There's still some guns out here. Not too many. They are mostly used as clubs now. Running out of bullets. But anybody smelling this is not going to take any chances and come in."

The sharp smell made Miranda sneeze. "Smoking that can't be good for you," she advised.

"Coat your nose again," he responded.

Miranda shook her head. Breathing through her mouth meant that things dropped into it while she slept. She had woken up choking once the night before. Once was enough. She lay down and drifted into an uneasy sleep.

SANCTUARY

CHAPTER TWENTY-THREE

As Alex followed Birna's stiff back out of the sleeping area, he was resolved. He would give this new life a day or two, and then he would demand that his father contact his mother or Tara and arrange for his return to Sanctuary. With all its flaws, he had never seen a child abused in Sanctuary. These children . . . what were they, exactly, with their names of numbered vegetables? Agricultural workers? Slaves? And what had his dad called them? The lucky ones?

Birna opened a door, and he was in a large room filled with wooden boxes on stilts so they were at least three feet high. His dad was studying one of the boxes. Alex composed his face so it didn't show the dread and disgust he was feeling. He didn't need to bother. His father sensed his presence, but he didn't look up.

"I have two gods," he said, as Alex approached. "You're going to work with one this morning. Would you like to meet him?"

Alex nodded cautiously. As he approached the box, he saw that it was filled with rich brown flaky material that bore no resemblance to the dust he had spent the last few days stumbling through. Dirt. Alex had only seen dirt in carefully tended pots at the nicer parks in Sanctuary and in a special room of the hydroponic city gardens. He took a deep breath. The smell was rich, like the best coffee essence, but pure, like a hit of oxygen at one of the very pricey bars in Sanctuary. He realized he had no real comparisons to what he was smelling. It smelled like life, the life he had hoped to have when he left Sanctuary.

His father guided his hand into the rich mixture. "This is my religion," he said. "My god makes this." He scooped a handful of the rich crumbling matter and held it under Alex's nose. Alex sniffed deeply. He wanted to bury himself in the scent and never return.

"This is my dream of a god, actually," Alex confessed.

Peter smiled. "Welcome to my worm farm."

"Your what?"

"This is the most nutritionally rich soil in COS. Almost three hundred thousand microbes in a tablespoon. It's where I breed my god, my superworm."

He reached in and pulled out a fat, wiggling worm and placed it on Alex's palm. Alex stared at it, fascinated. In all the stories he had watched, he had never seen such a creature. It was brown and segmented like something mechanical, but almost translucent. It wiggled on his hand as comfortably as it had in the dirt, seeming not to know it was being held by a giant who could flatten it into nothingness.

Peter studied his son as Alex studied the worm. He didn't shrink away or laugh, the first reaction of all his young apprentices. He simply stared at the worm with his slanted green eyes, so much like his own it hurt him to look at them. Peter ended the intensity of the moment by lecturing Alex about the earthworm, which lived to extract nutrients and then excrete even more microorganisms back into the soil. Alex listened, fascinated, and gently stroked the worm. No other apprentice had ever reacted with such intelligence and reverence. Peter silently thanked his ex-wife for the terrific job she had done raising him. Many times since leaving Sanctuary, he had been convinced he had made a terrible mistake. Now he felt the sun breaking through the eternal cloud cover. He gently took the worm from Alex.

"It took many years and a lot of deaths, to find some pockets of soil in the everlasting dust, places where earthworms were still plying their trade." He lifted Alex's chin so that Alex was looking at him and not at the worm burrowing back into the soil.

"Sanctuary would have you believe that you can have survival without sacrifice," he said. "It's not true. We are growing crops again, trees, raising animals. But only because people gave their lives so we could start over. Many scouts—men, women, even children—died finding me what I needed. Some pockets of soil, a few working worms. I have spent many years, and sacrificed many worms, to develop the right diets for them. They eat anything, even the detritus of the man-made stuff that destroyed us. You are going to spend the morning looking at worm casts under a microscope to determine which boxes of soil have the best conditions for worms."

He held up a hand at Alex's puzzled face. "I know you don't know what a microscope is. You will soon figure it out." He was silent for a moment, thinking. The woman who had found the microscope in a ruined high school lab had been a good friend and an even better lover. Large buildings were dangerous; marauder gangs occupied most of them. She had found one of the old-fashioned kind, working just from a rough drawing—a heavy metal tool that didn't require complex power supplies—along with the slides he needed. She had made it almost to the COS city gate before succumbing to her injuries. She managed all of this without knowing how to read and write. Future generations, Alex's children, would owe her a lot but would never know her name. Her real name was Margaret, but she had insisted on an enclave name so was known to others as Corn Three. She had been carrying his child, but he felt less sad about that. He looked directly at Alex, until Alex squirmed and broke his gaze. Children complicated things. One was enough.

He led Alex past the boxes into a white room with long, scrubbed wooden tables. The room was empty except for the two of them. He positioned Alex in front of a microscope, a heavy black thing

193

shaped like a question mark, with two eyepieces. He showed Alex how to adjust the eyepieces and focus on a smear of soil on a glass slide. Peter turned a knob which created a powerful light at the base. The smear of soil, which looked so uniform, transformed in the light into differently shaped, overlapping and interlocking circles. Peter explained what the different circles were, and what to look for on each of the slides, each of which represented a box of soil. This was a different Peter. He used terms like "pedotubules" and "cutans," features that broke the soil into identifiable structures with deposits. Alex listened, fascinated. This was a scientist, not a garbage collector. His father showed him the types of minerals they were looking for, by color and density, deposited in cutans and pedotubules created by worms burrowing through.

"We don't want the man-made substances that infest the earth around settlements," his dad said. "That just perpetuates our destruction." Alex nodded, his eyes narrowed and focused on what he was seeing.

Finally, Peter left him alone with the microscope. Alex studied each slide in turn and took notes on his newsline, which fortunately was still functioning, drawing power from his own body chemistry. He had never understood how the newsline worked, how anything worked, really. He was always focused on why, but now he was beginning to see the power of how, to regret his choice of story maker when he could have been learning to make something that would improve the world. Maybe it was rebellion against his mother, maybe rebellion against Sanctuary. It looked like he was getting a second chance to make a life, if only . . .

He put away thoughts about what discomfited him about City of the South. He had been here less than a day. It wasn't fair to judge based on the little he had seen. He focused instead on the purity of the earthworm, which took in nutrients and then pushed out more. If only he could spend his days like that, making things

GRACE J. AGNEW

better without second thoughts, like his dad. He was so focused
he didn't hear anyone else come in until someone gently jogged his
elbow. He turned, expecting his father, and then jumped, knocking
into the microscope and sending a glass slide flying to the ground,
where it shattered. A girl stood there with a tray containing more
soil samples in little heaps.

She was slender but short, about his age, with flowing, curly light
brown hair, something you never saw in Sanctuary, where everyone
kept their hair short for sanitary reasons. She laughed and brushed
her hair across her forehead, revealing a scar, pink, puffy, and shiny,
from the edge of her eye to the curve of her mouth on the right
side of her face. As he did a double take, she turned to face him
squarely and lifted her chin in a challenging way. She scraped her
hair back from her face and tilted her head so that he was facing
the scar, which looked not unlike one of his father's earthworms
in shape, if not in size or color.

"Go ahead. Get a good look," she said. "Peter tells me we are
going to be working together, so you need to get used to me. I don't
want you sneaking peeks when you think I'm not looking."

Her voice was clear and unblemished from the outside dust. She
spoke as well as anyone in Sanctuary.

"How—"

"None of your business," she answered smoothly. "I just don't
want you jumping every time you see me. We don't have that many
slides."

"That's not fair," Alex responded, stung. "You're the first person
I've met after Birna and the children who brought me food. You
startled me. Who are you, anyway?"

"My name is Agarita. Agarita One, actually, except there isn't an
Agarita Two, not yet. Maybe that will be you."

"My name is Alex," he responded stiffly. "I'm not thinking of
changing it."

She laughed again. "Nobody thinks of changing their name," she replied. "Other people think of it for them. But you are the boss's son, so perhaps it won't happen to you. Anyway, most people just call me Aggie."

The door opened and a shadow fell over them. Peter.

Alex jumped away, remembering how the children got in trouble last night for getting too close, but neither of the others moved. Aggie's lips twitched into a sardonic smile.

"Good. You two have met. Aggie is one of my top assistants. You'll be working a lot together. Do you want to show him my other god?"

Aggie didn't answer, but she nodded slightly and turned to walk out of the room. When Alex didn't move, she looked back at him.

"We have a full day," his dad said. Alex heard the same impatience in his voice that he had experienced on the road. Whatever his dad had expected, Alex was failing. He didn't know how to fix it except to obey without speaking, as everybody except Birna seemed to do. He followed Aggie out of the room.

When he stepped through the door, he was out in the world, or at least out in COS. A fine mesh roof above let in the outside air, a brown haze.

Aggie followed his gaze. "Nothing keeps the dust completely out," she said, "but in the crop shelters, the mesh filters most of it."

Alex sniffed, and the sweetness that filled his nose made him almost dizzy. He gulped the air.

"You don't have the nose mesh yet," she said. "I don't really smell it anymore." She led him down a path, and as they turned the corner, he stopped in astonishment. His father had been following silently and bumped into him.

"Pretty spectacular, isn't it?" he asked, the pride in his voice unmistakable.

"That smell," Alex said, "like spilled packfruit."

His dad frowned. He apparently didn't like reminders of Sanctuary. Alex filed that away, along with the other things he was learning. Whether he stayed or went, he needed his dad on his side. It hit him that he had never once worried about whether his mother was on his side. He brushed the thought away. His father was speaking, and he needed to listen.

"*Mahonia trifoliolata,*" his father said, "the agarita bush. It's blooming now. Those yellow flowers, that's the sweetness you smell."

Alex's dazzled eyes took in the green shrubs, knee high, stretching back to the stone wall that marked the edge of City of the South. They blazed with yellow flowers, tiny bells clustered against dark green leaves.

"Move closer," his dad said. Alex moved, drawn by the flowers but also by the excitement in his dad's voice. He loved what he was doing. Much like his mother.

The smell intensified when he reached the plants, almost making him dizzy. He leaned over a flower then jumped back when a prickly leaf scratched his nose. He turned quickly, but no one was laughing.

"The leaves are scratchy because you are not the visitor they want," his dad explained. "Here he comes now. My other god." Aggie tilted his chin with soft fingers. Alex jumped at her touch, and again no one remarked. His face was burning where she had touched him. He had been such a loner in school, and no one in Sanctuary touched anyone unnecessarily. Only his mother occasionally touched him, and she wasn't the physical type. He followed where she pointed, hoping his face wasn't as red as it felt.

When he saw what he was supposed to see, he stopped caring. A small nub of something flew toward the plant in a looping, curving track before landing on the flower that Alex had leaned over to sniff. He watched fascinated as its spindly legs dug into the center of the blossom. It was black and yellow with a furry texture much like his mother's cat. But this was no constructed creature. His dad clasped his shoulder and steered him past the plants, toward the wall. As they walked, the concentrated sweetness made Alex sneeze.

"It's midday," Peter said to Aggie. "Why only one bee?"

She shrugged. "It's fixing to rain again. They don't like that much."

Peter reached into a wooden box beside the bushes. He handed Alex a squashy hat with mesh that fell over his face. "Tie it under the chin," he advised. He and Aggie grabbed hats and tied them on with the expertise of long practice. Alex snuck a glance at the girl. When her face was covered, he noticed her long, slender neck and the wavy hair that cascaded down her back. They also pulled on bulky gloves. Alex reached in and grabbed a pair without waiting on his dad. He sensed his father relaxing when he didn't have to tell Alex every step to take.

"I use my best conditioned soil here," he said, "to grow plants for these guys." He pointed to perhaps twenty battered metal boxes on legs at the edge of the fence. "My bees," he said with reverence. As they got closer, Alex could hear a loud, strangely melodious hum. As it died in one place, it rose in another. The chorus of bees seemed to respond to their arrival, rising in volume as they approached.

"Before I got the bees, I had to hand pollinate everything I wanted to grow," Peter said loudly over the hum. "These are nature's pollinators. And more. We have begun to use their honey to sweeten cakes. And this year, the family will have their first mead."

"What's that?"

"An alcoholic drink." He frowned to himself. It would be a mild brew. He was hoping to wean the family off the distilled liquors they valued so much. It made them drunk and quarrelsome. And mean. He glanced quickly at Agarita One, at the side of her face where the scar was, hidden now by the mesh.

He lifted the lid off a box and pulled out a white, sticky frame to which several fat, velvety, vibrating nubs were clinging. He gently lifted a bee off the frame and placed it on Alex's gloved finger, where it sat, humming gently. Alex said nothing, but Peter could tell by his eyes that he was overwhelmed.

"Where did you find them?" Alex asked.

Peter hesitated a moment. "My parents had them," he replied, "in the woods, near our old farm. My older apprentices went with me to rescue them. Aggie was one of them. There were still some boxes left, and some bees hanging around. We used the boxes as models to construct more. And the bees came." Alex could hear the gratitude and wonder in his dad's voice. He didn't think much of people, that was obvious, but these small creatures really were his gods. He shifted his feet uneasily as he thought about his own interactions with people in Sanctuary.

"We finally have enough bees and enough honey and beeswax do so some things we need to do," his dad continued. "And the bee sting can also be powerful medicine for some illnesses."

"You mentioned family?" Alex asked. It stood to reason that his dad hadn't been alone all this time. But he found himself dreading the idea of half siblings, a stepmother. He looked again at Aggie, wondering if there was any resemblance.

Aggie and his dad exchanged a glance before her gaze dropped respectfully, awaiting orders.

"I had hoped to introduce him to extracting honey today," Peter said, "but it might be better to get it over with."

"They know he is here," Aggie agreed. "The scouts will have reported, or Birna."

His dad sighed. "If I could just be left to work in peace," he muttered to himself. Aggie shot a sideways glance at Alex and shook her head slightly. He took the hint and said nothing.

SANCTUARY

CHAPTER TWENTY-FOUR

Miranda had been sure she wouldn't sleep in the smelly house, falling apart in the wind as things fell off the roof with a loud thump and sometimes bashed against windows that were more ropy vine than broken glass. Murray stretched out and was soon snoring lustily, competing with the wind and outside debris. Miranda lay silently, shrinking protectively inside her ratty blanket whenever something sifted from the ceiling. She thought about the antiseptic cleanliness of Sanctuary, despite which deadly viruses and bacteria cycled through the population several times a year. It was understood that these diseases came from outside, from the few people admitted legally and the many others who found a way to slip in, even though official Sanctuary immigration had been closed for a decade. When she and Alex returned—if they returned—they would be quarantined for at least a month, assuming they were even allowed to return. And where would they go if they weren't? She looked at Murray's back, surprisingly broad for a tall, slender man, and felt reassured. Tara Jordan had sent him; she had promised him a reward for her safe return. Tara knew she wouldn't come back without Alex. When they returned, they would be greeted with suspicion and avoided. Somehow, they would get past all that. She might lose her place as top world builder, but with Tara's help she would get Alex back on track. He would have a lot of stories to create, that's for sure. She chuckled sleepily to herself, which was a mistake; dust and grit charged in the moment she opened her mouth. She coughed and spit as silently as she could, mindful of Murray between her and the door.

What seemed minutes later, she woke as she found her pack slipping from beneath her head. She sat up in alarm. "What are you doing?" she asked sharply.

Murray held a finger to his lips in response. "*S-h-h-h!* I don't hear anyone outside, but we are too close to City of the South for loud talking."

"What time is it?" Miranda asked in a sibilant whisper.

"It's midmorning. I let you sleep. You needed it. We'll reach COS before nightfall. That's all that matters."

"Finding my son is what matters," Miranda responded tartly. "Is that going to be hard to do?"

"Don't get ahead of yourself," Murray advised. "We have to get into City of the South first. They aren't too fussy about letting people in. If you have no business there, someone will put an end to you sooner rather than later, so no worries about that. And you're marked, so if you overstay your welcome, someone will turn you in for the bounty. But there's still a door with guards to get through."

As he spoke, he was rummaging through her pack, eyeing things speculatively and putting some aside.

"What are you doing?"

"The only people who get in without official business are scavengers bartering things they found on the road for food. We have to pull together some things for trade." He pulled out the lean-to and an old scaleskin Miranda had packed for Alex. He rubbed some dirt on a couple of packfruit and waterskins. "These are all things we might have pulled off a dead body," he said conversationally. "Not too much and not too clean. This will buy us a stay of at least a week to find your son."

He packed the things he selected into a sack and then began stuffing supplies, including the knife, in the pockets of his ratty coat. "Pack anything you can carry, including your newsline, in your guardian cloak," he advised. "We have to leave your pack behind and just bring my smaller one. We need enough to barter but not enough to be killed for. Our story is we found a dead Sanctuary guardian. That will explain your cloak. Stick close to me, and don't say anything. You talk too much like Sanctuary."

"What do you sound like?" she asked.

"Ah sou li Co," he replied without missing a beat.

"Why do they talk like that?" she asked.

"Years of swallowing dust," he replied.

"Don't you do the same?"

He looked at her without response. His shoulders and face were taut. She realized he was nervous about entering City of the South. The bravado of the previous days' march was gone. Wordlessly, she packed as much as she could into her pockets. Murray reached over her, took things out, rearranged things until he was satisfied.

"You can't march into City of the South with pockets bulging," he said drily.

She realized he wasn't nervous for himself; he was nervous for her.

Murray led the way as they followed the road to City of the South. They stopped when the narrow road intersected a larger road, bigger than any streetway in Sanctuary, filled with people pulling carts of many sizes, forms, and materials—rusty metal, wood, substances Miranda didn't even recognize, things that didn't exist in Sanctuary or even in the stories of yesteryear. The carts were so dense that Miranda stopped, not certain how to join the confused mingling of feet and wheels without being knocked down, or worse. Murray took her arm and guided her into the throng, somehow managing to blend with the carts. Miranda noticed that

Murray adopted a rhythm, almost a singsong movement, to weave in and out of the mass.

They were surrounded by cursing, spitting people pulling carts or wearing laden packs, with scarcely a breath separating one person or family from another. Miranda felt crushed and had to actively fight the urge to pull away from Murray, cut diagonally across the roadway, and escape.

The people around them moved silently except for the constant coughing and hawking. If someone doubled over, others pushed them aside or took advantage of the opportunity to rifle a cart or rip a pack roughly off someone's back. Out of the corner of her eye, she saw a young woman, maybe a girl, go down. A man pulled the girl's pack away with a laugh, but the crowd grudgingly moved around her, giving her room to recover and get up, although a few aimed a stray, listless kick in her direction while the girl screeched in reply. Miranda was relieved to see that no one actually trampled her into the roadway mud. She thought about her marauder encounter. Was there any daylight between that creature and this girl? Probably not much.

The constant coughing, punctuated with curses, was monotonous. Despite the nose coat, Miranda had a constant tickle in her throat. She had grown used to her own coughing, and Murray's, but she never spit in his presence, and he seldom did in hers. She kept her eyes to the ground to avoid the gray, gelatinous blobs that liberally studded the roadway. Some of the blobs had wiggling things trapped in them, parasites from rough living no doubt. Miranda felt her stomach heaving at the sight. Murray told her they would get food and clothes in the market after gaining entrance to the city. A city no doubt teaming with creatures like this. She doubted she would ever eat again.

They made their way to the city door, a large, slanted affair of rusting and bent metal at least as high as four people standing on one another's shoulders. It was impossible to see the city inside the walls. A painted sign over the double doors of the entrance-way read "City of the South" with a grinning sun, but one corner of the mouth had peeled away, turning the grin into a leer. The sun seemed to squint at each person as they went under. Miranda pulled her head in as if expecting the sun to hawk and spit on her as she went through. The city name was partially obscured by dirt and age, "City o the Sou." People in faded gray coats, protection against the dust, were checking each person walking in. Some were pulled roughly aside and either hustled away or sent back out onto the roadway, where they were kicked and jeered as they attempted to go backward. She noticed that they immediately began to sell or barter their goods with the people in line to enter, as if the turning away was expected and all part of the day's business. Movement was slow at the city doorway, giving her time to study the wall and the people around her. The roof arcing up to the wall blended into the fog, only its outline faintly visible. It had started as a dome but was squashed and bent in places like a well-worn hat with a broken crown. As she got closer, she realized the roof was mesh.

Murray muttered in her ear. "It lets the sun and rain in but keeps most of the dust out. It's full of holes now, with few people to repair it. Very dangerous work, and no one to heal you if the fall doesn't kill you." She shuddered and turned instead to look more closely at the people waiting for entrance. Aside from a few kicks and curses as someone stumbled into another, they mostly waited patiently. It was very different from the chaos of the roadway. People were on their best behavior.

"So many people living outside the city," she said. "How does this happen?"

He lowered his voice to respond. "The land all around is dead, and COS can't feed everybody with the food they grow, so the population is smaller than Sanctuary, and it's easy to get banished.

But City of the South doesn't make much of anything but food. So they're pretty open to visitors, particularly if they might have something to barter. They also expect us to be easy to swindle."

Miranda looked around at the people moving forward—they were thin and muddy, their faces lined and teeth, even for the children, crooked or nonexistent. It was a tough life for people outside the protection of a city wall; that much was clear.

"The way they talk," she said again. She had listened to the monotonous mumbling on the roadway without understanding most of it.

Murray smiled. "It's generally not a good idea to speak too much unless you want a mouthful of dirt. The speech is pretty economical. You don't need more than a syllable to get a word across."

Miranda didn't answer. *I need more*, she thought. *How will I find Alex if I can't ask questions and understand the answers?* She would never make it in COS without Murray. She was filled with gratitude toward Tara for sending him her way.

At last, it was their turn at the door. A harsh lantern, glowing blue-white in the mist, swung in their direction, causing Miranda to squint and shield her eyes with her hand.

"Wha tha?" a voice grated in their direction.

Murray turned his face to the light.

"Murr," the voice acknowledged. Apparently, he was well-known in the city. "Who tha wi?"

Murray didn't attempt to speak the abbreviated language. "Someone I found on the road, an exile from Sanctuary. Broke too many rules. She has some fine things she's going to let me barter." He motioned for the guard to step down from his perch.

The guard was huge, with a gnarled fist of a face and puffy lids turning his eyes into slits. He leered knowingly at Murray and looked Miranda up and down. His grin said Murray was paid with more than barter. Miranda found her face turning red and looked down at the dusty path. Murray opened a pocket and showed the bag of coins nestled on top. The guard reached in and took it very smoothly, before Miranda could even react. Murray tightened his grip on her arm to stop her if she tried. He opened the pack on his back. The man made a show of rummaging through the pack with one hand while the other transferred the bag to his trouser pocket.

"Twa wee. The we co fo tha," the man said finally. He motioned them to walk through the bright beam of the lantern. It was doing double duty as light source and scanner, Miranda realized, trying not to hunch under its voracious glare so that she didn't appear like she had something to hide. Murray had thought better of the dead guardian story. She realized the wisdom of sticking largely to the truth, in case they were able to cross-check against city data. She was probably already banished from Sanctuary.

The blinding glare of the lantern created its own second wall. She stumbled through it and stood dazed as her dazzled eyes turned everything into electric blue shadows bobbing about. Once she could see without blinking, she turned to Murray and said the first thing that came to mind. "Why do you speak good English?" she demanded. "Not these phlegmy, meaningless syllables."

"They aren't meaningless. You'll get used to it," Murray replied. "These are people who are cared for and protected by nobody. Their throats are broken from years of swallowing dust. The higher classes and protected families are sheltered from the dust. They talk the same as you and I do."

"But why you?" Miranda persisted.

"I haven't always been what you see," he replied. "Give me another year, though; see how I sound then."

Miranda wasn't satisfied. "Where do you live? That guard knew you. Is City of the South your home? You can't live outside."

"You ask a lot of questions," Murray replied. "People in COS don't like that. It generally means you are a spy but not very good at it. You need to save your curiosity for when it matters, finding your son."

His change of tone alarmed her. She was totally dependent on this man, and he was right; finding her son was what mattered. She stopped talking. They walked down the path in silence.

At first she thought her eyes were still light dazzled. The roadway narrowed as it entered the city. Buildings lined the street. The buildings were crumbling brick, patched with metal and wood where brick had fallen, and holes had bloomed in the wooden walls underneath. Black mold and green moss blossomed in strange patterns on every surface.

Murray turned her to face him. "You better know a little about COS before we go any farther. The city was founded by two families, former marauders who were strong enough to force others to do what they wanted: the Esters and the Stallways. The Esters exiled what was left of the Stallways, so now there's just the one family. They rule by fear. It is easy to get banished, thrown into prison, or put to death here—and lots of spies to report you for a price. They are surrounded by the administrators, people who make things run and are well rewarded for that, even though the results are spotty. They make sure the rulers have good lives. That's all that matters. They speak as good as you or me. Another way they control is to take family members in service. If the servers work well, their families benefit. If they don't . . ." He didn't finish the sentence.

"Can I assume that you are one of the administrators, and that's why you talk so well?"

"No. But you can feel free to make that assumption about your husband."

Miranda saw that the people they met were curious, so much so that they turned and stared as they passed. She fingered her guardian cloak self-consciously and wondered how soon the Esters, and probably Peter, would know she had arrived.

Murray turned down a side street, more like a footpath between the buildings, barely large enough to drag a cart through. The buildings were smaller, hovels rather than houses, with sketchy structures held together with old pots, machine parts, and cloth, like garbage heaps with openings serving as windows and doors.

"City of the South people are scavengers," Murray remarked quietly. "They have to be. And self-taught in survival trades like carpentry. Except for their server relatives, they are left entirely to their own devices by the rulers. They can usually figure something out." He gestured at a building pointed on both ends.

"Is that a boat?" Miranda asked.

"It's a house, but repaired with the scavenged parts of a boat. Which is all the more ingenious because there's no body of water nearby."

"Scavenge," Miranda replied, drawing out the syllables. "Is that the word they use for stealing?"

Murray smiled. "Yes, this is a city of scavenge and barter. Anything you can find or take and defend is yours. What you can't take, you can trade for. There are few guardians in City of the South except to press folks into service. Lots of fighting, but very little murder. People depend on one another to survive. The person you kill may be the person who would have bartered for something you need. On the other hand, theft, rape, anything that involves taking; these aren't crimes in COS. The only crime is to take something from the family or their administrators."

The crooked, twisting road was oppressive. The tumbledown upper stories of the buildings lining the street created a covered walkway that sheltered them from rain but blocked out a lot of the light that emerged from the cloud cover and filtered through the rusty mesh. The mesh created a dappled pattern on the muddy ground, creating a rippling effect like walking through water. The road was paved with stone but cracked, causing Miranda to trip. Miranda had the sense of eyes watching their every move, but when she looked up at the windows of buildings, they were dark and empty, more like holes gouged through decay than anything intentional to bring in light or air. "Are these buildings abandoned?" she asked.

Murray was amused. "City of the South is actually a lively place," he said. "It's early in the day, and people don't know what to make of you, is all. They are busy memorizing what they can see of you, in case it is worth something to somebody." He turned toward a tumbledown house, more hovel than home, and knocked on the rickety door. Miranda's heart sank. The shabbiest place of all. It figured.

CHAPTER TWENTY-FIVE

Aggie took the frame from Peter and placed it in the box. Alex was envious of her easy familiarity with his dad.

Peter sighed. "I guess we had better go. Knowing Birna, she's waiting for us." He strode out of the enclosure. Before Alex followed, he stole a last glance at Aggie. She was moving around the boxes and didn't look back at him. Alex found this surprisingly annoying. She didn't see people from Sanctuary every day. Somebody who looked different, who spoke as well as she did. She surely didn't meet the son of her boss every day. Was he going to be as invisible and ignored in City of the South as he was in Sanctuary? His dad set a rapid pace, and Alex soon forgot about the strange girl and worried instead about what else was in store for him before the day ended.

Birna was waiting with the same grim look on her face. She grabbed Alex by the elbow and pulled him into a room with a mirror and hanging sacks, but no shower that Alex could see.

"Strip down," she said.

"Just tell me what to do. I can manage by myself."

"You think this is fun for me? We do things differently here than in Sanctuary. I'll need to show you once, so you don't put out an eye. We need to get you looking as good as possible for the family."

The distain in her voice told him she didn't think the best he could look was a very high bar. Alex stole a look at himself in the mirror. Several rough days on the road had done their worst with his hair and clothes. He couldn't disagree.

He turned his back to her and stripped down. He wasn't going to face her, no matter what she expected. She grabbed some sacking, wrapped it around his back and shoulders, and began scrubbing. The sacking was gritty and surprisingly painful. He tried to pull away, but she was too strong.

She softened enough to explain. "We use fine rocks to abrade the dirt away. We don't have the power source of Sanctuary for a light shower, but the gravel does the trick."

After she had polished his back, arms, and legs to a brick red, she pulled out a very fine-tooth metal comb and began on his hair. Dirt, leaves, and some crawling things that made him shudder came tumbling out. She finished with something sticky that made his bristly hair shine. His nose wrinkled at the smell.

"You'll get used to it," Birna advised, "and it will keep things out that shouldn't be there."

She handed him a shirt and pants. "These are your father's. They will be too big for you, but better than the rags you arrived with."

Alex felt odd putting on his father's shirt and pants, both clean but soil stained and soft with many years' use.

Birna looked over her handiwork. "I guess this will do," she said.

Do for what? he wondered as he looked at his face in the mirror, swollen, polished, and red as a packfruit. But Birna seemed pleased enough. In truth, Birna was thinking back to when his father first set up shop in the back of COS, to start his gardens. The boy was skinnier than Peter but still reminded her of the way he looked back then, curious and eager, when it was just the two of them figuring things out.

Character is another thing entirely, she thought sourly. She could already see the mother's influence there. Her lips turned downward. "Don't keep your father waiting," she snapped. "Or the family."

Alex realized the moment, if it could even be called that, was over. He walked past her out the door without a backward glance

212

or even a thank-you. He hadn't asked for the ministrations, after all, and if he had his way, they would never be repeated.

His father was waiting in the main room, where the children and Birna had met them the day before. He was interested to see that his father had also changed his shirt and trousers, and his hair also gleamed and smelled with whatever it was that kept the bugs away.

His father looked him over. He raised one eyebrow at the clothes, which swamped Alex, but he didn't say anything.

"I've sent word to the brothers," he told Birna. "They're expecting us."

"Will you have dinner there?" she asked.

"I don't think so. They generally make meals a formal affair. We'll need to get him some new clothes before that would happen."

"I'll have something waiting for you on your return."

As his father led the way through a maze of rooms, some set up as labs, some with pallets similar to his own, he ventured a question to his father.

"This family we're going to meet. Is it your family?"

His father stopped in his tracks and faced Alex. "I should probably give you a quick history lesson. There were once two families who started City of the South. They brought in people to build COS, but they kept themselves separate from the people who served them. After a while, the marriage alliances didn't work out, and they began quarreling among themselves. Only one family, the Esters, had the sense to set up an administrative class to make the city work and keep the inhabitants in order. The other family, the Stallways, were driven away or killed, although there are remnants in COS. The Esters are known as 'the family' because they rule by blood not by elections. They keep the city intact, although they make a sketchy job of it."

This was the most Peter had said to him since they had first met outside the Sanctuary wall. He said as much.

213

Surprisingly, Peter grinned. "You will soon learn to say as little as possible here. Information is barter, and everyone has sharp ears. Also, you want to keep the dust out. But you need to understand what you are walking into."

"So, you are in the administrative class," he hazarded.

"Chief administrator," his father conceded. "But all that really means is everyone below me is wondering how to pull me down. And now they will be wondering if you are a tool for that, my weak spot."

Alex stiffened. "You mean Birna?"

His dad paused. "Possibly. Not likely. But Agarita One, most definitely. We need her skills, but she is not to be trusted. Learn from her, but don't make a friend of her."

"Not likely," Alex said quickly.

His father smiled. "You wonder why I work with such young children? They are quick and eager to learn. Also, too young to spy, or at least to be successful at it.

"You're going to meet the two brothers who run the Ester family today. If they approve of you, you'll be able to stay. I doubt you will meet any other family members. But you never know."

Alex scarcely heard the last. His attention was caught by "You'll be able to stay." He didn't know that he wanted to stay, but he didn't fancy his chances alone on the outside if he was kicked out tonight. Surely, his father wouldn't . . . ?

"Pick up the pace, Alex. We don't want to be late."

━━━━━━━━━━

Walden sprawled in a big chair in the family study. When the Stallways ruled, they called it the throne room, which seemed pretentious to his father and not in keeping with the image of the wise and paternal family his father strove to convey, an image he maintained tolerably well unless he got drunk on spirits and looked among the servants and the town for women, sometimes boys, to entertain himself during the binge. It got so bad that families were hiding or maiming their children, and their guards spent more time pacifying angry town mobs than quelling the Stallways rebels. Fortunately, his father had made a timely exit. Wells were dug deep to find the scarce groundwater in City of the South. It was a pity the heroic guard who had tried to stop his father's drunken tumble had fallen in after him. The man was a hero. His portrait was in a closet somewhere, to be hauled out during infrequent festivals or awards ceremonies for townspeople. And his wife and children were taken care of and not subject to impress. A tragedy. He sighed automatically. But even more tragic, they had to permanently close that well.

His musings were cut short by the heavy tread of his brother, Darwin.

Darwin flung himself into the other chair, which creaked under his weight. For a COS chair, it was opulent, with worn but not yet threadbare upholstery and carved arms that were barely scratched. Walden refused to call it a throne.

"What are we doing here?" Darwin demanded. He resented anything that took him away from raiding the town for likely servants, particularly female, or coyote hunting with his own administrators, who had no other qualifications than administering death with a bow.

Walden had no use for his brother and seldom involved him in running COS. Darwin was his half-brother, the result of his father's first coupling, Walden refused to call it a marriage, to a Stallways woman who died under mysterious circumstances. The heavy features and inability to sit still or concentrate seemed evidence of the inbreeding that plagued the imbecilic residents of COS. His brother's name was a giveaway. His father had a strange sense of humor. What his brother did have, as Walden had learned to his cost when he tried to make himself sole ruler despite being the younger brother, was an instinct for self-preservation. They were dependent on the agricultural skills of Peter, but Darwin, who loved his food more passionately than coyotes or women, didn't trust Peter. Walden felt it was wise to involve Darwin in anything involving Peter. If there was a genuine reason to worry about Peter, Darwin would ferret it out.

"Peter has brought his son from Sanctuary," he reminded Darwin.

Darwin pounded the arm of his chair, which cracked in two. Walden suppressed his annoyance. The next chair he provided for Darwin would have no arms.

"We have plenty of people in COS! We don't need to be bringing people in who may be spies."

"He said he needs someone educated," Walden replied mildly. "Very few people here can read or write."

"You don't need a book to plant a potato. He's up to something. I'm warning you."

Walden didn't respond. As a matter of fact, Peter *was* up to something. In collaboration with Walden—another, hopefully final, attempt to put Darwin in his place. He was getting out of control. The drunken sorties into town, the rapes. The townspeople, who tolerated a lot because they had to, were getting fed up. And Darwin was picking them younger and younger, just like their father. He shivered fastidiously.

When he looked directly at his brother, he saw him staring suspiciously at Walden. He should never forget that Darwin, for all his idiocy, could read the expression on a coyote's face from half a mile away.

A servant entered. "Lor Pe hea," he announced. "Lord" was the honorific for the ruling brothers but also given to the highest administrators.

Walden nodded to indicate that Peter and his son should be brought in. Darwin sat up straight instead of lounging in his chair as he preferred.

Peter walked in with his son following. He bowed his head to first one brother then the other. "Lord Darwin, Lord Walden."

Many people got the order wrong, given that Walden did most of the ruling and Darwin was seldom around in an official rather than a pillaging capacity. They forgot Darwin was the elder, and frequently got a lash from the crop he carried with him for their disrespect. Peter never forgot.

Darwin only growled in return, so Walden spoke up. "Welcome back. I don't need to ask about your errand. We can see the successful result."

"My son, Alex," Peter said. He nudged Alex slightly.

"My lords," Alex said, bowing first to the big, beefy one and then to the slender, handsome one, who could be any age with his smooth face but gray hair.

He hoped his lips didn't twitch as they had when his father coached him. "My lords" sounded like something out of a really cheesy yesteryear story. One of those romances most women, but not his mother, watched avidly. With his sensitive features, Lord Walden could be one of those heroes. Darwin, on the other hand, could be the village lout.

"So, what do you think of City of the South? I imagine you are finding it very different from Sanctuary."

The words were innocuous, but the narrowed eyes and tone were not. No matter what his long-term plans, Alex had no intention of being banished on his first day. He talked enthusiastically about his father's work—the soil, the flowers, and particularly the bees.

Lord Darwin didn't seem to be paying attention, except for the occasional derisive snort, but Lord Walden was listening closely, his head tilted to one side. Alex found Darwin disconcerting, so he focused on Walden, until Walden's head straightened and he looked past Alex and Peter.

Alex turned as well and saw a girl, slender and tall, with dark hair that fell in waves to her shoulders.

"My daughter Ada," Walden murmured sardonically. "She's not supposed to interrupt family business, but since she turned sixteen, she seldom pays attention to rules."

"Dad, you know that's not true," she replied. "I wanted permission to go into town to see if my dress is ready for Saturday. I forgot you were having a meeting." She was speaking to her dad, but her eyes never left Alex.

Alex stared back, until his father nudged him and recalled him to the meeting.

"Your father knows my daughter Ada," Walden said. "Ada, this is Peter's son, Alex."

"I didn't know you had a son," Ada replied, with the slightest hesitation that told Walden that Ada not only knew who Alex was but also had a shrewd suspicion why he was here.

"Anyway, Father, about going into town."

"You know I'm not answering questions until my business is concluded," her father responded. "Alex was just about to describe his journey here."

"Oh, may I stay? I'm so curious about outside. I've never been past the city walls."

Her complaint could have been his just a few days earlier, but not sulky and rude the way Alex realized he spoke to his mother, who he would probably never see again.

Walden shared the slightest of glances at Peter and then looked full on at Darwin, whose face was a thundercloud as his mind worked slowly to rub two ideas together, something it seldom had to do.

"Actually, I think we'll let Peter and Alex go home for now. This is Alex's first full day in COS. I'm sure he's tired. But why don't you invite him to your birthday party?"

"That's a wonderful idea," Ada said. "And you too, Peter. It will be much more fun if it's not just the same old family."

"We would be happy to," Peter replied when it was clear that Alex was too tongue-tied to respond. He nodded to the men and to Ada, rapped Alex lightly on the neck to remind him to do the same, and then nudged him out of the room.

When they were out of earshot, he clapped Alex on the back. "That went better than expected."

Alex hardly noticed the pat. You don't notice a small clap of thunder after you've been struck by lightning.

SANCTUARY

CHAPTER TWENTY-SIX

Miranda heard something that sounded more animal than human respond to Murray's knock, and then the inevitable hawking and spitting. Murray took this for an invitation and pushed their way through a door that seemed barely to be on its hinges.

The house was small and compact, with only a few pieces of furniture and a scrubbed wooden floor. The house felt warm after the windy outside, but the meaty, fetid smell reminded Miranda of the suburbs they had just suffered through. She wrinkled her nose as she got used to the dim light through the blocked-out windows. The only source of steady light was the red glow of a battered black box with a pipe through the roof that Miranda just recognized from stories of yesteryear as a stove. The stove was the source of part of the smell, a sweetish, almost chemical odor that made her woozy. The rest of the smell emanated from an old man in a wooden chair, huddled close to the stove and spitting into a bent enamel pot at his feet.

"Da," Murray said, in greeting. The man, who seemed no more interested than if he had seen Murray a few minutes ago, waved a large glove-like hand dismissively. "Go wa," he said.

"That's not much of a greeting," Murray responded. He set down the pack.

The old man's eyes lit up with interest. "Wha you gah?" he asked.

"Nothing for you, but good for barter." Murray responded. "I'll get us something to eat with this. I'm guessing you have nothing in the house?"

In response, the old man snatched a bowl off the stove's hob with a greasy piece of cloth. Miranda could see something gray and grainy, an oatmeal or porridge of some kind, burned and crusty on the edges but still soft and bubbling in the middle. He began poking it into his mouth and staring suspiciously, first at Murray and then at Miranda, as if they would pull the unappetizing mess away. Miranda knew that her pockets and Murray's were stuffed with packfruits and water, but she said nothing. They would need all that, and more, to share with Alex on the trip back.

Murray took Alex's spare scaleskin. "This will fetch a bit," he said to Miranda. "I'll leave you here with my Da to get acquainted. He would be trouble if he could, but he's too crippled to do much damage."

"Is he really your father?"

"What passes for a relationship in COS," Murray replied cryptically. He turned to his da, who had been following the conversation by looking from one to the other with red, rheumy eyes.

"Da, this is Miranda. She and I will be staying for a few days."

His father looked her up and down, much as the guard at the COS gate had. "Too ol'," he said critically.

"Get your mind out of whatever rat hole it is skulking in," Murray responded. The words were harsh, but the tone was almost gentle. "She's the founder of whatever feast we have tonight. Keep her entertained until I return."

He slipped out the door. Miranda reluctantly pulled the only other chair, a stool with no back, closer to the fire. The smell was worse the closer she got to the old man, but the entryway was very cold as the wind whistled through the chinks of the battered door.

"How are you?" she asked the old man. If nothing else, this would be a good chance to practice understanding the strange glottal speech of the inhabitants. The old man had other ideas. He glared at her through his heavy slanted lids, put his gruel carefully on the floor to the other side of his chair. "Sta tha!" he commanded.

"I'm not going anywhere," she promised.

He watched her until his eyelids grew too heavy and he drifted into a noisy slumber, with many snores, snorts and hawkings in his sleep. Miranda closed her eyes to shut out the unlovely sight and nodded off herself without realizing it, until an acrid smell woke her up. She opened her eyes to see the man sprawling in his chair. A wet stain spread across his lap. He had wet himself in his sleep.

To distract herself until Murray returned, she looked around the room, careful not to creak in her chair and wake the old man. She had an idea he was better at entertaining her asleep than when he was awake. The house was a shotgun with an open door leading to what was probably the kitchen, then through to the bedroom. She could see through the open doors to a small wooden table and chairs and a frowsy single bed. She wondered where the bathroom was and decided she probably didn't want to know.

She dozed off again until Murray pushed the door open and woke her.

"Not too bad," he said. "We'll have these for dinner." He brought the small table out from the kitchen and set down three pastries, oozing with red that looked like blood. Miranda shivered superstitiously, remembering the coyote on the road. *Surely not—*

The old man grabbed a pastry and began gnawing on it with the few stubs that remained of his teeth. "Bee!" he said happily.

"That's right," Murray said. "I found a baker just closing down in the marketplace and picked up beet pies." He bit into the pastry, oblivious to the red juice that coursed down his chin. "Eat it," he told Miranda; "you won't do better at the best bakery in Sanctuary."

Miranda took a cautious bite. The juice squirted in all directions. She tried not to notice how battered the outside looked, with fingerprints clearly showing where the pastry edges had been pressed around the filling. It was surprisingly good, rich and sweet, with chopped green leaves adding a sharp savory taste and texture to balance the mushiness of the beets. She just knew what beets were from the hydroponics garden in Sanctuary. They didn't grow them in enough numbers for the town, so they were reserved for some committee members who had a taste for them. She noticed a grittiness as she ate that caught in her teeth. She probed the grit with her tongue. Murray noticed.

"They can't clean vegetables the way they do in Sanctuary," he said. "No water to waste. Besides, these are probably pilfered, so they wouldn't risk preparing them where anyone could see. Likely roasted in a house stove like this one."

Miranda looked at the smelly stove, stuffed with rags and oily rocks, and shuddered.

Murray and the old man had finished their pies. The old man was eyeing hers.

She was no longer hungry. "You can have what's left," she said.

He might not talk full English, but he understood it well enough. He snatched the pie from her hand and shoved it down in two bites before Murray could intervene.

"Food is different here," Murray said mildly. "And scarce. Beet pie is something special. You can't let the hygiene of COS stop you from filling your belly. Not if you want to find your son and then trek back to Sanctuary. The old man is better looked after than you might suppose. Don't give him your rations anymore."

He grabbed rusty tongs by the stove and pulled out a rock and sniffed. "A form of coke. They scavenge it from an old mine on the outskirts of town. I told them not to do that. If this place didn't have so many holes, they would be poisoned by this." He looked down at the cracked pot full of foamy yellow-brown sputum. "It's not doing his lungs any good."

Miranda wondered who "they" were. The house was too clean for just the old man. Did Murray's mother live here also? She was too tired to ask.

The man didn't like being ignored. "Wha tha?"

"We'll go out now before it gets too dark and look for some wood to burn," Murray said. "Better for your lungs"

The man reached for the stone, which Murray held at arm's length. "Coh," he said.

Murray showed Miranda where she could place her bedroll in a corner of the main room. Her heart sank as she unfurled her blanket on the floor. If she ever returned to Sanctuary, she would never take a soft bed for granted again.

"Are you ready to hunt for something to burn in the stove?" Murray asked.

"Did you mean it about actual wood?"

"You never know," he replied.

Murray led the way down the narrow, twisty street with the ease of a COS native. Miranda stared up at the claustrophobic buildings. Why did they jut the second story over the first, blocking out all light and making the city look like a hastily constructed jumble of sticks, cloth and mud that could break apart and bury you at any time? She found herself ducking and pulling her neck into her scaleskin in response to the looming buildings. And where were all the people?

When they reached the next street, Murray stopped and looked about. "I don't want to do any scavenging on the street where we are staying," he said. "Spying is an easy way to make money in City of the South. You're a stranger and will attract a lot of interest."

"But they've already marked us," Miranda said. "At the gate. Aren't they already keeping tabs on us?"

Murray leaned in. "Keep your voice low," he advised. "They mark everybody, but the tracking capabilities are very primitive.

They depend a lot on people to keep them informed. And it works very well for them."

The rain began to fall as Murray led Miranda down dingy streets with rickety buildings that looked abandoned and dismal—a steady, monotonous tumble of drops that turned the cloud-covered sky into a perpetually shaken sieve. Miranda found herself longing for a slashing downpour that stabbed and stung your exposed face and hands but made the world seem alive and fighting back, not abandoned. "Abandoned," that was the word. City of the South was a place that had given up. She thought of Alex, experiencing this somewhere, and shivered.

"I don't get it," she said. "All the stories you see of City of the South, there are people everywhere, robbing and murdering each other but also talking, laughing, drinking. This place seems deserted."

"City of the South is lively enough when it wants to be—on market days, for example—but the citizens are careful. You are dressed too well to be a beggar, who would be easy prey. You might be a family spy. Some family members are known to cover themselves in cloaks and visit the town. It's a safe adventure for them because they fool no one with their disguises."

"And, of course, I'm with *you*," Miranda hazarded. "No one is going to challenge me while I am with you." She was figuring out that Murray was not who he seemed. He only shrugged.

Miranda had another question. "Why do they build their houses such an awkward way? Blocking out what little light the sky offers?"

Murray looked up at the tottering houses. "This is a pilfering society," he said. "There isn't much open crime, except at night, but in the absence of regular employment and guardians, people break into the homes of others to take what they need. The second story is for watching and for showering missiles down on anyone unexpected who comes to your front door."

"They look like they will fall down," Miranda said, and shivered.

"Education, including learning a trade, is sketchy in COS," Murray said. "Builders are in short supply, and most work for the rulers. But after enough people were crushed in falling buildings, people have learned where and how to prop the buildings to keep them steady."

"But how do you get anything done?" Miranda asked in frustration. "How do you get something fixed when it breaks? How do you find food or clothes? Are there no stores?"

"There are some stores, mostly catering to the rulers. Very little coin except what the ruling families distribute when they visit for ceremonies. There are some pubs, where you can get a drink and a pie and even a warm welcome, if they already know you. But you have to be careful flashing coin or barter goods about. You might walk in alone but then leave with several interested people following behind."

Miranda wasn't satisfied with his answer. She stopped in her tracks as she realized what was lacking: any sense of people trying to improve their lot. This felt like a place where people were just marking time.

Murray led the way to what felt like the outskirts of town, being more tumbledown and seemingly abandoned than the city center. It was marked by tottering piles of garbage—discarded, filthy rags too tattered for housework and broken bits of buildings in pieces too small and rotted to use for repairs. And the smell. Pipes tentacled up from the ground; green, gray, and brown stuff the thickness of pie filling oozed from holes in the pipes. Murray pulled face masks and gloves from his pack. "There are sanitary pipes to pull the sewage out of the city proper, but they break down a lot, and repairs are sketchy," he said. "We don't want to stay here long. It's not healthy. Gather up pieces of wood and cloth for burning. Make sure whatever you grab is clean, and don't go near the pipes."

He grabbed some sticks and stacked them on the ground. "Make a pile," he said. "Enough to burn for a day. I wish we had a cart."

Miranda looked at the piles of trash, steaming in the warm rain, and shuddered. She grabbed what looked like sticks attached to cloth, a tent of some kind. As she shook it, small fuzzy creatures fell out and squeaked away. She jumped and squeaked herself with alarm. The cloth was coated with droppings. She couldn't bring herself to pull the cloth from the sticks, then she remembered her knife in its sheath and cut the cloth away. *Fifteen minutes of burning, anyway*, she thought. She knew it was just her imagination, but her skin felt squirmy and itchy, as if the things that lived in the garbage heaps were crawling up the legs and arms of her scaleskin. She couldn't help but compare this to the garbage disposal in Sanctuary, where magcarts brought refuse for recycling and disposing. Everything, including the magcarts, would be sanitized after use and gleaming. It was hard to believe that in Sanctuary, disposal was considered a dirty occupation.

She noticed that Murray had assembled a pile of battered wooden objects while she was woolgathering. The old-fashioned term made her smile.

"I'm impressed," she said. "How did you find all this?"

He surveyed the pile critically. "It's not much," he replied. "The depleted ground is getting too fragile to support two-story buildings. Each rainy season, more fall down. Any debris is scavenged for repairs. There's not much left for firewood. COS won't be a city in a few years, just a collection of hovels, if things don't change."

Miranda noted with surprise that he seemed sad at the idea, which was at odds with his carefree attitude on the road. She hadn't seen anything about City of the South that made her give a damn about its future. It could wash into the sea, if the sea still existed, for all she cared.

Murray looked at his pile and at her much smaller pile. "We'll leave yours for another time," he said tactfully. "We have enough for a couple of days, which may be all we need. Let's head back."

SANCTUARY

CHAPTER TWENTY-SEVEN

Alex was woken by his father rather than by a child or Birna. "Woken" was probably not the appropriate term. Alex woke up on his own to see his father sitting on a chair beside his cot. How long had he been sitting there? Alex knew he sometimes talked in his sleep. He looked sharply at his father, but Peter's eyes gave nothing away.

"We have a busy day," he said. "Let's get started with some basic things to get you more comfortable in COS."

Alex realized he had apparently passed some test involving the family, which he supposed was a good thing. Even if he didn't plan to stay forever, he didn't want to be immediately kicked out. His thoughts drifted back to the girl he had met yesterday. She was pretty, maybe even beautiful, but there were plenty of pretty girls in Sanctuary. She just seemed, he groped mentally for the term, she seemed more aware than the kids his age in Sanctuary. She seemed like someone he could talk to, maybe even hang out with. Thinking about her reminded him of the other girl he had met, Agarita One, with the scarred face. He mentally kicked himself for thinking first thing about her face. There was probably a sad story behind it.

While he was mentally processing the previous day, his dad was moving around his room. He positioned the chair next to a table with a basin and some sort of small rod.

His father motioned for him to sit on the chair and asked him to tilt his head back. Alex was still only half awake and did what he was told. His father seized the slender metal rod. Alex realized, too late, that there was something attached to its end that his father shoved up his nostril. It was painful and caused Alex to cry out.

He started to rise from the chair, but his father restrained him, attached another small square and shoved into the other nostril. His nose felt enormous, swollen and burning. He glared at his father through watery eyes.

"It will burn and itch for a while, but you'll get used to it," his father advised. "These are very fine nose screens. They don't interfere with breathing, but they keep most of the dust out of your throat and lungs. Birna also found you some clothes that will probably fit. Get dressed and we'll get breakfast and do a bit of work before visiting the town."

Alex didn't respond. He was angry that he was given no explanation and no choice in what happened to his body. His mother was not the easiest person, but at least she treated him like an adult, not a child. He sensed there would be many boundaries crossed by his dad, and this probably wasn't the time to take a stand. He was also excited about seeing the city itself.

After breakfast, his dad took him to the bee enclosure and left him. Aggie was dressed in her hat with mesh mask and gloves. She motioned to him to come out to the hives. He grabbed a hat and gloves from the box at the enclosure door and put them on.

He sniffed the air and was disappointed to find it wasn't as fragrant as the day before, although he could still smell sweetness. Aggie showed him how to pull the white, sticky frames out of their slots in the hives. She did it so smoothly, no angry bees swarmed out to investigate. She still hadn't looked directly at him, whether from indifference or because she was feeling as shy around a boy her age as he felt with her, he couldn't tell. They carried the frames back to the lab.

Alex saw that each frame was layered on both sides with a thick porous material in a beautiful waffle pattern that was clumped with white deposits. "This is the honeycomb that holds the honey extruded by the bees in place," she explained. "The white coating is called capping." She grabbed a knife on a nearby bench and expertly sliced the capping off. It came off in sheets and pieces, which she placed in a battered metal tray.

Alex reached over to touch the comb that remained. Hexagonal shapes created a large golden mesh. "It's amazing," he said. The honey came off on his fingers in sticky droplets. He started to brush his fingers off against the frame, but Aggie stopped him.

"Don't waste it," she said. "This is our reward." She ran a slender finger lightly over the comb and then placed the dripping finger in her mouth. Alex followed her example. Warm and sweet. He had never liked sweet things like packfruit, but this was different, as natural to swallow as water or air. He looked up to find Aggie smiling at him. She turned solemn as soon as he noticed. He looked away, but the moment had changed to something else. Something as thick as the honey dripping into a large bucket underneath the frame.

"How do you get the honey out of the comb?" His voice sounded stilted and odd. He wasn't sure what was going on. He wasn't attracted to this girl. In fact, he wasn't sure he even liked her. His reaction to Ada was much simpler. Once he'd met Ada, he hadn't given Aggie another thought. And yet. He was definitely feeling a warmth that wasn't just the honey coating his lips and oozing down his throat.

As if to help him out, Aggie brushed her curly hair behind her ear, exposing the red puffy scar to its full extent. Alex looked away, although once you knew about it, it wasn't really much of a distraction. He cleared his throat. "What do you want me to do?"

Instead of answering, she tilted his head sideways and studied him. "Your nose is bleeding," she said. "I'm guessing you had the nose screens inserted."

He nodded sheepishly. "It hurt," he said, "a lot."

"And you can't smell much," she said sympathetically. "Don't worry. It heals quickly. By the time of the party, you'll be able to smell the amazing perfume the girls wear."

"How do you know about the party? Are you invited?"

She laughed outright. "Don't be ridiculous. I'm nobody at all, just one of your father's workers. If I wasn't deformed, I'd probably be serving at it. But Peter lets me make and barter perfume on the side from the agarita blossoms. Once the bees have extracted what they need, your dad has no further interest in the flowers. I got a bunch of orders for perfume that had to be ready in two days. I figured it out. I guess they know there will be somebody new to dance with. That doesn't happen often in COS. So, what did you think of the beautiful Ada?"

Alex turned red from his neck to his spiky hair. Somehow, he was going to have to get comfortable working with this girl. "She seemed nice enough," he answered cautiously. "Very friendly."

"As long as it serves her purpose," Agarita One responded.

That seemed very unfair, but Alex didn't pursue it. He cleared his throat again.

"That will go away in a few days too," she told him. "And you've already stopped coughing. You will definitely be a sensation at the party." Her voice was gently mocking.

Alex refused to take the bait. "So, how do you get the honey out?" he repeated patiently. "I'd like to get started before my dad takes me into town." He couldn't keep the excitement from his voice.

"You're going to town?" she asked. "You and Peter?"

He nodded and wondered again how she was on such easy first-name terms with his dad.

"Yes, well, I'm going to press the comb against this fine mesh in the bucket," she said, showing Alex that halfway down there was a screen with a mesh so tiny it was almost invisible, just a distortion wavering in the bottom of the bucket. They leaned over the bucket together and bumped heads. "Sorry," he said, backing up so rapidly he almost knocked the remaining frames off the table. He straightened the frames in time, before he could look like a complete idiot. Aggie didn't say anything as she pressed her lips together to stop a smile from forming.

Once the honey was scraped and drained into a rich, gleaming pool, Aggie snapped off a small piece of the honeycomb and popped it in her mouth. She broke off another piece for him. Alex looked around, remembering the trouble he had caused with the chee.

"It's okay; we're just testing it," she said. The rationale she offered made him realize she was breaking a rule. He shook his head.

She popped the second piece in her mouth. "That's okay. You can have as much as you want in a few days, when it is served as a treat at the party." She placed the white shavings into a large pot and carried it outside to a tripod over a small pit with burning wood turning to ash. The white facings began to soften and bubble. Aggie described the consistency she wanted it cooked to and left him watching and occasionally stirring the facings.

"I'll take the honeycomb to the kitchen and be back to check on you," she said. Alex noticed that she broke off another large piece of the honeycomb and slipped it into her pocket.

When Aggie returned, she stuck a metal stick with numbers into the bubbling mix and pronounced the facings, which she now called beeswax, ready to go. She set out cans and jars ready for pouring to create the candles they used for nighttime light in City of the South, but first she placed a little of the melted wax in Alex's palm. As it coated his palm, he saw the lines spring to life through the translucent wax. "You have a handful of stars," Aggie told him. "That means a life of adventure."

SANCTUARY

"Not so far," Alex replied. His voice was husky, and he hoped she would attribute it to the nose screens. He wasn't used to strange people touching him.

She traced a line across the fleshy part of his palm, which sent a shivery reaction through his body. "This is the lifeline. Have you ever heard of that?"

"No," he replied. His voice was barely a croak. What was wrong with him, anyway? He had interacted with girls before, at school and on his very occasional dates. As she bent over his hand, her curly head brought up a memory—a documentary about gypsies they had watched in story making, a lifetime ago. Aggie was very much like the fortune-teller. He wondered if she had gypsy blood. Her curls brushed his hand and arm. He realized her hair was the color of the honey. Where her curls brushed his skin, it responded by burning, as if in a fire.

Her voice changed. "This is a funny break," she said. "It looks like a very short life, but then the line takes up again. Like maybe you have two lives."

Alex thought about his life in Sanctuary, where every day drifted almost imperceptibly into the next, and then about City of the South. It was hard to believe this was only his second day.

"Very possibly," he said.

A cough made both of them look up. Peter was standing just a few feet away, watching.

Alex saw that Aggie was disconcerted, for the first time since he had met her.

"We didn't hear you come in," she told Peter.

"I can see that," he replied drily. "How are the tapers for the party coming along?"

"I'm just going to pour some box candles, and then I will make them."

"Don't neglect them for your perfume," he replied. "Or anything else."

She didn't respond, just bowed her head.

Peter motioned for Alex to follow him.

Alex started to talk about honeycomb. Peter cut him short. "We'll move to the fields tomorrow," he replied. "That's where the real work happens."

Alex could tell by Peter's tone that he had displeased his dad again. Anger flared up against Aggie. He didn't ask her to grab his hand for her silly fortune-telling. Peter led him through a maze of rooms. He caught glimpses of children carrying digging tools and dragging sacks. They walked past an entire room of children gnawing on what looked like bread and chee. The children looked up silently as they passed. Those closest to the door scrambled back into the shadows. His dad didn't say anything, and neither did the children. Alex couldn't help but compare the children in COS to the schools and parks of his childhood. He remembered how hard it was not to yell and run around until you reached the park, to get rid of some of the fizzy energy that filled your little body. But there was no point in asking or commenting. Two days in COS were teaching him to say only what had to be said.

Peter led him to a courtyard with a double-locked door in a thick wall. He unlocked both locks with a key on wire around his neck. The wire was almost invisible, and Alex had never noticed its presence. There was apparently no one in the courtyard, but Alex had the sensation of being watched and, when he turned around, saw a movement that might have been someone hastily turning a corner or could just be his own jumpy imagination. He rocked from one foot to the other, in a hurry to get outside. Yesterday they had traveled to the family compound through underground tunnels. Today, despite the beauty of the bee enclosure, Alex felt the same claustrophobia he experienced in Sanctuary creeping over him.

The road, when they stepped outside, did nothing to dispel his hemmed-in feeling. Alex looked around while his dad carefully relocked the door. This was no Sanctuary streetway but a crooked street barely wide enough for the handcarts Alex had observed people pushing toward City of the South.

Buildings brushed up against the streetway, a jumble of two-story houses that jutted crookedly over the road, like block towers that a child would build. In fact, what he could see looked like a child's idea of a town. A few shabby beggars stepped forward as Alex and Peter moved into the road, but they turned away with mumbled apologies when they recognized Peter. Peter ignored them and led the way down the street.

Alex observed the buildings curiously. The downstairs windows were blocked with wooden shutters or stuffed with rags and paper. People hung out of the upstairs windows, watching their progress or talking with neighbors. Some called out to Peter in querulous tones in that abbreviated speech Alex couldn't understand.

"Ma so," a woman hanging ragged clothing stopped to say. She reached a hand over her rickety fence to pluck at Peter. "Twa mo," she said insistently. "Twa mo."

Peter smiled stiffly and pulled his sleeve away.

"What was she asking you?" Alex asked.

"Her son," his father replied indifferently. "She hasn't seen him in two months."

"Why is she asking you?"

"Who knows? He could be working on the farm. Or he might have been killed in the street."

They were walking downhill.

"So, where we are living is built on a hill?"

"The administrative complex. And surrounded by a wall. Easier to defend that way."

As they moved away from the complex, the road widened, and Alex saw more people milling around. They stopped to watch them pass in sullen silence but looked away whenever Alex caught their gaze.

GRACE J. AGNEW

As they rounded a corner, something came rushing out of a doorway and crashed into Alex, knocking him down. A man straddled his chest, crushing the breath out of him, followed by a small child who stuck his fingers roughly in the pocket of Peter's cast-off pants.

"I don't have anything!" Alex panted. Things were going dark.

The man was pulled roughly off Alex. The little boy jumped on him, taking his father's place. He was aware of his father holding the man at arm's length before kicking him very hard in the stomach. The man doubled over, and the little boy left Alex to grab Peter's knee. Peter shook off the little boy, but it gave the man time to straighten up. Alex saw he had something shiny in his hand.

"Look out, a knife!" Alex cried.

His father reached into his breast pocket, pulled out his own knife, and slashed the man.

Alex watched in horror as a wide red line bloomed on the man's throat. His angry face turned stupid and slack as he dropped to his knees.

"Da!" the little boy cried, placing his hands on his father's throat to stop the bleeding.

Alex was frozen in shock. His father grabbed his arm and pulled him along.

As he came to his senses, Alex dug his feet into the dust. "We need to get a healer!"

His father stopped. "Are you hurt?"

"No, the man," he said. "We may be able to save him."

"There's no saving him," his father said. "I don't fight to wound. If he's lucky, he's already dead. COS is not very gentle to armed robbers."

"His son," Alex started.

"Is following in his father's footsteps. He was trying to kill you."

They stopped at a building that had actual windows on the

ground floor. Through a window, Alex could see a man with a measuring tape in his hand dancing around someone who looked familiar. He was dazed and ill from the encounter with the robbers and hoped he wouldn't throw up on any of the bolts of cloth he saw stacked about.

"Lord Darwin," Peter said smoothly and bowed his head. A slight pressure on Alex's arm reminded him to do the same.

Darwin didn't say anything. His head nod in return was almost imperceptible.

"Tomorrow?" he said to the tailor.

"Absolutely, Lord Darwin, or the next morning at the—" The tailor broke off as Darwin's bushy brows furrowed together. "Tomorrow," he agreed hastily.

"Morning," Darwin said. The man gulped but nodded wordlessly.

As Darwin turned to go, he looked Peter and Alex over. "What have you been up to?" he asked with a sneer that was almost a smile.

"Alex worked with the bees this morning." Peter replied. "Honeycomb for the party."

"I need to see these precious bees. They seem pretty vicious." He nodded at Peter's shirt. "Looks like they have drawn blood."

Peter looked down at his shirt. "We had a dustup with some robbers," he said. "Easily handled."

"I'll send someone by first thing tomorrow," Darwin told the tailor. "And I'll see you and sonny at my niece's birthday party, if you make it back from the city in one piece."

Peter bowed slightly and then turned his back on Darwin to confer with the tailor.

Darwin strode out of the store and up the street. His face was a thundercloud. When he reached the street where the robber lay tumbled in the dirt, he paused for a moment, long enough for the man's son to charge out of a doorway and grab his leg. The brat was sniveling about something. Darwin tossed a coin into the dirt to shut him up, although it was more than he deserved, since they had failed to do what they were told. But there were people glaring and muttering from doorways. And he didn't have time to whip them all into silence.

The tailor held the measuring tape from Alex's waist to ankle. "Ta," he said.

"He is," Peter replied. "Just tailor some barter clothes you already have to fit him. I know you have a big order for Lord Darwin to see to."

As the tailor went into another room, Peter turned to Alex.

"Will you be all right if I run an errand?"

Alex nodded.

"I don't think I have to tell you to stay in this building. You will be safe enough here. There aren't too many tailors about. No one is going to threaten someone with his skill."

The tailor returned with several shirts and pairs of pants, none of them particularly clean. He motioned to Alex to put them on, even though he was exposed to view through the window. Alex was already learning that modesty was not a concept, much less a virtue, in City of the South.

He took off his shirt, which the little boy had torn, and pulled a new shirt over his head.

As he did, he noticed a woman in a cloak passing with her little boy. Just great. He was lucky he was still wearing his pants. The woman wasn't interested, anyway. As she passed, the hood of her cloak fell away, revealing long, curly hair and a puffy pink scar that curved from—

Alex almost cried out. Aggie! And the child with her, also in a hood and cloak. Wasn't that Corn Seven?

241

SANCTUARY

CHAPTER TWENTY-EIGHT

Miranda woke to the sound of Murray's gentle snoring a few arm's lengths away. She could hear his da snorting and gurgling in the bed in the next room. The woody smell from the stove was a slight improvement over the coal pieces of yesterday, but otherwise, as near as Miranda could tell, the homes of City of the South were the same as the outside—except, if anything, the buildings seemed in even more tumbledown condition. The sooner they found Alex and got out of here, the better.

Murray raised himself up on one elbow.

"What's on the agenda for today?" she asked.

He looked at her quizzically. "I'll sniff about, ask some questions," he replied. "You will be safe enough here."

Miranda's heart sank. A whole day sitting next to the smelly stove watching the old man soil himself. She didn't think she could bear it.

"I want to go with you," she protested. "I need to look for my son."

"Alex isn't lost in the wild," Murray explained patiently. "He's with his father, and Peter is a really big man in this town. He can have us thrown out of COS, if we're lucky, and in prison if we're not. It's not a question of finding your son, but getting you a private moment with him so you can make your case."

"Make my case!" Miranda said indignantly. "Alex is a minor! What Peter did is kidnapping."

"Possibly, in Sanctuary. But people Alex's age in COS are usually partnered and on their second kid by now. Anyway, Peter had a reason for luring Alex here, and Alex agreed with that reason. Unless that hasn't panned out, Alex is not going to come with you of his own free will, and we can't force him."

Miranda felt the hopelessness of her situation wash over her. "You're right," she admitted. "Alex came here of his own free will. Assuming they made it."

"That I was already able to determine," Murray said. "Ol' Pete is back. And he had a young stranger with him."

They looked up at a shuffling noise. The old man stood in the doorway. He tottered past them and leaned against the rotting jamb. They heard the splashing as he relieved himself.

"I'll have to hope that Alex is finding COS as unpleasant as I am," Miranda muttered to herself.

"He's living in the administrative compound," Murray responded drily, "so probably not. On the other hand, if he's a smart boy, he is already figuring out that life in COS isn't exactly what he expected." He nodded toward his da, who was now edging to his seat by the fire. "How old would you guess he is?"

"Seventy?" Miranda hazarded.

"He's not yet sixty."

Miranda was stunned. She thought of Tara, who was fifty-one and at the height of her powers.

"A COS life won't be a boring life," Murray remarked, "but even for the rulers, it's not very long. Something you might mention to Alex when you meet up with him."

Murray brought out three more beet pies. Miranda was as hungry as the old man, and when he looked over at her hopefully, she had nothing left but a shower of crumbs, and those she gathered up with a moistened finger and ate herself.

"I won't be too long," Murray promised. "We can gather more fire supplies when I return." He spoke as if going to the noxious city outskirts with their overflowing pipes was a treat. Miranda looked at the old man as he sank down to his collarbone on his chair for the morning nap. I guess treats in COS are relative, she thought wryly.

The backless stool that fell to Miranda's lot was not comfortable enough for prolonged sitting. Miranda tried her bedroll, but the floor wasn't much of an improvement over the stool. She walked around the house, from room to room, but there was not much to snoop other than to discover a very smelly lean-to that she guessed was where the old man did the other necessary evacuation. Her stomach moved queasily, and she realized she was going to need a similar place, but not that.

She was forced to go outside to see if she could find any sort of private area where she could be alone with her needs. She fingered the waterskins, packfruits, and coins in her pockets, prepared to barter for working plumbing or, failing that, at least some slightly more sanitary private space to be alone with her thoughts.

The street outside was deserted. She looked back at the old man before stepping through the doorway in case he had been told to sound the alarm if she left, but he was fast asleep by the fire. She almost skittered down the road, looking up hopefully at the second-story windows, prepared to make eye contact with anyone who showed up. A woman came to the window. Miranda stopped and craned her neck, shading her eyes against the relative brightness of the City of the South sieve roof. A shower of debris, small rocks and sticks, fell around her and into her open mouth. She could just make out a woman shaking and folding a rug, as well as the laughing mouths of several small children. There was no doubt this was deliberately done. Miranda's cheeks burned as she moved hastily away.

As she turned a corner, she felt something sharp bite into her heel and stumbled to one knee. She quickly righted herself and whirled about. A very small child, a young girl with dirty, tousled hair, was batting a ball with a stick. She grinned at Miranda with widely spaced teeth.

Miranda examined her ankle. A scratch was forming with red dots where the skin was broken.

"Did you poke me with that stick?" she asked.

The girl looked at her with round eyes and poked a grubby finger in her mouth in response. She was a cherubic looking child, despite the fact that her face was patched and brown with caked dirt.

"Don't do that again!" Miranda said sharply. She turned around to continue walking but whirled back when she heard movement, just in time to step away from the plunging stick. She grabbed the stick. The girl held on very tightly for such a small child and began to howl. Miranda jumped when she was poked sharply in the back. She dropped the stick she was tugging. A larger child, this one a boy, had poked her back with another sharp stick. As she glared at her new attacker, the little girl poked at her ankle again.

"Stop it!" Miranda cried out. Backing toward the wall of the house she was passing, she felt a stabbing pain in her side. A third child, a larger girl, this one maybe eleven or twelve. She jabbed expertly with her stick, placing it behind Miranda's knees and pulling her forward with a sharp thrust. Miranda found herself losing her balance, her arms moving in front of her to break her fall. She landed hard onto her knees and then rolled onto her back. The three children hovered over her solemnly, sharp sticks raised and pointed at her stomach. Beyond them, through her tears, Miranda could see people peering out of windows, but no one moved or made a sound.

"Help me!" Miranda cried. They waited expectantly. Miranda realized the most they would do is help themselves to their share of whatever the children took off her body.

She closed her eyes so she wouldn't see the sticks piercing her. She felt movement rather than pain. The youngest child began howling again. "Enough of that," a girl's voice said harshly. "Get off home before I call a guard."

Miranda opened her eyes to see an arm reaching toward her instead of a stick. She was almost too shaky to rise. She grabbed the slender hand gratefully.

"Are you okay?" the girl, a teenager, asked.

"Mostly," Miranda said cautiously. As she stood, the air around her turned cold and darkness lapped the edges of her vision. The girl led her to the wall to rest against it. Miranda doubled up with stomach cramps.

"Actually, I do need something," Miranda said. She lowered her voice, embarrassed. "A bathroom."

The girl laughed. "Come with me to my home," she said, "I'll fix you up."

The girl pulled the hood of her cloak over her face so Miranda couldn't see her features. Miranda realized it probably wasn't seen as an act of heroism to prevent the children from disabling and robbing a stranger. She felt even more grateful for what the girl was risking.

Her gratitude turned to puzzlement when the girl entered the same doorway Miranda had exited just a few minutes earlier. Her bewilderment grew when the girl called out sharply, "Da!"

"He doesn't need to spend the whole day sleeping," she muttered in an annoyed tone.

Miranda didn't respond. If this was her da, what did that make Murray? Her brother? He seemed too old for that. Her father? No relation at all?

The girl led Miranda through the shotgun to the kitchen. She opened a door that Miranda had assumed was a cupboard, but which proved to be an opening to a pitcher and water basin and a lean-to with the familiar-looking stool.

Miranda almost shed tears of relief. "I assumed the shack in the back was the only place."

247

The girl laughed slightly but turned her head away in embarrassment. "Da uses that. I used to try to keep it clean, but it's not possible. He can't work the latch to get in here."

Miranda brushed past her gratefully. When she returned to the main room, the girl had renewed the wood in the stove. She nodded toward the two bedrolls.

"I assume Murray brought you here?"

Miranda nodded cautiously. She didn't know how much to tell this girl.

"You don't seem like one of his usual rescues," the girl said. "In fact, you talk like Sanctuary."

"I am Sanctuary," Miranda was startled into admitting. The girl took off her cloak and hung it in the kitchen. When she returned, Miranda saw a red, jagged scar from her left eye down to her chin. The girl lifted her chin defiantly, daring Miranda to say anything.

"Gur . . . ya gah foo?" The old man said as he sat up from his nap.

In response, the girl reached into her cloak and brought out a golden crust of something, which the old man snatched eagerly. Something golden and sticky dripped down his chin.

"He had a pie for breakfast," Miranda said. The old man glared at her.

"I can't get here every day," the girl replied. "I try to overfeed him when I come."

"He seems very well taken care of," Miranda replied.

The girl snorted. "Not if you ask him." When she spoke harshly, Miranda could hear the resemblance to the da, even if she couldn't see it. Despite the puffy scar, the girl's features were delicate. She would be a beauty if she kept half her face hidden.

"How long are you staying?" the girl asked.

Miranda answered honestly. "I don't know. I hope not for very long."

The door pushed open, and Murray was in the room.

"What are you doing here?" he asked the girl. "Did you get permission to leave the compound?"

"None of your business, and why are you foisting guests on my da?"

"He's fine with it," Murray responded shortly. "She has a lot to barter with, so he's eating well. That's all he cares about."

The girl looked away. "He used to care about more than that," she muttered.

Murray didn't respond. "Have the two of you met?" he asked.

"I found her outside," the girl replied sullenly. "She wasn't doing too well. You should warn her about wandering around on her own."

Murray shot Miranda a look but didn't say anything.

"Thank you for helping her," he replied.

Miranda decided to take some control. Murray was working for her, after all, not the other way around.

She stepped toward the girl with a hand outstretched for shaking. When the girl ignored it, she dropped her arm to her side. She took a deep breath.

"I'm Miranda," she said. "I appreciate your help this morning. Your—Murray—is helping me retrieve . . . something . . . that I lost. I didn't realize this was your place, and that we would need permission."

The girl had the grace to look embarrassed. "It's not my place, or his," she said, nodding at Murray. "It's Da's. And he's right. As long as you supply food and fire, he doesn't care if you stay." She looked Miranda directly in the face. "And you are welcome to use my . . . things." She and Miranda smiled at each other over the shared secret.

"Can you stay for a while?" Murray asked? "You could help us find what we are looking for."

The girl's face closed down. "I've stayed longer than I should. I just wanted to look in on Da. I have to get back to my bees. How long are you staying?"

"Not long," Murray answered. "A week or two at most."

"I'll stop back," the girl replied. "We can talk then." She didn't indicate a day or time, just nodded briefly at each of them in turn and slipped out the door.

"Who is that?" Miranda asked curiously. "Why do you both call the old man Da? He can't be father to both of you."

"He's no relation to me," Murray responded.

"Should you have told the girl so much?" she asked. "What relation is she to you? Can we trust her?"

"I'd trust her with my life," Murray replied. Even though it was only midday, he stretched out on his bedroll and turned his back to her, indicating the conversation was closed. The old man was already slumped in repose after all the excitement. From what little Miranda had seen, people in COS seemed to sleep a lot.

"Well, she doesn't seem to like you very much," Miranda responded.

Murray didn't answer. Miranda stretched out on her bedroll. She'd let him get over whatever funk the sight of the girl had put him in before she asked anything else.

GRACE J. AGNEW

CHAPTER TWENTY-NINE

Alex didn't sleep well. He couldn't escape the eyes of the little boy, the way he had frantically pressed his fingers against his father's neck to try to stop the bleeding. If the man really did die, how would the boy survive? Did he have a mother, older siblings? Somehow, Alex doubted it. And he felt guilty, as if it were his fault by merely existing. He was a stranger, walking around looking at things like a tourist instead of watching for danger. If he hadn't been such an easy target, the man would still be alive. And his father! He had wounded that man—a mortal wound—with no more thought than killing a bug. No doubt he was sleeping soundly.

Somehow, Alex finally drifted off and woke to his father gently shaking him. He had a piece of bread with chee in his hand. Alex had been too shaken to eat dinner, so he was hungry and wolfed it down. His stomach was getting used to the food.

"You're going to see the heart of my enterprise today," his father said, sounding almost eager. "I needed to wait until you had nose guards in place."

He took Alex out the back door where they had entered COS a few days ago. They walked in a different direction about ten minutes and then Alex stopped, frozen in astonishment. The bee enclosure had been fascinating, but what he saw now he couldn't even put the words together to describe.

"It's paradise," he said simply.

His father didn't respond but placed his hand on Alex's shoulder and gripped it gently.

251

Alex saw mounds of green and gold as far as the eye could see, with leafy plants undulating in the breeze and paths crossing between them stitching a giant quilt. The fields were surrounded by a high rusty metal fence with jagged edges that Alex recalled as barbed wire from history stories.

"The three sisters," his father breathed into his ear. "Sweet corn, pole beans, and butternut squash. The pole beans pull nitrogen from the air to enrich the soil, the corn provides support for the beans. You'll find them twisted up the stalks. The squash keeps the soil cool and moist. Its broad leaves protect the soil from washing away when the rain comes crashing down, and as the plants die, they enrich the soil."

"How did you manage this?" Alex asked.

"It wasn't easy," his father answered, the pride unmistakable in his voice. "My grandparents had a farm. They grew pole beans. I had to find the farm and fight the squatters there, and of course everything was about dead, but I was able to save some bean shoots. I grew just beans for years, to enrich the soil together with the earthworms. We had to go looking for the corn and squash. We used stories of yesteryear to help us find likely locations. Many lives were lost."

He was silent a minute then continued. "We started with one mound, but once we had plants and we created decent soil, we were able to expand. We can feed the entire City of the South with these."

Alex thought about the skinny little boy he had seen yesterday. He didn't look like someone who ever got a full plate of beans.

"You'll be working with the corn team to harvest corn today," Peter said, leading the way carefully through the barbed-wire thicket to the first mound.

The enchantment didn't fade as they got closer. If anything, it intensified. The corn towered overhead, entwined by green vines that made Alex think of the fairy tale "Jack in the Beanstalk." The story had been a favorite, particularly the idea that you could climb a green ladder and escape to a magical land. He couldn't help but feel that the story had come true for him. If he could stay at this mound forever, safely encased in gold and green, never interacting with the inhabitants of COS, life would be—

A hand plucked at his shirt and he looked down into the solemn face of Corn Seven. The events of yesterday, particularly seeing Aggie hand in hand with Corn Seven, came flooding back, but Alex didn't say anything. He was pretty sure they hadn't seen him, and he sensed that they would be very alarmed if they knew.

He looked around and saw that Peter was gone. He heard loud rustling among the stalks and realized a small army of children—the corn kids, he mentally labeled them—were stripping corn off the stalks and popping them into cloth bags. Corn Seven showed him how to do it, with a quick lift and a twist. It took him a few minutes to learn, but then he was much faster than anyone else because he was taller. The others had to carefully bend the stalks to remove the corn, being careful not to damage the encircling bean vines. But no matter how comfortable the task became, Corn Seven was faster and neater. His straw-colored hair blended with the stalks so that it was hard to tell boy from stalk. He was almost a blur as he carefully stripped the ears from the stalks without damaging stalks, beans, or the squash roots that tangled underfoot and caused Alex and the others to trip. Alex watched and realized that despite his small size, Corn Seven was in charge of the others. They brought undersized ears to him to inspect, as well as finished bags to size up for fullness before they were tied. Alex was sure he was, at most, seven or eight. He was impressed to the point of a lump in his throat by the pride Corn Seven showed for his work, the gentle authority he exerted over boys and girls that were taller and clearly much older. His dad must have made this happen. Alex found himself rethinking his father, whom he had dismissed last night as practically a barbarian. Would he ever figure him out?

When his father collected him at the end of the day, he was completely exhausted but happy. He ate a quick dinner and tumbled into bed, untroubled by regrets or bad dreams. He worked with Corn Seven and the others for a couple of days. On the last day of harvest, Corn Seven invited him to join the others for a meal. Alex found that by listening to the corn kids as they worked, he was getting the hang of outsider English. His dad overheard the invitation. Alex looked at him, and his dad nodded.

Corn Seven took him to the empty dirt yard next door to the warehouse where they stored the corn. The other children were already stacking debris—old clothes, broken furniture. Corn Seven lit a candle, perhaps one that Alex had helped Aggie to make, and started the bonfire. He showed Alex how to stick his ear of corn on a sharp stick for roasting. Alex ate two. He had never tasted anything so good. If this is what he left Sanctuary for, if he could work with these children and ignore the things he didn't like—Birna, who still sniffed at him and only answered his questions when his dad was around, the city, the family—he would be okay. He still missed his mother, most often at night when he couldn't sleep, but the rest of Sanctuary seemed as unreal as a dream.

His stomach twisted when he thought of the family. He was eager to see Ada again. To see if the immediate attraction he felt still held, but he hadn't liked the brothers, and he particularly didn't like the fact that the elder brother, Darwin, clearly hated his dad and him as well. Tomorrow he would be having dinner with them, but he would rather just roast corn with his fellow workers, for the rest of his life if he could.

Peter made sure Alex allotted plenty of time to get ready in the clothes that had been tailored to fit him. Peter picked up the clothes alone. COS was a city best experienced in very small doses. The tailor had a bruised neck that he kept fingering gently, and he spoke in a whisper. Peter assumed that Darwin had not liked the bill. He overpaid the tailor by almost twice, which made the tailor teary eyed. Peter wasn't turning soft. This man was the only decent tailor left, and Peter hoped he might have need of his services for wedding finery soon.

When Alex presented himself for the party, Peter could tell that even Birna, who didn't like or trust Alex, was impressed. This was important, because Birna had been sent to him by the family. Her family had been their house servants from the earliest days, before there was much of a house to serve, and her loyalty ran deep. Peter had no reason to complain about Birna. She kept a large agricultural organization running smoothly. If the children obeyed out of fear rather than loyalty, the point was that they obeyed. It was rare that a worker had to be expelled. Peter knew that Birna was probably still a little in love with him. One night years ago, after an early, successful harvest on a very full moon, she had proven herself a tireless lover. But he had never repeated the occasion, and he still thanked the moon whenever it was full for watching over them and preventing Birna from becoming pregnant. When he took up with another worker, who did become pregnant, Birna said nothing. But she decided henceforth that all workers would be children. Fourteen was the cutoff age.

When a child turned fourteen, he or she was given a gold coin and a small pie in a ceremony and returned to their families. Peter didn't know what they did then. Private gardens were forbidden. The family controlled the food supply, which was doled out monthly, supposedly based on a complicated formula to reward good behavior, but more likely based on patronage and buying off silence after the rampages of Darwin and his rowdy hunting companions. Peter didn't think about it. COS was mostly a loss anyway, its people barely human. Peter had long-term plans, but they didn't involve COS.

"You look good, Alex," he said. Alex had filled out a bit on the fresh air, hard work, and food. Although the sun could rarely be seen through the cloud cover, it was there invisibly working, giving Alex's skin a ruddy glow. Alex had his unruly hair, but the grease they used tamed it, although it still spiked into tufts, just as his did.

"Shall we go?" he asked. Alex nodded, and they walked side by side to the tunnel that connected to the family compound.

Alex felt unreal walking beside his dad. He felt disembodied, except his hands and feet were cold with excitement. He was anxious to see Ada again, but he had already realized that the secret to a good life in COS, for him at least, was forgetting that the brothers existed, and he suspected his father felt the same.

Peter and Alex were invited for dinner before the small dance planned for Ada's sixteenth birthday. Peter made sure that Alex understood that being invited to the dinner beforehand was an honor. It was an honor Alex felt he could probably do without.

Peter and Alex were greeted at the door by Walden; his wife, in some ways an older version of Ada but dark and exotic with slanting eyes; and then by Ada herself, a vision in a blue floor-length gown. Alex felt hot and cold, his heart beat so loudly he could hardly hear the introductions. His father kissed Ada's mother's hand. Was he expected to do that? Instead he brushed her fingers lightly with his, conscious of all the callouses on his fingers from plucking corn. He did the same with Ada, and the shock of her cool fingers on his tingled down to his toes.

"Darwin has said he will be detained and will join us sometime during the meal, so we'll go right in. I know the young people are eager for dancing." Ada's mother had her same clear voice.

"We're having Ada's favorite meal—noodles, and of course fresh corn that Peter sent up." The mother nodded graciously at Peter.

GRACE J. AGNEW

Wine was poured into actual stemmed glasses and not the battered
cups used in COS or the utilitarian growfiber vessels that were also
used for soup in Sanctuary.

Darwin proposed a toast to Ada, which gave Alex the excuse he
needed to look directly at her, something he hadn't had the nerve
to do after the first glance. He found her looking back at him.
Her eyes were large and brown with thick fringed lashes, the only
feature that didn't resemble her mother. Unfortunately, they were
crinkled with laughter, which Alex was all too familiar with from
the girls in Sanctuary. However, when they raised the glasses in
the toast, Ada leaned over the table to tap her glass against Alex's,
something she didn't need to do.

He took a cautious sip after the toast and coughed as the sharp,
citrus-flavored liquid went down.

"Alex isn't used to wine," his dad said in amusement. "I doubt
that he got any in Sanctuary."

"Now, Sanctuary is a place that interests me," Ada's mother said.
"Is it as bad as it seems, with guardians everywhere watching your
every move? Have you ever been arrested by a guardian?"

"That's not all that common," Alex said. "The DPs—digital
personas—keep people from getting into trouble. You rarely see a
guardian. Most people live their lives very freely."

"That's what I keep telling Mother," Ada spoke up. "She needs
to stop listening to the stories she sees on COSLine. Sanctuary is
a very civilized place. I'd like to visit."

"I can't help but wonder why you left Sanctuary," Ada's mother
said, a hint of ice in her voice. "What did you expect to find here,
if Sanctuary is all that you say?"

Alex tilted his head in thought. He had been wondering the
same ever since he left.

"Sanctuary is a pleasant place," he finally said. "I have lots of
good memories of growing up there, but as I got older . . ." he fell

silent, lost in thought until a slight cough from his father made him realize nobody else was talking or even eating. They were waiting for him to finish his thought.

"As I got older, I realized that Sanctuary had no future other than to maintain what it had in the present. Keep the population stable, keep them working for the common good, try to keep the viruses out. It wasn't a city; it was a museum to the way people remembered living. And those people were dying out."

It was the longest speech he had given since reaching COS, maybe the longest speech he had ever given. His face turned red and he ducked over his noodles, which were long, flat, and cream colored. They tasted very pleasant but were slippery and had to be chased around the bowl. Alex was glad of the excuse they gave to look down. He missed the look that Walden and his father shared. A look that Ada and her mother also saw.

"Well, I hope you are realizing you have a wonderful future in COS," Walden said smoothly. "We are very happy to have you here."

Ada stood up. "To the future!" she said. Everyone stood and clinked glasses.

The door to the dining room pushed open and Darwin Ester stumbled into the room, clearly the worse for a number of drinks. The woman with him was wearing a half-ripped dress with wine stains down the front. She was in a drunken daze but managed to smile at everyone in the room with a wide mouth missing half its teeth.

"Sorry we're late," Darwin said. "I had to pick up my date. This is—"

He looked at the woman. "I don't know what the fuck your name is. I only remember your cunt."

Ada's mother gasped, but Ada just looked bored.

Walden stood up. "I think we'll skip dessert, since I am sure my wife is serving many nice things at the party. Shall we take a moment to prepare and then walk over?"

Peter stood up quickly and nodded to Alex. The two of them walked out into the courtyard, which was paved in stone that looked blue in the faint moonlight.

"Darwin's an ass!" Peter said savagely, forgetting his maxim to say as little as possible. "He's the result of ridiculous inbreeding. Walden had enough sense to marry a woman from Asia City."

Alex nodded thoughtfully. That explained the exotic curve of Ada's lips.

"Lady Meiru herself is the product of an alliance with Sanctuary. Her mother grew homesick and returned with her to Asia City. When it was clear that Asia City wouldn't make it, she tried to arrange a marriage for her daughter with Sanctuary, but they are too modern for that. Walden saw the sense of it. And Lady Meiru has probably done better than she ever would in Sanctuary."

While they were talking, Alex could hear the loud rumbling of voices in the dining room and then a drunken giggle that broke off into a squawk as the sound of a hand slapping flesh made the French doors rattle. The front door banged, and the dining room was silent.

Walden came out into the courtyard. His nostrils were pinched and white, and he was breathing heavily. He took a cigarette from his breast pocket and lit it.

He offered the pack. "Would either of you—?"

Alex shook his head hastily. Walden seemed calm, but Alex could see that his hand was trembling slightly.

"Alex, I wonder if I might have a word alone with your father? We have a nice garden just beyond the balustrade, thanks to your father."

Alex mumbled "of course" and walked away quickly, but he still heard Walden say to Peter, "This is unbearable! Something has to be done."

Beyond the paling, which Alex realized Walden called the balustrade, Alex found a small pond. There were shadowy fish swimming in it. They were skinny and pale but undeniably real. Alex was mesmerized. He had seldom seen live animals other than the ferrats that scurried boldly through Sanctuary.

A slight cough made him whirl around. Ada stood there, a blue shimmering presence that mimicked the fish gliding around the pond.

"Sorry about my uncle," she said. "He's pretty awful at the best of times, but after a few drinks . . ." Her voice trailed off and she shivered. "My dad sent him and his lady friend packing. He won't be spoiling my dance."

"That's good."

"I wanted to ask you in private if you know how to dance."

"Not really," Alex replied. His dad had shown him a few simple steps, but it was beyond embarrassing to dance awkwardly with his dad.

"We do old-time dancing here," she said. "My grandmother introduced it. English country dancing, it's called. It dates way back before all the troubles. Lord knows where she learned it. She wasn't that old." She laughed, and Alex obediently echoed her. She showed him some steps, set, and up and down. His dad had shown him the same. They weren't that hard.

"There's not much touching in dancing, but this next step is called arming." She crooked her elbow in his. Alex could feel his arm trembling, but if she felt it, she didn't say anything."

Ada looked up at the house, and Alex's eyes followed hers. Their fathers were watching from the courtyard.

"Everything else requires more people to demonstrate," she said. "I'll dance the first dance with you and show you the steps. I asked them to keep the dances simple for you."

She said this matter-of-factly, not in a condescending way. Alex realized she was a very thoughtful girl. This was unexpected, given her parents. Without thinking, he crooked his arm in invitation.

Her lips quirked in a smile, and she nestled her arm in his. Alex looked directly at Walden and his dad. Neither man gave anything away, but they didn't seem displeased.

The gathering was small, some couples the parents' age and only six or seven unattached teenagers. No wonder Ada appeared interested in him. He had the dual appeal of novelty and scarcity. After the first dance, he was separated from Ada as the other boys and many adult men asked her to dance. Alex didn't lack for partners; in particular, the teenage girls came back for multiple dances. They were also very kind in showing him the steps, which were fortunately pretty basic. At one point he danced with the Lady Meiru. His father had partnered her and brought her over smoothly to Alex for the next dance. She was nice enough but had a set smile on her face and refused to look him in the eyes. Most of his partners asked in the first breath what he thought of COS and in the second what Sanctuary was like. It was clear that they wanted to hear that COS was better, and he was able to oblige in all honesty by describing his dad's amazing farm. At last intermission was called, and Lady Meiru directed everyone to the refreshment table.

Alex saw honeycomb cut into flower shapes that made him think of Aggie. For some reason, he felt guilty. Aggie spoke as well as anyone here. Was it only her scarred face that kept her from being invited? He felt a hand on his arm that felt the way hers did when she guided him in the bee enclave. He jumped and spun around. Ada was there.

"Get me a glass of honey punch, and we'll go sit somewhere," she said, brushing a wet curl off her glistening forehead. "I've done my duty for a while, I think."

Alex got two glasses of the golden liquid and turned to find Ada was gone. She was walking across the dance floor to a balcony that ran the length of the ballroom. Alex followed her, understanding that she didn't want to be observed walking together.

When he got outside, he had lost her. He saw several couples huddled together, but not a girl alone.

"Over here," she called in a soft but penetrating voice. She was sitting on a bench in the shadows. She patted the seat beside her, and he took it. The bench wasn't large, so he was touching her dress, and if he moved, he brushed her arm or leg through its rustling cloth. So he tried not to move. She smelled like the agarita blossom, and he realized she was one of the purchasers of Aggie's perfume. She had managed somehow to attend the event even if she didn't get an invitation, he thought wryly.

"So, tell me what you really think of COS," she said. "Not the appropriate things you said when people asked."

Alex hesitated. "I'm serious when I say I like COS," he said. "The present is messy here, dirty and dangerous, but it has a real future. My dad is doing things to heal the soil that Sanctuary hasn't even thought about. The gardening is hydroponic there, which is good enough for an enclosed city but does nothing for the damaged land. My dad is restoring the earth. Just a small pocket of it, but a small pocket that can grow." As he talked, he realized what bothered him. His dad was healing the earth, but he was just one man. There was a limit to what he could do. Did the children get to take what they learned and create new farms? It didn't appear that they did.

He expressed some of this to Ada, who listened intently, her luminous dark eyes fixed on his face.

"I think you may be romanticizing these children," Ada said. "Your dad is teaching them a trade, which is more than most of them would get in COS. Many are fairly limited in intelligence."

Alex shook his head stubbornly. "Not all of them," he said. "Maybe not most of them." He was thinking about Corn Seven but realized it might be dangerous to say too much, even to this girl.

"No, not all of them," she agreed. "I actually sponsored a school to teach some of the more promising children to read and write.

But it was a struggle for most, and when they learned, they had no place to apply it. They became targets of the other children, who were threatened by their learning. Many of them died. That was too hard to live with. I had to stop." She sounded sad.

"You said what you liked about COS was its future. I don't see it. You say Sanctuary is a dying place." She waved an arm bitterly. "This is a dying place. The administrative compound is small, and very political. You have to be careful what you say and do, every minute. There are spies everywhere. My father and my uncle hate each other, and each wishes the other were dead. My uncle is always threatening to marry and produce a legitimate heir. As it is, COS is filled with his bastards." Her voice was bitter, and she twisted the folds of her dress with her hand.

"We live in a fairy tale, dependent on the people of COS to keep our homes clean and feed us. They resent and fear us. We have to lock our bedroom doors so our own servants don't kill us in our sleep. And our numbers get smaller every day, while their numbers grow larger and larger. I want so much to get away from here, to a place where everyone is equal and everyone is treated the same."

"You could build that here," Alex said. "If your father is the ruler, he could decree that everyone is the same."

"You haven't been listening," she said. "The people of COS have been too damaged by the outside. They aren't very bright, and they don't live very long. You can't hold a conversation with them; you can't teach them to think beyond the next meal. Believe me, I have tried. I wish it was different here."

The distress in her voice was real. He looked in her eyes and saw they were bright with tears. She turned her face to his. She was very close. And it happened. They kissed. Her lips parted under his, and his tongue sought her mouth. His arms went around her soft shoulders. After a moment, she pulled away gently but rested her head on his shoulders. Alex sat very still, feeling every nerve ending, every cell in his body. He was electric with feeling and wanted to pull her even closer, but instead she sat up, smoothed her skirt, and moved away on the bench.

"Here you are," a voice said smoothly. Walden stepped over to the bench.

"It was hot," Ada said. "We were getting some air."

"We're going to start the second set," her father said. "You'll dance with me. I am sure we can find a suitable partner for Alex."

"Perfect," Ada said. "What a wonderful party this is." She stood up and took her father's arm without a backward glance.

Alex sat still for a moment, wondering whether Ada had felt the same as he had. Then he wondered what Walden had seen, and if he was angry. He was just getting up to join the others before his own father came looking for him when a woman stepped out of the shadows and a voice he knew better than any other said, "Hello, Alex."

CHAPTER THIRTY

Miranda negotiated the dumped contents of a slop bowl expertly as she walked the narrow City of the South streetway. The streets took getting used to, as claustrophobic as tunnels. If you stretched out your arms, you could touch the crooked, crumbling buildings that lined them. More than anything, she was homesick for the wide streetways of Sanctuary. There was something about a clean, shining street that seemed to stretch on forever that made you feel your options were limitless. They were designed to create that illusion, but Miranda didn't feel manipulated. She was part of the team that designed them, and she felt as excited by the design as the people they were developed for. More than anything she missed intention, the deliberate design of things for the common good. Everything in COS felt haphazard, dropped or even vomited up, with no one to straighten or clean. Even the smelly slop from the upstairs window would just sit here until a hard rainstorm washed it into the sewers.

Miranda had spent several days after the party in a depressive funk. When his questions elicited no answers, Murray had wisely left her alone to work through whatever she was thinking. She couldn't bear Da's smelly little house, so she walked the nasty paths of COS aimlessly, with Murray following closely enough to keep the thieves away. After two days the girl, whom Murray called Aggie, returned and asked Miranda to help her with something. Miranda looked listlessly at Murray, who nodded.

The "something" proved to be a school, a large room with children of all ages sitting cross-legged on the floor. Miranda distributed large flat, whitish rocks and sharpened pieces of coal, which served the students as makeshift writing tablets and pencils. She thought of the newsline, which took notes from your speaking and, when properly trained, even from your thoughts. How could Alex prefer a primitive life like this? Aggie showed pictures—of houses, people, even a bumblebee —with the names written under them. The children carefully formed their letters and tried to sound out whole words rather than stopping at the first syllable.

Miranda wondered what the point was, given the terrible place where they lived and the lack of any evident employment that would utilize reading, writing, or even talking in whole words, but she had nothing better to do and welcomed the break from her bitter thoughts.

After about an hour, Aggie said she needed to get back to her bees. She asked if Miranda would continue working with the children for another hour before dismissing them. Miranda agreed and conscientiously set the alarm on her newsline.

She walked among the children, helping them with the complex compound noun "bumblebee." She found herself, almost against her will, moved by one girl, who managed a very respectable spelling of "bum bee," but struggled to get beyond the first syllable. "Buuu," she said.

"Bum bul," Miranda enunciated clearly. The girl focused intently on her mouth, her eyes narrowed and brow furrowed in concentration. The narrow eyes reminded Miranda of something, or someone.

"Bu bul!" the girl said triumphantly.

"Very good!" Miranda said. The girl grinned in triumph, and then Miranda placed her. The last time she had seen those narrowed eyes, that grin, the girl had been standing over her with her sharpened stick, ready to drive it into Miranda's unprotected stomach. Miranda stepped back involuntarily.

"Excellent," she said in a shaky voice. "You have almost got it."

The girl grinned again. She gave no indication of remembering Miranda. *Would I have been more memorable if she had killed me?* Miranda wondered. *Or maybe she would only remember the good meal she was able to purchase with my coins?* She checked her newsline. Forty-five minutes. Close enough.

"You all did very well," she announced. Without being told, the children deposited the slates and coal pieces into buckets by the door. Many smiled shyly as they left. The girl who came close to spelling and saying bumblebee raised her fist in triumph at her younger brother and sister, who Miranda now recognized as her other attackers, as they left the schoolroom. What did their attendance at this school mean, if anything? Were they hoping for something better than a life of crime, or were they just killing time? The girl seemed too proud of her accomplishments for the latter.

Murray was outside on the stool at Da's house, leaning against the doorjamb and whittling. He had been very patient with her since the party at the administrative compound. He would be wanting to know her plans. She just wished *she* knew them.

Without speaking, he went inside and got the old man's chair, which must mean the old man was in bed, since he never left the house. He sat on it, even though it was the better seating, rightly guessing she wouldn't want it. She took the stool.

"I did see him, if that's what you were wondering. Right after he kissed a very pretty girl. I'm sure that was his first ever kiss, and he did quite well for himself in selecting a partner."

"Ada, the daughter of Walden, one of the rulers of COS," Murray said.

"You seem to know everything," Miranda said. "You probably know already what happened."

Murray shook his head. "I wasn't there," he said. "It was hard enough to smuggle you inside. Anyway, I would have been recognized. But I know the party was held for Ada's sixteenth birthday. And her father wants a suitable husband for her. The pickings are slim in the administrative compound, and Peter is probably too old. Alex would be an excellent choice."

Miranda turned her stool to face Murray squarely. "Are you serious?" she asked, her voice rising. "Did Peter lure Alex to City of the South to marry him off? Is he some prize calf for breeding like in one of those everlasting Western stories he used to watch?"

Murray stood up. "Let's take a walk," he said. He led Miranda for what felt like hours expertly through the streets of COS, to the outskirts they visited each night for fuel, and then past the decaying waste area to the wall itself, where a small house, more like a shed, stood inconspicuously in the shadow of the wall. He unlocked the door and motioned her to proceed him inside, to a single room neatly outfitted with a stove, bed, chair, table, and candlestick. There was even a small, clean rug on the floor. After Da's shack, it seemed like paradise.

"What is this place?" Miranda asked.

"Where I stay when I am in COS," Murray said. He sat on the chair and motioned Miranda to the bed. She sat gingerly on the blanket.

"Not with your da?"

"He's not really my da," Murray said. "His place is convenient when I need to be in the city."

"And to see Aggie," Miranda said. Murray didn't respond.

"What happened with Alex? Was he surprised to see you?"

Miranda looked off past his concerned eyes. "Not surprised so much as shocked. He didn't expect me at this fancy party, dressed as a COS serving woman."

Murray had arranged with one of his many contacts for Miranda to work in the kitchen at the party, washing the dirty crockery as the servers brought it back. She snuck to the door as often as she could, even though she had gotten thumped twice with a punch ladle for doing so, the second time so hard on the head it raised a bump and she saw stars. She had given Murray a coin to bribe the head cook, but the man still expected a hard day's work from her.

She saw Alex dance, not too badly. When she saw him leaving the dance floor, she evaded the head cook, who was supervising the loading of serving trays, and slipped through the door. Everyone seemed to be moving toward the food, so by creeping along the wall, she was able to slip outside and follow Alex at a distance. She watched him sit on a bench with a girl, and then she saw them kiss. They seemed to melt into each other, their heads so close together they looked like some mythical creature rather than two people. Fortunately, the girl broke away first and then rose and went away with an older man. Miranda moved without thinking, before Alex could follow. She knew it would be her only chance.

He fell back onto the bench when she spoke to him, and then he rubbed his eyes, not once but twice. She didn't know if it was disbelief or if he was hoping she was an unwelcome apparition that he could make disappear.

"Mom?" he said. He sounded like four-year-old Alex when she interrupted his night terrors with a hand on his shoulder.

"It's me," she said. "I followed you from Sanctuary."

"How? When?" He was at a loss for words.

"I've been here almost a week. I hired a man as a guide. A friend of Tara's."

She made it sound simple. He would never have any idea of the terrors of the road, the girl she got killed, the miseries of City of the South in Da's squalid house. She had found him, and none of it mattered.

"You shouldn't have come," he said. "I was going to get word to you. To let you know I was all right. Ada, the girl you saw, would help me. You didn't need to come."

"Alex, you can't stay here. This isn't your home," Miranda's voice was urgent. He would be missed. There wasn't much time. "You're still a child."

"Not in City of the South," he said flatly. "I'm an adult here. And almost an adult in Sanctuary. I was learning a role. I would have left home soon anyway."

"But that was different," Miranda said. He would have gotten a flat not too far from hers. He would have built a life with work and friends but still seeing his mother at least once a week. And soon there would be a girl who was more than a friend, a wedding, and then a grandchild that Miranda would babysit. Not this strange place where most of the people were savages, and a very lucky few lived out a tarnished fairy tale behind walls that were as much a prison as the city walls themselves. He couldn't want this.

"City of the South isn't perfect," Alex said. "In fact, it is pretty much a ruin, just like the rest of the outside. But we are starting to heal it. And that's all I ever wanted."

"We?" Miranda asked, envisioning the girl who had just left.

"Dad and I," Alex said. "I'm working with Dad. We're growing food. We're rebuilding the earth, the soil. Just a little bit, but we will heal more and more."

"Alex, you could do that in Sanctuary. Outside integration . . ." Her voice trailed off, as Alex just shook his head with a finality she couldn't ignore.

"Then I can stay here too," Miranda said. "God knows City of the South needs world building. I can make myself useful."

"Your place is Sanctuary," Alex said. "You belong there. You matter there. I didn't. But I matter here."

"Do you not want me to stay?" She looked Alex directly in the face and saw first dismay and then pity in his gaze.

"Don't decide right away," he said. "Think about it and get word to me."

"How do I do that?"

"Whoever got you in here in the first place will know how. Listen, I better get back. Dad will come looking for me." He stood up and hugged her tightly.

"Are you happy here, Alex?" her voice was shaky, but she wasn't going to cry. Alex had made it clear often enough that he felt blackmailed by her too-ready tears.

He thought a moment and then replied. "Not yet, but I can be. I hope you can be happy too." The finality in his voice made it clear that her happiness couldn't depend on him. He melted away into the darkness. She sank on the bench he had vacated.

She had relived this scene a hundred, maybe a thousand times in her head. But she found she couldn't bear to relive it aloud with Murray. She said only, "He wasn't happy to see me. He doesn't want to leave."

Murray didn't answer.

Finally, she brought out the rest. "I offered to live here with him. He doesn't want me to stay."

"Did he say that?"

"He's too nice a boy for that. But his eyes did."

"He's a nice boy because you raised him to be."

Miranda stood up and paced the small hut angrily.

"Yes, I raised him. By myself. Every day of his life since he was four years old. But he picks the parent he never knew. The one who abandoned him."

"Is he picking the man," Murray asked mildly, "or the life?"

Miranda stopped pacing. "What do you mean?"

"All the things you have told me about Alex were about how he didn't appreciate Sanctuary. How he felt trapped there. I've known a lot of Sanctuary folk. He's not the only one to feel that way."

Miranda started to argue but stopped. Murray was right.

"Maybe what he liked best about his father was that he was offering him an escape."

"But why doesn't he want me as well? Was I so terrible as a mother?"

Murray looked away. "The problem with being a parent," he said, "is that kids often see more than you want them to see."

"What does that mean?"

"I think you figured out that Aggie is my daughter. I loved her mother, but she left me for Peter when Aggie was very young. I was young myself, and angry, so I left, wandered around. When I heard that Margaret had died on one of Peter's errands, I came back. But it was too late. Aggie was already almost grown, living with Margaret's da. She was very bitter and wanted nothing to do with me. You know that scar on her face? Did she tell you where it came from?"

Miranda shook her head. She had imagined all sorts of terrible things.

"She did that herself. Beautiful girls are rare in City of the South. They are claimed as prizes by administrators, mostly Darwin's crew. She had a narrow escape from someone, maybe from Darwin himself, so she decided to make herself unappealing. Da was no use as a protector. He would have been happy with the coins that came his way. And I . . . wasn't around."

Miranda was silent, imagining how that cut would have hurt. And how it would hurt in an even more lasting way to hear that story from a wounded child. "I'm sorry," she said.

"That's what she sees when she looks at me. A coward who ran away when he could have been of use. When Alex looks at you, he doesn't see that. He sees a mother who was always there for him, all through his childhood, when his father abandoned him, as I abandoned Aggie. If he makes another choice now, you have nothing to feel bad about. You raised him proper and did what you could. You prepared him to make a choice that you can trust."

Miranda was moved beyond measure that Murray shared this with her. She owed him, and herself, complete honesty in return.

"He sees fear," she said slowly. "That's what he sees when he looks at me. The outside was so terrible. Each day brought some new horror. And losses. Giving up my best friend, my dog, Fred, to come inside. Where it was safe, where we were protected. I loved Sanctuary from the moment we stepped through the wall. It had to be worth the sacrifice. But somehow I knew. . . I was scared for Alex every day of his life. When his father left, I told myself the fear was that Peter would come back for Alex. But my real fear was that I knew Sanctuary wouldn't be enough to make Alex happy. That it wouldn't be enough to keep him safe.

"Alex can maybe do great things here. But he still won't be safe. He probably won't live to be my age. Maybe he'll get sick, or . . ." She couldn't voice the thought. "But he wants to take risks. To build a life that makes a difference. A dangerous life. And he knows if I am here, he won't. He'll let me stop him. Because when all is said and done, he loves me."

As she said it, she understood all the bitterness of Alex's teenage years. He wasn't bitter because he hated her but because he loved her. And because that love could stop him from living the life he was meant to live.

She looked Murray squarely in the eyes. Haunted, pain-filled eyes, she now realized. "I'm ready to go back," she said. "Alex is right. My place is in Sanctuary. But his place is here. Before we go, can I get word to Alex? I want him to know I understand his choice, and it's okay."

"Aggie can get word to him," Murray said. "She can fix it so you can see him again before you leave."

Miranda laughed through her tears. "I'm sure she can," she said. "A very resourceful girl, your daughter. And she can't have gotten that solely from her mother. But if I see him again, I'll lose my nerve. I just want him to move on, maybe with that beautiful girl he was kissing, and not worry about me. I'll be all right."

Murray placed a hand on her chin and brushed her tears away gently with the other. "I know you will," he said. "And so does Alex. Or he wouldn't let you go."

Miranda reached both arms around his neck and kissed him. They fell onto the bed and he pulled fiercely at her clothes until they came off. She climbed onto his chest and let his lanky body swallow hers as they dug deep into each other's hurt and lonely places. She poured herself into him. His scarred, hardened body melted like candlewax and she was nestled inside, feeling only his beating heart, while his mouth and hands traveled over every inch of the outside of her. When they finished and lay in a pool of salty water that reason told her was sweat but that felt like the ocean, she knew that previous couplings, with Peter, with Tara, had been as unreal as a holo. They might have been DPs. Once he returned her to Sanctuary, she might never see him again, but she would always have something inside her that he had permanently planted. Who knew what it would create?

CHAPTER THIRTY-ONE

Alex looked up from breakfast to see his dad eyeing him speculatively. When he had left his mother to head back to the party, he'd almost bumped into his dad. What did his dad see? He was amazed at the guilt he felt, as if he had betrayed his dad by meeting with his mom. He never asked her to follow him. Those first few days on the road, he was stunned by the desolation of outside and disappointed in his dad, in part because he could tell his dad was disappointed in him. He was a soft Sanctuary boy who would never have survived a single day without three tough men to pick him up every time he fell down. And he fell down a lot. He was beyond homesick for his mother and fantasized about her showing up with a posse of Sanctuary guardians and taking him back. It would be such a neat and satisfactory ending to a huge mistake. He wasn't responsible if his mother dragged him back. He could return to resenting her and Sanctuary, while at the same time feeling profoundly relieved.

But his mother didn't show up on the road, and he decided that she had been unable to interest Tara and the authorities in physically rescuing him. He thought they might try diplomatic channels instead. He had half expected Walden to say, "You're the young man who has caused so much upset in Sanctuary." But Walden had said nothing, his sole interest in Alex being that he was Peter's son. It never once crossed Alex's mind that his mother would really follow him. Her hatred and fear of the outside were palpable.

City of the South was no picnic, that's for sure. He still didn't think much of the city itself, and if he never wandered its streets again, he was fine with that. But the work his father was doing was real, and he wanted to be part of it. He meant what he said to his mother. He wasn't going back. And he knew his dad would back him up.

And yet. What about his mother staying in COS? He knew, if offered, she would jump at the chance. He had always known he was her whole purpose in life. His dad had his own plans, and Alex still didn't know how he fit into those plans, but he knew that if he didn't work out, his dad would shrug his shoulders and move on. If that boy had killed him on the COS street, it probably would have upset his dad at the moment, but he doubted he would have lost the night's sleep over it that Alex lost over the boy's father—a man that he didn't even know, who had tried to kill him. Alex wanted to feel angry and hurt that his dad had so little interest in him, but truthfully, the knowledge was surprisingly freeing. It meant Alex could make his own plans, long-term plans that might not involve his dad. For the first time in his life, Alex could live for Alex. Or at least, so he had thought. Until his mother showed up.

He resigned himself to the fact that he would have to intercede for her. The brothers would be suspicious, particularly Darwin. His dad might try to argue, but he could tell by the grudging respect in his dad's voice when he spoke of Miranda that he hadn't won many of their fights. She would be allowed to stay. And she would do good work for them. She would do her level best to make City of the South into an acceptable version of Sanctuary. People would lead better lives, talk better, read and write. She wouldn't make many friends, but she wouldn't care.

But no matter what she did, he would do what he wanted with his life. He was a different person from the sulky Sanctuary boy she remembered. She would soon see that. And if his plans didn't keep him forever in City of the South, he would be sure the next time he left that she didn't follow. He had just decided he could make it work when his father spoke.

"How about a change of pace today?" he asked. "Something new."

"That's fine," Alex replied. "But I did like the corn, and I understood harvesting the beans are next."

"I've got good apprentices working with the crops," his father said. "I want you to understand planting and harvesting. It's important to understand the entire enterprise. But I want to give you something of your own to manage. My latest venture. Something different."

His tone had changed, and Alex found himself responding. He bolted down the rest of his bread and tea. Miranda was temporarily forgotten.

His father closed the door to the wall behind them, but this time he led Alex away from the fields. As they crested a small hill, he saw a large stone building with a fenced-in yard.

"That's the barn," his father said proudly. Alex remembered barns from stories of yesteryear. As they got closer, he heard the noises, a chorus of bleats. Animals! He couldn't help himself. He broke into a trot.

"I keep a herd of goats and a smaller herd of sheep," his father said. He lifted the large latch on the double-paned door. "The goats will come out this side and the sheep out the other."

They slid the doors open. Alex tried to move quickly, but the goats, all of them short and wiry, bumped against his knees as they tumbled out. They had barrel bellies and short bowlegs with hooves that were surprisingly nimble as they pranced toward long, hollow food troughs. The sharp smell was overpowering at first, but he got used to it quickly as he watched their antics, butting each other with long, curved horns as they shoved their way out of the barn. Alex helped his father distribute hay to the troughs.

"They will also spend the day grazing. I use them to condition fields for planting. Their excrement does wonderful things for soil."

Alex was impressed with how much his dad knew. First plants, now animals.

"Goats are omnivorous and hardy. And wicked smart. We found a few that had survived, created their own herd. Once we had sufficient breeding pairs, we were on our way."

The bleating of some goats was louder than others.

"Those are the breeding mothers. We let some feed babies, but others we milk. That's where we get the cheese you eat most mornings."

Alex realized the white stuff the children called chee was actually cheese. He had heard of cheese and read of cheese. "The cheese stands alone," a line from his mother's dogeared book of children's poems, bubbled up in his thoughts. It was one of the few remnants of her outside childhood that he had inherited and kept.

One goat nudged first his dad and then Alex, repeatedly. She stood out from the others because she had no horns, and her fur was a rich auburn color.

"Rosie," his dad said, attempting to sound annoyed. He pushed her away, but Alex saw him reach into his pocket and pull out a small piece of honeycomb, which he tried to slip to the goat without the other goats, and Alex, seeing. The honeycomb made him wonder if his dad had been to visit the bee enclave and Aggie, who seemed to work alone. He was surprised at the feeling that shot through him. Was it annoyance or . . . jealousy? Was he ever going to work with her again? Why should he care, now that he had met Ada, the most beautiful girl he had ever seen, even compared to all the cosseted girls in Sanctuary? Aggie would be even prettier, except for that—

278

His dad snapped his fingers in Alex's face to get his attention. "One of your first tasks will be to learn to milk. And here's the girl, Goat Eleven, who will teach you how to do it."

Alex realized that a tall girl, at least twelve or thirteen, with a round red face and a body surprisingly fat for City of the South, was standing near the barn door. She showed Alex how to separate and herd the loudly bleating females back into the barn and tether them. Then she showed him how to milk the teats with a sharp downward jerk to stimulate the gland and then a rolling pressure to push all the milk out the small hole at the point into a waiting bucket. Some goats seemed resigned to the process, but others kicked with their sharp hooves or butted with their bony horns. Fortunately, the horns were curved and ended in a point close to their bodies so they couldn't stab, but they were rock hard and could quickly leave a bruise. Alex got the most abuse, but he didn't mind. He realized he was new, and they were testing him. He loved the smell that came off the steaming, frothy milk, as well as the rank, grassy smell of the goats themselves. Although they nipped at him, they nuzzled each other, and he realized they were helping each other through the morning ordeal. He saw Goat Eleven guzzle the milk straight from a teat when she thought he wasn't looking. He deliberately turned away to give her the opportunity, glad to see at least one of the workers eating her fill.

After the goats were milked, Alex helped Goat Eleven carry the milk across the field to the same warehouse where the corn had been gathered. He saw Aggie at a distance, talking with a man who was counting bottles of honey on a table. If she saw him, she gave no clue. After the milk was received by a woman with a face sour enough to be Birna's twin, Goat Eleven smiled one last time. She had a sweet smile except for the loss of one of her front teeth. She had smiled all through the milking, but she never laughed, no matter how many times a goat got in a well-placed kick or butt somewhere on Alex's body. She also never spoke.

Alex walked back to the goat pasture. He saw that the handful of sheep were also out in their yard and being tended by a small boy. He was sure his name was Sheep something or other. The boy looked at him curiously and waved. Alex waved back.

His father was long gone, so Alex studied the goats. There wasn't much to do. He kept the water trough supplied from a barrel of water in the barn. The goats were thirsty and drank a lot of water, which made Alex uneasy. Water was a scarce commodity in COS, just as it had been in Sanctuary. Except for the morning tea, Alex generally didn't get a drink until dinner. He understood why the goat and sheep herds were small.

Alex spent the next several days with his goat herd. Once the goats were used to him and responded, albeit reluctantly, to a switch on their rumps, he was able to take them out to the pasture, where they came into their own, prancing, jumping, and playing. The younger goats did play fighting and played with sticks and stones like children anywhere. *Anywhere but COS*, Alex thought. He had several children working with him, and they focused intently on the goats, breaking up the play when it got too rambunctious when, really, they should be joining in. Alex got to know the social habits of the goats, which goats were friends and liked to stand together and flick each other with their tails. The mother goats with their kids made him squirm, wondering about his own mother. It had been four days since he saw her. Where was she now? She might have gone back to Sanctuary, but he doubted it. Not without getting word to him.

Rosie took a liking to him and shadowed him in the yard and in the pasture. She wanted nothing to do with the other goats. She considered herself human, with her hornless head, which his dad called "polled." He said that Rosie was the first goat to trust him. Catching her enabled him to catch the other goats in her small, wild herd. If Alex ignored Rosie too long, she nipped him to remind him to scratch behind her ears. He found himself comparing Rosie, with her moods, to the cat his mother had created. How had they ever thought it possible to add personality to a mechanical thing?

His dad showed more interest in the goats, in Rosie particularly, than he showed in the people of COS or even Alex. Alex had a very dim memory, one of the very few, of finding a ferrat nest with his dad, behind a red dumpster painted like a dragon. He could still remember the gentle way his dad had exposed the nursing mother, who hissed and bared her teeth until she realized they were no threat to her suckling babies. Alex realized, like him, his father preferred animals to people. Discovering his similarities to this man who abandoned him and his mother made him uncomfortable, so he focused on the goats instead.

At night, when he put the goats back in the barn, he made a special effort to fix Rosie up with water and hay and give her the forehead massage that she loved. She closed her eyes, with those strange horizontal pupils in golden irises and ridiculously long lashes, and rubbed against him while he kneaded her head. The other goats were jealous and would give Rosie nips and kicks when they thought Alex wasn't looking, but Rosie didn't seem to mind. She gave back as good as she got. Whatever Alex decided, whether to stay in COS or go, he would take Rosie with him.

The goats absorbed his attention, but thoughts of Miranda cropped up like goat kicks to the belly. He thought about getting in touch with Ada, to see if she could help with his mom, either to intercede with her father so Miranda could stay or to arrange for an escort to take her back to Sanctuary. He had decided to ask his dad how he could arrange to see Ada when his dad brought an invitation to tea the following day. Alex was too relieved to take much offense from the smirk on his father's face. If he was honest, his interest in Ada as a girl was fading. The kiss had been something out of a dream, and Ada was a beautiful girl, but maybe too beautiful to be real. He wanted to learn everything he could and then strike out on his own, and it was hard to imagine this girl, a vision in her flowing blue gown, helping with goat milking or harvesting corn. How would they even develop a relationship if they only saw each other at dances and teas, under the watchful eyes of both sets of parents?

He gathered the goats for breakfast and a quick milking so he could devote several hours to the arduous task of cleaning off several layers of goat dirt. But the girl who stood at the barn door this morning wasn't Goat Eleven. Alex was suddenly very conscious of his smell, which rivalled the entire herd smell, and of the straw in his bristly hair.

"I wasn't sure I would ever see you again," he said. "I didn't know if you ever left your bees." Of course, he did know. He had seen her in town, leading Corn Seven furtively down the main shopping street.

Aggie smiled. It was a warm day, and she wasn't wearing a hood. Instead, she wore a dress that hid none of her lovely curves, her tiny waist. Alex forced himself to focus on her face, on her scar. He found himself wanting to trace that scar, from her eye to her chin. He looked away, aware that he was red and sweating, and that she knew the walk from his bedroom was too short to account for it.

"Good morning to you too," she chided. "Goat Eleven wasn't feeling too well this morning. She helps herself freely to the goat's milk, and sometimes it gets the better of her." Alex said nothing. He hoped Goat Eleven's habit wouldn't get her in trouble with Birna.

"Well, let's get started. Peter said you have a social engagement with the family this afternoon."

Again, the easy familiarity with his father. A familiarity no one else—not Birna, not Walden, not Alex himself—had achieved. "When did you see my father?" he asked.

"This morning," she replied. "We had breakfast together in the bee enclave."

Alex envisioned the bee enclave, green and white, the overpowering sweetness, the long grass where a couple could . . .

"You get along well with my father," he observed.

"I've been working here since I was six," she replied. "I'm sixteen now. You can get to know a person pretty well in ten years."

The jealousy shot through him like a poison arrow. No mistaking this emotion. Ten years that Peter had been away from Alex. Ten years watching this girl grow up instead.

She looked into his eyes and understood.

"He knew my mother," she said, "quite well." Her eyes dropped.

"Are they still . . . ?" Alex didn't finish the sentence.

"She died when I was five. Your dad made me an apprentice not long after."

The set expression on her face warned Alex to drop the subject. There was silence in the barn except for the tinkling sound of milk hitting metal pails.

When they finished, Aggie leaned toward him. He could smell the blossoms and clover of the bee enclave on her. He closed his eyes so she wouldn't see him respond.

"I have a message from your mother," she said quietly. His eyes popped back open. He took both her slim shoulders and turned her toward him.

"What? How do you know my—?"

"I've met her several times. I like her, Alex. I see a lot of you in her."

"You don't really know me," he replied hotly. He was tired of people thinking they knew him so that they could plan his life for him based on understanding nothing about him at all.

"You're right," she said. "I shouldn't have said that. She's been staying in COS with my—with a friend of mine. She's fine. She asked me to get a message to you."

"What message?"

"She's leaving COS tomorrow. Returning to Sanctuary. My—the guide who brought her is taking her back. He'll keep her safe. She wanted me to give you this." She handed Alex a note, which he read slowly.

Alex,

I have given this a lot of thought. You are right. My place, my future, is in Sanctuary. Yours never was. I am leaving tomorrow. I'm not going to see you again. It's safest for you and will make it easier for me. If you are able to send word from time to time, I would really appreciate it, but I'll understand if you don't. You're a man now, Alex. A fine man. I wish I could take credit for what you've become, but I honestly think you became who you are in spite of me, not because of me. I trust the choice you are making. Have a wonderful, meaningful life.

Love, Mom.

"No," Alex said. Aggie was watching him closely. "Did you read this?" he asked.

She shook her head. "It wasn't addressed to me."

"She's leaving tomorrow. She doesn't want to see me."

Aggie was silent for a moment. "Well, that's really her choice, isn't it?"

Alex shook his head. He felt relief that his mother was returning to Sanctuary. It was her best chance, and the life she willingly chose. But she couldn't leave without knowing . . .

"She has to know," he said. "That I love her. That my decision to remain in City of the South is not about my father, not about her, but about me."

"I'm sure she knows that," Aggie said gently.

"She doesn't. I can tell by the letter. If she understands that, there will be no regrets."

Aggie just shook her head. "They will get an early start," she said. "I don't see how—"

He shook her slightly by the shoulders. "You know exactly how," he said. "You're smart and resourceful. You don't work for this place; you make this place work for you. You get in and out of the administrative enclave all the time, whenever it suits you. I want it to suit you tomorrow."

Aggie shook her head, but he didn't let her go.

"All right," she said reluctantly.

SANCTUARY

CHAPTER THIRTY-TWO

Murray said nothing as Miranda wrote a note on the scraps of paper with the pen he found for her in his pack. Before getting her tears under control, she had wasted several pieces where the ink ran too much to be legible. He took her back to Da's, where Aggie was visiting. She readily agreed to deliver the note. Murray missed nothing about Aggie. He could tell she was excited about seeing Alex again. She was so much like her mother, which probably meant that Alex, whom he had never seen, was a lot like his dad.

The next morning Murray left Miranda with Da. He said he had errands to run before they could leave City of the South. She was listless, and he knew she had slept poorly. Murray took back roads, where the alleys were so narrow he could barely squeeze through, to evade the rudimentary sensors in COS. When he reached the administrative compound, he used the same door as Aggie—a servant entrance that had been closed off long ago and secretly reopened—to slip inside unnoticed. He knew exactly where Peter would be, having followed Aggie's mother there, long ago.

Peter was frowning over numbers on a long piece of paper. Crop yields, or something similar. Aggie had told him lots of things about Peter and his work, no doubt to wound him, although he sensed that she didn't really like Peter any more than she liked him.

"Hey, Pete," he said quietly. Peter looked up, and the worried look on his face was replaced by a sneer.

"Look who is gracing COS again with his presence," he said. "Checking up on Aggie?"

Murray shook his head. "I'm here on an errand this time. I didn't come alone."

Peter looked uneasy, but he didn't ask any questions.

"Tara Jordan sent me. Remember her?"

Peter nodded and put down his pen.

"I ended up escorting someone you know very well. A lady who wants her son back."

Peter didn't pretend to misunderstand. This was maybe the only thing Murray appreciated about Peter. He cut to the chase.

"He's my son too," he said. "And he came of his own free will. He wants to be here, and he knows if he doesn't, he can leave at any time."

Murray shook his head. "You and I both know better. A soft Sanctuary boy on the outside? He wouldn't last a day. I'm sure you had an armed escort when you picked him up."

Peter reddened. "Only because I wasn't willing to take risks with my son. If he wants to go, I'll send the same escort back with him." He stood up. "Let's go ask him now. Get this over with."

Murray stepped in front of him to stop him. "Relax," he said. "He's already seen his mother. He told her he's staying."

Peter sat down heavily in his chair as he processed this. "He's seen her? How? Where?"

"Don't worry about it. I arranged it so nobody else knows."

"So why are you here?"

"I came to ask you," Murray said slowly, "to let Miranda stay. He won't leave, and she won't leave without him."

Peter shook his head. "Did Miranda send you? Because the answer is no. I have no doubt she's gotten around you. In fact, I'm sure the two of you have hit it off really well. I think we both know we share the same taste in women." He grinned mirthlessly as he eyed Murray.

Murray clenched his hands at his sides. He was here for Miranda. He wouldn't mess it up with his temper.

"Miranda's not good for Alex. She had him wrapped in cotton wool back in Sanctuary. He has his freedom here to do what he wants."

Murray doubted that. Based on things Aggie had let slip, he suspected that Peter was even more controlling than Miranda.

Peter thought for a moment and came to a decision. "Alex has said nothing to me about this. Does he want his mother to stay?"

Murray tried to keep his face blank, but he saw that Peter had read the situation correctly.

"If Alex asks me to let his mother stay, then I will consider it. But unless he asks . . ." He smiled. He already knew the likelihood of that.

Murray turned to leave.

Peter said to his back, "When do you plan to leave with Miranda?"

"Tomorrow morning."

"We're having tea with the family today. I am sure you remember them well. He'll have plenty of time to ask me. If he wants his mother to stay."

Murray left without responding.

Alex sat at the beautiful table with its intoxicating white flowers, small sandwiches, little cakes, and tea that tasted like tea and not dead leaves and twigs. And all he felt was irritation. The fragrant blossoms were agarita branches, which felt like an intentional provocation, because he was sitting across from a beautiful girl but could think only of a young woman with a scarred face and her blouse stained with goat's milk in all the wrong—or very right—places. His hostesses, the Lady Meiru and Ada, were stunning in pink and ivory dresses, but so perfect in every way that they seemed like holos. In fact, Ada seemed like the DP a horny Sanctuary teenager might create, something Alex himself might have created before he knew any better. But now he did.

The conversation was formal and stilted. Lord Walden asked his dad about the crops, and his father responded. Alex twisted in his chair. Time to shake things up a little.

"I've been wondering . . ." He cleared his throat self-consciously when all conversation stopped and everyone at the tea table focused on him. "Are there other fields in City of the South besides the ones we manage? I mean, do the citizens get involved?"

Everyone stared at him, until Ada broke the silence with a little giggle.

"I'm sorry," she said. "It's that word, 'citizens.' I am trying to picture the people of COS growing their own beans or raising their own honey."

Peter broke smoothly into the awkward pause that followed. "That's eventually the goal," he said, "but the people of COS currently lack the skills and temperament to grow crops successfully. We hope they will get there in time, as enough children learn the trade. But we can't risk scarce seeds or soil right now."

"But you have a lot of apprentices," Alex said in frustration. "And from what I have seen, they're very good. They could go home on weekends, and—"

"That's enough, Alex," his father interjected in a steely voice.

"It's our job to grow enough to ensure that the populace is adequately fed," Darwin said. "When you have been here longer, you will see that the distribution system is fair and equitable. We may not be Sanctuary, but no one is starving in COS."

Alex thought of the few people he had seen in COS. Not one of them, not even Aggie, looked well fed. But now was not the time to say so. In fact, looking at the set faces around the table, he realized he had really put his foot in it. Maybe he should reconsider staying any longer in COS.

After the sandwich plate had been handed around a second time, Darwin suggested that Ada might want to show Alex the grounds in daylight. Alex thought she rose with some reluctance, and she was as tight lipped as his mother whenever he managed to upset her. He had a swift image of married life with Ada and didn't like what he saw. Based on the way she swept from the table and didn't look back to see that he followed, she felt the same.

Once they were out of earshot of the table, she rounded on him. He saw fury blazing in her brown, almost black, eyes.

"What is the matter with you?" she hissed. "You've been here two weeks. And you think you know what's best for us? You have no idea what City of the South is really like. Walk the streets, any street, at night, by yourself, without your father to protect you, and you'll find out."

"I know," he said apologetically. "I've already had my own encounter in City of the South. It's just that if the people had their own—"

"If the people had their own what? Gardens? Food? Then the people with the largest gardens would fight to take over the smaller gardens. The people with smaller gardens would raid the larger gardens, at knifepoint, so they had more than they were willing to grow themselves. These people are the ones who survived on the outside. That means they were stronger and more cunning, but it also means they don't have any limits to what they will do to survive."

"My uncle Darwin is a pig, the result of inbreeding with that sort, but my father is trying, very hard, to bring civilization to a place that doesn't want it. You would not believe the horrible crimes he has to adjudicate once a month. They would turn your stomach. The fact that you are still standing means that whatever happened to you in COS was nothing. Life isn't easy for us, isolated, trying to turn a bunch of savages into a city. If we didn't control the food and water supply, we'd have no power at all."

Her voice had risen almost to a scream. Alex was silenced. She was right. He was judging after two weeks without really understanding. The way he had always judged Sanctuary. No wonder his mother was perpetually angry with him.

He mumbled an apology.

"I thought you would be different. I thought you would understand. Nobody does, not even my parents. I have been so alone." She was talking more to herself than him. "I don't want to see you again for a while," she said. "I'm very disappointed."

She walked away and left him standing there until his father came to collect him; they walked silently home through the tunnel.

CHAPTER THIRTY-THREE

Murray was gone when Miranda woke, before first light. She packed her meager belongings. Her heart was heavy, but her pack was light. She hoped they had enough provisions to get them back to Sanctuary. She wasn't looking forward to the trip through the outside, but she would be glad to be back in Sanctuary, even without—

Her brain froze with her heart as she refused to think about her failed errand. What would become of Alex in this terrible place? Could he hide safely in the administrative enclave, which she had only briefly glimpsed but envisioned as a very poor imitation of Sanctuary? The door opened, and she stood up with her pack, eager to leave this evil place behind her. Da snored wetly in the bedroom. She hoped they wouldn't need to wake him up to say goodbye.

"I'm ready," she said.

"I'm afraid there's been a delay," he replied. "We'll have to wait until tomorrow."

"Tomorrow?" Her heart sank at the idea of another day in this smelly hovel, with nothing to do but worry about . . .

Murray stepped to one side. Another figure, wrapped in early-morning shadow, stood in the door.

"Hi, Mom," Alex said.

Miranda froze for a minute then ran and hugged him tightly to her. He wasn't as thin as she remembered. Somehow COS, with all its privations, had filled him out. She held him at arm's length, studying his sunburned cheeks, the crinkles already forming around his eyes. She had to admit that COS suited him. He was a man now, not a boy.

"Didn't you get my note?" she said. "I understand why you want to stay. I'm fine."

"I just wanted to make sure," Alex said, "to tell you. . . . You can stay, too, if you want. I'll make it right with Dad."

Miranda closed her eyes and tried to envision her life here. She would live with Murray in his little hut. She would avoid Peter as much as possible. She would design things. Her vision broke down as she tried to imagine the people she had met in COS fabricating the things she designed. It wouldn't be easy, but the rulers would see the value of it. They would take the things, and—

She shook her head. She was a builder, not a politician. She couldn't make the rulers share things or turn COS into a civilized town with fabricated stuff. The things she made would just increase the divisions, not heal them. Alex was a different person, with his innate distrust of authority. She wanted to improve the status quo. Alex wanted to change it. She would be dangerous in a place like COS, but this city needed Alex.

She shook her head and tried to smile. "It's not for me, Alex. It's not that I wouldn't fit in. I would probably fit in too well. Like your dad."

He didn't take offense. He just nodded. Alex was more than a truth teller; he was a truth seer.

"I'll be okay," she told Alex. "I'll miss you terribly, but I'll distract myself. I still have my cat to finish." Alex smiled, and Miranda laughed through her tears. "I can't promise not to worry about you. I don't know if someone like you can be safe anywhere, but surely not here."

A slender figure stepped through the doorway and stepped forward to stand beside Alex. Aggie. She slipped her small hand in his, and Alex found himself squeezing it.

"He has friends," she said. "He won't be alone. And Murray will get word to you about us at least once a year. You have my promise."

Alex looked down at her, clearly startled but pleased by the word "us."

This is news to him, Miranda realized, *but welcome news.* Somehow, she felt better leaving Alex in Aggie's hands than with that unknown girl in the administrative enclave.

Miranda pulled Alex to her again. Aggie had the rest of her life with him. She could give his mother one more moment. "I know it hasn't always seemed this way, but all I want for you is a good life. A life that matters. If it doesn't include me, that's okay. Really."

Alex hugged her back. "My life will always include you," he said. She looked into his eyes and saw that it was true. And then she was ready to leave.

Alex tugged her hair one last time and then took Aggie's hand again. "We'll be in touch," he promised. And they melted through the door. Miranda heaved a big sigh. "I'm ready to go home," she said.

"We'll have to wait one more day," Murray replied. "We need to make an early start if we want to avoid too many nights on the road."

Alex was quiet as Aggie led him through the dirty, narrow streets of City of the South. The goodbye with his mom had been final enough, but it didn't seem real that he would never see his mother again. Every step on the muddy street felt insubstantial, as if he had stepped off a cliff into nothingness. For sixteen years his mother had kept him safe. Every day in City of the South, even the days he enjoyed, he always had a sense that it was all make-believe, that he would look up and see his mother standing in the doorway with a disapproving frown as he slowly came to himself and realized he had immersed himself too deeply in the story cube. Nothing about this place had felt real until he felt his mother's final hug. When he knew for certain that he would never see her again.

He looked at the rickety houses, the dirty people who mumbled at him and held out their hands. He had traded beautiful Sanctuary, where he had a role and a future, where life might be dull but was never dangerous, for . . . what, exactly? He stopped to say that he had made a huge mistake, to find his way back to the house where his mother was, and he realized he had no idea where they were.

"Is this the right way to the enclave?" he asked.

"We're not going to the enclave," she replied. "I want to show you something."

"We'll be missed," he objected. She gave him a small, secretive smile and turned away. She quickened her speed, forcing him to break into a lope to keep up with her.

She led him through streets so narrow they were footpaths, to empty lots where dust blew into funnels, to the wall of the city itself. He felt the momentary quickening of hope. She didn't want to stay either. They were going to leave COS and meet up with his mother and her guide somewhere.

Aggie led him to a vine-covered portion of wall and expertly pulled the vines away. "This is a private exit only a few of us know," she said.

He followed her for what felt like hours. He was getting worried. His dad kept close tabs on him and would have noticed his absence. Who was taking the goats to pasture? He had expected to be back early enough to do that.

His head was down as he worried about how easily things could go wrong in City of the South, until Aggie stopped with no warning, causing him to plow into her. And his worries vanished like turning off the story cube. He rubbed his eyes in disbelief.

"What is this?" he asked.

"My forest garden," she said proudly.

He didn't stop for more questions but ran instinctively into the heart of the leafy green illusion. Trees of various sizes, close together so that they looked like a small green city, didn't melt away when he got close enough to touch but proved to be trees, real trees, with leaves and scratchy bark. Bushes and leafy plants covered the ground and arrested his movement. He looked up, through the leaves patterning the cloudy sky. So many shades of green, from the lightness of a lime packfruit to a deep green that swallowed him up as he stepped into it.

The leaves whispered around him, and something small and—blue?—flew overhead.

"Is that a—"

"Bird? Yes, a jaybird, it's called. We're growing berries, and a few birds have found us. There's an actual nest in here."

"How did you do this?" his voice was a hoarse whisper. He still couldn't believe this wouldn't melt away like a holo. The most wonderful holo, but still . . .

"It's a forest garden," Agarita said proudly. "Not just being gentle with the earth but actively working with her, letting her be the guide. I started with root plants, there are potatoes here, and onions. I got some small, wrinkled ones for barter a year ago. That gave me the idea. The root vegetables fertilize the soil and provide structure for the berry bushes to take root. I have blueberries and blackberries."

She pulled back a waving branch to reveal a glistening blackberry, each small globule glowing against a branch thick with slender thorns. "Be careful you don't get stuck," she said. She plucked the berry off and popped it into Alex's mouth.

He bit down carefully. It was sweet and sour at once, and the juice ran down his chin. Aggie caught it with her finger.

"I have small fruit trees—apricot and pear—and then larger apple trees to form a canopy. The canopy shade keeps out the dust and wind, and the bushes and root plants trap the moisture. All we had to do was follow what nature wanted. She did the rest." Her voice had dropped to a husky whisper. Her hand was still on his cheek. She dropped it and took his hand.

"One last thing," she said.

She picked her way through the dense foliage, following a trail so small Alex could never have found it. In the very center of the forest was a small clearing with a bed made of multiple blankets.

"When I can get away for the night, I sleep here," she said.

She looked up at him, turning her face so that the scar was fully exposed. "What do you think?" she asked.

"I think I finally know why I came here," he replied. He traced her scar with his finger. She didn't move. Then they kissed.

She pulled away and dropped onto the blankets. He sat beside her. Before he could move, she grabbed him and pulled him tightly to her.

He felt the familiar hardening and began to sit up, embarrassed, but Aggie pulled him back down. He looked at her, puzzled, unsure of her intent until she pulled her dress up over her head. Her breasts were perfect mounds above a flat, almost-concave stomach. Her flawless skin was almond colored, without any of the marks and blemishes of normal people. He tried to shake his head, but the air was as thick as water around them. He found he could only move toward her beautiful body, not away. She was tugging at his clothes, and he helped her. They came together, thrashing against the blankets while green branches and leaves closed over them. The first time was fast, but Aggie rose above him, her perfect breasts positioned so his head, his mouth, would naturally go there.

"Let's try this again," she said with a breathless laugh. "Slowly."

They melted into each other. Her last thought before she gave herself entirely to what they were doing was that she was making a memory to last for the rest of her life. Whatever happened, whether Alex went or stayed, if he disappointed her like everyone else, she would always have this.

After they finished, Alex held Aggie closely, his arms and body covering and sheltering as much of her as he could. He tried to analyze his feelings. Happiness, of course, and a feeling that he wanted to be with her for the rest of his life. Was this love? Maybe. But the biggest feeling was . . . relief. He had made the right decision, after all. He stared at the tree branches sheltering them and knew all he wanted to do was create more and more spaces like this, with this girl showing him how. His life had a purpose.

———

The waving branch reached down from the tree and clutched at him, pulling at his shoulder. He brushed it away, but it didn't stop, so he grabbed it, grabbed—fingers. His eyes popped open. He felt protectively for Aggie, who stirred in her sleep beside him, while his other hand gripped the hand that touched him. A small, grubby hand belonging to . . .

He looked up into the wide, concerned eyes of Corn Seven. When Corn Seven saw he was awake, he began to shake him even more urgently.

"Ge uh!" he said.

Beside him, Aggie sat up in one smooth movement. Corn Seven began to jabber excitedly at her. Aggie listened intently. Alex wondered if he would ever understand COS speak.

"We have to go," she said. "Our absence has been noticed. We fell asleep."

Alex found himself strangely reluctant to move. "Let's stay here," he said. "It's far enough away from COS to be safe. There's food here."

Aggie shook her head. "We have to give your mother cover until she is safely away. And I'm not ready yet. I want to take at least one beehive when I go."

Alex found himself thinking about Rosie. He'd like to take her away before she became goat stew, which he knew his father was reluctantly considering.

"Besides, this is too close to COS to be safe. I want to leave it for Corn Seven and the others while we start something even farther away. We have at least a year of learning and planting first."

Alex's heart sank at the thought of returning to the enclave. He would need to keep his head down and avoid the family. Ada didn't need to know about him and Aggie. Even if she was through with him, she needed to be the one to break it off.

Corn Seven was urging them to dress. If he thought it odd to find them naked together, he gave no indication. His fear communicated itself to Alex, who realized he had risked a lot to come and warn them. He remembered the child from his first night who had been knocked unconscious simply for failing to move fast enough. He pulled on his clothes quickly and followed Corn Seven and Aggie out of the forest. Although the cloud cover made changes less noticeable, he could tell it was darker, cooler. It was almost night. Where had the day gone?

They didn't notice a figure hiding behind a clump of trees. They dawdled as they walked, holding hands and watching the moon making a rare appearance through the ever-present cloud cover. Corn Seven tried to hurry them along, but the path was completely empty. He was worrying about nothing, and they weren't eager to get back while it was still daylight.

The figure following them took a shortcut across the barren landscape and reached the wall an hour before they did. Once inside, the cloaked figure pulled the hood back and smoothed her thin hair.

CHAPTER THIRTY-FOUR

Darwin was restless. Walden observed him shifting in his chair, muttering what were probably curses and shooting dark looks at Peter. It wasn't good to let Darwin get into this state, particularly since he was so suspicious of Peter and had taken a dislike to the son. Darwin hadn't spent any time with the boy, but he was aware that Ada was of an age to marry, and that Alex was a suitable choice for Ada. Darwin was smart about some things. Sex was one of them. It never paid to underestimate him.

Walden had gone off the boy a bit himself. He had the arrogance of youth and was very sure he had City of the South all figured out. Walden's wife didn't like him and didn't think him right for Ada. She wanted to find someone from what was left of Asia City. Of course she would. More importantly, Ada seemed less interested, and she was notoriously hard to persuade to do something she didn't want to do. All in all, it seemed Darwin was suspicious about nothing, but it wouldn't do to have open warfare between him and Peter. Thanks to his spies, they were reaching the point where Peter was expendable. Good agriculture wasn't that complicated. The hard part was assembling the tools and the process. Now, thanks to Peter's training, even the drooling idiots of COS could grow plants. After this season, Peter wouldn't be a problem.

Darwin stood up from his chair. "And why is the bean crop less this year?" he said angrily.

Peter responded smoothly: "As I just explained, rainfall is down. But planting an additional squash variety for next year will help with moisture retention."

"Next year doesn't help for this year," Darwin roared. "You should have done something for this year."

"We started a preserving project," Peter said. "We will have to be careful, but we should have the supplies we need to see us through the year. And next year—"

Darwin strode over to Peter and grabbed him by the throat. "I said, I don't want to hear about next year. I thought the addition of your precious son was supposed to—"

Peter pried Darwin's hands off his throat, straightened, and stared Darwin down. "Alex just arrived. He will be a big help, but he can't solve last year's rain." He stepped forward, forcing Darwin to step back in response. It wasn't a good idea to make Peter angry. Darwin was a bully and, like all bullies, a coward when he didn't have his gang with him.

"I think we'll end here," Walden said smoothly. "Thank you for the report, Peter."

Peter gave Darwin a long look, until Darwin looked down and mumbled something. Peter strode from the room.

Darwin turned angrily to Walden, but Walden forestalled him. "What are your plans this evening?" he asked." Would you like to have dinner with my family?"

"When do I ever want to have dinner with you, your bitch wife, and your brat?" he snarled.

"I figured you probably had plans with your men," Walden answered smoothly.

Darwin hesitated. "Damn right, I do!" he said, striding from the room to gather whoever he could find for a night of carousing in COS.

Walden heaved a sigh of relief. Darwin was combustible. No one was safe when his energy and his lusts were too pent up. He spared a moment's pity for the taverns and any unfortunate women who would cross his path. He hoped the cleanup wouldn't be too onerous—or expensive.

Darwin was dressing for a night out. This didn't involve evening wear but beltless pants he could pull down quickly when he found a likely girl to throw against a wall—and a knife if she gave him any argument or had a father or husband nearby. He answered a knock on the door with a feral growl.

A cloaked woman entered the room. Servants, particularly female servants, generally knew to stay out of Darwin's way. His rooms were cleaned, his food set up, when he was out. The woman pushed her hood to one side. Birna. He had what passed for fondness for Birna. She had been his nanny as a child, a very permissive nanny. He liked to play with animals, particularly ferrats. They squeaked really loudly and moved fast. It was almost a fair fight, except there was no way out of the room, and he had the knife. No matter how many he killed, Birna could always find more. And when he turned a strapping fourteen, she went from being a nanny to something else. She had been a good-looking woman when she was younger. He had once toyed with the idea of taking her on a coyote hunt, but his brother had sent her to spy on Peter instead. His eyes narrowed. She had been the one to alert him to the tailor's visit. This visit must have the same purpose.

"What's up?" he asked, almost mildly.

"I've come about the boy, Alex," she said, "and that girl Peter is so fond of. The one with the scar."

His face darkened. She was one of the few who had gotten away. He had always intended to have another go at her, but that goblin face put him off. He didn't know who had done that to her, but he heartily approved.

"What about them?"

"They've started their own garden," she said, "in competition with COS."

"Is this Peter's doing?"

She paused. "I don't think so. I don't think he knows. It's the girl's doing. He gives her way too much freedom to come and go as she pleases. And she knows too much. The boy hasn't been here long, but he's a willing participant." She paused. "Very willing." She smiled, making sure he got her meaning.

"How do you know this?"

"They were at the garden today. I followed them. They are still on the way back. I know a shortcut. If you leave now, you can catch them."

The rage that had been gathering in Darwin for weeks, ever since he caught Walden and Peter plotting, bubbled up behind his eyes. He could hardly see Birna for the red.

"Are any men out there?"

"A couple," she replied.

"They will have to do. It shouldn't take many of us to handle those two." He would finish what he had started with the goblin. It was getting dark, he wouldn't have to look at her face.

The men came upon them at the turning where Birna's shortcut began, close to the city gate. Corn Seven was walking in front with a large stick, which he aimed at the man who led the way. Lord Darwin himself. Corn Seven barely came to Darwin's waist. Darwin easily thrust the stick aside and swung his long knife. Corn Seven dropped to his knees, wide-eyed, blood pouring from his throat. Alex was weaponless, but he grabbed Darwin's arm before he could slash again. One of Darwin's companions slammed his meaty fist down on Alex's head. Alex fell to the ground.

Aggie rushed at Darwin with her fingers extended. She raked her nails across Darwin's cheek, drawing blood and leaving a wide track that was a good imitation of her own scar. He roared and grabbed her first by the hair and then by the waist. He wrapped his arms around her so she couldn't claw or kick. Once he had her secure, he turned to leave. His evening's entertainment was set. He just needed someplace quiet. He didn't check on Alex. It didn't much matter if the boy lived. He would probably suffer more in the morning when he picked up the pieces of what was left of the girl.

His two companions watched his retreating back until they could no longer hear the screams of the girl. One of them kicked the little boy. He was gone. The older boy was stirring slightly, but they knew he had been invited to Lord Walden's party for his daughter, and they had no orders from Darwin. They looked at each other and shrugged. They had been promised a night of carousing and didn't need Darwin to make that happen. They followed the main path back to town.

SANCTUARY

CHAPTER THIRTY-FIVE

Alex woke to the dripping of a light rain on his face and the smell of something meaty and sickly sweet. The ground where he lay was sticky. Opening his eyes sent stabbing pain through his head, so he shut them again. Where was he? Was it time to take the goats out? The events of the previous day came crawling back into his consciousness. He sat up abruptly—and vomited all over the ground beside him as the dizziness took hold and spun his head. Just a few feet in front of him, he looked into the empty eyes of Corn Seven. Eyes that would never see another harvest.

Aggie! Alex looked around wildly, but she was gone. He remembered the men. Three of them, and one of them had been Darwin. Then everything had gone dark.

He forced himself first to his hands and knees and then upright. Nausea and pain washed over him in dark, cold waves. He vomited some more but forced himself to look around through squinting eyes until he got his bearings and figured out the way back to town. He was sad and horrified about Corn Seven, and he would do something about it later—at least give him a proper burial—but nothing mattered right now except finding Aggie. And if she was—his mind refused to think the word "dead"—nothing would matter except taking the life of whoever had done it, regardless of what happened to him. But it couldn't be. She was too smart at navigating City of the South. Whatever had happened, they would get through it. He just had to find her.

His thoughts were as scrambled as his walk as he made his way shakily back to the city. He saw a tall figure in the distance and hoped it was Darwin. He clenched his fists. He would make Darwin tell him where Aggie was, what had happened to Corn Seven, and then he would wrap his fingers around his beefy neck and . . .

The figure got closer. Through blurry eyes he saw the spiky hair and slender frame of his dad. He broke into a stumbling run.

"Dad! A terrible thing has happened! Aggie and I were ambushed on the way to COS. And Corn Seven. Corn Seven is . . ." he broke down crying. He threw himself at his dad. Peter held him briefly at arm's length and then let him go.

"What were you doing outside the walls?" he asked, his voice taut with anger. "It's strictly forbidden. You know that. Agarita One certainly knew that."

Alex froze at Peter's use of the past tense. "Is she—?"

"Dead? Not yet, no thanks to you, but definitely in danger. What were you thinking? You've ruined everything. A decade of work. I don't know if I can smooth this over."

Alex stared at his dad. "Corn Seven is dead," he said.

"I heard you." His father brushed that impatiently aside. "I don't think you realize the damage you've done, Alex. You'll have to leave now. Fortunately, your mother and her guide, the mercenary, are still here and can take you back. This was obviously a mistake. You were too old. Sanctuary had already ruined you, made you too soft."

"If caring about my friend makes me soft, I'm proud to be that way. You don't give a shit about your workers."

"I'm sorry about Corn Seven," his father replied. "But this is his third harvest. He knew the rules better than anyone. If he'd followed them, he'd still be—"

Alex hauled off and hit his father in the mouth. Peter reeled back and clenched his own fist into a ball. He raised his hand, then dropped it.

"Bringing you here was a risk," he said quietly. "I took it, and it's my fault things didn't work out. You can't help who you are. You are your mother's son. There isn't much of me in you. I sensed it, but I didn't want to see it."

"If you think that's an insult, you're wrong," Alex said. "I can't wait to leave, but not without Aggie. Where is she?"

"She's in jail," his father answered. "She's going to get thirty lashes at noon today. Darwin's doing. She broke the law, and this is the result. Another one of my mistakes. I gave her too much freedom. I could trust her mother with my life, and I did. But Aggie is not her mother."

"She knew better than to trust you," Alex said bitterly. "She's smarter than I am."

"I'm going to do my best to get her punishment changed to banishing. Let's hope she's smart enough to keep quiet until I can arrange something."

He looked at Alex through narrowed eyes. "You are going to wait at the door where I brought you into COS for your mother and her guide. I will get Agarita One and bring her there. Then the four of you need to head as fast as you can to Sanctuary. Darwin knows the outside well, and once you are beyond the walls, you are beyond any protection Walden can provide. Do you understand?"

Alex shook his head stubbornly. "I am going with you to rescue Aggie," he said. "I won't step one foot outside the city without her."

In answer, his father grabbed his shoulders and shook him. The movement made the nausea rise again in his throat, and he turned away to be sick.

"You are in no condition to come with me," Peter responded. "Besides, I intend to tell Walden and Darwin that you're dead. They will be more inclined to show leniency to Agarita One if I tell them that."

Alex didn't respond.

"I know you think I don't care. About you. About Aggie. I do. I admit I care more about the work that will outlast all of us, that will heal the planet we damaged, but I loved Aggie's mother, and I promised to take care of her daughter."

"Did you love my mother?" Alex asked.

His father was silent.

"Your loss," Alex said bitterly. "She was too good for you."

"That's probably true," his father responded. "We'd better get going if I am going to put a stop to Aggie's punishment."

Miranda sat by the stove. A child brought Murray a message of some kind. Miranda recognized her from school. She was upset about something, but Miranda was too dispirited to get up and investigate. She was grateful that Da had gone back to his bed for a nap. She needed to be alone with her grief.

"I have to go out for a bit," Murray said. Miranda nodded. He didn't tell her more, but she figured it couldn't be about Alex or he would have said, so it didn't matter. She stared into the smelly stove and poked the burning trash whenever the flame seemed to be dying out. She didn't hear Murray return until he loomed over her.

"You're back. What do we need to—?" She looked up and fell off her stool in surprise. He reached out a hand to help her up.

"Hello, Miranda."

"Peter!" There was no mistaking her ex-husband. The cowlicky hair, the glinting green eyes. It could have been a much older Alex standing there. But it wasn't.

"Where is Murray?" he demanded.

"Yes, it has been a while," she replied. "I'm fine. And how are you?"

"For God's sake, Miranda!" he replied impatiently. "This isn't a social call. Can you think about someone besides yourself for once? Where is Murray?"

"I don't know. Some girl came for him and he went out. She seemed upset. Alex? Did something happen? Is he okay?"

"Something did happen. Something very bad. Alex is okay, for now, but if he stays here, he won't be. He has to go back with you."

Miranda would never forgive herself for the joy that flooded her. Alex was leaving with her. She lowered her eyes so that he wouldn't see the happiness. Something bad had happened. He wasn't leaving by choice.

"What's wrong," she asked quietly.

"He got involved with illegal activities," he said harshly. "And with a girl. They both have to leave."

"A girl? The one at the party?"

"The party? Is that how you—? No, not that one. One of my workers."

"Aggie," Miranda said.

"How do you—? Never mind. She's in serious trouble. I'm going to rescue her, while you and Murray meet up with Alex at my COS door and wait for me to bring her."

"I'm going with you." Murray stood in the doorway.

"You can't," Peter said. "It's too dangerous. If anything happens, you have to get Alex and Miranda back to Sanctuary."

"Not without Aggie," Murray replied. "You two aren't the only ones with a child."

Miranda looked between the two of them and then went to stand beside Murray.

"The four of us leave," she said quietly. "Or none of us do."

SANCTUARY

GRACE J. AGNEW

CHAPTER THIRTY-SIX

Peter was silent, marshaling his words. "Aggie's safety matters to me as much as Alex's. I've known her all her life, and I loved her mother very much."

Miranda was surprised at the stab of jealousy that shot through her, but she kept quiet and retreated to the shadows. She had gotten over Peter long ago; anyway, this was about Aggie.

"You won't have a shot at getting Aggie released," Peter said to Murray. "The Esters have always regretted letting the Stallways live unmolested. The brothers feel less and less bound by the treaty enacted by their father. If they remember the relationship between you and Aggie, it might be her death warrant."

Murray shook his head stubbornly. "I'll stay behind you. In the shadows. If your persuasion doesn't work."

"You have no idea what the atmosphere is like in the enclave. There are spies everywhere, and the punishment arena is tightly guarded. You can't hide, and when you are discovered, there is nothing more I can do. Our only hope is to make Aggie seem like a nobody—an agricultural worker who broke the rules and has already been punished for her crimes."

Miranda saw Murray flinch at that last sentence. She looked away from the pain that filled his eyes.

"What's the plan?" he asked quietly.

"Aggie has been sentenced to thirty lashes in a couple of hours. I am going to appeal to Walden to reduce the sentence to banishment."

"Why do you think he will listen to you?"

"We're having problems with some crops this year. They need my knowledge to limit the damage so there is enough food for everyone after the harvest. I will threaten to leave with you."

"They might kill you for that threat," Murray observed.

Peter shrugged. "They might. But they won't manage a successful harvest without me. I think for Darwin, his belly will win out over his anger and his hatred of me."

Miranda, who had slipped into the shadows, felt a flicker of admiration. She hadn't believed Peter capable of caring for anyone but himself, but he was willing to risk his life for this girl.

Murray made a decision. "Miranda, are you ready?"

In answer, she grabbed her pack. Peter looked at her, seeming to actually see her for the first time. "Sanctuary has agreed with you," he said. "You've worn the years much better than I have."

Miranda answered with a slight nod of the head, although truthfully, the weather-beaten-farmer look suited him. But his praise meant nothing. She was only interested in her son.

"Alex is?"

"Waiting for us at my door," he said, "on the outside. Only a few people have the key, so he should be safe enough."

Murray grabbed his own pack. "Let's go," he said.

Alex was pacing outside the door. The wind had picked up, spiraling dust over his shoes, sometimes high enough to get into his mouth and even sting his eyes. They would have rough going on the trip back to Sanctuary, but Alex didn't care. He just wanted to see Aggie again. He blamed himself for whatever had happened to her. He had forced her to take him to his mother, which was strictly against the rules. Then she showed him her forest to comfort him

314

after he and his mom had said goodbye forever. She had probably slept with him for the same reason. He should have insisted that they return immediately, before their absence was noticed. There would have been other times when they could slip away. Other times when they could—

Where was his dad? This was taking a long time. Every time he heard a thump or a scratch, he looked anxiously at the door, but it was always just the wind, blowing debris around.

Finally, the door opened. His dad, his mom, and a strange man stepped through. His mother ran to him and hugged him. For a minute he gave into the embrace gratefully, like a little boy who had stubbed his toe.

"Alex, your head!"

"Never mind. It'll heal. What about Aggie?" he demanded of his father.

"I'm going to get her now. I may be a while, so you will all have to wait. Do you have enough supplies for the children?" he asked Murray.

"We'll make do," Murray replied,

Peter turned to go back into the city. "I'll return as fast as I can," he said. The door closed and locked behind him with finality.

Alex rushed to the door and pulled on the handle. When it didn't give at all, he kicked the door hard, although the act made his head and stomach swim.

A hand gripped his shoulder, and he looked up into the leathery face of a man with Agarita's deep blue eyes.

"I have another entrance," he said. "It's farther from the administrative area, so I have to leave right away. Stay here with your mother. I'll bring her back." He strode away into the dust.

Alex watched him with burning, tear-filled eyes. Then he shook his head. "Stay here," he ordered his mother. "I'm going too."

"Alex! You can't! You're injured. And you broke the same laws. You're in trouble too."

She was protesting to the wind. Miranda began to run before she lost sight of him. They'd have this argument at the other door.

Alex reached the door shortly after Murray closed it carefully behind him. It was well-camouflaged, and it took him a few frantic minutes to find it. The wind had picked up even more, and he didn't hear his mother come up behind him. As she reached the door, it closed for the second time. Fortunately, it wasn't locked.

Aggie woke in a pool of sticky wetness. She reached to touch it and screamed as pain rammed through her like a hot knife, like his—she couldn't bring herself to think the word. She pulled her knees protectively under her chin despite the pain and mewed like an injured cat while hot tears ran down her cheeks. Two years ago, she had been caught by Darwin and his men after dark in COS. She had managed to get away, and fortunately had the administrative compound to escape to. She had heard from other women who weren't so lucky that Darwin hated deformity as much as he loved large breasts and a curvy belly, neither of which she had. There was a voluptuous woman with a small harelip who made an excellent living from her body, who had offered herself to Darwin in a tavern and been pushed roughly away. Aggie had known since she was twelve that her beauty turned heads, but she didn't want to make a living from her body. She was smart, she was learning things, and Peter was her protector. She also didn't want her da, her mother's father, who had taken her in until Peter recruited her for the crops, arranging a marriage for money and goods. When she saw him negotiating with a man with no hair and few teeth, she decided. She took a gardening hoe from Peter's workshop and hacked a gash across her face. Not so deep it would cause infection, but deep enough for a lasting scar. The best part had been Murray's shock when he saw it—Murray, who had abandoned the family when her mother took up with Peter and who had taken too long to come after her when her mother died.

She found that she liked being the girl with the scar. It made her fearless in a way that other girls could not afford. Despite the scar, she still attracted glances, and she had intentionally lost her virginity to a boy her age. The short relationship convinced her that she had made the right choice to devote her life to agriculture and to one day starting her own forest garden, far away from COS, with some of the workers she had met and trusted. She didn't understand the point of bringing children into a world like this and then struggling to feed them, as most women did.

She had learned how the earth really liked to grow by wandering far from COS with her mother and finding pockets of growing things protected by rocks from the wind and dust.

And then Alex arrived. And messed with her judgment. She decided her dream could expand to include him, which was a huge mistake, even if Peter would have allowed it. The pain and the blood below; her puffy, split lip; and the black eye she could feel forming when she gingerly felt the soft, swollen flesh around her eye told her what a mistake she had made—what a fool's paradise she had inhabited because Peter's protection and her own arrogance had convinced her that she alone of the agricultural workers could come and go as she pleased.

She refused to think about what Darwin had done to her last night before slinging her into the cell like a bale of hay. But she couldn't stop from thinking about Alex and Corn Seven, and what her carelessness might have cost them. Despair rumbled through her like bile. If they had paid the ultimate price for her carelessness, she didn't want to live either. But until she knew, she had to stay alive. She began to cautiously scissor her legs, stifling her screams until she was used to the pain enough to get up on all fours and then slowly, shakily, to her feet.

━━━━━━━━━

When Peter reached the administrative compound, he stopped to beat down his anger. He needed to be calm and rational with Walden. Most people viewed Walden as the reasonable one because he seldom lost his temper, but Peter knew from long experience that there wasn't much to choose between the two brothers. Both of them operated solely on the principle of "What is in it for me?" only Walden had a veneer of civilization and manners that impressed the unwary. Neither son was the visionary the father had been until the drink ruined him, despite the high-sounding names he had bestowed upon them. And neither brother would ever back down unless he believed he was getting the best of a deal. Peter would have to be careful to use the threat of his departure only if necessary, or the result would be his joining Aggie at the dock.

━━━━━━━━━

"I do understand what you want," Walden said, playing for time. "I just don't understand why it matters to you."

Peter had decided on the necessary falsehoods on the way over. "I lost my son yesterday," he said, allowing a small tremor in his voice. "I can't lose my daughter too."

"Your daughter?" Walden's eyebrows shot up in surprise. "I understood the scarred girl was a Stallway."

"Her mother promoted that lie," Peter said. "But as she grew older, I saw resemblances that made me think otherwise. I believe she is my daughter. And I feel that way about her."

Walden studied him closely. He had always admired the fact that Peter was such an emotionless man, focused on his work. His own life would be much simpler if he didn't care so much about Ada. This train of thought made him angry. Peter's harebrained scheme to bring his son to wed Ada had been a stupid idea from the start. He should have listened to his first instinct rather than being persuaded by Peter's arguments. It would be best if Peter went back to being an automaton, at least until this growing season was over and he could replace Peter with the workers Birna had picked out. Birna had persuaded him that each worker was good but expendable, so he would never be hostage to another man's talents again.

"I think we had better leave things as they are," he said mildly. "I understand from the prison warden that the girl is somewhat the worse for wear but likely to live. With any luck, she will withstand Darwin's beating and learn a valuable lesson from it."

Peter was trembling in earnest now. He had persuaded himself that all he felt for Agarita One was the obligation to her mother, but now he was forced to confront the truth that he was fond of her in her own right. Her pluckiness reminded him of her mother, but he also saw his own influence. In a different place and under different circumstances, he would be pleased that Alex preferred her to Ada. He couldn't afford to dwell on the phrase "worse for wear." She was alive, and that was all that mattered.

He chose his words carefully. "I don't think I can turn off my feelings for her that easily," he said. "She's my blood, after all, as was the son I lost yesterday." He paused to let his silence remind Walden that death was a harsh punishment for simply leaving COS. "I'm not sure I would want to go on in this life if I lost both." He turned to one side as if overcome by emotion, but really to give Walden some face-saving time to consider.

Walden sighed. There was no end to the trouble that brat Peter had winkled out of Sanctuary was causing, even in death. But it was clear from Birna's reports that they needed Peter this year to wring as much as possible from disappointing crops. The towns-people were increasingly restless, and if the rations were cut even shorter . . .

"I don't know what I can do," he said petulantly. "Darwin is incredibly stupid, but he is two years older. I can't overrule his decision."

"Can the sentence be commuted to banishment?" Peter asked. "A young, defenseless girl is unlikely to survive in the outside. Particularly if the marauders who wait outside City of the South were to spot her."

Peter spoke as artlessly as he could, but the message he was sending was that the sport would be much greater for Darwin if he and his men hunted the girl outside the city walls. He would have to trust that Murray would be able to evade them.

He saw the sideways glance and the secretive smile as Walden put two and two together, but then he shook his head.

"No. The girl didn't just sneak away from her duties. She built a forbidden forest outside the city walls. Who knows how many people are aware of this? She must have a public punishment. But here is what I will propose. I'll reduce the strokes to ten, and I will give them myself. Afterward, she will be banished." He held up a hand to forestall Peter's objection.

"Don't worry. I will strike lightly with a special whip I have for children. She will be in good enough shape to make her way on the outside."

Peter submitted. It was the best he could do. He would have to hope it was enough.

Peter stood in the shadows behind the punishment arena. Workers in the administrative enclave had been gathered to witness Agarita One's punishment. Most of them looked sullen and not as if anticipating a treat, as they usually did when a thief in City of the South was sentenced. Walden, standing on the stage, observed the same. The citizens were getting surly and restive. He had put a stop to Ada's visits to the city, because even with guards it was no longer safe. He had done a lot to make the food distribution more equitable. Without him, and his foresight, they would be howling savages, like the less-than-human marauders who endlessly circled the city gates.

Resentment flared in him like a match. These people were mostly unskilled and illiterate. The only people capable of building were the ones he personally employed or arranged training for, but there was no gratitude. The more he gave them, the more they wanted. And now, servants like this girl were stealing the training and probably stealing supplies. He had no doubt of his fate, and that of his wife and daughter, if the people no longer depended on him for food, water, and supplies.

The guard brought in the girl. She was smaller than he expected and a bit bruised and torn, but she didn't look too bad after a night with Darwin. Maybe Darwin had rudimentary misgivings about savaging a girl he thought was a Stallway.

Walden stepped in front of her and read the punishment. He brandished the special whip that raised a welt but didn't break the skin. She looked like she could handle ten lashes easily.

The crowd didn't seem to agree. An angry murmur swelled through the crowd. "She jus ma foo!" a woman he recognized as one of his wife's housekeepers called out.

He held up a hand. "The land can only bear so much working," he said, although he had no idea if this was true. "She is untrained and did more harm than good."

The angry buzz grew louder. He raised the whip to get this over with and end the spectacle. It was a good thing this girl was leaving. Darwin would probably finish her off outside the city walls, but no one would be the wiser.

As was the custom, he asked the girl if she had anything to say.

He could see that it cost her physically to square her thin shoulders and stand upright. She faced the crowd, not him.

"I appreciate all I have learned in the enclave about growing food," she said, "but it doesn't make me blind to the mistakes, and the harm we do with our practices. We have begun to heal the soil, but we still plant as if we were the masters. You have only to go outside the city to realize we are the vanquished, cowering behind our walls. One bad drought, too much or too little rain, and we are finished. But the Earth knows how to grow, if we let her. She wants to bloom and not be barren. She can nourish her own soil, retain the water she needs, if we work with her, not against her. The forest garden I started is one way. The Earth wants ground cover, and layers of plants that pull from the sky and the Earth to nourish the soil. We can plant vegetables and fruits that feed both of us. If we let her, she will nourish us both. We need to keep the forest garden going. And we need more people working the soil and growing enough food for themselves and their families. The earth that we need to heal and the needs of the people are too great to hoard the farming."

Walden's lips creased to a thin line. "Are you finished?" he asked. She nodded. He also turned to face the restive crowd. "This city only exists because my father had the foresight to establish it," he said, ignoring the other family. "You only exist because my brother and I continue to protect you from marauders, to feed you and shelter you. Every day, there is a long line of people wanting to get in. Some are allowed to barter, most are turned away; a very few are allowed to stay. If you feel you would be safer outside, feel

free to go." He waved his arm in the direction of the front gate.
"There are many who would be happy to take your place. Join this
girl, who will be banished as soon as her punishment ends. But
don't follow her to her so-called forest. It has been destroyed. It
was a pile of weeds and dangerous animals. The two boys who
accompanied her lost their lives trusting that forest."

Aggie bowed her head to hide her tears. It was true then. She
had cost Alex and Corn Seven their lives.

A burly man rushed the stage from the rear. At first Aggie
thought it might be Peter, or Murray, but then her heart dropped
to her feet.

With a roar, Darwin snatched the whip from his brother. "This
girl is traitor scum! She wants to destroy City of the South." He
pulled the whip away from his brother. "Not ten lashes, not thirty
lashes—fifty lashes to this trash who would destroy us all!" He
flicked the whip against Agarita's back. It tore into the already torn
dress she wore but didn't break the skin.

"What is this?" Darwin snarled. "Bring me a real whip!"

Walden turned to leave the stage. There was no controlling
Darwin when he got this way. The girl wouldn't survive, and maybe
that was for the best. He was in for weeks of damage control, of
bribing the family, if she had any, to say that she was plotting to
destroy the townspeople and kill its children. He saw Peter, his
face white and set, standing backstage, although he had ordered
him to stay away.

He mouthed "I'm sorry" to Peter. Peter would be a tougher sell
than the town. He went to put his arm around Peter's shoulders to
lead him away, but Peter roughly shook him off and strode to the
stage. He jumped at Darwin with his long knife drawn. The knife
penetrated Darwin's vest but no further. The vest was made of the
close wool that servants sheared from the sheep but reinforced
with scrap metal. Darwin had learned to prepare for trouble at

323

these public punishments, punishments that Peter shied away from, preferring not to know. This lack of knowledge cost him dearly as Darwin whipped the lash around Peter's neck. Peter struggled to pry off the lash that was choking him. He slashed uselessly with his knife as Darwin strode behind him, shoving his own knife deep into Peter's back and drawing it down to do the most damage. Peter dropped to his knees before sprawling at Aggie's feet. His empty eyes and slack mouth caused Aggie to scream.

Murray rushed the stage with his own knife drawn. Darwin stepped away from the body as the two men circled each other. Miranda watched from the front of the crowd, where she had managed to push and shove her way in. The bloody scene in front felt unreal, telescoped into a story beamed from a cube. It seemed like only moments ago that she and Peter had met in Da's smelly hut. He couldn't be here one minute and then gone forever, with no preparation to deal with his loss. He was older, and ruddy from the outdoors, but looked the same as when the two of them had been raising their son. She had lost sight of him in the crowd milling around the stage, awaiting the punishment. Her eyes scanned the crowd frantically. When she couldn't find him, she looked up at the stage, where a guard had entered from the side with a knife and was moving toward Aggie, on her knees, cradling Peter's lifeless body in her arms.

She looked away from the body, the crying girl, the blood, and into the eyes of—Alex, following the guard onto the stage. She almost cried out in protest, but a firm shake of his head stopped her. He locked onto her with his steady green gaze and then looked at Aggie, who had risen unsteadily to her feet to confront the guard. Miranda looked at Murray, who was wrestling Darwin on the ground for his knife.

Aggie's eyes remained fixed on the guard, so she didn't see Alex sidling behind her. Alex held Miranda's eyes with his steady green gaze, and he smiled. A lifetime passed while his eyes spoke. He told her life would mean nothing without Aggie, and she knew that was true. In a very short time, he had given his heart to this girl, had risked everything for her. Miranda could barter for his life, for his safe return to the city, but only the shell of Alex would return, not the man he had become. He glanced again at Aggie, backing away from the guard, and reached into his boot to pull out a knife. But he didn't move. He looked at Miranda. He knew what his death would do to her, and he wanted her permission, her forgiveness. She took a deep breath and nodded. He smiled, and his smile wiped away all the mistakes she had made as a mother. His smile told her he loved her, without reservation.

As he loved Aggie. She looked away and shut her eyes tightly as he made his move. She heard the scuffle, another scream from Aggie. When she was able to look, two more bodies stained the ground, the guard and Alex. Miranda wouldn't look at the bodies. She glared instead at Aggie, who looked back at her without recognition. Miranda found her voice.

"Run, you little fool" she screamed. "He died for you!"

Aggie's head snapped back as if she had been slapped. Then she turned and ran. Darwin let out a roar and released his grip on Murray, which was his undoing. Murray drove the knife deep into his groin. Darwin dropped with a scream as the blood gushed out. He wouldn't go marauding again. Murray ran after Aggie, and both were lost to view. Miranda fell to the ground and blessedly lost consciousness.

She woke sputtering to rain splashing into her mouth and nose. The sky had opened up with a howling storm. She sank into the mud and opened her mouth wider to the rain that pelted her. She choked and sputtered but wouldn't turn away. She would drown like a ferrat in a puddle and join Alex. She lay there until the rain blotted out both consciousness and light.

SANCTUARY

CHAPTER THIRTY-SEVEN

Miranda sank into wet and cold but rose into fire. She was burning, and someone was trying to put the fire out with a wet cloth. She pushed feebly at her would-be rescuer. She had to get to Alex. He was just there, beyond the flames, calling to her. An arm pulled her up and held something to her mouth. She felt something cold brush against her lips and force its way in a trickle down her swollen throat. She gasped and lashed out.

The hand grasped her neck firmly. "I must get this down you, if you want to live."

Miranda shook her head. Living was not in her plans. The voice was familiar. She squinted against the light. The scarred lip; she had seen that before.

"You know me," the voice said. "Aggie."

"Aggie," Miranda croaked in reply. She opened her eyes wide, even though the movement made her head crack open with gusts of pain. "You survived."

"Because of your son," she said, "and not by choice."

Miranda shook her head. "Can't say that," she panted. "You have to live for both now." She turned away. She needed this girl to live a meaningful life, to justify Alex's sacrifice, but she would never be able to forgive her and refused to look at her now.

Aggie understood and let Miranda's head drop gently back on the bed. She would never forgive herself either.

Miranda felt the fever breaking over her in waves, like the sea. She was too far away from the control of city healers for any effectives to work. The relief of knowing she was beyond help was immense. A face floated on the waves toward her. Alex smiled and waved at her as he floated on the fever sea. Beside him, Peter was leading the way to the far shore. Ever the explorer. Peter straightened up at Alex's touch and saw her. He smiled as well. A beckoning smile. Miranda almost cried with happiness. She hadn't been the best mother or, truthfully, the best wife. The blame for his departure lay partly at her doorstep. But they both forgave her, and they wanted her with them. She strode toward them without looking back.

CHAPTER THIRTY-EIGHT

Three years later.

When she walked in the door to her hut, she realized he was back. She watched Murray wrestling with Alex on the floor. Alex was panting. His green eyes, so like his father's, were crinkled and teary with laughter. She looked at him and saw Alex as a young boy, who he might have been with a father to tease and poke him as his grandfather was doing.

"How is she doing?"

"All right."

"Did you speak to her?" In response, Murray tickled Alex's tummy as the little boy squirmed with laughter. No response was answer enough. Agarita didn't say anything. She understood the shame he felt that he couldn't save his grandson's father. But Miranda was a grandmother too, and she needed to know that. Agarita sensed that things between Murray and Miranda weren't finished either, whatever Murray thought. But the timing would have to be his. He made excuses to visit Sanctuary frequently, so she knew she just needed to wait. She owed it to Alex to heal things with Miranda.

She heard a bleating at the door, and Alex ran to open it. Rosie tumbled in and play-butted Alex in the stomach. They tumbled together in front of the fire while Murray watched. Murray had risked a lot to steal Rosie, but he hadn't protested when Agarita insisted, although he took some breeding goats as well for his trouble. Their herd was coming along nicely. They had milk and the occasional meat dinner.

Aggie was just coming back from a class she taught in the use of daggers. Girls in her small town were outfitted with daggers at an early age and taught when and how to use them. Unlike City of the South, girls lived their own lives and made their own future plans. They went everywhere and did everything they wanted. But nothing was ever taken from them unless they gave it freely. The lessons she had learned from COS were hard, but lasting.

At another glance from her, Murray ended their game and picked Alex up to take him to bed. Alex gave a whoop of surprise that could easily turn to tears, but Murray imitated him, and they whooped together as he carried the boy into the other room. Aggie smiled. He was good with Alex. Who would have expected it? Maybe with Alex, he was finally raising a child right.

She could hear the sounds of covers turning down, of Murray's grumbling voice and Alex's high one. The old argument about going to bed, an argument Aggie could hardly understand. Many nights she tumbled into bed, too tired to change clothes or eat. She and Murray had started with just the two of them, but gradually others had shown up, refugees from COS and the outside—in ones and twos, sometimes whole families. They welcomed some, but not all.

It was work to build a town around a constantly enlarging forest garden, and it was aging her beyond her years. There were already silver strands in her curly hair. Some men still eyed her sideways, despite the scar, but she was done with that. Her heart was bound up only in her work and in Alex. It was scary to love another person so much. Her feelings for the first Alex, which invaded her dreams, felt like nothing compared to what she felt for his son. She felt that she finally understood Miranda, and what she, Agarita One, had cost her.

Murray came out of the bedroom. "He's wanting an Alex story," he announced. She had grown used to his daily presence, his weathered, expressionless face. He was a quiet, reliable presence in their lives, in her life. She was amazed at how fond she had grown of him. She couldn't imagine coming home at night and not finding him here. Fortunately, except for trips to Sanctuary and scavenging missions with the older children, he never had reason to leave. She knew her mother had chosen Peter partly because Murray's wandering ways made him seem too unreliable. Now he was content to stay at home and help her raise Alex.

As he took his standard place by the fire, she thought about their comfortable evenings together, after Alex went to bed and when she wasn't too tired. She shared her plans for the town. He didn't say much, but he would occasionally make a suggestion that told her he was listening closely. Tonight she plied him with questions about Sanctuary, about Miranda.

"She's semi-retired from world building, doesn't get out much," he said. "I guess it is to be expected."

So he *was* checking up on her, which was what Aggie really wanted to know.

"Tara, on the other hand, is the same. If anything, she seems younger. But Sanctuary—"

"What about it?"

"I don't think it has much longer. The signs of decay are there. I said something to Tara, but she cut me off. But it was clear that she knows."

Agarita considered that and smiled. Things might come to head with Miranda sooner rather than later.

Tara was home alone when Miranda arrived at the flat. "Alex stayed at work. He's finishing up some things." She gestured toward the kitchen. "I have a surprise for you," she said, and smiled broadly. "Guess what I found at the food emporium." She didn't wait for Miranda's reply. She knew Miranda hated to guess things. "An actual apple! A bit wrinkled, but still . . ."

"Terrific. We'll have it when Alex gets in. Maybe do a story."

"I wouldn't count on Alex," Tara said. "I think he has plans."

Miranda lifted her head from the story cube where she was browsing through selections. "Oh?" she asked, responding to Tara's tone. "Someone he met at work?"

Tara shook her head. "I think he met her at a music club. If it's serious, I'm sure we'll meet her before too long."

Miranda looked at Tara. With her glowing, unlined skin and athletic body, she was more like Alex's older sister, or at least a very young aunt. They shared a closeness that Miranda would never be able to understand, much less experience.

"I just hope he remembers that he has a date," Tara said. "He had a real breakthrough with the aging today." The aging was a sore spot with Miranda. Tara and Alex felt it was critical. Miranda didn't see the point of it. If you managed perfection, or at least a close proximity, why would you ever choose to destroy it? They felt that the ability to grow and change required knowing you were mortal. Alex was always trying to push the boundaries of who he was. Just like the first . . . she pushed away the thought.

She knew there were essential things she would never know about Tara II and Alex, a consciousness they shared that she was shut out of, but they would never experience bitter loss the way she had. Although Tara II . . . in her mind, she still called her that. But she was returning openly to her role as committee member tomorrow, after a long convalescence, so it was important to break herself of the bad habit. *Tara, Tara, Tara,* she imprinted the name in her mind.

She unwillingly thought back to her return to the city three years ago, weary and sick and wanting only to die in the howling wet misery of the outside. She had no memory of the journey back, mostly carried by Murray. Tara had been waiting at the gate. Tara had taken her home and slowly brought her back to life with her work. Not the cat, which was just a new apprenticeship for Miranda, but the real android, the one Tara was designing: Tara II.

"It's not narcissistic," Tara insisted. "I care very much about the city. And no one understands it as I do. I needed to build someone who could preserve what is best about the city for all time, to re-create it when the time came. And someone that I completely understood. Tara II is me, only without my fears, my failings. But she isn't quite right. She needs the outsider's eye. I've been hoping and waiting for your return."

Tara II brought Miranda out of her fog of grief. What was special was how Tara II participated in her own development. Working with the two Taras, co-creating with the creation itself, was a world building experience Miranda had never even hoped for—the ultimate experience, in fact. She could almost forget outside were it not for the ghosts that visited nightly. Peter sometimes, but always Alex. He seemed to be asking for something.

The poor sleep and the nightmares didn't stop her from throwing herself into her work. Tara II absorbed every waking moment. She could forget everything until bedtime, when she slept on the floor beside her bed. One of the funny aftereffects of her time on the outside was her inability to sleep on anything but a hard floor, with just the barest of blankets for covering.

The three of them did their job well. Tara II was human in every sense but the frailty of human flesh. Then Tara got sick with another virus that was making the rounds in the city. It started slowly and lingered, but it was seldom fatal, except for the elderly and those with weakened immune systems. Tara looked good, but she was in her fifties, and she drove herself very hard. Tara II nursed her around the clock, and in the end, she gave the FD when Tara herself was too weak. Miranda would never forget the look of love and gratitude that Tara showered on Tara II as she gently administered the medicine, holding up Tara's frail head until it fell back onto the pillow. Nor would she forget the fear and sadness that brushed across Tara II's face like a shadow before it recomposed to its usual cheerful calm.

Miranda knew Tara II couldn't be asked to live this experience twice all by herself when Miranda's time came. She was too human for that. She needed a companion, and it needed to be someone Miranda knew well—the thought processes, the fears and dreams, the story at the core of the person. She never even considered immortalizing herself. That night, as she let herself into her lonely flat, she turned on the story cube for the first time in three years and watched Alex, age four, playing with his big blue rabbit DP.

With Tara II's help, and soon with the help of Alex himself, they created a person who was more real than anyone Miranda had ever met, including perhaps the son she had physically birthed. Or maybe it was just that she had never really seen Alex until the very end, had only seen the distortion she had created through the haze of her own fears, projected onto the boy despite her best intentions. But now the worst had happened. The shoe had dropped. She had no fears left. She could see Alex, her son, as he really was. And she could give birth to him again. She saw Alex plain, and the result was nothing short of miraculous.

The creation process added the one thing, to both Tara II and Alex, that Miranda and all the people Miranda knew had lacked—self-knowledge. Tara II and Alex understood themselves and their motivations at a level Miranda could never hope to emulate. She worried over the right steps to take, while they always seemed to know. They loved her, but they exchanged glances of puzzlement at the limitations of the person who was both their mother and creator.

Miranda marveled at the way they studied each other and tinkered with themselves. She had been content months ago to declare a victory and perhaps plan the next person, but they seemed to feel essential pieces were still missing. Their bodies were made of growfiber, which required a certain level of nutrient to stay supple, but otherwise they had no fears of illness or death. It amazed Miranda that they considered this a bad thing, that they discussed algorithms for aging—adding wrinkles and a lack of elasticity to skin, brittleness to hair, and stiffness to joints. These could be added at will, but they were arguing to make them automatic—something Miranda, who was beginning to find the flat's moving stairs a bit of a trial, fought against. Miranda could see how aging would enable them to fit in, but she wasn't sure how much longer that would matter.

Sanctuary was fraying at the edges. The young people were restless and rebellious against their roles, and more of the outside got in every day, including viruses, like the one that killed Tara. Better to focus on building companions, each of whom carried an essential part of the city consciousness, to heal and rebuild whatever could be fixed on the dying planet.

But Alex insisted, and Tara II concurred. Although Tara II was the older and the more experienced, she usually followed Alex's lead. Miranda often felt proud of her work, but she hadn't believed it when Tara had told her, toward the end, that Miranda was the world builder Tara had only hoped to be. It wasn't her skill, she knew, but her subject. She had never really known what it was to be totally consumed by her work until Alex. She was an expert world builder, and Alex had been—and would always be—her world.

Tara II (*Tara*, she corrected herself) called her from her thoughts to the table, where an apple was skillfully arranged in slices on a plate. One of the positive changes in the city that Miranda was just waking up enough to appreciate was the availability of new and strange foods from the outside. Thinking of the outside reminded her of COS, a time she could never share with Tara and Alex. She hadn't given Alex memories of the outside or of any of the people she now associated with that awful time. No Aggie, and no Peter. Alex would probably go outside one day, perhaps quite soon, given how the city was changing, but he would forge his own memories based on who he was now. She had given him the insecurities of a man who grew up with only a mother, but not the insecurities of being abandoned by a restless father. This Alex knew without a doubt that he was loved. It was the best armor she could give him for what lay ahead.

Tara took a small slice of apple and picked at it delicately. She talked about their discoveries at work today, moving her hands with animation. Miranda listened and supplied the right answers to questions, but she kept glancing toward the flat door. Tara intercepted a glance and said, "I didn't really expect him. He's been distracted lately. This girl may be someone who matters."

"Why do you say that?"

"I discovered—not snooping, you understand, but we share a research cube. Alex has been researching sperm."

Miranda stopped her fork in midair. A slice of apple fell onto the table unheeded. Sperm and eggs, procreation itself and not just the act of it, was something they hadn't been able to solve. But Alex had all of Miranda's analytical skills and, more than that, he had time. She had no doubt that just as she had surpassed Tara, he would surpass her. After the initial shock, the idea pleased her. Perhaps there was no need to create more android people. Life, and Alex, would find a way.

"How did your errand go?" Tara asked.

"Fine."

Miranda used her DP to alert her when Alex or Tara returned to the flat late at night. They had full lives without her, and friends she had never met, but she just liked to know they were back safely. She turned her DP off tonight. She didn't expect him back, and it seemed wrong to keep tabs on a grown man, even in such a small way. Alex might register; he might leave the city sooner than she expected. Was she ready to let go? What did parents do when their children left the nest? She had run blindly away from the prospect with her blood son, who existed now only in story cubes. She wouldn't make the same mistake with the second chance she had been given. The idea of Fred escaped her closet and crawled unbidden onto her blanket, arranging it with his scratchy nails until he had created a comfortable if messy nest. He settled with a sigh onto her feet. He needed some work, but she was much more skilled than she had been three years ago. And there were lots of parks in the city. Miranda smiled to herself in the dark.

SANCTUARY

EPILOGUE

Adele walked all the way to the corner and back. Then she walked around the back of her building. The effort winded her a little. She didn't go out much. Her needs were simple, and Harmonium could run most of her errands. In fact, she had almost sent Harmonium on this quest, but something in her decided she needed a little adventure. She tried to get out at least a few times a year anyway.

The ringing of the flat bell had woken her from a very pleasant memory, her first meeting with Albert at a dance. She was pretty enough, but so shy that she faded into the wall at most dances. Her only companions were the girls without partners, girls who appreciated having someone to talk to. All eyes were on Albert that night. He was short but strong, a vigorous, athletic dancer. He strode over to ask the woman next to her to dance—a flashy blonde without a partner only because she was trying to attract Albert's attention. But before he could ask the blonde, he saw Adele. And the rest, as they say, was history. Or magic.

She thought about Albert a lot, when she wasn't actively talking to him. She didn't get many visitors, but that was okay. Albert was all she needed. Except for occasional encounters with neighbors, her last visitor had been—*what?*—three years ago, when Alex and his mother—*What was her name?*—brought that cat to them. Accompanied by Harmonium, Adele had occasionally visited the streetways that Albert designed, but then she'd stopped. Things seemed different, or perhaps she was just too old to move about the city any longer. The streetway was crammed with people moving vigorously but in a disjointed way. Few people seemed to have DPs. A young man knocked into her. She had Harmonium take her home. It was safest to stay inside.

She wished Alex hadn't stopped visiting, but she understood what it was like to be young. No doubt he had met a girl his own age and forgotten everything, and everyone, else. She hoped so. The way she found Albert at that dance—

A neighbor interrupted her memory. Alex's mother had been seen downstairs, outside the building. She had asked about Adele, but she didn't want to come in. She would wait for a few minutes if Adele would come down. If Adele hurried, she might just catch her. So Adele hurried, fussing with her shoes and a scarf while Harmonium tried to help her. But there was no trace of a blonde woman with startling blue eyes when Adele got downstairs.

She was behind the building now. There was a small alleyway between her building and the next that was dark and forbidding. The city was changing. You saw stories on the newsline of hooligans, in the city itself, not safely off in places like City of the South. Something squeaked at her feet, and she jumped. A small shadow brushed past her—some trash blowing about, except that she recognized the graceful arch of a small back as it rounded the corner into the alley. It couldn't be . . .

All fear forgotten, she edged cautiously into the alley. There it was, at the very end, huddled in a corner. As she approached, it arched its back, hissed, and spit. She was blocking its exit, so of course it was terrified and prepared to fight. She talked soothingly. "Where did you come from? Have you lost your mum? Don't be frightened. I won't hurt you."

The kitten watched warily. Without warning, she swooped. The kitten struggled and got in a few good scratches, but she carefully wrapped it in her scarf so it couldn't move.

"It's okay," she said. "You're going to be just fine." She could feel the cat's rapid heartbeat and delicate ribs through the scarf. Harmonium would find it something to eat. She unwrapped the scarf enough to see it was a boy kitten, with hooded green eyes. Cats' eyes were usually yellow. It was a white cat, which she knew really meant it was all colors, not no color. She was humming the tune she had first danced to with Albert when the sun came from behind the clouds and she knew she had a bright future after all. "I think I'll call you Rainbow."

ABOUT THE AUTHOR

Grace Agnew is a nationally recognized data specialist and librarian who has advised the National Science Foundation and its grantee universities on large-scale data projects to monitor the Pacific Ocean and other large ecosystems. She is the recipient of more than $12 million in grants from the National Science Foundation for data research projects. She was author or coauthor  for these highly competitive grants, with a grant award record much higher than the academic average—a tribute to her ability to develop innovative strategies and describe them in a compelling and clear manner that convinces world leaders in data management that her strategy is the best, indeed only, strategy to fund. While this is her first novel, she is the author of three well-received nonfiction books on data management, all of which were bestsellers in the field of library science.

In previous positions, Grace managed collection development for the two largest public library systems in Georgia, so she also understands what people want to read, and why. *Sanctuary* incorporates her strong understanding of climate change, its near-future effects, and the steps people can take to heal the planet. Unlike many books in the "cli-fi" genre, her plot combines unflinching realism with hope.

In her (very) spare time, Grace enjoys gardening, travel, swimming, hiking, birding, opera, and spending as much time as possible enjoying the world while we still can.